THE MOTHERHOOD WALK OF FAME

For much of Shari's working life she was a night club manager, standing on club doors arguing with crazy drunk people in Glasgow and Shanghai. She now lives in Scotland with her husband and two children and spends her days writing books, screenplays and two weekly columns for the *Daily Record* newspaper. It's great . . . but she does miss the crazy drunk people . . .

For further information on Shari Low, visit her website at www.sharilow.com

Visit www.AuthorTracker.co.uk for exclusive updates on Shari Low.

SHARI LOW

The Motherhood Walk of Fame

AVON

AVON

A division of HarperCollins*Publishers*
77–85 Fulham Palace Road,
London W6 8JB

www.harpercollins.co.uk

A Paperback Original 2007
1

First published in Great Britain by
HarperCollins*Publishers* 2007

ISBN-13: 978-1-84756-003-2

Set in Minion by Palimpsest Book Production Limited,
Grangemouth, Stirlingshire

Printed and bound in Great Britain by
Clays Ltd, St Ives plc

With huge gratitude to the two fabulous women who guided this book to print: Sheila Crowley at AP Watt and Maxine Hitchcock at Avon. Ladies, thank you – working with you has been an absolute joy.

To the rest of the wonderful team at Avon – I love my new home!

And to the others who give their unfailing support: Linda Shaughnessy, Rob Kraitt, Teresa Nicholls and the rest of the team at AP Watt. I'm counting my blessings . . . Sxx

To Betty Murphy – we'll never stop missing you.

And to my big guy and two little ones . . .
Everything, always . . .

Now can one of you go put the tea on.

PROLOGUE

I knew something was wrong. As I bit down on an apple Danish, one of my five daily fruit and vegetable portions as recommended by Government health guidelines, I had that vaguely edgy feeling of unease – the one I normally get when PMT is raging and I want to commit acts that'll guarantee me a starring role on *Crimewatch*.

Actually, I never watch that programme. The minute the theme music starts I have to switch over, because a feeling of crushing guilt comes over me even though I know that I don't own a balaclava and I was nowhere near the Kensington Post Office three weeks ago last Thursday at 10.24 a.m.

Still, I couldn't put my finger on exactly what was bugging me. It was just another normal Monday morning. And up until that point, everything had been pretty much uneventful. My husband, Mark, had risen at some ungodly hour, staggered to the bathroom, peed with his eyes still shut, shaved with one eye open, returned to our bedroom and dressed in the dark. Due to this well-practised regime, all his business clothes were of the same colour to avoid ritual humiliation and ridicule.

He tripped over his briefcase at the bottom of the stairs, before picking himself back up, grabbing a banana from the fruit bowl and checking his reflection in the hall mirror. At that point, by some power of cosmic wonderment, his transformation was complete. Gone was the zombied, scruff-ball dosser who couldn't even manage to pee in a stationary receptacle without leaving splash marks on the surrounding area; and in his place was Mark Barwick, corporate lawyer and all-round babe-magnet.

He then got into his flash sports car, flicked on the flash radio and set off on his mind-numbing commute from our Richmond semi to his flash office in a flash tower block in a flash area of London.

Of course, I'm assuming all of the above because it would take medical intervention and explosives to wake me at that time in the morning. But his routine hadn't varied in the seven years we'd been together so I doubt that he somersaulted out of bed, had a quick espresso and a chocolate croissant then spent twenty minutes deciding which tie suitably expressed his mood that day.

And anyway, Mark only has one mood – stable. No ecstatic ups. No wrist-slitting lows. Just . . . stable. Which is a good thing. Great. Fantastic. How I love having a stable, dependable guy who is the perfect balance for my rather more *changeable* disposition. I do. And never, ever have I been tempted to call him a boring, predictable git. At least not out loud. Oh, okay, but only to my pals.

I took another bite of the Danish and realised that gnawing, restless feeling was still there. That ruled out hunger then. I ran through the other possibilities.

Kids. One deposited at preschool, and the other one had just started nursery that very week. Mac, the oldest at four, was in his third month of preschool and he loved it. Touch wood, I hadn't yet been called up to the headmistress for a dressing-down, primarily, I suspected, because I'd endeavoured to keep him on the non-violent side of Power Rangers by telling him that cameras in the lampposts around the school allowed me to watch his every move via the internet. I'm sure the teachers must wonder why he keeps looking heaven-wards and shouting, 'I didn't mean it, Mum, honest!'

Mac definitely has his mother's genes. His vocabulary is starting to broaden now but they'll be ice-skating in hell before it includes the word 'stable'.

Mac's little brother, however, is a whole different splash in the gene pool. When I was pregnant for the second time I told Mark that I wanted to name the new baby Big. I figured we were a shoo-in for a McDonald's sponsorship deal. But in the end we settled for Benny, and he's the cutest, most adorable little thing on earth. Not that I'm biased. But honestly, he should be doing the conga in a cowboy suit in a nappy advert.

Anyway, my kids were fine, so I crossed them off the 'Why am I discontented today?' questionnaire. They were wild, mad, crazy, and no doubt destined for borstal, but for now they were fine.

Maybe career? I find it difficult to discuss my career in isolation as it's actually inextricably linked to my family background. You see, I am not, as appearances, birth certificates and DNA suggest, the daughter of a haughtily superior schoolteacher and a woefully inadequate finance salesman who shared every penny the family ever had with his pals Johnnie Walker and Jack Daniel's. I am, actually, the secret love-child of Jackie Collins and Sidney Sheldon. I haven't quite worked out how I managed to find my way to a Scottish maternity ward all those years ago, but I'm sure that Jackie had a good reason for giving me up for adoption. Maybe the Mafia were after her and she feared for my safety. Perhaps she didn't want me to grow up spoiled and superficial and thought I'd become a more grounded, soulful person if my childhood was spent in an area of urban deprivation on the outskirts of Glasgow (in which case, *Mom*, I can assure you that it worked – I'm lovely, now please come and get me). Anyway, whatever the reason, for my whole life I knew that when I grew up I wanted to be a writer, just like my real parents. I'd write a ton of salacious best sellers, go to live in LA, have a kidney-shaped swimming pool and do dirty things to brooding Italian studs.

Sadly, it hasn't quite worked out that way. My first book, *Nipple Alert*, did pretty well for a debut. *Fab!* magazine even said it was a 'riotous romp'. Okay, so they say that about everything with a pink cover, but it's a start. My second book, *Pre-Mental Syndrome*, sold pretty well too. Not Marian-Keyes-oh-my-God-let's-buy-a-Ferrari well, but it sold out its first and second print run. So I should be loaded, right? Wrong. Why did no one tell me that unless you sell ten gazillion books the dosh doesn't trickle in until about 347 years after you're dead?

So to keep the bank manager off my back and my secret credit card in the black, I write a pathetically pretentious weekly column on the joys of motherhood for *Family Values* magazine. Which should really be called *OK Ya!*, because it's nothing but an upmarket, incredibly naff suck-up to upper-class and celebrity mothers. Excuse me, my gag reflex is trembling again. The magazine demands that it's written from the perspective of the perfect mother, so to write it I need a massive stretch of imagination and a sick bag on hand for the really nauseating bits. But hey, I'm a mother with a Tonka-truck of bills so I'll take the money and keep on churning out the gospel according to a mother that I'd want to kill if I ever met her.

Life hasn't exactly turned out how I imagined, has it? Sunny Beverly Hills? Great career? Kidney-shaped pool? Italian studs? I got pissing-down Richmond, a ridiculous job, a puddle out the back door, and I suppose if Mark clutched a pizza and kept his mouth shut he might just pass for someone who once spent half an hour in a transit lounge in Rome.

I opened the back door and lit a Benson & Hedges. Filthy habit. I'm so glad I stopped doing it in public years ago. Far better to freeze one's arse off in secret in the valiant pursuit of an iron lung than to acknowledge to your husband and children that you have the willpower of Pavarotti in Pizza Express.

I could hear music coming from next door. I use that term loosely. It sounded like the greatest hits from the Nepalese panpipe charts. Then I caught sight of two feet dangling upside-down in midair, through next-door's kitchen window. There's only one thing bloody worse than a neighbour who listens to Nepalese panpipe music, and that's a neighbour who listens to Nepalese panpipe music while they're doing yoga. How's a girl supposed to enjoy toxic free-radicals and poisonous chemicals destroying her skin and clogging her lungs when the neighbour is spoiling the environment with spiritual music and invigorating exercise?

It shouldn't be allowed. Especially when the neighbour is supposed to be your best friend. If she were any kind of pal she'd be out here with a sneaky Silk Cut and a Bakewell slice.

Friends. In the past I'd have waged my worldly goods on at least one of them having a situation that could be responsible for this gnawing feeling, but nope, nothing dramatic, disgraceful or worrying sprung to mind there either. Kate next door is nauseatingly happily married to an architect called Bruce, a nauseatingly great mother to a Walton-like brood, nauseatingly toned and together, and has a nauseatingly glam part-time job as a fashion stylist. Just as well I love her a nauseating amount really. Although, I do realise that it breaks the solemn code of friendship: thou shalt not have a friend that's skinnier, smarter or more successful, as envy giveth thou frown lines and wrinkles.

Kate and I have been best friends since we were kids on a council estate about five miles from Glasgow.

There was a gang of us: me (Carly Cooper, now Barwick – or it would be if I had ever got around to officially changing my name after I got married), Kate, Carol, Sarah and Jess. And we stuck together through thick (Carol flunked O-level cookery), thin (and she makes Posh look like she's got a high-grade Dairy Milk habit), richer (Sarah married a millionaire), poorer (after she escaped a life of abuse and poverty with her first husband), sickness (Jess once had an affair with politician Basil Asquith, who turned out to be the MP for Very Sick and Perverse Sexual Habits) and health (yoga, panpipes).

Strangely, we didn't do that normal thing where you lose touch after school, then find each other twenty years later through Friends Reunited, drag your partners along to a reunion party, only for pheromones to fly like pigeons on steroids and the next thing you know you're throwing your car keys in a bowl and it's a wife-swapping scandal in the *News of the World*. Or does that only happen in the Cotswolds?

We all, via jobs, men or missing each other, ended up living in London together for years and although we're a bit more scattered around now, we're still pals. We're kind of like Girls Aloud, only with lower breasts and slight hints of jowls.

In fact, some of us are real family now. Carol, once Scotland's favourite model and for many years the international face of the Visit Scotland tourism campaign, married my brother Cal, also a model and once the face and bollocks of the Calvin Klein underwear range. What was I thinking when I was in the womb? I was obviously so busy floating around doing frivolous things like developing internal organs that I left all the best-looking genes to my brother. Anyway, they now live in one of the really big expensive houses up on the edge of Richmond Park with their twins in the attic and my other brother Michael in the basement. Michael asked them if they'd mind if he slept over one night. That was four years ago.

Jess lives in France now with partner Keith and her son Josh. I think she went for the peace and quiet. She was a major tabloid story here when her affair with the MP was rumbled and splashed across the *Sunday Echo*. Lord, do I have any normal friends? Anyway, she then married the journalist who exposed the story, had Josh, discovered her husband was a no-good cheating bastard, left him and met Keith – a lovely builder who adores her. They renovate old properties in a wine region in the South (could be Champagne, Chardonnay, Lambrini . . . I'm never sure) and keep chickens.

And Sarah? Aw, get ready to say 'aaaah' and have your faith in human nature restored. Sarah left school, went straight into a horrendous relationship with a psycho, had two kids, finally fled from Sleeping with the Enemy a year later, met Nick Russo – celebrated restaurant owner and the man I lost my virginity to, although I'm sure the two aren't connected – fell in love, married him and now they're in New York over-seeing the opening of Nick's fourteenth restaurant.

Lord, when I read all that back I realised nope, I don't have any normal pals. Although for the first time in about, well, forever, we were all settled, happy, in

8

good relationships and there wasn't a drama, dilemma, disaster or devastation in sight.

Nope, all was well with the world. My life was a paragon of peace and tranquillity.

Or at least, that's what I thought.

But sometimes those inexplicable gnawing feelings are more than just your hormones reminding you of their existence. They're subliminal signals from the Goddess of Womanhood that it's all about to go the way of the Wonderbra generation – unanimously tits up.

Family Values *Magazine*

PUTTING THE YUMMY IN MUMMY
THIS WEEK . . . MAKING TIME FOR YOU

Remember, ladies, it's not just the children who need to be nurtured. What about Mummy and Daddy? Yes, we all get tired, stressed and our priorities change, but it's essential that you take time for yourself and your relationship. Make sure you get to that weekly Pilates class, think about taking up a new hobby or interest to stimulate your mind and, most importantly, find time to pamper yourself.

Have one afternoon every week that is just for you – how about a manicure, a facial or a cheeky little pedicure to reduce those stress levels and leave you looking gorgeous at the same time? Don't lose touch with your inner self – take at least fifteen minutes every day for reflection and contemplation. And remember, girls, when you travel the road to contentment, take your cosmetics with you. Colour on those cheeks, gloss on the lips . . . just a few moments of maintenance every morning will leave you feeling refreshed and ready to face the day.

If you've had a particularly hard week, there is

nothing like a gentle massage to ease away the memories of those sleepless nights. And for that gorgeous, sensuous treat, ladies, you don't even need to leave the house. It's important that we don't forget our partners, so remember to set aside one night a week and fill it with love and lust. Make a mouth-watering feast, light those candles, turn the music down low and remind each other that desire and parenthood can co-exist in glorious splendour.

The result? Happy parents, happy children, happy home.

The Motherhood Walk of Fame

★ *Step One* ★

I knocked on Kate's door and then wandered on in without waiting for a reply. It was probably just as well, because her body was tangled in a position that looked like it was a therapeutic pose for someone suffering from acute constipation.

'Morning, Madonna,' I greeted her, while switching the 'off' button on the CD.

'Morning, Fag Ash Lil. How's you?'

I made some kind of yeeeeurghhh sound that I felt conveyed just the level of discontentment.

'Very articulate,' she said. 'You know, with those profound, descriptive abilities you should really be a writer.'

I pulled the CD out of the machine. 'One more word and the panpipes get it,' I warned her. I glanced down at the CD pile and shoved the top disc onto the CD player, which just happened to be 'Ancora' by Il Divo.

Il Divo – an Italian term for which I believe the exact translation is 'great arse and a fine set of lungs'.

I poured a coffee (decaf), sat down at the kitchen table and put my feet on another chair. Kate didn't bat an eyelid but I knew the minute I left she'd sponge down both table and chair with Flash antibacterial. Her whole house was spotless. Not in a freaky 'I'll stab you to death if you drop crumbs on my angora shag pile' kind of way. Just in a super-organised, highly efficient, natural earth mother kind of way.

Kate had been mothering all of us since we were kids. When I was six, she refused to play in the snow with me unless I put gloves on. When we were teenagers she used to put condoms in my bag on the way to the pub. When my boys were babies she insisted on disinfecting my kitchen on a weekly basis because she said that I was – and I quote – 'obviously brought up in a lighthouse because I didn't seem to be capable of getting into corners'.

Her kitchen was a gleaming showroom of wood units, marble worktops, plants, copper pans, pottery things that served no obvious purpose, kids' paintings and collages made from leaves and wool. In my house the kids' stuff made the kitchen look cluttered and messy. In this house it looked charming.

Like I said, the laws of womanhood would normally decree that I would have to hate such perfection, but with Kate it was impossible because she was so goddamn humble and lovely. She was gentle. She was beautiful. If your granny knitted the perfect woman it would look like Kate. Even her children liked her. All three of them – Cameron, Zoe and Tallulah. What were the chances of having three children and all of them thinking that you're great? My earliest memory is of my mother irritating me incessantly by trying to put ribbons in my hair to make me look like a girl when it was plainly obvious to everyone else that I was a boy. Looking back now I can only assume that my willy fell off somewhere during the long journey with Jackie from Beverly Hills.

Kate disentangled her limbs then folded them into a different position as effortlessly as a bit actor from *Wallace & Gromit.*

'Are you sure you've still got a skeletal system or have you done a Cher and had bits of it removed?' I asked. I could honestly say that in my whole life, despite numerous experiences involving alcohol and imaginative sex, the back of my head had never come into contact with my ankle.

She laughed. 'This one is great for the pelvis and the sex life,' she said. 'Do you know that scientists reckon that a woman has seven G-spots?'

'Yeah, well you'd better call out some Sherpas and a tracker dog cos six of mine are missing.'

The front door slammed and Carol breezed in, all copper tendrils, size-eight hipsters and shopping bags.

'Jesus, it'd freeze the balls off a brass gorilla out there,' she said, shivering for effect. She'd never been very good with metaphors. She gave me a hug, then looked at Kate.

'I know I'll regret asking, but what are you doing?'

'Counting her G-spots,' I interjected.

Carol looked puzzled. 'Why the plural? I thought we only had one?'

Thank you!

14

'Nope, according to some anthropologist expert we've got seven,' said Kate. Although how she could talk when she was staring her privates in the face was beyond me.

Carol giggled. 'Oh, well there's something for Cal to look for later then,' she announced.

I made a very immature teenager, grossed-out face à la *Hollyoaks*, circa 2001.

'Carol, we have laws! I've told you before – do not talk to me about your sex life with your husband. Due to the fact that he's also my brother, it gives me mental images that will eventually lead to a psychiatrist's couch or an appearance on a daytime talk show. Anyway, let's not talk about sex because my memory is in no mood to be tested this morning.'

Sad, but true. I couldn't remember when I'd last had one of those 'alcohol and imaginative sex' encounters. Don't get me wrong, Mark and I could do that whole jungle hot and heavy thing. Once upon a time.

The first time I had sex with him I was still a teenager and the earth moved. And not just because we were in a standing position and I was wearing platforms the size of Mini Metros. We had an on–off thing all through the hormonal teenage years, and then lost touch until years later, when we bumped into each other at Cal and Carol's wedding. Actually, that's a lie. We didn't exactly bump into each other. For reasons that I'll summon up the courage and the accompanying mortification to reveal later, I had stormed off in a flurry of embarrassment, tears and snot, only for Mark to appear out of the blue and rescue me.

Within months we were married and it would have been impossible for me to be happier. Life was bliss. On weekends we'd climb into bed on Friday nights and stay there until Sunday, getting up only to shower, answer the door to the pizza delivery guy and change the batteries on the TV remote control. I couldn't believe my luck – Mark Barwick, the gorgeous, smart, funny, laidback sweetheart of a guy, who had been bailing me out of trouble since before puberty, had actually taken me on. I should probably add 'brave' to that list. And not only that but he shagged me silly from dawn till dusk and seemed to enjoy it. Who needed yoga?

My wedding present to Mark had been to throw out every method of contraceptive I possessed. Foolishly, I flushed ten packets of pills, fourteen condoms and a diaphragm down the toilet. It kept a plumber in business for weeks.

But we were soon to hit a blockage of a different kind.

Six months of lost weekends later we were surprised that I wasn't pregnant. A year passed and we were verging on astonished. Another eighteen months on and we were seriously worried. And two years after that we discovered that I had polycystic ovaries. And that was before they were trendy. Now everyone's got them. They've become one of the barometers of modern-day chic. Everyone who's anyone has had a boob job, Botox, goes to Barbados in the winter, South of France in the summer, is on the waiting list for the new Chloe bag, shops in Harvey Nicks and has polycystic ovaries. Even Victoria bloody Beckham has them. Oh, the irony. I had to have *one* thing in common with that incredibly thin, jet-setting, millionaire, diamond-laden, David-Beckham-shagging woman, and it's the fact that our ovaries don't work properly. And to add insult to injury, despite the dodgy ovaries she's still managed to shoot out three kids. Although calling them after a bridge, a missile and a bloke with a fondness for balconies was a bit harsh.

However, in my case, the whole reproductive thing seemed to be on strike.

For Mark and I that meant sex became a battle to conceive rather than an enjoyable pastime to while away the hours between a Friday and a Monday. All of a sudden it was ovulation tests, fertility drugs, thermometers, laparoscopies and endless gynaecologists sending their Marigolds up to places that no one except your partner should ever visit.

It was horrible. Bollocks. Unfair. And really, really crap.

It was all those clichés that you read about in the *Daily Mail* when Felicity from Chelsea decides to share her infertility experiences with the world. Yes, I called my husband to come home from work because I was ovulating and wanted the eggs fertilised. Yes, I did the legs up against a wall after sex. Yes, every month on the day before my period was due I would get all desperately optimistic and do a pregnancy test. And then another sixteen just in case it was a faulty batch.

And somewhere in the middle of all that the romance kind of slid away. Actually, that sounds too gradual and gentle. In reality it went downhill like an Olympic skier on a Lurpak lid. It broke my heart.

Then one day, something really strange happened. It was the launch party for my second novel and I'd spent the whole day in a flurry of excitement, dread and panic. What if no one came? What if the book didn't sell? What if that cow from that glossy celebrity magazine gave it a bad review? (Incidentally, she did, and one day I swear I'll track her down.) Anyway, flurry, flurry, flurry ... and then I realised that I felt ill. Nauseatingly, gut-twistingly ill. And much as everyone tried to tell me that it was excitement, nerves, stress, etc., etc., I knew differently. I *knew*. I just knew. A trolley dash round Superdrug, a quick detour into Marks & Spencer's toilets and seventeen more pregnancy tests confirmed that I was not, in fact, a stressed-out, over-excited basket case. I was pregnant. Cheggers. Up the duff. Banged up. Or as Carol would say – I had a cake in the cupboard.

Some women were born to be pregnant. Demi Moore. Kate Hudson. Catherine Zeta-Jones. They glow, they bloom, they blossom. Unfortunately I wasn't one of them. I peed. I sweated. I swore. I went from slim to sumo in about three weeks and spent the rest of my pregnancy humping around the collective weight of ten adult seals. By the time I actually gave birth I was the size of an aircraft hangar.

So it's fair to say that in those months, our sex life was rather infrequent. Definitely less often than a new moon and only slightly more frequent than an eclipse of the sun.

After what seemed like the gestation period of an African elephant, babe was born, ooohs, aaaaah, gurgle,

gurgle, and we called him Mac. In actuality we could have called him Contraceptive because that was the effect. He was either sleeping between us, or on top of one of us, or we were taking it in turns to walk the floor with him while the other grabbed a quick hour of shut-eye on the couch.

But here's the weird thing. I've heard of this same situation happening with other couples and normally there is one of two fairly predictable outcomes. After a few months, the sex life reverts to situation normal. Or alternatively, the bloke gives up waiting and takes to shagging his secretary.

In our case, it was neither.

On the bright side, Mark didn't go off with his secretary – and I'd like to hope that has more to do with the fact that he adores me than the reality that his secretary weighs sixteen stone, has nostril hair and answers to the name of Harry. Instead he just kind of shut down on the sexual side. Gone. Fun over.

I suppose I should have paid more attention to it at the time, but to be honest I was grateful. After all, it's not as if I was throwing my knickers at him and demanding he ravish me once a night and twice on weekends and bank holidays.

Aaaw, I thought, he's just so considerate. So undemanding.

I thought it was all perfectly normal, to be honest.

And at least I did get the mandatory birthday and Christmas shag.

Nine months later, Benny came into the world. Two babies in sixteen months. And despite the probability that my privates could now be a prototype for a new Channel Tunnel, we were ecstatic – years of infertility and now we'd somehow managed to buy one, get one free.

It was great for our hearts and souls, bad for our sleep patterns and nuptials.

Another zombie-like year later, this time with two babies in tow, I realised that my idea of an orgasm was now a thin and crispy pepperoni and anything with Liam Neeson in it. I've always had a thing for him.

However, it wasn't the end of the world. I loved Mark. He loved me. He was amazing with the boys. He kissed me like he meant it. He told me he loved me a dozen times a day. We'd cuddle up on the couch every night and enjoy those blissful six and a half seconds before one of us fell asleep. We both revelled in every little new thing that our kids did.

'Guess what, honey, Mac said "mummy" today.'

'Mac ate a whole banana.'

'Benny managed to projectile vomit all the way to the other side of the coffee table.'

We were happy, contented and together. We still laughed at the same things, understood each other and led a pretty peaceful existence – apart from one time when I suffered a particularly nasty reaction to the dangerous combination of sleep deprivation, a hormonal blip and a few glasses of vino and tried to pummel him with a packet of Pampers for forgetting our anniversary.

But I was happy. Ecstatic. We had so much going for us: my husband was my favourite person over two feet tall, we had two gorgeous boys, a nice house (apart from the mucky corners) and great friends.

The positives definitely outweighed the negatives. I could live with the fact that my writing career wasn't exactly setting the world alight, Mark was working horrendously long hours, and despite his flash salary the exorbitant cost of London living meant we only had £3.63 in our savings account.

I can remember the exact moment it struck me that I should be concerned about my sex life. Or lack of it. It was late in the evening and I was sitting on the couch. Mark was lying sleeping with his head on my lap. I desperately needed to pee but couldn't work out how to manoeuvre myself from underneath his head without waking him.

The closing credits of *Taggart* had just rolled and I'd even refrained from belting out the 'No Mean City' theme tune at the top of my voice. I was aimlessly flicking through the Sky channels, trying to find something to watch, when I came across a documentary on the merits of naturism. At least I thought that's what it was. Until the naked woman having a picnic in a field started sucking her own nipples and was then joined by a big hunky farmer in a state of excitement. Well, what the sheep in that field must have thought!

It was shocking. Scandalous. Outrageous. Although I did make a mental note to sign up for a subscription to *Country Life*. But most of all, it was very, very . . . *horny*. I even forgot the urge to pee as I got tingles in an area that had been a distinctly tingle-free zone for longer than I cared to remember. Almost without clear direction from my brain, my hands went wandering – one under my bra (grey, overstretched, another mental note: must go lingerie shopping) and one down to the button on Mark's jeans. I fumbled for a few minutes, before finally popping it open. God, I was losing my touch. In my younger days I could undress a bloke with one hand, in the dark, while simultaneously biting his ear, talking dirty and parking the car.

Anyway . . . fumble, fumble, fumble, much squeezing of own nipples, breathing getting heavy (mine), zip coming down (his), penis located, gentle extrication from boxer shorts, gentle rubbing, then a little faster, a little faster still, then definite reciprocal hardening, then . . . *SWAT!*

He swatted my hand away like I was a mosquito attempting to land on his Ambre Solaire.

Okaaaay, I thought. He's obviously still sleeping. He's confused. He thinks he's on a sun-lounger in Fuengirola and under attack by a predator. Of the winged variety.

So let's try that again.

I psyched myself back into a lustful mood. The fire-place was now wearing my jumper and my bra was dangling from a lamp. My jeans were open, one hand was going south and the other was going back into Mark's boxers for a repeat ambush.

I ran my finger around the tip of his cock, slowly, softly, as he hardened again. Meanwhile my clitoris was throwing a 'Welcome Back' party as the DNA codes in my fingers consulted their long-term memory as to what to do.

I gasped as the tingling reached my toes. My nipples

hardened and I was starting to sound like Paula Radcliffe after 26 miles.

Oooooh yes. That's it. Oh yes, I remember. Why *oh why* had I ever stopped doing this – was I crazy? Oh yes, just there. There. There. That's it. Oh, he's so hard now. If I could have manoeuvred on top of him I would have done, but fuck it, I was doing just fine where I was. Yes. Yes. There. Oh my . . . *SWAT!*

And this time it was accompanied by one open eye.

'Honey, what are you doing?' he murmured sleepily.

Now, call me picky, but there was a time when I wouldn't have had to draw him a diagram.

I adopted my sultriest look, threw one tit over my shoulder (flexible tits are one of the benefits/drawbacks of two years of breastfeeding) and leaned down to kiss him.

'I'm playing with your cock while whipping myself into an orgasmic frenzy,' I whispered playfully.

Okay, so this is when, if it were a movie, he would open his eyes, smile, run his finger gently down my face and whisper that he loved me – before proceeding to bend me over the back of the couch and roger me until I screamed in orgasmic delight. Then I'd flop into his arms, satisfied and exhausted, content in the knowledge that I'd be walking like a cowboy for the next week.

Sadly, it wasn't a movie. It was a three-minute commercial for the merits of chastity and abstention.

Groggily, he removed my hand from his nethers, turning his head to kiss my belly. 'I love you, you mad woman,' he whispered.

I could have burst with happiness. Right up until he rolled over onto his other side so that I could only see the back of his head and murmured, 'Babe, I'm too tired. But you go on ahead. Knock yourself out.'

Who said romance was dead?

I peeked at the TV screen to see that Farmer Giles and the milkmaid slut were indeed still on course to shag until the cows came home. I flicked off the telly, as deflated as a certain part of my husband's anatomy. I'd been rejected. Knocked back. Dizzied. Dinged. And I didn't like it one little bit.

Over the next few days I couldn't get it out of my head. I drew up a list of reasons for the collapse of our sex life:

1. Mark works far too hard in a very high-pressured job.
2. We have two young children.
3. He's always tired.
4. I'm always tired.
5. We never go out as a couple and so have disconnected from each other.
6. I make no effort whatsoever with my appearance any more.
7. He's stopped seeing me as a sexy woman.
8. I only wear fabrics that are washable at 40 degrees and dryable on a radiator.
9. The kids are always in our bed.
10. I couldn't find my make-up bag if my life depended on it.
11. We never get a chance to really talk.
12. Don't think he'd want to anyway.

13. I never flatter him.
14. He never flatters me.
15. My bras are all grey and overstretched.
16. When we met I was wild, exciting, unpredictable and horny.
17. Now I confuse porn with a naturist documentary.
18. When we met he was sexy, fun, interesting and horny.
19. Now he confuses a wank with a mosquito.

It was quite obvious, really. Somewhere in the midst of all the stress, infertility, pregnancy, babies, financial constraints and daily monotony we'd lost that spark. Hell, we'd lost the whole bloody blowtorch.

That night when he came home for dinner, I was a woman transformed. I had clean hair. I was wearing make-up. I'd alerted Friends of the Earth that a forest was being eradicated before shaving my bikini line. I was wearing tight, sexy jeans and a low-cut sexy top (black, silk, borrowed from Carol, and definitely not dryable on a radiator). The lights were dimmed. The candles were lit. I'd prepared a meal without the aid of a microwave and the kids were next door at Kate's house.

'What's all this?' he said with a grin when he finally got in just after eight. I'd forgotten how handsome he was at the end of a long day. His dark brown hair was ruffled, his face all rugged and stubbly. His green eyes, squinting slightly through tiredness, had the effect of making him look sultry. His tie was loose. His shirt sleeves were rolled up. I could have climbed on top of him right there in the hallway just like the old days.

Why had it been so long since I noticed all of this?

Perhaps because normally the minute he walked in the door I thrust a malodorous baby and a nappy in his direction, then raced back in to other child who was in his bed, screaming the place down because his mother had dared to leave the room in the middle of a story about three little pigs under house arrest.

I did my very best pout – the one that I hoped made me look like Angelina Jolie, but was probably a bit nearer a puffer fish who's just been smacked in the mouth.

'You, my big stud, are going to be pampered, preened and fussed over. I've made you a gorgeous meal. There's wine, there's food and there's romance. And in return, all you have to do is shag me senseless. What do you think?'

Was it my imagination or did he hesitate slightly?

He tossed his jacket, pressed me up against the kitchen wall and kissed me like he'd just remembered how it was done. Oooooh, I liked that. With one hand he pulled up my top and whisked it right over my head (definite ripping sound – mental note to remember to give it back to Carol with a grovelling apology and a box of After Eights). I tore off his tie, then his shirt, and pressed my tits up against him as my tongue searched for his tonsils and my legs came up around his waist. Suddenly, he pushed them back down and took a step back, a playful look on his face. His eyes ran from the top of my body to my feet. Then, and believe me, I'm getting a hot flush just thinking about this, he dropped to his knees, opened my jeans and tore them down, to reveal – yes, drum roll and trumpets please – new, sexy lace knickers that actually matched my bra. Then he leaned over and ran his tongue very slowly up the inside of my thigh. My fingers were in his hair as I gasped, trying desperately not to come and spoil what I was sure were going to be the most deliciously filthy and downright buttock-clenchingly horny moments of my life.

He ran his tongue over my other thigh. Then at the top, he paused and moved my slut thong over to one side. And then slowly, sexily, gently, he blew. Thank God I'd done the bikini line or the resulting whiplash could have taken out an eye.

It was all too much for me. I yanked him up by the follicles, deftly unbuckled his belt, undid his button, wrenched down his zip then pushed down his boxers, releasing the most magnificent erection I'd seen since before that first little blue line appeared on a stick all those years before.

And when faced with that kind of apparatus, what else is a girl to do but climb on, hold on and scream until the neighbours call the police.

We've done it, I thought smugly, as we snuggled down, very sore, very sleepy and very happy. We'd rediscovered each other. We'd reconnected our hearts and re-engaged our libidos. Oh yes, baby, we'd relit our sexual fires.

But little did I know that Mark's obviously lived in damp conditions because the bloody thing kept going out again. While my sex drive was once again motoring along like a Formula One car with no brakes, Mark's was spluttering to life once every week or two, going out for a quick spin then crawling back into the pit lanes for a refuel and a rest. Over the following weeks, months and years, and much to my general discontent (although to the pleasure of Ashif, who ran the grocer's at the end of the street where I bought batteries for a certain adult toy on a far too frequent basis) our sex life was reduced to the occasional mildly satisfying romp. Whenever I broached the subject with Mark, it was always the same – he was tired, he was under pressure, he worked long hours, he loved me, it would get better, now cuddle in, go to sleep, and cross my heart I'll make it up to you at the weekend.

Occasionally he did. But more often than not life, kids, bills, work and sleep took over. Still, it could be worse. We still laughed. We had the family we always wanted. We genuinely loved each other. And Ashif was now able to send the wife and kids to Center Parcs for a fortnight. In the grand scheme of things, surely a less than perfect sex life was a small price to pay for all the other great things in our lives.

Definitely. Absolutely. It was.

'CARLY!' I snapped my head up, spilling my coffee on my tracky bottoms. It didn't matter. They were washable at 40 degrees and dryable on a radiator. Well, if he wasn't going to sustain the effort then neither was I.

Carol was laughing. 'What are you thinking about – you were on another planet there.'

Which was ironic, since Kate was now doing something that required bending her spine into an unnatural position and sticking her arse in the air. I decided I was far too refined to make a joke about Uranus.

'Sex,' I replied truthfully.

Of course, what goes on between Mark and me, in the privacy of our own home and within the sanctity of our marriage is sacrosanct, and I would never, ever divulge the intimacies of our lives with anyone.

'Mark still not putting out?' asked Kate.

Busted.

'He'd need a satellite navigation system to find my clitoris these days,' I admitted.

'So that's why you're looking so pissed off today then,' Carol interjected.

But no, I was sure she was wrong. After all, my sex life had been crap for years – why would it suddenly upset me now?

'Nah, I don't think so. I'm just having a down day. No idea why.'

'PMT?' Kate asked.

'No, that was last week – remember the whole dry-cleaners weeping over a ketchup stain/threatening a traffic warden expedition,' I said ruefully.

'Work?' asked Carol, with a wary look on her face. Carol had the same reaction as most men when faced with an emotional woman – she donned a crash helmet and checked out the nearest exits. It wasn't that she didn't care. It's just that when God was giving out empathy and sympathy she was down in the 'superficial aesthetics' department picking out the best face, the best body and getting a manicure, pedicure and permanent teeth whitening.

'Work's work,' I replied with a shrug.

'See what I mean?' grinned Kate, talking to Carol but gesticulating to me. 'I just told her that with her acutely incisive powers of descriptive narrative she should really be a writer.'

There's nothing worse than a pal with a gift for irony. Except a pal with a gift for irony who now had her legs spread like an acrobatic porn star.

'Will you stop with that bloody yoga?' I demanded petulantly. Carol had just put a chocolate éclair in front of me and Kate's bendy stuff was putting me right off. She looked at me, took on board my distress, considered our lifelong bond, evoked the emotion of all we'd been through together, then carried on regardless.

I took another gulp of cold coffee. Work. Well, I suppose on a scale of phenomenal excitement to turgid banality it was somewhere in the middle. I was gutted that my books hadn't propelled me directly onto the world stage and my bank manager's Christmas card list. I always thought that the minute my novels hit the shelves my adoring public would form an orderly queue that would stretch for miles. I'd be the new big thing. I'd be windswept and interesting, Richard and Judy would be my new best friends, and newspapers and magazines would clamour for my opinion on the really important issues.

Crisis in the Middle East? Let's ask Carly Cooper for her informed opinion as to the path to resolution.

Are 'new' men really just 'old' men with cosmetics? Carly Cooper will know.

Is a daily orgasm essential for great mental and

physical health? Actually, for obvious reasons I'd probably have to pass that one on to Jilly Cooper.

Obviously, my stellar rise to hot author of the year and 'she with the finger on the zeitgeist of modern social culture' hadn't quite happened. But then, I suppose that, like the whole sex thing, I'd been too busy with babies, house and banalities to notice.

I was under contract to write one more book for the publisher who'd purchased my first two, but I had to admit I was struggling to conjure up the motivation.

I really liked the people who worked at my publisher's – all six of them. One of the factors contributing to my pitiful income and my definite non-arrival as a literary force was probably that I was signed to a small independent publisher who did minuscule print runs and had the advertising budget of the average office Christmas kitty.

With both books I'd already released, the first issues sold out within a few weeks – not difficult when most shops held a grand stock of about four – never to be replenished, because the publisher had already moved on to the following month's titles.

If book deals were like recording contracts then I was the second runner-up on a past season of the *X Factor* who had a couple of tiny hits and was looking forward to a career on the cruise ships.

Still, I was grateful for the heady excitement of actually seeing my name in print, and following the old adage that as one door closes, a crow bar and a bit of brute force opens another, I did get my weekly column out of it. It might not be much, but it paid for the weekly jaunt around Sainsbury's, with a bit left over for the holiday fund.

Was I disappointed? Sure I was. But then, I hadn't quite given up yet. I still had nine months left before my deadline for the next book, so I'd work at that, submit it, and fulfil my contract. Then I'd decide what I *really* wanted to do when I grew up.

Writing had seemed like a great idea when I thought it was a step on the journey to fame, riches and my biological mother, but the harsh reality was that it actually involved endless hours of solitude spent sitting in a room making up imaginary friends. In some countries they locked people up for that. I was convinced all that solitude and angst was detrimental to one's mental health and I already had the proof that it had fairly detrimental physical effects – all the pondering inevitably caused boredom-fuelled comfort eating which, unchecked, could lead to a mightily fat arse.

I squirmed as I registered that my waistband was just a tad tighter than comfort demanded. Perhaps I'd skip the chocolate éclair.

I watched Kate finally getting up from the floor. Thank God that was over. Then, like Jean Claude Van Damme in the presence of really bad men, she suddenly kicked her leg up, twisted it around onto the kitchen worktop and did a ballet/stretchy thingy.

That's it, my appetite was completely gone now. Mainly because I knew that if I so much as attempted that manoeuvre my kidneys would fall out, my skin would burst like an overripe marrow and I'd need stitches in my secret garden.

'Right, it's been a wee slice of heaven, but I need to go. Benson & Hedges, the ironing and children are calling.'

'Where is my gorgeous little Benny the Ball today?' asked Carol. I know, how rude! He might have a slight weakness for extra puddings, but a space-hopper he was not.

'He started nursery yesterday. I've to collect him at three.'

'Oh no,' said Kate, in a doom-laden voice. My head spun around to face her as inwardly I groaned. Dear God, don't let one of her muscles have snapped or her back have frozen in that position. Her legs were still at a ninety-degree angle to each other, and if we had to take her to hospital in that position then one limb was going to have to go out through the sunroof.

'What's wrong?' I asked fearfully.

'You're not getting wild jungle sex,' she stated.

I appreciated the recap on my love life but was pretty sure we'd already moved on from that subject.

'And nothing is going on work-wise to make you remotely inspired or enthusiastic.'

Correct. Did she want to see me cry?

'And Benny has just started nursery.'

Look, didn't I just say that?

'Carly, you know what's going on, don't you? You, my darling, are suffering from acute non-stimulation of the neural passageways and cranial cavity.'

'*What?*'

She laughed. 'You're bored! Out of your head. Off your tits. Restless. Fed-up. Your va-va-voom has vucked off.'

I processed this for a minute. How could I be bored? I had a house to run, a book to write, a husband to manipulate into giving up sexual favours, two demanding children to be fed, watered and diverted from a life of crime, friends that did bloody yoga . . . Oh, shite, she was right. I was bored rigid.

Where was the excitement? Where was the adrenalin rush? Where was that little flutter of anticipation when I woke up each morning wondering what the day would bring? Bored. Rigid. In fact, I couldn't remember the last time that I'd been this bored.

'I remember the last time you were this bored,' piped up psychic Carol, scaring the crap out of me. The day that Carol got in touch with the thoughts and feelings of another woman was the day that the skies would be awash with large pink animals that snorted and whiffed of bacon.

'It was right before you left,' she continued. 'You know, before you did the whole mid-life crisis, desperate cow, psycho stalker, any port in a shower thing.'

Well put, I thought. She was right. Much as I cringed with embarrassment at the thought.

Okay, so here it is – the thing I alluded to earlier that should really only be mentioned after I'm dead, when my body has been handed over for medical research and the scientists are dissecting my brain in a bid to understand the primitive behaviour of deluded, hormone-fuelled, biological-clock-powered women.

You see, I once made a huge cock-up. Massive. Mortifying. Actually there were several. About a year before I met Mark at the wedding, I had what can only be called a mental aberration. At that time I was single, in a job I hated (selling toilet rolls – you couldn't make it up), living in a grotty rented flat and generally discontented with where my life had gone. Especially when it had at one time shown so much promise. In the preceding ten years, I'd worked in London, Hong Kong, Amsterdam, and Shanghai. I'd visited New York and Ireland. I'd had wild, crazy jobs managing nightclubs in some of the most exotic places on earth. I'd met some amazing people, I'd been engaged six times, I'd bought gorgeous clothes, and I'd earned and spent a fortune . . .

Nope, even when I hide it in the middle there it still sticks out like a nun in an S&M basement. *I got engaged six times.* Two informal promises and four full-blown sparkly-rings-phone-the-vicar ones.

Yet there I was, at the end of it all, living on my lonesome and existing on ready meals for one. And if Ashif had known me then, his family would be going to Barbados twice a year.

So I did the sane, rational thing – I made a plan. Sadly, that's where the 'sane and rational' bit ended. I quit my job, relinquished the lease on my flat, grabbed my credit cards and went off round the world to find all the guys I'd been engaged to just in case any of them really had been Mr Right and I'd been too busy signing up as a certified commitment-phobic to notice. It was insane, deranged, desperate and a bigger disaster than George Bush's contribution to world peace. The ignominy of the memories is too hard to bear, so I'll give you the pamphlet edition as opposed to *War and Peace.* Or should I say the *Nipple Alert* version, as the following story provided shame, embarrassment, disaster, and the plot for my first novel.

First there was Nick, the man who'd taken my virginity on a hot night in Benidorm. Actually, 'taken' isn't strictly true. I'd lobbed it at him at the approximate speed of an Olympic javelin. But when I rediscovered him in a restaurant in St Andrews, we discovered we had all the sexual tension of custard. Luckily, Sarah was with me, and they fell in love, married and when we're all together now I manage to blank out the fact that I know what his penis looks like.

Then there was Joe, a nightclub owner in Amsterdam. By the time I tracked him down he was a millionaire entrepreneur and paragon of chic – and so camp he made Elton John look like Vinnie Jones's harder brother.

Next was Doug, who, ironically, dumped me first time around because he caught me shagging Mark – in the days when Mark didn't think a libido was one of those inflatable things you lie on in the pool on holiday. Anyway, second time around Doug proved that he had the thirst for vengeance of a Sicilian mob boss and totally humiliated me, so I was forced to move on to . . .

Tom. Bless him. An Irish farmer with the body of a Greek God. By the time I found him again he was happily married and had the body of a Greek taxi driver called Stavros who existed on ten thousand calories a day.

Then there was Phil. A complete honey, who was my

Shanghai Surprise – never more so than when I discovered that he'd become a big name on the American comedy circuit and had married Lily, the beautiful flower who'd worked with me in a nightclub in deepest darkest Shanghai.

So that left all my hopes pinned on Sam. Sam Morton. The martial arts expert who I fell madly in love with when I lived in Hong Kong. The one that I knew, just *knew*, was right for me when I set eyes on him again all those years later. The one who adored me, who said he'd prayed every moment for me to return to him – that is, when he wasn't really busy doing other things, like shagging half the wealthy female population of South East Asia. Oh, yes, Sam had become a gigolo. A hooker. A man who could fucky-fucky-long-time for mucho dinaro. And thereafter I couldn't look at him without thinking 'wire brush and disinfectant'. And believe me, I tried. I even agreed to a holiday on a paradise island to heal our tortured relationship. Result? Loads of sun, sea, sand . . . and a clitoris that spent the whole time on its own little vacation. Yep, the passion was officially gone, replaced by friendship. Platonic friendship.

So my great international manhunt fell spectacularly on its buttocks – as did I when the entire congregation at Carol and Cal's wedding (except my dad, who was deep in an alcoholic slumber) found out that the man who had accompanied me to the wedding – and whom I'd begged to masquerade as my boyfriend for the day to save my embarrassment about the whole round the world/still single debacle – was actually South East Asia's most prolific rent-a-dick.

My mother claims she is still taking the anti-anxiety pills.

But strangely, it didn't faze Mark, my first love, my childhood sweetheart. He stepped in when my life was falling apart and (literally) picked me up and rescued me. That's when I realised that throughout my whole life, through every crazy scheme, drama and disaster, Mark Barwick had always been there at the right time, said the right things and saved the day. Yep, his Y-fronts should be worn on top of his trousers at all times. He's my soul mate and I thank God every day for sending him to me. Well, except when I've got PMT and could happily keep the local hitman in business.

I wouldn't change a thing and I've never doubted for one moment that we were meant to be together. Mark is my penguin. Or my swan. Or whatever bloody bird it is that only has one love and mates for life. And the thing that I love most about him? It could be that he accepts me for what I am – warts, cellulite, irrational obsession with reality TV and all. It could be that he's a genuinely decent bloke who couldn't shaft someone if his life depended on it. It could be that he has the best buttocks I've ever seen. God bless all those teenage games of footie down the park. It could be that there's no one on earth whom I'd rather was the father of my children.

But honestly? I love him because it just feels right. Oh, okay, the buttocks help.

And luckily he's the most non-jealous easy-going man in the universe, because some of my exes have become really good friends. Nick, obviously, on the grounds that he's married to one of my best pals. Joe and his partner Claus now own nightclubs all over the world, including one in London, so they pop in regularly for dinner. Phil and Lily still live in New York and we do the whole 'Christmas card, drunken phone call every three months' thing.

And Sam . . . Bugger, my mobile phone was ringing. 'Don't move,' I screamed at Kate, still conscious of the fact that if she pulled a muscle while in that position she was going to have to have a very open-minded physiotherapist.

I snatched it from beside the coffee machine, burning my hand in the process.

'Hello,' I wailed.

'Is that Carly Cooper, literary genius and all-round sex-goddess?' drawled those familiar transatlantic vowels.

'Nope, it's Carly Cooper, crap columnist, bored off her tits and wouldn't know a good shag if I won it in a tombola.' I was trying to be casual, but I have to admit, I was more than a bit freaked out. It was the second time that some kind of weird psychic synergy had cropped up that morning. And I MUST remember to stop divulging intimate details about my sex life to my pals.

'Ah, well, that may be about to change, my darling.'

'Which bit?' I asked, puzzled.

'All of it, my love.' His English accent was back. The one that teenage girls lusted over, middle-aged women fantasised about, and men (except those in Joe and Claus's very-camp camp) despised. You see, on the other end of the line was Sam Morton, male hooker turned international A-list movie star, by way of a screenplay he wrote about his life that went on to become a movie with him in the leading role. Obviously the world was ready for a male take on *Pretty Woman* (with the most amazing abs on God's earth thrown in for good measure) because it grossed over $100 million. Sam had made the Big Time.

'Oh yeah, and how's that, Mr Big Shot Movie Star?'

Kate and Carol realised who I was talking to and shouted a simultaneous 'Hi Sam!' in the background.

He laughed. 'Tell the girls I said hi. Oh, I suddenly got a twinge of homesickness then.'

'Yeah, cos it's really tough spending all day shopping on Rodeo Drive and having your ego stroked by young, pneumatic starlets,' I retorted. 'Anyway, enough about you, tell me why my life's about to change?'

'That's what I've always loved about you – your depth, humility and your interest in the lives of your friends,' he said.

'Sam, I'm sitting in a semi in London on a cold, rainy day having a mid-life crisis about the pitiful state of my existence. You, on the other hand, have probably just disembarked from your chauffeur-driven limo after spending the night in the VIP lounge of an exclusive club, having free Cristal champagne chugged down your neck while your adoring masses worship at your Prada-clad tootsies. Forgive me if I don't feel your pain. Now, I have to go and collect Benny from nursery, so much as I love you madly and would adore to extend this cosy chat I must leave. Go call up Julia Roberts for a blether.'

'Nah, I'd hate to wake her – her twins have been giving her sleepless nights over the last couple of weeks so she's exhausted. Anyway, I haven't told you how your life's about to change yet.'

'Oh, I thought you were just being your usual optimistic, dramatic self.'

'No, it was a statement of fact. Remember I told you that I gave a copy of *Nipple Alert* to my agent? Well, he loves it, he thinks he can sell it and he reckons it'll be huge. He wants you in Hollywood, Carly Cooper.'

I was stunned. My chin was down somewhere around my knees.

'Wha— Whe—'

He was still laughing on the other end of the line.

'No rush, honey. Any time later this week would be just fine.'

Oh. My. God. I was going. To Hollywood. To fame. To stardom. To success. To Jackie and Sidney, my biological parents.

After all these years, the mother-ship was finally calling me home.

★ Step Two ★

There are two things in life that I know inside out: one is the local kiddies' indoor play area and the other is my husband. He doesn't like change. He doesn't do spontaneity. He definitely doesn't do plain fecking crazy. So I did have the wherewithal to recognise that if I ambushed him with the grand announcement that we were all off to Hollywood the very minute he walked in the door he'd be about as thrilled as J.Lo in anything polyester.

So I waited until he'd dumped his briefcase at the door, hung up his jacket and kicked off his shoes before me and the kids did a conga past him singing, '*We're all off to LA, we're all off to LA, da da da da da, HO, da da, da, da, da.*'

He laughed, that gorgeous face crinkling up into a grin that gave me goose bumps. Mac threw himself into his daddy's arms. 'Daddy, daddy, we're going to Hollywood and, and . . .' he was in a frenzy by this time, 'Mickey Mouse is there, and, and Pluto and, and Spiderman and, and, and . . .' He didn't get a chance to finish. Wisely, Mark recognised that such an extreme level of excitement could mean only one thing: incontinence. He whisked Mac into the downstairs loo before he peed his pants.

'*Spiderman, Spiderman, does whatever a spider can . . .*' sang wee Benny in something approaching the cartoon's theme tune. What did that say about me as a mother? Could they rhyme off the birds in the skies? No. Could they spot a petunia at a hundred paces? No. Could they tell you the name of the Prime Minister? No. But they could win *Junior Pop Idol* by chanting the theme tunes to every cartoon that was ever made.

We definitely had to get out more. Oh well, in LA we'd be far too busy surfing and going to Tom Hanks's house for tea to spend any time in front of the box.

'So, do you want to tell me what's going on?' said Mark when he emerged from the downstairs loo. He didn't look too pleased and I guessed that it probably had something to do with the damp patch on the front of his Hugo Boss suit. Damn.

'Sam called today – his agent has read *Nipple Alert* and feels sufficiently excited by it to request that I come over to LA while he promotes it to the world's biggest movie studios. I've done a cost-versus-risk analysis and while it is, of course, a speculative journey, I feel that it has sufficient merit to warrant extracting funds from our account and making the trip. I've cleared it with our accountant who has confirmed that a large portion of the outlay will indeed be tax deductible. I recommend that we start scouring the internet immediately in order to minimise our outlay by booking the most economical flights available and use the air miles that we've accumulated over the years to further reduce costs. I would anticipate leaving in approximately three weeks, giving you plenty of time to clear your current caseload.'

You just know I'm lying, don't you? Was it the 'cost-versus-risk analysis' bit that gave it away?

What I actually said, in a babbling rushed voice that was donated especially for the occasion by the Gods of Helium, was, 'Sam called, we're going to LA, they want my book, Mark, they want my book! Oh my God, I can't breathe! Anyway, so we have to go to LA and we have to go this week, so I looked on the internet and all the flights are fully booked, so fuck it, I used my credit card and got us all on a flight on Friday, business class, British Airways. You get those lie-down seats and free pyjamas. And your own telly screen. And, oh my God, Mark, I'm so excited. I haven't found us anywhere to live yet, but Sam says we can stay with him till we find somewhere. Can you believe it, Mark, can you believe it?' At which point I spun round, reached behind me for his hands, slapped them on my arse, grabbed wee Benny and started another conga, singing, *'We're all going to LA, we're all going to LA, da da da da da, HO, da da da da da . . .'*

I was halfway into the kitchen before I realised that Mark wasn't behind me.

I stopped, turned around and saw that he was still standing at the end of the hall, and the whole 'crinkled-up cute grin' thing he had going was definitely gone.

'Pardon?' he said.

I knew I was clutching at straws, but for a few seconds I hoped that it wasn't a pardon in the 'for fuck's sake, have you lost your mind' sense and more one in the 'sorry darling, in all the excitement I missed some of that last statement – free pyjamas, did you say?'.

'What bit did you miss?' I asked hopefully.

'The bit where my wife lost the plot altogether and, if I understand correctly, booked flights we can't afford, for a trip we can't take, on the premise that some agent thinks that her book might, perhaps, maybe appeal to someone in the movies.' Then his tone changed altogether. 'Incidentally, congratulations on that part, honey, you deserve it.'

'Thanks,' I mumbled.

'Carly, I'm sorry but I can't take any time off right now. You might not have noticed, since the last time you asked me about my work was about three years ago . . .'

Ouch. Bulls-eye in the dartboard of brutal honesty for Mr Barwick.

'. . . but I actually have a lot on my plate just now and there's no way that I can . . .'

'We're all going to LA, we're all going to LA, da da da da da, HO, da da da da da, HO.'

It was Mac, on the way through the hall, having divested himself of his wet undergarments and replaced them with a Batman suit.

Benny spotted him. And, naturally, burst into song.

'Da na na na Da na na na Da na na na Da na na na BATMAN!'

Woah. My husband and I were in crisis talks, having

45

one of the most important discussions we'd had in years and I couldn't hear a word he was saying because I was stuck in the family home equivalent of Nickelodeon Channel hell.

And said husband was looking at me like he was trying to decide whether to have me certified or shot.

How to play this? I could shout, I could holler, I could blackmail. I was sure I had some dodgy photos of him somewhere. In the end, I decided to let one of my other personalities take over. If anyone could swing this, it was Saint Carly of the Blessed Martyrdom.

'But Mark, we *have* to go. Come on, *please*. Mark, look at my life. I cook, I clean, I organise your life and I spend most of my day dealing with the aftermath of other people's body fluids.'

Mac and Benny had the decency to hang their heads at this point.

'This could be great! This could be our big chance for financial reward, for a life of fame and stardom, for glitz and glamour . . .'

I could see I wasn't winning, so I pulled out my trump card.

'. . . for a NANNY!'

He still didn't blink. God, he was good. Saint Carly gave it one last shot.

'Come on, babe. In five years I've never asked you to do anything for me. Do this for me, please.'

His face softened. I could taste victory. We were going! Now where was my passport, my travel adaptor and the list I got off the internet of all the stars' Hollywood addresses?

Or maybe not.

'Carly, I'm sorry. I'm really pleased that they're interested in your book, but we can't go just now. Mac has school. I have work. I can't just take time off on a whim. And most of all, we can't afford it. Can't you tell them we'll come over in a few months' time when we're a bit more organised and on our feet?'

Over my dead Tinseltown-bound body!

'But we can't. Mark, Hollywood doesn't work that way!' said I, trying to sound like I knew what I was talking about. I'd seen *Fresh Prince of Bel-Air* twice, I watched *Beverly Hills 90210* for years and I never missed an episode of *Baywatch*; I was a seasoned LA veteran.

I took a huge breath then went on the offensive.

'Mark, they're interested in me this week, but it'll be someone else next week if I don't get over there and make the most of it. And Sam says we should plan to stay for a month – four weeks without preschool for Mac is hardly going to scar him for life. He's four – they're still painting with their fingers and singing songs about blind mice for God's sake. As for your work, Mark, you *need* a holiday. The whole legal backbone of this country is not going to crumble if Mark Barwick takes a month off. And don't even get me started on money. If lack of money were a barrier to everything I wanted to do in life then I'd have done nothing. To hell with it, that's what credit cards are for, I say!' I finished with a dramatic flourish and accompanying triumphant hand gesture.

I peeked at the boys. Mac's expression showed he was definitely on my side – I think it was the whole school-avoidance thing that swung it. Benny, however, just looked puzzled. Then, a split second later, his face lit up and he blurted out, '*Three Blind Mice, Three Blind Mice . . .*'

That boy was a walking request show.

Mark didn't notice – he was far too busy getting pissed off. Or as close to pissed off as Mister S. T. Able ever got.

'Carly, we know that's your attitude to money and that's probably why you had more debt than Peru when we met.'

He must have spotted the blaze of anger that went across my eyes because he switched to a more concil-iatory tone. 'Honey, it's just too tenuous for us to risk blowing a fortune, not to mention my job. If Warner Brothers were on the phone right now with their chequebook at the ready, I'd say go for it. But how many people are in Hollywood right now trying to sell a script? Hell, the whole city is made up of wannabes who are convinced they're the next big thing. Tell Sam thanks, but we'll pass. We'll maybe go over for a fortnight later in the year. The kids can do Disney and you can perhaps set up some meetings then.'

I was furious. What do you call a Taurean with the hump? Raging bull. Or 'me'. But I was suddenly aware that the kids were watching the whole exchange, their heads swivelling from side to side like something out of *The Exorcist*.

I morphed into Mary Poppins. 'Right, guys, come on then, bath time,' I said in a singsong voice.

'Don't want a bath,' Mac replied petulantly. 'Want to go to see Spiderman.'

'*Spiderman, Spiderman . . .*' Oh, Christ. I scooped Benny up, and invoked Method Number One in the Parental Code of Discipline and Behavioural Adjustment – blatant bribery.

'Mac, fifty pence for sweets if you're in that bath in five minutes.'

He shot up the stairs. That boy will do anything for cash to finance his E-number habit.

I crossed the hall to follow him with Benny wrapped around my neck, drooling milk down the back of my shoulder.

Mark was standing at the bottom of the stairs. 'I'm going,' I said deadpan, when we were face to face. 'This means a lot to me, Mark, and I'm going.'

I carried on up the stairs, furious that he'd so ruthlessly burst my little happy bubble of optimism and excitement. How often is the repetitiveness of everyday life interrupted with such an exciting prospect? One of my biggest ambitions in life had always been to sell one of my books to someone in the movie industry. Anyone. I didn't care if it was the bloke who drove the tour bus in Universal Studios and he bought it for a tenner. But all my beloved husband could think about was the cost, and the fact that it wouldn't allow him the statutory two-week lead time to fill out his company's administration form, number 2334: Holiday Request Form for the Anal Retentive.

In fact, Sam wasn't the only major A-list movie star who knew how serious I was about my dream. Kate

Winslet knew too. Oh yes, we were close personal friends once. For about five minutes.

A few months before, the boys and I had been having a picnic in Richmond Park. It all sounds very Enid Blyton, but in truth it involved two Happy Meals from the nearest McDonald's and a rug I got free with an order from a catalogue. We were lounging in the sun, when another family plonked down not far from us. I nodded a friendly hello, a gesture that was reciprocated by the blonde woman who was unpacking a picnic from a real hamper. Flash cow. I was furtively shoving my Happy Meal boxes under the rug, when I realised that I'd seen her before somewhere. It came to me in a flash. Checkout number six at Waitrose. She was the girl from Newcastle who was trying to break into glamour modelling. Suddenly the blonde with the picnic shouted to a little girl who was with her. Nope, no Geordie accent. But ... oh, good grief, Kate Winslet! I was sure of it. I considered bursting into the theme tune from *Titanic* just to check.

'Mac,' I hissed, 'go and play with that little girl.'

'Can't,' he replied, completely matter-of-fact.

'Why not?'

'She's a girl. Don't play with girls.'

'Mac, please. Just this once.'

'Nope.'

I was getting desperate. I needed an 'in' and I wasn't above resorting to desperate tactics to get it. Ever since *Nipple Alert* had been published I'd carried a copy around in my bag, just waiting for the day that I would bump into Steven Spielberg in Woolworths and present him with the material for his new blockbuster.

Time to call out the big guns.

'Mac, a Spiderman magazine, a pound for sweets and you can watch *The Simpsons* every night this week if you go and play with her.'

He knew when he was beaten. But five Curly Wurlies would cushion the blow. Off he wandered with his football, and soon he had a game going with the little girl – two-touch soccer with Benny as a goalpost.

I wandered over as casually as I could. 'Ah, kids – they just make friends so quickly, don't they?'

Ms Winslet smiled, a grin that was no longer on her face ten excruciating minutes later after I'd feigned surprise at recognising her, told her how great she was, thrust my book into her hand and given her my phone number. I'm sure she was surreptitiously pressing a panic button on her hi-tech, A-list mobile phone to summon her security by the time I collected up the kids and left. I walked quickly just in case the police had already been tipped off about a demented stalker who was casing Richmond Park giving out free novels. Oh the shame.

Mark had laughed when I told him the story – then reminded me to carry his mobile number at all times so that I could get hold of him to post bail. That was in the days when he still had a sense of humour, before it went the way of Miss Winslet's maiden voyage on that big cruise ship.

The splashes as I bathed the boys snapped me back to the present. I watched as Underwater Action Man whupped Scuba Spiderman in a fight for supremacy of the octopus squirty sponge and then we sang four choruses of 'Row, Row, Row the Boat'.

'Look at me, Mummy, look,' shrieked Mac as he made a bubble Mohican on his head. I know I'm biased but my boys are extraordinarily gorgeous. Sometimes I wonder if I had sex with Brad Pitt *and* George Clooney.

The strange thing is, neither of my boys look particularly like Mark or me. Mac has jet-black hair, almond-shaped blue eyes and the most gorgeous smattering of freckles across his nose. Benny, on the other hand, is blond with the hugest green eyes, long black eyelashes, a little upturned nose and perfect little lips. At that time both the boys had spiky inch-long crew cuts – I'd love to say it was fashion but it had more to do with an outbreak of nits that had reached our house about four weeks earlier.

'Fart! Fart!' screamed Benny, momentarily turning the bath into a Jacuzzi. He then laughed so hard that it set off a choking fit and I had to whip him out, calm him down and make him sip water.

When was the last time I'd done that? Laughed uncontrollably, I mean, not farted in the bath – I gave that up when I got married.

God, I couldn't remember. I now spent my life cooking, cleaning, working, smoking, sleeping and trying in vain to resuscitate a sex life that was in second-stage rigor mortis. Where was the fun? This wasn't life, it was monotony.

And of all places, LA would be such an adrenalin rush. Running in slow motion across *Baywatch* beach. Skipping down Hollywood Boulevard. Going around on the big wheel on Santa Monica pier. Stalking Liam Neeson. Catching up with my best pal Kate Winslet.

How amazing would all of that be?

As for the boys, let's see: they could spend a whole month freezing their bums off here, staying indoors because the rain was pelting down, painting with potato shapes for the four hundred and tenth time already this year, or they could have a blast surfing in the sun, playing baseball in the park and going to Disneyland.

And I hadn't started on the fundamental reason for going. What if . . . Oh, I could hardly even think about it without wanting to shriek and dream about what I'd do with my first million. (Botox, incidentally, followed by lots of Prada, first-class flights and generally swanning around acting starry.) But what if some big-time, legendary, iconic studio actually bought the film rights to one of my books? That's like winning the lottery. It's like discovering an elderly relative you never knew has died and left you a fortune. It's like robbing a bank. It could be the start of a brand-new life, not just for me, but for *all* of us.

I read the boys their stories, tucked them in and kissed them goodnight. No sign of husband. He'd obviously done what he always does when there's a conflict in sight – decided to avoid it altogether. If Mark Barwick were alive in Wild West times he'd have chosen the day of the Alamo to nip to the nearest IKEA and stock up on soft furnishings for his cabin.

Mac yawned as I ruffled his hair. 'Love you, Mummy.'

I kissed his cheeks, then his forehead, then his chin, then blew a raspberry on his chest. 'I love you too, gorgeous.'

'Mummy . . .'

'Yes?'

I stood by and mentally prepared myself for one or more of his standard 443 stalling gestures. Can I have an apple? I want another story. Sing me a song. There's a ghost under my bed. Is it Christmas tomorrow? I need a pee. Can I have a drink? What age am I? How many sleeps until I'm ten? Why is there no ice in ice cream? When I grow up can I be the Pink Panther? Where did I come from? So how did they get me out of there? Yuk, I'm never doing that. What goes faster, Batman or a jumbo jet? Why is Shrek green?

'Mummy,' he murmured again, his eyes already closing. 'Are we really going to Disneyland?'

I kissed his forehead. 'Yes, we are, baby. We definitely are.'

'And Mummy . . .'

'Yes, babe . . . ?'

'Why is Shrek green?'

I lay in bed that night with Mark lying next to me, pretending he was asleep. Or actually, maybe he was. It was amazing how many things I could think of that irritated me about my husband when I really tried, and the fact that he didn't in any way hold with the old saying that you should never go to sleep angry was one of them. He could. Easily. We could have an argument that was verging on volcanic and he would still have no problem whatsoever rolling over and grabbing forty winks right in the middle of it.

My brain, however, was racing.

Whichever way I analysed it, there was no justifiable

reason not to go to LA. Mark would come round. I had four days until the flight and if those days went the way of our normal major disputes (of which, I had to admit, there had only ever been five or six in the twenty-odd years we'd known each other), then he'd avoid me for about a day, spend the next day acting as if nothing had happened, finally get around to looking at things from my point of view on day three, and on day four either compromise or capitulate. Capitulation would be good, but I figured I could handle compromise. We could cancel the business-class flights and go standby. Or perhaps wait until the following week at the very latest. Or change airlines and save money by flying via Bangladesh.

One way or another, we'd get there.

There was no way that Mark would make me pass up this chance when he realised how much it meant to me. It might be a gamble, it might be reckless, it might be completely misguided – but it just might be fabulous. And there was only one way to find out. I knew Mark would come round. There was absolutely, definitely no way he'd make me do this on my own.

'I can't believe you're doing this on your own,' said Kate as she steered her perfectly clean, perfectly green, hybrid car around the big Concorde statue at Heathrow airport.

'Me neither,' concurred Carol.

I sighed. 'Don't get me started.'

I couldn't quite believe it myself. The usual post-meltdown reaction had gone right to schedule. For a whole day.

On Tuesday evening (Day One: Avoidance) Mark had come home from work around eight. The boys were already down for the night and I was at the kitchen table pretending to create a literary work of genius on my laptop. He said hi in a flat, dismissive tone. I didn't respond. He looked in the oven for his supper. I let him discover for himself that the oven was bare. He flicked on the kettle and pulled one cordon bleu, exquisitely prepared Pot Noodle from the cupboard. I continued to type. By this time my fingers were rattling across the keyboard, forming perpetual repetitions of *Mark is a Tosser, Mark is a Tosser, Mark is a Tosser*. He made his Pot Noodle, grabbed the paper and went into the living room. About an hour later I heard him moving around upstairs, going in and out of the boys' room. He always kissed them goodnight before he went to . . . bed! He couldn't be going to bed! Didn't he want to talk about this at all? Aaargh! Well, bugger him.

And anyway, we were still on Aftermath, Day One of Operation Big Sulk. He was bound to have changed his tune by Wednesday.

He had, but only in a musical way.

Come Wednesday (Day Two: Pretend nothing has happened) he was whistling 'Hunka Hunka Burnin' Love' as he came in the door. Bloody whistling! My life was in turmoil, my heart was breaking, my soul was scarred . . . Okay, so I'm exaggerating a wee bit, but I was mightily pissed off. And he was *whistling*.

Tap, tap, oven bare, another Pot Noodle, bed.

Finally, Day Three, he spoke.

'Carly, we have to talk about this.'

Ah, I knew he'd come around and I was delighted that he was actually doing it a day ahead of my estimation.

'You're right,' I said softly, putting on my very best humble face and trying my hardest not to gloat.

'Did the airline give you a refund or do we need to ask them in writing and provide some kind of official explanation as to why we cancelled the trip?'

I was astonished. This was when he should be packing his suitcase, ordering his dollars and launching a search party for his Speedos – last seen in 1989.

'Mark, we're going. I won't miss this. I'd regret it forever.'

He looked more irritated than angry. 'Come on, Carly, be reasonable. It's crazy.'

'I know! That's one of the main reasons I want to do it. When was the last time you did something really, really crazy, Mark? So crazy that you wanted to scream with the sheer giddiness of it.'

'The day I married you,' he said calmly.

Oh. Sails now wind-free. And his facial expression hadn't changed so I couldn't tell if that had been a good comment, as in crazy-great, or a bad comment, as in crazy-should've-been-locked-up, so I just ignored it.

'Please, Mark, this really means a lot to me.'

'Carly, my job means a lot to me – mainly that it keeps a roof over our heads. I'm in the middle of a major deal. If I pull out now I could lose the client and a shit load of commission – commission that we could really do with.'

'Fuck it, there'll be other deals, other commissions.'

'Jesus, are you never going to grow up, Carly?'

I don't think the first response that came into my head – 'Definitely not, and where did you put my pogo stick?' – was the answer he was looking for, so I didn't say it out loud. Once upon a time that would have made him crease with laughter. Where had that guy gone?

'Yes! I will, I promise. I mean, *I have*. Look at me: I iron, for Christ's sake. I now know that Dyson isn't the name of a rock group. I pay tax. I make the boys wash their hands after they pee. I say things like, "If you don't behave then Santa won't bring you any toys." I'm a fully fledged bloody adult.' I was tempted to add, na na na na boo boo, but thought it might blow my well-made point.

'Then use some sense and don't go.'

'I'm going.'

'I'm not.'

And he didn't. Day Four (Capitulation and compromise) and here we were, charging up to the departure terminal at Heathrow, one woman, two pals, two children and six suitcases. And no Mark.

He had tried again to change my mind the night before, but it was futile, despite tugging my heartstrings so hard that they almost snapped.

'Carly, you can't do this. How can I be apart from the boys for a month?'

I knew it would devastate him, but on the other hand there was a simple solution – he could find a way to come. He'd been with his company for twenty years – twenty years of slog and success. I was positive that if he asked them for a month off they would agree. But I was also convinced that the problem wasn't with bureaucracy, it was with Mark's refusal to do anything that hadn't been analysed, prepared and planned to the degree of a military operation.

For once I was awake that morning when he left. As I lay in the dark, I heard him go into the boys' room, kiss them and murmur something. A few minutes later, thud (trip over briefcase), rip (banana off bunch), door open, door shut, car engine on, car engine fades as he drives off down the street.

I wrote him a letter, giving him the flight details, Sam's address and telephone numbers, and got the boys to draw kisses across it before leaving it propped against the cornflakes. I *still* didn't think that he'd let us go alone. Come on, we were a team. Soul mates. Best mates. Okay, so perhaps we'd let things slide lately and hadn't been paying each other enough attention, but we were definitely in this for the long haul, weren't we? Definitely. So he'd made his point. Let's move on. Santa Monica Boulevard, here we come.

'What are you doing?' asked Carol. 'Any minute now security will arrest you because you look like you're casing the place.'

My eyes flicked manically from one door to another. We were standing in the middle of a packed terminal, at the entrance to the security area that leads to the departure lounge, and I was rooted to the spot.

'I'm waiting for the snot bit,' I replied, still searching the crowd.

'What?' said Kate.

'You know, the snot bit. *Officer and a Gentleman*, he carries her out of the factory. *Top Gun*, he goes back to the café and puts their song on the jukebox. *Dirty Dancing*, he pulls Baby out of the corner. *Friends*, Rachel gets off the plane. *Pretty Woman*, he decides to overlook the fact that she's a slapper and climbs up a ladder. The romantic ending. The bit where the hero comes rushing in and you go all warm and bubbly, despite dripping with snot.'

'Ladies and gentlemen, would all passengers on Flight BA0283 to Los Angeles please proceed directly to your departure gate, as this flight is preparing to board.'

'That's you, honey,' prompted Kate, her eyes misty. Oh crap, we were having a snot moment without the big hunk charging to the rescue. Could we do *nothing* right?

That's when I saw him. It wasn't hard. At over six foot Mark was usually one of the tallest in the room. Over a sea of heads, I could see an inch of that familiar dark hair coming towards us. I swear it was like a slow-motion B-movie ending, only without the crap music that sounded like it was composed by someone's auntie on her organ after a dozen gins. He was fifty feet away: my heart started to race. Forty feet: a huge grin crept across my face. Thirty feet: I went up on my tiptoes, wanting to see the expression on his face as he rushed towards me. Twenty feet: I started to wave. Ten feet: I stopped breathing. Nine, eight, seven, six . . . A shriek was starting in my stomach and working its way north. Five, four, three. Aaaaaaargh! There it was – one shriek, at a tone so high-pitched that every dog within a ten-mile radius just had a heart attack. Two, one . . . That's how long it took me to realise that the shriek wasn't mine. It belonged to what looked like a Swedish au pair called Inga, and she was now sucking the tonsils out of a bloke who was the spitting image of my husband from the forehead up.

It wasn't Mark. He hadn't come. He really hadn't come.

I swallowed.

'That's us, Mum, that's us. Come on!' yelled Mac excitedly. Shallower than a foot spa, that boy. He was leaving his father for a month, his mother was devastated, we were going to the unknown, facing an uncertain future, and don't even get me started on the fact that I'd be in debt until I was sixty after this trip.

'Come on, Mum, our plane's ready. D'you think I can wear the pilot's hat, Mum? Do you, do you, do you?' He was going hyper again.

I raised my eyes to heaven. Dear God, if I promise never to ask you for anything else again, please hear me now. Please, please, please make this trip worthwhile. Please make Mark come charging in that door right now. And please do not let Mac pee his pants in the middle of a security check at Heathrow. They'll think it's fear and have us strip-searched before you can say 'And what exactly is that white powder up your jacksy, madam?'

'You have to go now, Carly. If you're going . . .' Kate said tentatively.

I swallowed again, and then scoured the room one last time. Bastard.

I took a deep breath, threw my handbag over my shoulder, my carry-on bag over the other one, grabbed both my boys' free hands (their other hands were pulling Postman Pat trolley bags) and leaned over to kiss Kate and Carol.

'We're going,' I said with a rueful smile. 'We're definitely going.'

We were going to LA, we were going to have a ball, and, most importantly, I was going to show Mark stubborn-arsed Barwick that it wasn't just some crazy flight of fancy. I was going to make a success of this trip. I was going to sell the film rights for one of my books to a movie studio and get a cheque with more zeros than Stephen Hawking's IQ. I was going to make this pay off big-time and show Mark that all he needed in life was a little more faith in his wife.

That's if I ever forgave him. And I wasn't sure that I would.

Family Values *Magazine*

PUTTING THE YUMMY IN MUMMY
THIS WEEK . . .
TRAVELLING WITH THE FAMILY

Gstaad, Aspen, St Moritz, Monte Carlo, Bermuda, Antigua . . . It's vital for the all-round development of children that they experience other countries and cultures. Of course, getting them there can be a mine-field of pressure points and explosive incidents; however, a little planning can make the journey seam-less, crisis-free and perhaps even add to the excite-ment of the adventure.

First of all, ladies, take your nanny. Yes, it may add to the expense, but it's <u>your</u> holiday too and you deserve the rest, so look on it as an investment in the quality of your life.

Secondly, prepare, prepare, prepare. Take snacks for the children – organic rice cakes never go wrong. Pack an assortment of toys and puzzles to keep those enquiring minds busy. And don't forget to request that the airline block the row behind or in front to give you plenty of space to spread out and relax.

As soon as you board, change the de rigueur Chanel

travel suit, remove all make-up and slather on the moisturiser. La Prairie is le essential! During the flight, keep the Evian flowing, the Clinique spritzer nearby and a short nap will re-energise those batteries.

Then, shortly before landing, leave your nanny in charge of changing the children into fresh clothes, while you reapply your make-up, restyle your hair and don your Dior. You'll sashay down those aeroplane steps feeling a million dollars . . . and looking like it too!

★ Step Three ★

'Ladies and gentlemen, we'd like to thank you again for travelling with us today, and remind you to take special care when opening the overhead lockers as items stored there may have moved during the flight. When those of you travelling with young children have retrieved your belongings, please make your way to the nearest exit, where a member of the cabin crew will aid your disembarkation and reunite you with your will to live.'

It had been the longest two hours of my life. Actually, it was a ten-hour flight, but Los Angeles is eight hours behind us so the net effect is that you travel halfway across the globe in the time it takes to watch the *EastEnders* omnibus.

It was lunchtime when we touched down and already I looked like a bag lady. My short blonde spiky hair (think the secret love child of Billy Idol and Annie Lennox – but tone deaf) was standing even more vertically than normal. My jeans (size 12 but very stretchy) were stained with the orange juice that Mac managed to tip over me before we'd even reached international airspace. My white T-shirt could have doubled as an in-flight menu. On the top right-hand corner was the chicken in a tomato sauce that we'd had for our main meal – unfortunately Benny had eaten his with his fingers and was then overtaken with an irresistible urge to cuddle his mother. In the middle was the dressing from the side salad, flicked there by Mac with an accompanying 'I hate tomatoes.' Somewhere in the middle was the raspberry cheesecake – delivered there by a wandering spoon. And finally, there was the coffee splatter. That one was all my own work. I'd just got the coffee to my mouth when, completely out of the blue, Benny asked me if I had a baby in my tummy. Splurt. Oh, the indignity. Had he never heard of air-travel bloat? Perhaps I'd better give the after-dinner choccies a miss anyway.

I just hadn't anticipated the impossible logistics of travelling alone with two small children. You cannot go to the toilet to fix your face, freshen up or pee unless you take them with you, because the minute you are out of sight they are likely to either a) try to open a door causing depressurisation of cabin and mass death, b) hide and give you chronic heart failure when you come out to discover an empty seat, or c) start wailing at the top of their voices – at which point a social services employee on their way to an Eradication of Child Neglect Conference in Nebraska will pop her head up from the row in front, take down your details and give you a lecture on child separation anxiety.

The alternatives, however, are limited and decidedly uncomfortable: you can either cross your legs or take the two of them with you. Try getting one adult and two children in an aeroplane toilet – it's like getting the entire cast of *Chitty Chitty Bang Bang* in a dodgem.

I'd had such high expectations of our first business-class flight. I thought Mark and I would kick it off with a glass of champagne, while the boys busied themselves with educational games and witty banter. Then we'd all change into our free pyjamas and snuggle down for a snooze, before being awakened by the aroma of our cordon bleu meal being brought to us perhaps with a fine wine (that would be one that didn't come with a screw top and cost less than £2.99 for a two-litre bottle in our local Spar) and one of those square chocolate mint things to accompany it.

Er, no. Cue sound of needle being scratched across vinyl. Or that sound they make when someone gets a wrong answer on *Family Fortunes*.

In reality, I skipped the pyjamas because getting two children undressed and dressed again is far too much hassle to be undertaken unless there is a proper bed, sports or muck involved. In the midst of all the drama, I had of course forgotten to pack games, books and jigsaws to pass the time, so the boys watched cartoons for a whole ten minutes before the first fight erupted over custody of the one and only Game Boy. Now, here's a point of law that is unique when it comes to the under sixes. The Game Boy belongs to Mac. However, his brother wanted to play with it, even though at two and three-quarters the only thing he can do with it is switch it on and off, press random buttons and chew it. It seems fairly logical then, that since oldest child is the legal owner of the item he should be allowed to dictate who plays with it and when. Wrong. The laws for the under sixes state quite clearly that whoever screams loud enough in a public place wins the toy. Nobody ever said life was fair.

They battled it out over the bloody computer game for about four thousand miles, with me maniacally making shushing noises, threatening them with prison and, finally, removing the game altogether. At which point they both started wailing and two dodgy-looking businessmen in the next row looked up from their laptops for long enough to give us the filthiest looks.

I leaned over to the boys and did my very best evil, venom-filled whisper. 'Right you two! See those two men over there?' I gesticulated to the hard-faced suits.

The boys nodded, wary expressions creeping across their faces.

'Batman and Robin in disguise,' I whispered.

'*Da na na na . . .*' Benny started.

'Sshhhhhhhhh!' I clapped a hand over his mouth, and then leaned over, collected Mac's chin from his knees and returned it to its normal position.

'They're in *disguise*, Benny. That means it's a secret that they're here. They're on the lookout for baddies. Now, do you think they'd approve of this behaviour?'

They both shook their heads.

'Correct. Now, before Batman comes over here and gives you both a piece of his mind I think you'd better stop fighting and act like model citizens that Gotham would be proud of. Do you understand?'

They nodded, still transfixed that their superheroes were sitting only yards away.

Just at that moment, the air hostess walked past the end of our row. 'Batgirl,' I whispered to the boys out of the side of my mouth.

They gasped. 'I knew it,' said Mac.

'Oh, really?' I asked. 'How did you know?'

'Because she's a rubbish air lady – she's spilled my juice twice.'

The superhero presence worked – not another argument for the rest of the flight.

There was, however, 4,356 repetitions of 'Are we there yet?', 3,245 repetitions of 'I need to go to the toilet', and three repetitions of 'I'll have a gin and tonic please.'

I drew with them. I made jigsaws. I played 'I Spy' for an hour until I was bored to the back molars with 'W' (wing, window), 'S' (seat, shoes, socks) and 'T' (television, T-shirt, trousers). The choice of objects on a plane is not exactly vast. Not that it mattered to Benny because he's yet to master the alphabet, so he just answered 'banana' to everything.

By the time we touched down, I was frazzled, exhausted and considering putting my offspring up for adoption.

'We're here, Mummy, we're here. We're at Spiderman's house!' screamed Mac as the wheels hit the tarmac. At which point, his wee joyful face and sheer excitement made me fall madly in love with him again and I would gladly have given him my kidney should he require it.

'*Spiderman, Spiderman, does whatever a spider can . . .*' sang Benny, to the amusement of the cabin crew who wanted to keep him as an airline mascot.

We grabbed our bags, clamoured down the aisle and hiked the half-marathon to the immigration hall, at which point I almost fainted when I saw the queue. I'm British, so I should love queuing, but unless there's a new pair of shoes or a pizza at the end of it then I'm not interested. Especially with two children in tow.

We'd been standing in line for about ten minutes when my pants started to vibrate. Not my actual pants – I mean my trousers, but I'm just getting into the LA lingo.

I pulled out my mobile phone. 'You have one new message,' the screen informed me, but there was no sender telephone number. I figured it would be Sam letting me know where he was going to pick us up. I pressed 'read'.

'Sorry we didn't work this out. Hope u arrive safe. Tell boys I love them. And I love you. Call me.'

I swallowed hard as tears stung at the back of my eyes. Don't cry. Don't cry. The immigration officers would already be within their rights to knock me back on account of the fact that I looked like a dosser, so pitching up at their desk and snotting over their computer would give us a good chance of getting a one-way ticket back home.

Suddenly the queue moved. I stepped forward three centimetres to keep up. At this rate the kids would be old enough to shave by the time we got to the baggage hall.

'Mummy, in America will we get motorbikes like the Power Rangers?' asked Mac.

I hadn't quite picked up what he said over the noise

of three thousand people tutting and moaning about the wait.

'I SAID WILL WE GET MOTORBIKES LIKE THE POWER RANGERS?' Mac bellowed.

Three thousand people turned to stare at us. Benny took the opportunity to give them a tune.

Away in a manger, no crib for a bed,
The little Lord Jesus lay down a sheep's head . . .

I closed my eyes. Dear God. Anyone. Please rescue me. Sam, where are you?

Sam. It suddenly struck me that I hadn't given a single thought to the fact that I was going to see Sam again. I'd been so caught up in the whole going/not going thing that I hadn't given a second thought to Sam.

The queue moved again so I stepped forward another three centimetres.

Sam Morton. The love of my life. Well, one of them, and since it ran to double digits it wasn't such an exclusive club.

I'd first met Sam in my early twenties, when I'd been transferred from my job managing a nightclub in a hotel in Shanghai to a club in a sister hotel in Hong Kong. On the night I arrived I decided to do an incognito reconnaissance of my new place of employment. Unfortunately, I'd been in deepest darkest Shanghai for so long that I was a year or two out of touch with the fashion trends. The look I was going for was Madonna in her rebel years, but instead I looked like I'd love you

71

long time for a tenner. My dress could have doubled as an inner tube: black leather mini with a zip going from breast to thigh. That was in my pre-gravity days when there was still a bit of space between those parts of my anatomy – two kids later I could have covered the same area with a thick belt. I wore killer stilettos (so called then because they were wickedly gorgeous – so called now because attempting to walk in anything that high would be considered suicidal) and my hair was trussed up on top of my head like an exploding pineapple. Think Pebbles from the Flintstones after she'd grown up and decided to support her prehistoric crack habit by going on the game.

I'd made my way down to the club, only to be faced with an Adonis at the door. Six foot two inches tall. Brown hair. Twenty-seven. Londoner. Ex-army. Crew cut. Eyelashes that Naomi Campbell would have killed for. Square jaw-line. Suntanned. White teeth. Broad shoulders. Defined pecs. Washboard abs. Slim hips. Bum that looked like two melons on a tray. Nipples alert. Ovaries putting out a 'first ride free' banner.

Obviously those last two physical conditions were mine, not his.

He was the most beautiful man I'd ever seen in my life. I wanted to push him into the janitor's cupboard and do filthy things to him. I wanted to talk dirty. I wanted to . . .

Oops, the line moved again. Another three centimetres forward. And was it just me, or was it getting really hot in here now? Still, at least the kids were quiet. Mac was engrossed in wiping out another galaxy on his

Game Boy and Benny was now curled around my neck snoozing.

Anyway, so I wanted to ... Everything. Just everything. There wasn't a lewd act that I didn't want to commit with Sam Morton, but unfortunately our hotel chain's code of conduct had a very strict DEFTS rule: Don't Ever Fuck the Staff.

And of course, never one to break the rules (and much to my excruciating agony), I remained chaste. For about a whole fortnight. Then Sam turned up at my hotel room in the middle of the night, revealed that he had the biggest penis I'd ever seen in my life (and, I must admit, has yet to be surpassed), took my breath away and ravished me in ways that I couldn't even think of repeating without pulling a muscle. About six times, if I remember correctly. The earth didn't so much move as crumble. The man was amazing. Stunning. And so sweet. He even spent some of his wages every week taking care of three old homeless Chinese guys who lived outside his apartment block.

I adored him. I completely and utterly adored him. Although I did get a bit of a shock when, much to my initial mortification and bashfulness, he asked me to marry him in front of hundreds of drunken revellers on New Year's Eve.

Of course, I said yes. Well, you don't like to say no, do you?

That sentiment might go a long way to explaining how I managed to get engaged six times before I was thirty.

Life was just great. Sam had a day job teaching martial

arts and he planned to eventually set up his own coaching academy, but he continued to work in the nightclub to get some funds together. Meanwhile, I loved every minute of being in Hong Kong, and for the first time in my life I felt settled. Like I belonged.

Naturally, then, it was time for fate to intervene and turn my whole life into the emotional equivalent of a ten-car pile-up. When my contract at the hotel ended, my bosses announced that I was being transferred to either London or Dubai. I refused, but it was pointless.

Dubai. London. Dole. Those were the options.

I begged Sam to come with me; he begged me to stay. In the end, I went, promising him that I'd come back when the next contract was over. I'm not sure he ever really believed me, which was just as well, because it was more than five years later when I finally tracked him down. The minute I saw him again . . . ah, I knew. I knew that we could definitely be great together and I promise it was based on our love, our inherent connection and our mutual feeling of shared destiny. Okay, so the fact that he had a penis the size of a marrow was a contributory factor, but I'd like to think I was deeper than that. Slightly.

However, it wasn't to be. I discovered that after I'd deserted him, Sam had undergone a career change and transformed himself into the most popular (and expensive) high-class male escort in South East Asia – not exactly what I'd anticipated as a career for a potential husband.

'Do you, Sam Morton, promise to love, honour and cherish Carly Cooper? Do you promise to keep her in sickness and in health, for richer and for poorer, and by the way would you also stop shagging anyone who throws their credit card in your direction?'

Much as Sam tried to persuade me otherwise, I knew it would never work. Shortly afterwards, he gave up hooking and wrote the screenplay of his life, which landed on the right desk at the right time. I've no idea if it was a female's desk and if Sam's privates also landed on it, but I prefer to think he got it on merit.

The movie was huge. Massive. And, surprisingly, Sam was great in the lead role. Who knew he could act? Apart from the one very strange woman who booked him for Wednesday afternoons to pretend he was her husband and answer to the name of Harold.

It was the first of many roles for Mr Stud. And great ones too. He became Richard Gere when the real Richard Gere was getting on a bit and too busy pissing off the Chinese government to strut his stuff in romantic dramas.

We stayed friends. Whenever he was in London for a premiere or to shoot something at Pinewood he'd stay with us and allow us to bask in his reflected glory. To the world he was Sam Morton, A-list superstar and all-round sex god. To us, he was just Sam. Friend. Ex-boyfriend. All-round good guy. With the biggest donger in the northern hemisphere. I chose not to share that not-so-insignificant tidbit of information with Mark. He might have been born without a single jealousy gene in his body, but there was nothing like penis envy to upset a bloke's equilibrium.

Mark actually really liked Sam. But then, liking Sam

was easy. He was sweet, great company, utterly without ego and he brought lavishly expensive pressies when he came to stay. He and Mark got on well and had loads in common (apart from a familiarity with my reproductive organs). A mutual love of football and beer and man-to-man avoidance of any conversational topics that included emotions, feelings or gossip seemed to have developed into a mutual respect for each other. It was all very modern and adult. Mark had even demonstrated his admirable lack of jealousy once again by suggesting that we ask Sam to be Benny's godfather. Sam was thrilled – and I'm sure one day Benny will echo that sentiment when he realises that his godfather has direct access to hordes of hot chicks.

'Ma'am, can you step forward please.' Hallelujah! My back was breaking with the strain of carrying three stones of little boy and what seemed like the entire aircraft's carry-on luggage. The rather formidable gentleman checked our passports, scanned things, tapped his computer, took some kind of weird photo and fingerprinted me. I refrained from pointing out that I was coming to crack Hollywood, not the bullion safe at Fort Knox.

We trundled through to baggage reclaim, grabbed a trolley, dashed to the carousel and dragged off our cases. By the time I'd loaded everything up, I couldn't see where I was going and, bloody, bloody arse, my trolley had a wonky wheel and kept veering to the left.

I dragged it through customs, Benny awake and on my back now, Mac sitting precariously on one of the bags. I'm sure the customs officers would have stopped me if I hadn't looked like I was three seconds away from demented hysteria.

I got another five yards up the steep walkway. What sick bastard designed a corridor so that people had to push luggage-laden trolleys UP a hill? Just when I thought I'd got the hang of it, Mac swayed to the side causing a full-scale dissolution of the suitcase mountain.

Bollocks. I pulled and heaved everything on again, then started back up the hill. Around the corner . . . Crash. Everything back off. My hands started to shake. Benny started to moan. Mac . . . well, Mac didn't give a toss but that's only because he has the thirst for adventure of an adrenalin junkie on speed and this whole new experience was whipping him into a frenzy.

A frenzy . . . Oh no.

'Do you need to go to the toilet, Mac?'

'Nope.'

Fingers crossed that he wasn't lying or being overly optimistic. But I speeded up just in case.

I loaded everything back on and pushed upwards. Round another corner, one last burst of energy and . . .

Sam. He was standing against a railing looking like he'd just stepped out of Man at Armani. He smiled and opened his arms. Mac ran into them.

'Uncle Sam, Uncle Sam!' he screamed, delighted.

I reached two things at exactly the same time. Sam and the end of my tether. As he reached over to envelop me in a hug, I burst into tears. And not pretty Demi Moore/*Ghost*-type tears. Not even mildly sweet Kate

Hudson tears. I'm talking full-scale Gwyneth Paltrow, nasal fluids, racking sobs, off-the-scale-in-humiliation-and-embarrassment tears. Sam looked horrified, but that might have been because my make-up-smeared, tear-drowning face was in contact with his two-thousand-dollar jacket.

'Hey, hey, what is it? What's wrong, honey?'

'Uncle Sam, Uncle Sam, we're going to see Spiderman!' screamed Mac. '*Spiderman, Spiderman, does whatever a Spider can . . .*' wailed Benny.

There wasn't a single person in the building who wasn't looking at us. I pulled my head off his clothing.

'Sorry Sam, it's . . . it's . . . been emotional,' I said apologetically.

'Don't worry, it's okay. And there's me thinking you were just overcome with joy at seeing me.'

I suddenly realised he was looking behind me expectantly.

'So where's Mark? Did he get held up in customs?'

'He's not coming.'

'What? Why?'

At which point I gave him a sane, rational update on the situation. Unfortunately, however, it came out as 'yyyeeeurrrghhh' and was accompanied by a fresh round of hysteria. I gasped for breath and eventually regained the power of speech.

'I'm sorry, Sam. Sob. I'll be fine in a minute. Sob. Then we can just get out of here and we'll forget this ever happened, okay?'

'Okay, honey, no problem.'

But actually it was a problem. At first I thought a

bulb on one of the overhead lights had popped. Then another. And another. LAX definitely needed to revisit their maintenance policies. Then another. Then . . . 'Hey, Sam, who's the lady?' 'Sam, over here.' 'Sam, this way.' 'Who is she, Sam?'

Suddenly we were surrounded, the flashlights were going off everywhere and we were marooned in a sea of paparazzi. Sam grabbed Mac and I frantically grabbed Benny. Sam shouted to someone to get our bags, and then put his child-free arm around me. 'Just put your head down and walk fast,' he shouted. Security guards materialised and suddenly I got an inkling of how Moses felt. The sea of denim and Pentax parted, and after only a few minor tussles we burst out of the doors and into a waiting limo.

'Okay guys?' I asked the kids breathlessly. They both nodded. And I made the very mature, responsible, parental decision to ignore the fact that Mac was making a particularly rude gesture to a photographer who'd knocked off his baseball cap.

I looked up at Sam with my scrunched-up face and swollen eyes.

He grinned. 'What d'ya think of the LA welcoming committee? We put that on for all the new arrivals.'

'Impressive. You might want to do something about that whole trolley/fecking great big hill combination though.'

He laughed. And despite being about as stable as Mariah Carey on a rope bridge, I found myself joining in, and . . . oh no. It must be jetlag. Stress. Insanity. I was in a stretch limo for the first time in my life. One of my sons was singing, 'Is This the Way to Amarillo' on the seat in front of me. The other was flicking a V sign at a photographer. My husband was missing. I had the complexion of a vine-grown vegetable. Sam Morton, Hollywood megastar and all-round demigod, was grinning at me. And, dear God, help me ... My nipples were winking right back.

CARLY CALLING . . .

Carly to Kate and Carol:

Hv arivd safe - flight nightmare, sam
colectd us - God, he's ugly. On way
to slum in Hollywd Hills now. Lifes a
bitch. PS: Anyone spk to Mark?

Carol:

Glad all ok - kiss my nephews for me.
Not spkn to Mark - but don't worry,
he'll come around. Lv ya, Cxx

Kate:

Give ugly bloke our lv. Mrk came here
4 tea 2nite - not happy - sorry, babe,
ul hv 2 accpt that he wl not cm around
2 this. Tk care, kiss boys, miss u, Kxx

★ Step Four ★

'Does he ever just talk?' Sam asked as Benny splashed around in the pool, defying the laws of physics and biology by swallowing water and singing at the same time. He was on verse three of the *Jungle Book*'s 'Bare Necessities'.

'Not often,' I replied. 'If he wants something really badly, like the food and water required to sustain life, and there's no relevant musical reference, then he might try stringing a sentence together. I've decided it's a small price to pay for his obvious talent, but if he's not making millions in a boy band by the time he's sixteen then I'm trading him in for another model.'

'Why on earth would you want him to be in a boy band? Think of the pressure,' Sam countered.

'Yeah, but think of the chicks! He'll love me for it.'

There was a shriek from the pool as Mac dive-bombed into the centre. Did I mention that we were at a pool? A *private* pool. With streams and waterfalls and dinghy things. And a fountain in the middle. Of course, I'm not so superficial that I'm impressed by such materialistic ostentation, but if I was a guy I'd have had a hard-on.

Sam's house had completely surpassed my expectations. Since my sole experience of LA real estate came from MTV's *Cribs*, I expected a sleek glass exterior, black and chrome interior, Louis Vuitton wallpaper, with solid gold Jacuzzis in every bathroom and plasma TVs dropping out of the ceiling every twenty feet. I was thinking flash, I was thinking bling, I was thinking a bugger to get around it all with a bottle of Windolene.

Instead, the house was like an old Spanish hacienda. Granted, it was the approximate size of Alicante, but it had a rustic charm – sort of a cross between a five-star hotel in Mexico and Zorro's weekend pad.

The only slightly worrying thing was that the house was built into the side of a hill in the upmarket and very beautiful Pacific Palisades area. Good points: amazing views over Santa Monica and right to the beach. Bad points: three words: San. Andreas. Fault. But hey, since I was sitting by a private pool with a fountain, I decided that I'd concentrate on counting my lucky stars and worry about irrelevant things like an earthquake sending us crashing down a mountain to an excruciatingly painful death some other time.

Benny waddled over, soaking wet, hair standing upright.

'Sleep,' he mumbled.

'See, I told you he could talk,' I said to Sam, as I enveloped Benny in a towel and he climbed on top of me and nuzzled in for a snooze. I never, ever want my boys to stop doing that. For the rest of their lives it should be mandatory that they snuggle down with their head on their mother's shoulder for a nap. Granted, it will be somewhat embarrassing when they are twenty-two and their girlfriends are watching.

'So . . . ?' ventured Sam cagily.

'So what?'

'Sooooooo . . . When are you going to tell me what happened with Mark?'

Ah, I was wondering how long it would take him.

We'd been there for four glorious, sun-baked hours. I was just beginning to acclimatise to the heat. I was busy trying to forget that I'd had lustful and impure thoughts about my ex-boyfriend. I was thinking how much the man I married would have loved this, once upon a time before he was kidnapped by the zombie cult of the London Commuter and turned into a workaholic android. I was getting goose bumps watching my boys having the time of their lives in the *private* pool. I was wondering whether I'd get arrested if I popped over to Jackie's house and announced that her long-lost daughter had come back to her and, oh, by the way, could I be in the will now? I was having orgasmic tremors at the fact that Sam's housekeeper, Eliza, was unpacking my luggage. Although what she thought of my seven grey bras, I'd rather not know. Mental note: underwear shopping required on a major scale. I hadn't updated my gussets since my last doomed seduction attempt, so to hell with the credit-card bill, my nethers deserved a treat.

The one thing I wasn't doing was emotional distress and contemplation.

'Sam, do you want to see me cry again? It's already taken three icepacks for the swelling in my eyes to go down.'

He shrugged his shoulders and stayed silent. Doh! I always hated it when he did that. He knew me too well. He knew that I was hopeless at letting things lie, at allowing things to remain unspoken. If he'd immediately changed the subject, I would have been fine, but the minute there was an uneasy silence my gob became jet-propelled and I coughed up information like a mob grass with his willy in a vice.

And how could I possibly pour out my heart to the near-naked Adonis who was lying less than three feet away from me? I was far too busy contemplating much more serious issues like how if I squinted in a certain way his chest looked like a silhouette of the Andes.

I hadn't phoned Mark yet. I couldn't. A paralysing medical condition, Latin term *Sulkus Extremis*, prohibited my fingers from pressing the buttons on the phone. Besides, it was after midnight in the UK now and far be it from me to disturb His Indispensable Legal Holiness from his slumbers. My stomach lurched. God, I missed him. Or at least I would once the whole blind bloody fury thing subsided.

Back in the present world, the pause was so pregnant it was about to give birth to triplets, so I crumbled and told Sam everything that had happened between Mark and me lately. Well, not quite everything. I might have vaguely alluded to the woeful reality that my sex life was about as exciting as a weekend at a plumbing convention but I refrained from going into

85

too much detail. Somehow it seemed disrespectful to discuss our inadequacies in that department when Mark's son was in earshot. Benny might look like he was sleeping but kids were like sponges – bendy and high on absorption. I didn't want it all coming back to him twenty years on when he was lying on a psychiatrist's couch. 'Doctor, I feel tortured and unable to maintain intimate relationships with women and I'm sure it's all down to the trauma of hearing my mother bad-mouthing my dad's performance when I was two and three-quarters.'

I stuck to the facts: I wanted to come here, Mark refused, so I was sitting by a pool in LA and he was on 'Pot Noodle for one' for the next month. A cloud of despondency had crept over me just by contemplating the state of my marriage.

'What do you think?' I asked Sam, when my rambling came to an end. 'Woeful or what?'

'Woeful,' he agreed.

'Cheers for that incisive, intuitive analysis. You're obviously wasting your life being a multi-million-dollar-a-year actor when you could have a very successful career with Relate.'

I shrugged off the gloom. The sun was shining and I have a gene that makes it physically impossible to be on a downer while lying on a sun-lounger. Time for salacious gossip.

'Anyway, enough about me. Which young nubile star of a weekly beach-based drama are you tampering with this week?'

He smiled and rolled his eyes. 'Don't laugh.'

I grinned. 'I won't.'

'You will.'

'I won't.'

'You will.'

'Look, Sam, trust me. I'm a knackered mother of two with jetlag and a missing husband – I can assure you that I lost my sense of humour long ago. I'm a dour-faced cow, I promise. I will not laugh. I will not even smile. I'll be a paragon of passiveness and nonchalance. So spill.'

'I'm single. Haven't seen anyone for over a year.'

At which point I spluttered into such convulsions of mirth that I woke up Benny.

'You. Are. Kidding,' I spluttered. 'Or lying.' I shushed Benny back to sleep lest he burst into song and ruin the moment.

Well, well, well. Sam Morton, single. Same sentence. Never thought it could happen. And for a whole year?

'Not even any one-night stands or illicit fumbles?'

'None.'

'But why?'

I was astonished. Let's put this in context. It was like a gifted artist locking away his paints. Or a serial shoplifter boycotting Marks & Spencer during the January sales.

Was he sick? Was he stricken with unrequited love for a world-famous but very married actress? Had his publicists hushed up the fact that he'd actually spent the last twelve months in jail?

I knew whatever it was must be serious. Profound. Deep.

'Can't be arsed,' he confessed in a non-profound, definitely-not-deep tone. 'It's just not worth the hassle. Carly, I spend most of the year away on location or promoting a movie. There's no stability, no permanence. And to be honest, not many opportunities to meet someone.'

'What about your co-stars?' I replied, still dumb-founded.

'Yeah, great idea. But can I just remind you that I spent the last nine months shooting a prison movie with Bruce Willis, Will Smith and The Rock. Somehow I think that flowers and a subtle chat-up line would have resulted in mourners being directed to my grave-side.

'And besides, sounds crazy, but I'm trying to shake off the assumptions.'

I was confused. 'What assumptions?'

'When I came here it was because of my movie. There it was – life story, no secrets. Closet open, skele-tons out. I was Sam Morton, that bloke who'd been an escort for rich women. I was pretty sure it would be a one-movie wonder and once the curiosity factor wore off I'd take the money and run back to Asia. And that would have been fine. But it didn't happen. I got more roles, the dosh went up, and the publicity was positive considering this country is the last bastion of the morally righteous. But then, they love a reformed sinner, and by making *Play the Game* I'd spent two hours and ten minutes in a public confessional. So I stayed and made a go of it, and it worked. But now when I meet someone they've already made their mind up about me. Some of them just want to find out if the sex lives up to the hype. Some want publicity or the cash from a shag and spill. And the decent ones – well, I think they'd probably run a mile.'

That last thought hung in the air. I could see his point. Putting to one side for a moment the fact that he was now loaded and therefore devastatingly attractive to very shallow women, gold-diggers and religious cults, Sam's dodgy career history meant that to most females he sat on the 'Great Catch' league table somewhere between bird flu and a sexually transmitted disease. But, as I'd thought many times over the years, at least he was honest. How many toxic bachelors fuck every girl in sight, swearing undying love to each and every one of them, all the while knowing that if they were linked up to a bullshit detector it would be wailing like a smoke alarm in a sauna?

Sam was always honest. And although it seems like a contradiction, he had integrity. And honour. And a good heart. And a female would be crazy to overlook that just because he'd dabbled for a while in a career that involved being butt naked and asking for credit-card details at the end of every shift.

Yep, she'd be mad. Crazy. Nuts.

I kissed Benny on the head and glanced in Mac's direction. He was wrestling with an inflatable alligator in the shallow end.

I couldn't look at Sam because I didn't want to see his expression. Would it be matter-of-fact? Probing? Accusatory? Sad?

Because, after all, I knew the real Sam Morton and

I loved him. Once upon a time I'd loved him more than anyone else on earth. Yet still . . . hadn't I run for the moral hills when I'd found out about his venture into the escort services?

There was a long, pensive silence while I digested this. I had. I'd bolted. I hadn't even had the courage to try and overlook that one transgression. How unforgiving was I? After all, it wasn't as if he'd been caught with twenty-seven bodies under the floorboards. He had sex with lots of women. So did Tom Jones, and women still threw their knickers at him.

But then, I thought with a sigh, wasn't it all just a case of fates and destinies? If I'd given Sam another go then Mark and I wouldn't be together. Although I suppose I should really qualify that with 'together – in a 5,382 miles apart and having the kind of stand-off normally championed by men with sombreros' kind of way.

And if Mark and I weren't together then I wouldn't be living in London. Nor would I be permanently skint. I wouldn't be fighting my way through 4x4 traffic hell every morning to get the kids to school. I wouldn't know the names of all the ladies who work on the checkouts at Asda. Oh no, I wouldn't have all those wonderful gifts that came with choosing to love Mark Barwick. Instead, I'd be living in Pacific Palisades, borrowing cups of sugar from the Hanks next door, asking my chef what was for tea and counting my Prada bags. I'd have to suffer the superficiality of private jets and unlimited charge cards. I'd have bloody blisters from trundling up and down Rodeo Drive. Oh, it would be shite. A nightmare. Horrible. And worst of all, I'd have to suffer the trauma of going to bed every night with a man who made Brad Pitt look average, who was anatomically gifted and who hadn't commanded the highest rates in the free world for his sexual proclivities just because he was nice to talk to.

God, I'd had a lucky escape. Phew. Giddy relief.

Excuse me, I'm just off to find a whip with which to flagellate myself until I weep.

I was roused from my contemplation by Mac, who had sauntered over, leaving a trail of conquered inflatable animals behind him.

'Mum, did you see me, did you, did you, did you? I killed ten whole dinosaurs!'

'I saw you, honey, and you were fantastic! So brave and fearless and not in the least bit worrying!'

Sam laughed, and in an instant the tense atmosphere was dispelled.

'So listen, how would you like to go and see the REAL Spiderman tomorrow?'

Mac screamed and literally jumped for joy. I hoped that puddle around him was caused by the fact he'd recently alighted from the swimming pool.

'Yes, Uncle Sam, can we, can we, please?'

I wondered what age he'd be before he stopped repeating every question at least twice.

Benny squirmed on my chest – no doubt roused by a combination of Mac screaming and hunger.

Two minutes ago I'd been deep in thought about lost love and regrets – now I was contemplating disinfecting a poolside deck and pondering how I was going to break the news that it was unlikely that Sam's freezer contained fish fingers and chunky chips.

Motherhood – situation normal.

I smiled at Sam. 'Thanks, Sam, they'll love it. So where are we going to spot Spidey then – one of the theme parks?'

'Movie lot – Sony are shooting *Spiderman 3*. Tobey Maguire's a mate and he said it would be cool if we stopped by.'

Like I said, this would be a shite life. 'Oh, okay then. Great,' I said casually, doing my best to act like I bumped into Tobey Maguire twice a week in the chip shop.

'Eh, actually, you're not going.'

'I'm not?'

Oh, I immediately got it – it was the whole paparazzi thing. He didn't want to damage his reputation by being snapped with someone who looked like she modelled her look on Lisa Simpson.

'Nope, you've got a meeting. A breakfast meeting actually. The Peninsula Hotel, 9 a.m., with Ike Tusker – über agent and all-round Hollywood player from TDA.'

I gasped. Ike Tusker. Sam's agent. From TDA! Talent Development Agency – the top agency in the world. The company that represented Catherine Zeta-Jones, Cameron Diaz, Julia Roberts, George Clooney, Brad Pitt, Tom Hanks . . . and perhaps me!

This was huge. HUGE! And I was ecstatic for a whole five minutes before I began to panic. My one and only decent suit had just spent 24 hours in a suitcase. My roots were showing. My nails were hacked. My eyebrows were sending out mating signals to all caterpillars within a ten-yard radius. I had nothing prepared – no pitch, no presentation – and I'd spent so long in the company of children and isolated from the cut and thrust of corporate life that I wasn't sure I still had the capacity to speak in words of more than two syllables, let alone have an intelligent, informed conversation.

But HOW exciting! The adrenalin pumped around my blood vessels and switched my brain straight on to 'hyper' setting. I was scared to death, but this, *this* was what I'd been missing for so long – the excitement, the thrill, the sheer bloody madness of feeling wild and reckless.

Just then, Eliza appeared. I was relieved to see that she wasn't brandishing a grey bra and a *Victoria's Secret* catalogue.

'Sam . . .'

I liked it that she called him by his first name – it reinforced Sam's lack of pretension and disregard for ego-boosting bollocks.

'I'm just nipping down to the store, can I get anything for anybody?'

She leaned over and ruffled Mac's hair as he opened his mouth. Never one to miss an opportunity for E-numbers, I could tell he was about to chance his arm and ask for one of everything on the sweet shelf. I unleashed the wrath of the main source of discipline in our family – my right eyebrow – and raised it as far as it would go. Mac spotted it and immediately closed his mouth and looked sheepish. God help us if I ever had Botox because behaviour in our house would run out of control.

'Thank you, Eliza, but we're fine,' I said, then realised that I'd forgotten to pack possibly the most essential item of all – pull-up pants for Benny. We had mastered the daytime potty training many months before, but overnights were yet to be tackled.

'Actually, Eliza, could I come with you – I need to get some pull-up pants for Benny.'

You see, I'd be rubbish at being rich. While it would take me a whole five minutes to get used to first-class travel and ostentatious spending, I felt really uncomfortable with servitude.

'Not at all, sit where you are – I'll pick them up for you. You're talking about trainer pants, right?'

'Right. Size: large. Let me just get my purse . . .'

'That's not necessary. We have an account at the store.'

Oh. How do I get one of those? As she wandered away, leaving me to lounge and generally work hard at soaking up the sun's rays and sipping a cocktail, it did cross my mind that maybe I could get used to this after all.

'Right, guys, who's coming in for another swim?' Sam leapt up, grabbed Benny and ran off with Mac chasing behind him, all three of them squealing with laughter.

He wasn't stuck in his office debating fine points of law. *His* head wasn't stuck in a newspaper. *He* wasn't asleep. *He* wasn't sulking. *He* was fun, exciting, and fantastic with my boys. Yep, this really would be a crap life.

*   *   *

By seven o'clock that evening I was falling head-first into the pizza Sam had phoned in for dinner. You can't beat a balanced diet: extra-large pepperoni in one hand, garlic bread in the other. The boys were exhausted too. Benny was lying across the sofa with his head in my lap and a piece of pepperoni stuck to his chin, while Mac was lying on the other sofa, trying to keep one eye open as he pretended to be able to read the words in a comic. Sam lay on the floor, head propped against Mac's sofa.

'Bedtime, guys,' I declared with a yawn. I checked my watch and did a quick calculation – three in the morning UK time. If I was a shallow, narrow-minded person I just might give Mark a call to irritate him. But no, I was being very mature about the situation now. After all, I was an adult and a responsible mother of two – I had to deal with things in an efficient, intelligent manner, so a few hours before I'd sent Mark an efficient, intelligent text.

'DAD, WE'RE HAVING THE BEST TIME EVER! THE POOL HAS A FOUNTAIN AND I KILLED AN ALLIGATOR TODAY. WE MISS YOU BUT MUM SAYS SHE DOESN'T. LOVE M&B XX'

Very dignified, I'd thought. A beep alerted us that a text had come straight back.

I MISS U GUYS TOO. WL CALL YOU 2MRW. LOVE YOU. DAD. PS: WELL DONE ON THE ALLIGATOR. XX

There had been a knot in my stomach ever since. There was no use denying it – private pools and cock-tails aside, I missed my husband. Uuuurgh, and that made me even more furious. Imagine how great it would be if Mark were here – just perfect. Instead, it was . . . well, it felt like winning a medal at the Olympics, then discovering that the whole family had nipped out for a fag at the podium/national anthem bit. I wanted him here.

I gave myself a shake. He wasn't. End of story. Work was far more important to Mr Mark Barwick and I'd better get used to it. Oh crap, my eyes were filling up again. Jetlag. Definitely bloody jetlag.

'You okay?' Sam asked.

I nodded. 'Just . . . just wish . . .' Hold on a minute, what about Sam? Let's get some perspective here. This bloke was one of my oldest friends, he had facilitated the chance of a lifetime and he'd welcomed us here with open arms – the last thing he deserved was me moaning and dripping snot on his cashmere carpet. How pathetic was I, face like a wet weekend when I should be damn well revelling in every minute of this. I owed it to Sam. I owed it to myself. And I owed it to my boys. After all, how many people got a chance to escape the monotony of life for an all-expenses-paid stay in the swanky pad of an A-list movie star? Mark Barwick, eat my shorts. I was going to grab Hollywood by the throat and squeeze it till it sang. Or if that didn't work I'd fall at the feet of every movie mogul and lick his boots until he realised my genius and got his chequebook out. Or had me arrested. Either way, I was going to make this worth it.

'Heeelloo?'

I snapped out of my deliberations. Sam was looking at me with an expectant, amused expression.

'Sorry, Sam, I was just wishing that . . .' Quick recovery required. I gave myself a mental shake. 'Just wish that I looked slightly more groomed and slightly less like someone who's been backpacking through the Third World for a year.'

He eyed me up and down. Ah, sweet, he was going to say, 'Don't worry, love, you look great,' and my fragile ego would soar.

'Don't worry, love . . .'

How well did I know that man?

'I know a make-up girl who can work wonders. She should be able to get you looking half-decent in no time.'

Hear that banging noise? That was my fragile ego thudding its head on the marble coffee table.

Sam reached over and grabbed the phone, then pressed speed-dial. 'Hey, Jojo,' he said, 'I wonder if you can do me a huge favour?'

I decided not to stick around to listen to him explain the gargantuan scale of the task. 'C'mon, gorgeous,' I whispered to Mac, while picking up Benny and heading for the bedroom. We were in the guest suite. Or, more accurately, a bloody great big room that could have my whole house deposited in the middle and still have space round the edges. Sam had offered to put in a couple of extra beds, but since the main bed in the room could accommodate Tottenham Hotspur, I declined. Besides, I liked snuggling up to my boys. I wanted all the hugs I could get.

Mac stripped and pulled on the pyjamas that Eliza had left at the end of the bed. If Sam asked if I'd like to take home a souvenir of my Hollywood experience, I was going to ask for Eliza. Pushing my luck, I know, but for this level of pampering I was prepared to risk it.

I stripped Benny while he slept and cast around for the pull-up pants. When I spotted them I shrieked with laughter.

'What, Mum, *what*?' giggled Mac, clueless to what was going on but happy to join in with any excuse for hilarity.

'Look at Benny's new pants,' I whispered.

Mac searched around and gasped when his eyes fell on them. These were no ordinary pants. These were to little boys who pee in their sleep what Ferraris are to grown men with small genital organs. They were the haute couture of the incontinence world. The jewel in the crown of the preschool wardrobe. They were ... Buzz Lightyear pants.

'Benny, Benny, it's Buzz, it's Buzz!' shrieked Mac, jumping up and down. Ah, the great Mr Lightyear – the intergalactic space ranger who had once been the love of Mac's life – right up until Spiderman muscled in and replaced him. Toddlers – so fickle. Anyway, I have to say I was relieved because, while it lasted, Mac's obsession with Buzz Lightyear had resulted in a compulsion to spontaneously jump from a great height shouting 'To infinity and beyond', resulting in two split lips, a dislocated elbow, suspected concussion and more bruising than Rocky at the end of ten rounds.

Benny opened one eye, and then went from sleep to

hyperactive in three seconds. 'Buzz Lightyear, Buzz Lightyear!' he shouted.

Oh yes, I could tell already that my boys were going to be serious conscientious academics, perhaps scientific geniuses who would no doubt go on to discover the cures for many of today's terminal diseases. Right after they put on glass helmets and saved the world from the Evil Emperor Zurg.

Benny yanked off his clothes and put his pants on. I would have been impressed if he didn't have both legs through the same hole. I rearranged him and he strutted across the room, one fist held aloft. 'To infinity and beyond,' he yelled.

I grabbed him by the buttocks. 'To your bed and beyond, little man,' I told him as I tickled him furiously and he squealed with laughter.

It was only later, as the two of them lay beside me breathing softly in their sleep, that I realised I hadn't washed faces, brushed teeth, or prepared clothes for the next day. Was this some laidback LA downward slide – within a week would I be feeding them hot dogs for breakfast and having competitions to see who could spit the furthest?

I made the executive decision that for just one night I wouldn't give a flying fart about such trivialities as personal hygiene and grooming. I kissed them both on the forehead and whispered goodnight. I was in LA. I was on the cusp of fame and fortune. And I was having a threesome with two gorgeous males – life didn't get much better than that.

*　　*　　*

Sam shook me awake about ten minutes later. Actually, it was early morning but it definitely felt like ten minutes later. My eyes were swollen shut and my mouth had all the moisture of a desert-dweller's flip-flop.

'Sorry, Carly, but Jojo's here,' he whispered.

Groan. 'Morning,' I slurred. Since the boys were born, I hadn't quite mastered mornings. I'm sure that one side of my head looked like it had collapsed and there was definitely drool – a clue, perhaps, as to why Mark had lost the urge for a pre-dawn shag.

I grabbed the robe Eliza had very kindly left over the chair at the side of the bed and pulled it on, before padding through to the kitchen.

'Well, hi there!'

Aaaargh! Christ Almighty! It was some ungodly hour in the middle of the night, I felt like I'd been stroked to sleep by a jackhammer, I was struggling to remember my own name, and now I was being assaulted by Heidi Klum in yoga gear.

Jojo was Amazonian. She had long blonde hair that belonged in a Pantene advert, the smile of an Osmond, her body had been carved out of marble and her breasts were in their correct anatomical position. I hated her on sight.

'Great to meet you,' she grinned, dilating my pupils with the gleam from her molars. 'Here, I brought you a skinny mocha chocca decaf cappuccino with a vanilla shot.'

Suddenly it was all clear. She wasn't human. No one this bright, shiny and perfect could be made from flesh and blood. She was an android on an advance party from the Planet Starbuck.

I took the coffee and did my best to muster a smile and a greeting. I took shallow comfort from the fact that she was an enemy creature from outer space and as soon as Buzz Lightyear and his lightsaber woke up she was toast.

'Okay, so what do we need here this morning?' she asked in a singsong voice, but clearly eyeing my general appearance with trepidation.

'Jojo, have you heard the story of the loaves and the fishes?' I asked her.

She nodded. Good to know they taught religious education on Starbuck. 'Think that scale of miracle, then double it. Make me gorgeous.'

Sam laughed in the corner. Jojo glanced from me to Sam then back to me again. Then burst into giggles.

'Hey, I'll give it a shot. You know, I always wanted to put on my CV that I'd worked on *Mission Impossible*.'

I nearly choked on my skinny mocha bollocksy thing. The irreverence. The cheek. The bare-faced bloody insult. Suddenly I felt . . . I felt . . . like I was back at home in the metaphorical bosoms of my girlfriends. Maybe I was going to like Jojo after all.

Cancel that last statement. There was no maybe about it: I bloody loved Jojo. By the time she left, nearly three hours later, I was fervently hoping that she was a lesbian so that I could offer to have her babies in thanks for the wonder of her talents. I was a woman transformed. Gone was the hair of Billy Idol, and in its place was a blonde Hepburn elfin cut. Gone was the face that had been put through a mangle, replaced by cosmetic perfection. Even my eyebrows had been reduced from insect status to immaculately groomed arcs. And my nails? Well, they weren't strictly mine any more, they belonged to a Chinese plastics factory, but they were so brilliant I wanted to spend the whole day in a crowded street just waving.

I gave her a hug as she left. Very LA. 'Thanks, Jojo, you've been a godsend.'

'Hey, no problem. I'll catch up with you guys later.' She leaned over and kissed Sam, then jumped into some kind of flash convertible thing and whizzed off.

I nudged him in the ribs. 'She *likes* you,' I grinned.

'Nah, that's just Jojo. She overflows with the cup of human kindness to everyone. She lives with Cameron King – big-shot director.'

Strange, I was sure I'd detected a definite longing there, but obviously not. Anyway, whatever. Jojo came, Jojo went, and I wanted to drop to my knees and thank God and space travel for her visit. I glanced at myself in the hall mirror. I was ready. I was *so* ready. Now there was just the matter of two little boys to get ready. We were scheduled to leave in an hour. The plan was that Sam would drop me at the hotel, take the boys to the shooting location a few blocks away, then come back for me when I called him after my meeting. Sam Morton. Hollywood A-lister. Demigod. Richer than a small Arab state. And my taxi driver.

I wandered back into the bedroom, no resemblance whatsoever to the creature from the black latrine who'd left it only a few short hours before. The boys were still sleeping – Mac in the shape of a starfish, and Benny curled up, but clutching the waistband of his Buzz pants. I shook him awake first. He opened one eye, then the other, then gaped.

He immediately spotted that something was different. Jeans and stained T-shirt mum had been replaced by chic, suited, lipsticked mum. Only one person could have accomplished this transformation. He gazed down at his pants in wonderment – it was amazing what Buzz Lightyear could do in just one night.

I scooped both boys out of bed and deposited them at the breakfast table, holding them carefully in the underarm position so that no snot or any other fluid could find its way from them to my smart togs.

Sam wandered off to his study to make some calls while I, with one eye on the clock, shovelled their breakfast down them. So far, so good. We were just about on schedule, with no surprises, minimal resistance (but Mum, I hate cornflakes, I want pizza for breakfast), and no casualties.

Then I was ambushed. By Buzz Lightyear.

'Okay, Benny, time to get dressed now, honey.'

Silence.

'Come on, babe – time to get dressed.'

'Nope.'

'What, pet?'

'I'm not taking off my Buzz pants.'

'Come on, honey, Mummy's in a big hurry today, you have to get ready to go.'

'Nope. Not taking off my Buzz pants.'

Hell. The enemy was engaged.

It was an unanticipated hitch in the battle plan. I checked the clock – almost time to leave. I had two choices: surrender, let him keep the pants on and make my meeting in the grown-up world on time, or fight it out and risk being trounced.

I made a split-second decision, based on years of experience at the front line. As all mothers know, once you get them out of daytime nappies there's no going back. Weakness is fatal and likely to result in once again having to lug extra-large boxes of Pampers back from Tescos and a twenty-pound-a-week dent in the shopping budget. I had to stick to my guns. Besides, he'd had the pants on all night and they were sagging down to his knees.

The way forward was clear: Buzz was coming off and nothing would deter me from my mission. Except, that is, a small boy who bolted to the bathroom like his Buzz-clad buttocks were on fire. And, of course, proceeded to lock the door.

Well, I tried everything: from gentle bribery through cajoling, coercion, and leading up to blatant threats of adoption. Nothing worked. It was a siege situation and the negotiator was out of ideas.

Twenty minutes later, I sought out Sam in his study.

'Do you want the good news or the bad?' I asked him.

'Give me the good,' he said with a grin.

'I think you're a lovely person and I'm sure you'll go to heaven for all the very nice things you do for your friends.'

He still had that gorgeous, knee-trembler of a grin on his face.

'Okay then, let me have it. What's the bad news?'

I grimaced. Twenty-four hours under the man's roof and already we were causing chaos and mayhem.

'Benny's locked in the toilet. I've tried everything to get him out and he's not budging. I think we're going to have to break down the door.'

Ten minutes, a loud crack, several splinters and a bruised shoulder later, we finally broke through enemy lines. Buzz was eventually defeated, leaving only one severely upset wee boy who probably wouldn't talk to me again until he hit puberty and needed pocket money for drugs.

We bundled the boys in the car, with Sam probably wondering what the hell he'd let himself in for, and headed towards Beverly Hills for my meeting. My nerves were shot. My heart was racing. But hey, compared to the savage, danger-fraught minefield that is motherhood, breaking into the movie industry should be a doddle.

Family Values *Magazine*

PUTTING THE YUMMY IN MUMMY
THIS WEEK . . . MY HEART, MY HUSBAND

Ladies, remember that first flush of love? The butter-flies in the stomach, the breathless anticipation of the first kiss, the spa days to whip yourself up into an irre-sistible frenzy, those romantic seductions by the fire-side in an Aspen lodge . . . Oh, aren't courtships wonderful? And then there was the engagement, the wedding, the holiday homes in Paris and Milan (so useful for the seasons) and then the most amazing gift of all – the children. Where there used to be two, there are now three – or four, five, or six in the case of multiple births and devout Catholics. As we all know, ladies, even with a full complement of nannies and a night nurse to ease the burden, those early days are simply exhausting: so many people to receive, thank-you cards to write, baby clothes to choose. But in the midst of this dramatic adjustment, we mustn't forget the other person whose life has changed forever – your partner. The man who was once the centre of your universe has made way for another person to take a piece of your heart. This we must acknowledge and reward. Never lose sight of the person whose love has brought you the miracle of family.

Now, girls, we're not in the Forties any longer. The days of standing by the door to greet your husband with his slippers and a drink are long gone (although Harrods are currently doing a roaring trade in the most incredible chichi suede mules for men – apparently David Furnish is a fan). However, simple touches will keep the sparkle in your relationship: perhaps run your beloved a bath after a long flight, have the housekeeper prepare his favourite meal, and, most importantly, remember never to reject the intimacies that you once shared.

The Forties may indeed be gone, but perhaps today we could learn something from our forebears' mantra that 'a happy husband is a happy home'.

★ Step Five ★

'Okay, Sam, advice, coaching, therapy, Prozac . . . hit me with anything you've got,' I wittered as he dropped me off at the hotel.

He laughed. 'Relax. Ike's a good guy – if you like ruthless megalomaniacs who'd sell their granny for a deal.'

'*What?*'

'I'm kidding! He's a good guy, honest. Now don't worry, just smile, go in there and be yourself.'

Myself. A woman who was wearing grown-up clothes for the first time in years, who was so excited that her heart was ready to pound right out of her push-up bra and who hadn't quite recovered from a wrestling bout with a fictional spaceman.

Not to mention a woman who was so damned irresistible that her husband would drop anything just to be with her. Not.

Yep, Mr Tusker was sure to be bowled over.

'Right, boys, be good. Remember your manners, tell Sam when you need the toilet and DO NOT ask Spiderman to reveal his true identity, okay?'

'*Spiderman, Spiderman . . .*'

Benny was off again and the doorman at the Peninsula was giving me strange looks.

I kissed the boys, gave them a hug and told them I loved them. I got the usual chorus of 'Love you, Mum' in return. I know they say it in mantra fashion with no discernible emotion or meaning, but I care not a jot. Heart melts. Every time. I kissed Sam on the cheek. 'Thanks for this and . . . everything.'

A very loud horn blared from a Maserati that was waiting behind us in the driveway. I resisted the urge to give him the V sign and it was just as well because I suddenly went blind – not because of some sudden neurological failure, but the result of half a dozen flashes shooting like bullets from the bushes nearby. Paparazzi again. Bloody hell, how did Sam live like this – it was a scandalous state of affairs that raised some serious questions about the modern-day obsession with the cult of fame. Were we going to be faced with constant intrusion into our privacy? Was there nothing they wouldn't do to get a good shot? Did the public thirst for salacious details have to extend to a breach of a celebrity's human rights? And most importantly, did they get my best side?

I rushed inside. Oh, it was posh. Cream marble floor, columns, gold décor – if they moved the bloody great vase of lilies from the middle of the foyer they'd have the perfect setting for a stage version of *The King and I*. Right, I will not be so impressed that I crumble into a blabbering mess, I vowed, throwing back my shoulders, pouting my lips and doing that walk I'd seen on the fashion channel where you sway your hips while adopting the gait of a two-legged Bambi. I was working it, working it, oh yeah, baby, working it . . . right up until I walked past a queue at reception, tripped over someone's laptop case and missed cracking my teeth on the edge of the reception desk by an inch. Only catlike reflexes saved me as I reached out and grabbed the marble desktop with two hands. There I was, near horizontal, white-knuckled and suffering from severe mortification – another one of life's little moments of dignity. Before I could straighten up, the receptionist leaned over the desk to see who the knuckles belonged to, as if this happened on a regular basis. 'Can I help you, madam?'

I shuffled to my feet, wondering if my blazing face was an attractive contrast to the décor. 'I'm meeting Ike Tusker.'

'Ah, Mr Tusker, he's already in the restaurant. If you'd like to go back across the lobby, and just before you reach the entrance turn right. Go along to the end of the corridor, turn right again and the maître d' there will be able to assist you.'

I ignored the fact that half the people in the vicinity had witnessed my triple salchow and scored me zero out of ten for artistic impression. They probably all thought that I'd escaped during the night from a Malibu rehab clinic and was under the influence of mind-altering substances. Sod it. Rehab was trendy. If it was good enough for Kate Moss . . .

Head held high once again, I strutted back across the lobby, ignoring the curious stares. I was cool, I was calm, I was Jackie Collins's biological daughter, I was in Beverly Hills and I was meeting Ike Tusker, agent to the stars. It was going to take more than one minor incident of public humiliation to take the shine off my day.

When I reached the restaurant, the maître d' was there waiting. Strange, he looked exactly like the bloke at reception. Twins. How unusual for them both to be working in the same place.

'Hi,' I greeted him. 'I'm here to meet Mr Tusker.'

He eyed me with confusion. 'Pardon me, ma'am?'

Suddenly, I realised the problem. I'd experienced this very same syndrome when I lived in New York. The Scottish accent – if it didn't sit somewhere between Sean Connery and *Braveheart* then some Americans had trouble deciphering it.

I repeated the request, this time speaking slower and more clearly. Nice maître d' man flashed Jojo-esque teeth at me then led me over to a corner table. I tried not to look to the left or right while I was en route. Sam had told me that this was THE place for the big names in the movie industry to meet, so I didn't want to run the risk of seeing Liam Neeson sitting at a table and being compelled to fall at his feet and offer him sexual favours in front of every mover and shaker in Hollywood.

Ike got up as I reached the table, snapped his mobile phone shut and held out his hand. Christ, he had Jojo's teeth too. Was there a shiny teeth supermarket around here?

'Carly, Ike – pleased to meet you,' he announced as

111

he shook my hand – firm grip, but not in a 'I'm trying to reinforce my masculinity and let me tell you I can bench-press 400 pounds' macho kind of way. Just strong. Firm. Controlled.

'Thanks for seeing me – I know you're busy so I do appreciate it,' I replied.

Good start, I thought – a touch on the grovelling side but not so obsequious that he thought I was star-struck. Although, naturally, I was. I was desperate to check if Mel Gibson was tucking into his brekkie at the table behind me. Was Travolta sucking up decaf just behind that pillar?

I sat down on the green padded banquette and immediately the waiter appeared. Wow, triplets. What are the chances? Come to think about it, Ike had a few similarities too. Tall, broad-shouldered, great tan. Dark hair, not too short, gelled back but in a Beckham/Brylcreem way as opposed to dirty mac/hangs out in a park kind of way. Startlingly blue eyes and, of course, Jojo's teeth. Yep, there was definitely a similarity thing going on here between several of the guys . . . Maybe they were cousins.

The waiter gave us both menus and I immediately opened mine. Oh, I could murder a big breakfast. How long had it been since breakfast didn't comprise a bit of toast clenched between my teeth while pulling on two children's jackets, grabbing bags and sprinting to the car? I was going to have the works. I'd have bacon. I'd have eggs. I'd have sausage. Wonder if they did fried bread? Oh I'm sure they would if I asked. Maybe a potato scone was pushing it, but mushrooms and . . .

'Three-egg-white omelette, herbal tea,' Ike announced without even glancing at his menu.

'And you, ma'am, what can we get for you this morning?'

Pants. Now I was going to look like a prime candidate for Overeaters Anonymous if I went for the full shebang. And I'd already escaped from one rehab that morning.

'Er, I'll have the same please,' I said with a smile. Although I knew it didn't have the same dazzling effect as everyone else in LA because I seemed to be the only person in the city without Jojo's bloody teeth. I made a mental note to ask Sam where I could get them.

'So, I'm really excited about your book and I definitely think we can do something with it. It's high concept and that's exactly what everyone is looking for right now.' Ike stormed right in there like the movie-industry equivalent of the SAS.

'Great,' I replied enthusiastically, trying not to show that I wouldn't know a 'high concept' if it arrived on top of my three-egg-white omelette. 'I'm thrilled that you think it's got potential. And excuse my naïveté, Ike, but what exactly will happen from here?'

He went on to explain the master plan. The all-important strategy. The vital essence of our route to success. And I tried to listen, I really did, but I was sure now that it was indeed Mr Gibson at the next table, although I might have been a bit out on Travolta. Either that or he had a great make-up person on *Get Shorty 2* and had just spent a month in a pie shop.

However, I got the gist of the plan. Ike had couriered

the book over to some contacts from the major studios and production companies the previous afternoon. It had also gone to a handful of actors that they represented. In total it went out to about ten people. They'd then come back to him if they were interested and he would set up introductory meetings with me.

I suddenly felt deflated. He'd only just sent it out? But these people could take weeks to read it. Months, even. I'd come all the way over here and all I'd achieved was a new hairdo, one meeting with an agent and a potential divorce.

Gasp – it *was* Travolta, definitely. And he certainly wasn't ageing as well as Olivia Newton John.

But back to . . . oh, that's right– I'd come all the way to LA thinking I was going to get snapped up the minute I stepped off the plane and the whole pitch process had only just kicked off. Mark was right. Argh, I hated that! But he was right. I should have waited until the interest was a little more definite. Instead, I'd been so desperate for a bit of glamour and excitement that I'd jumped the gun quicker than Dick Turpin after a case of Red Bull.

'So, I'm hoping that we'll get some feedback by the middle of next week. Of course, if it was already in script format then I'd definitely say we'd have our responses by Monday, but my assistant has put together a great synopsis and some key excerpts so I don't think the fact that it's in novel form will be too much of a problem.'

Next week? Good grief. I couldn't get Sainsbury's to deliver my groceries in that timescale and here he was saying that we could send out a book to some of the busiest people in a crazy-busy industry, and they'd read it and get back to him with an answer.

'But . . . but . . . That's great, Ike. Amazing. I'm just startled. I thought the whole process would take a lot longer.'

He leaned towards me and lowered his tone slightly. 'Look, normally it would, but to be honest, my main focus is on looking after my people so I don't do submission work – I'd normally hand that over to another department in the agency. However, this time I've made an exception. I've already called everyone and primed them that this is on the way and it's hot. I have to tell you that Cameron is already interested and I've told Demi that the mother role is perfect for her. She's been wanting to play older for a while now – likes to keep on surprising people.'

If the waiter hadn't broken the moment by appearing with my breakfast I would have keeled over. (And if that had indeed happened I'd like to think that Liam Neeson would have immediately sprung from a table and snogged me back to life. And if he wanted to cop a feel while I was semi-conscious that would have been just fine.)

Cameron. Demi. Last week the most exciting thing that had happened to me was a catalogue delivery and now I was sitting in Beverly Hills discussing how I was going to be Demi Moore's new best friend. And Ike Tusker, agent to the entire stellar world, didn't normally take on novels or submissions but he'd made an exception for mine. *Mine!* I was so lucky. I was gifted. I was special. I was spectacularly talented. I was obviously . . . Oh crap, I was deluded.

'Ike, can I ask you something and would you be totally and utterly honest?'

He hesitated. Never a good sign. 'Sure, go ahead.'

'Are you only dealing with my book because Sam is your client and he's pulled in a favour?'

Long pause. I'd hit the nail on the head. Hole in one. Bulls-eye. Bingo. Fuck.

'Okay, Carly, let me be straight with you.'

My stomach lurched. Thank God I hadn't gone for the fried bread and mushrooms. I hated it when people announced that they were going to be honest. I always wanted to interject and say, 'No, please do humour me by telling me nice things. I couldn't care less if they're not true. Just patronise me and I'll choose to believe you and that way we'll all be happy.'

I nodded my head and not without considerable apprehension.

'If you'd sent this book to my office it would never have got past my assistants. Even if it had, I'd never have got around to reading it. Did I look at it because Sam asked me to? Sure I did.'

There it was. I was the Hollywood-agent equivalent of missionary work. A charity case.

'But at the same time, I've got a reputation and if I didn't think it was great I wouldn't have done anything with it. Carly, I laughed my ass off by page five. Laughed. My. Ass. Off. So did I take it on because of Sam? Yes. But do I genuinely think it's got great potential? I do. I definitely do.'

Oh, he definitely did. I loved Ike Tusker. I loved Sam Morton. I loved Los Angeles. Strange, normally my buttocks were frequent visitors to the bitter-and-twisted bench and now suddenly I loved the whole wide world.

'So, rewind a second, Ike. Tell me what else will happen. Hopefully we'll get some interest and introductory meetings . . .'

'I'd say that was pretty definite,' he declared with confidence.

'. . . So what will happen after that?'

'Okay, the purpose of the introductory meeting is to run through the project as a concept, for you to meet them and for them to get a sense of where you're coming from.'

London. Pissing-down rain. Overdraft.

'Now, this is where it differs depending on who it is. As far as the names on our studio lists are concerned, we're already talking heads of development, so we've cut out a few people on the food chain. And if those guys are interested, then they'll make a recommendation and set up a further pitch meeting with the final decision-makers. If they like it then it's that time . . .'

'What time?'

He grinned. 'It's money time.'

Money time. Cash. Mucho dosho.

'However, if we don't get that far straight off the bat, then that's where the talent comes in. If an actress reads it, loves it and thinks a role would work for her, then we can pitch it to a studio or production company with her name attached. The studio takes it on because with

117

the star attached it's already got weight. And then we're back to money time,' he finished with a grin.

Oh, that M word again. I liked that.

'Ike, can you tell me what kind of figures we're talking about here? Just, erm, ballpark. You know . . . is it new shoes, new wardrobe or new house?'

He laughed and for the first time I noticed that even when he smiled the corners of his eyes didn't crinkle up. I spied with my little eye something beginning with B. And on a man, as well! Either he didn't have kids or he'd been able to establish some other form of discipline. I must remember to ask him when I got to know him a bit better. Like after our herbal tea.

He sat back in his chair. 'Carly, I'm not going to lie to you. The days of the studios doling out million-pound cheques for material are pretty much gone now unless you're a big name.'

Bollocks. There goes the trolley dash round Prada. Oh well, Primark would just have to do. In a dim light with the right accessories you could hardly tell the difference anyway.

'I don't want to set your expectations at levels I can't meet, so let's be realistic. A book like this, a studio might take an option – that means they've got a hold on it for a year and you can't sell it to anyone else – for, say, fifty to a hundred grand.'

Gulp. Fifty to a hundred grand? I was sure I could hear my credit cards chanting. Gimme a P. Gimme an R. Gimme an A . . .

And the boys? Skiing lessons. A trip to Disney. Fuck it, I'd just blow the lot and buy them Donald Duck.

118

Meanwhile, back in the real world ... I think Ike mistook my silence for disappointment.

'However, if it's love at first sight, or if they sense that there's going to be other interest and we get some kind of bidding war going, then they'll skip options and go straight to purchase. And for that we're probably talking somewhere around two hundred to half a mill.'

For the second time in half an hour I felt faint. Half a mill. Half a million dollars. And holy crap, he was still talking.

'Of course, that's when the real talking starts. We'd want you in on the adaptation, writing the first draft of the script. Or consulting, at least. So we'd try to get you on board and help push it through development. Obviously that would mean you sticking around here for a while, or depending on timescale maybe going back to the UK and then returning here when they need you. Would that be a problem?'

I gave it serious thought and contemplation before replying. He deserved honesty. I couldn't ask him to stake his personal reputation on starting a process that could possibly derail six months down the line because of the constraints of my personal circumstances. After all, coming for a month had put my marriage on the same stability footing as the Middle East – so what would the repercussions be of moving here long-term? This was definitely something I had to think long and hard about. I had to analyse it. I had to discuss it with my husband. I had to consider the effect on my boys. I had to weigh up the financial reward versus ...

Unfortunately, no one had thought to transfer any of these deliberations from my brain to my gob. 'Nope, that wouldn't be a problem at all. In fact, it would be fabulous.'

Fabulous.

And as I shook his hand and said goodbye twenty minutes later, it was all I could do not to snog him – in a purely businesslike appreciation for services, no tongues kind of way. It's not that I was counting my chickens before they were in the bush (as Carol, she of the mixed metaphors, was fond of saying), but Ike had given me a glimpse of the kind of life I'd dreamed of since I was a flat-chested, pre-pubescent reading *Hollywood Wives* by the light of her electric-blanket switch under a duvet in a council house in Glasgow. Imagine living out here. Imagine working in this industry. Imagine seeing something I'd written turned into an excuse for popcorn, hot dogs and groping in the back row.

And I can't deny the whole financial side wouldn't be too hard to take either. If I was earning serious money then Mark could work fewer hours. Or maybe not at all. We could travel. We could live on an island while I wrote my next book under a coconut tree. The boys could learn to surf and water-ski and they'd be two little bronzed beach-bums. And we'd have loads of time together – I wouldn't be a stressed-out basket case. Instead I'd drink pineapple juice and wear flip-flops and bikinis. Of course, I would have to leave our beach haven and scrub up for the premiere of my new movie. Or perhaps Matt Damon would collect me as he went past on his private jet.

I noticed my hands were trembling and I wanted to hug people. And that was without alcohol. Suddenly I realised two things. Firstly, I was bursting with excitement. If nothing ever came of this, then I'd be grateful just for this moment of sheer bloody blissful anticipation. Secondly, I wanted to call Mark to tell him all about it. I checked my watch: 10 a.m. That would mean 6 p.m. in London. He'd still be at his desk, attempting to earn a medal for dedication to duty. Or perhaps he'd bunked off for the afternoon and was shacked up in a cheap hotel with one of the girls from the telephone pool. In which case he deserved to be interrupted.

Sod it, it was time for this pettiness to be over. I missed my husband and I wanted to share this with him. Wasn't marriage full of ups and downs? Okay, so we'd just staged the marital equivalent of the downhill slalom, but I knew it was a temporary blip. I dialled our home number. We just had to start talking again. Start communicating as adults and forget all the petty childishness.

I dialled the direct line to his office. He answered on the tenth ring with a harassed, 'Yep?'

'It's me. I'm still not speaking to you but I just wanted to tell you something.'

I expected him to laugh, to giggle with relief that I was holding out an olive branch. Instead, a pause, then, 'Hi.'

Not 'Hi darling!', not 'Babe, thank God you called, I couldn't live another minute without hearing your voice.' Not even, 'We're out of Pot Noodles, where's the nearest place to buy them?'

Branch trampled, olives mush.

'I just wanted to tell you that I've had the meeting with Sam's agent in the Peninsula Hotel – oh Mark, we're talking swanky with a capital fucking fabulous, or at least we were until the point when I fell on my arse, but that's another story. Anyway, Ike, the agent, he's really positive about the book, and Demi Moore might play the mother, and the big-wigs at the studios got it yesterday and they might buy it and it could be for up to half a million dollars, Mark – half a million! Could you imagine that? This could be so great, Mark, and . . .' If the olive branch hadn't worked, maybe the white flag would. 'I miss you, Mark. The boys miss you. Please come over.'

A deep sigh, then silence – a silence that lasted so long I thought he'd fallen asleep over his desk. And for anyone who thinks that's a ridiculous notion can I just remind you of the whole wank/snoring situation that I relayed earlier. Since this was an emotionally charged, highly fraught situation that definitely involved sensitivity, feelings and possibly hormones, avoidance via sleep, feigning bad telephone line or acute, immediate laryngitis would normally be Mark's first reaction.

'Where are the boys?'

'They're with Sam, he's taking them to see Spiderman.'

'Spiderman is a 12 rating, they're too young for it.'

'Not the movie. Spiderman. The real one. Sam is mates with Tobey Maguire.'

'Who's he?'

'Spiderman. The real one.'

'Oh. I thought that was George Clooney.'

'Nope, he was Batman . . . Mark, who cares! Did you hear anything I just said?'

Jesus H. Christ. Our relationship was in turmoil and I was calling him with potentially life-changing news and at the same time attempting to build bridges, and all he could muster was a casual conversation about a blue and red bloke who liked to climb walls.

'Carly, I'm sorry. I'm tired. It's been a long day. Look, I'm pleased you're excited about the meeting and I hate the way things are between us, I really do. But I'm not coming over. I can't – my workload is crippling just now. I told you already, I'm working on a huge merger and it needs constant attention and care – if I fuck it up it would be a nightmare. And look, I want you to make a deal with me. I know you said that you were going for a month, but honestly, babe, I don't want you all to be away for that long. So please, if nothing happens in a fortnight, just come home.'

Typical Mark. Realistic. Straight-talking. Sensible. With all the giddy delight of haemorrhoids.

'And I know you think I'm saying all this just to burst your bubble, Carly, but I'm not. It's just because I want my family home. I miss you guys.'

I could have cried. In fact, I nearly did. Then I noticed that the receptionist bloke was clearly trying to guess what rehab centre I'd escaped from. I decided tears probably weren't a good idea – I'd be in the Promises Clinic in Malibu before I could persuade them that the only drugs I took were Disprin. So instead of histrionics, I settled for mild fury and petulance.

'You know, Mark, I didn't expect excitement. I didn't dare think you might be pleased. But I thought at least you might have looked deep inside yourself and some-where among all that anal retention found a modicum of bloody support. And as for attention and care – your bloody wife needs some too!'

I thought that was quite good – after all, there were a couple of three-syllable words in there.

'For Christ's sake, Carly, will you get off your high horse?'

'No, I bloody won't. Jesus, Mark, when did you turn eighty? Do you want our lives to be one endless slog where you only get to see your kids when they're sleeping and you've only got the energy to fuck your wife on an annual basis?'

A passing woman gasped and drew me a filthy look. I was sure it was Sharon Stone. Yeah, like she could pass judgement. If I'd wanted to see those parts of the female anatomy I'd have been a gynaecologist.

'Come on, Mark, at least be a little bit . . .'

Beeeeeeeeeeeeeeeeeeeeeeeep. He'd hung up. Hung up! I momentarily wondered if anyone had ever been arrested in the foyer of the Peninsula Hotel for screaming 'Fuck, Fuck, Fuck', while jumping on a Motorola. I quickly decided that probably wasn't how I wanted to achieve fame in Hollywood. Instead, I did that thing you do when you're mortified. I glanced around frantically to see if anyone was watching – strike one, the desk clerk. Strike two, Sharon Stone – then slapped a huge smile on my face and said in a voice borrowed from Marilyn Monroe especially for the occasion, 'Oh, sweet cheeks, I love you too. No, you hang up. No, you. Oh, go on. Kiss, kiss, kiss.'

I pretended to hang up, then flopped down on the lobby chairs and texted Sam, as arranged, to let him know I was done.

I desperately wanted to call Kate or Carol for moral support, vindication and suggestions for really bad swear words, but the time difference ruled out calling for the ovarian cavalry – they'd both be up to their chicken nuggets in kids' dinners.

Instead I settled for texting Kate. 'Emergency! During night, pls go nxt door & assault my husband with blunt object.'

It would never stand up in court. And even if it did, hopefully the judge would be female and I'd get away with it.

'Excuse me, Ms Cooper?' The doorman interrupted my conspiracy to commit a serious assault. 'Your car is waiting outside.'

'Thank you,' I beamed, then panicked. Tip! He'd spoken to me therefore I needed to tip him. Bollocks, how much should I give him? I scrabbled in my purse and snatched out the first thing that came to hand. Exit one happy doorman with $20. No wonder he held the door open with a smile. Christ, he had Jojo's teeth too.

Flash, flash, flash, surreptitious flick of hair and Vicky Beckham pout. Oh, I know I'm pathetic, but I couldn't help myself.

'Hi guys,' I yelled as I jumped into the car.

'*Mum, Mum, Mum, Mum!*' came the double chorus

from two wee boys who were so excited they'd gone pink.

'One at a time, guys!' I laughed, before turning to Sam. 'How were they?'

'Great,' he replied with a particularly gorgeous grin. 'We saw Spiderman and I was so excited that I almost peed my pants. What about you?'

I shrieked with rediscovered excitement. 'Fabulous! Apparently by this time next week I could be sitting on ten mil, with a house in Beverly Hills and Paris Hilton will be begging me to be her shopping buddy.'

He leaned over and squashed me in a huge hug. 'Way to go, Coop, your first step on the Hollywood Walk of Fame. I think this calls for a celebration.' He turned to the boys in the back. 'What do you think, guys, who wants to go to the beach and have a party?'

It would take days for those seats to dry out.

CARLY CALLING . . .

Carly to Kate and Carol:

Dear Friends, had meeting with v. big shot - says I'm going 2 b a huge star. Pls know that I'll always b grateful 4 ur support along the way. Now pls delete me frm ur contact list as I'm getting far more important friends.

Carol:

Dear huge star, remembr Confucius say, pride comes b4 a smack in mouth from pissd off ex-pal.

Kate:

So can I sell story to Nws Of Wrld now? I'll say we had lezzy affair - could do with dosh.

★ *Step Six* ★

If God were to appear in front of me and say, 'Okay, dollface, I'm designing the perfect lifestyle and you're the perfect chick to help me,' I would have just shown him my holiday photographs from the weekend following my big-shot Tinseltown meeting. We're talking hypothetically here, thus getting around the fact that Benny buried the camera in the sand ten minutes after we arrived at the beach and we never found it again.

After a quick stop at the house to change following my meeting that Saturday morning, we piled back into the car. Half an hour (and several death-defying near misses on the Scalextric set that LA calls a freeway) later we pulled into a car park by the sea and Sam unloaded a kitbag and a hamper. Given my new, super-swanky, pampered lifestyle, I waited for Eliza, a personal chef, two waiting staff and a secretary to jump out of the boot too, but sadly he'd given them the day off.

We took a child each and I followed his lead, edging around the side of a huge restaurant called the Cheesecake Factory, to the closest thing to kiddie heaven

128

on earth that doesn't include the Tweenies – Mother's Beach. Which isn't, as the title might suggest, an exclusive zone for women with postnatal breast droop and stretch marks.

'Caesarean sections to the left, epidurals to the right, and all those who had episiotomies, it's your turn for the pedalos.'

Instead it's a glorious bay in the very affluent surroundings of one of the world's largest manmade marinas, Marina del Rey, and it was designed so that the water has no current and is therefore perfect for children. Add in a great picnic area and a playground on the beach and the result is two ecstatic boys and sand in places that it definitely shouldn't be. Surprisingly it wasn't packed out – just a handful of families all looking like they'd escaped from the pages of the Boden catalogue.

We spent the whole day there playing Frisbee, building sandcastles and hiding valuable personal objects, then went back to Sam's, changed and went to the Hard Rock Café for dinner, where more shiny waiters who bore a disturbing resemblance to the staff in the Peninsula served us with a perfect smile. I was beginning to think LA was just one massive feat of genetic interbreeding, but hey, the blokes were easy on the eye and I'm superficial, so it wasn't a hardship.

It was funny to watch Sam too. I stopped counting as he constantly got interrupted and asked for autographs and photos. Sam. My ex-boyfriend. The man who was standing on a nightclub door earning less than ten quid an hour when I met him, yet he handled this life of royalty like he was born to it. Which thankfully he wasn't or he'd be related to the Windsors and have a predilection for large teeth, premature hair loss and an aversion to gainful employment.

Later we got home and put the boys to bed, then spent the rest of the night drinking beer out of the bottle and singing at a zillion decibels on the karaoke system in Sam's outdoor bar terrace. I think it was extremely churlish of the neighbours to phone the police and very generous of the officers to let us off in return for two signed photographs and a chance to sing Gloria Gaynor's *I Will Survive* to a professional backing track in a very camp manner.

On Sunday, the highest-paid tour guide in the world unapologetically played to his three-foot-high audience and took us further afield. Disneyland, California. The Holy Grail. Or, '*Jesus, Mum, it's Mickey Mouse's house!*', as an overwhelmed Mac announced when we entered the park gates and he spotted the castle. I decided to classify his outburst as 'praying in thanks' rather than 'blasphemous and deserves to be punished'.

And, thankfully, it seemed that we'd outwitted the evil paps. In fact, surprisingly, Sam didn't get recognised at all – a pair of big dark glasses, a baseball cap and a T-shirt declaring 'Milwaukee Chiropractic Convention, 2006' gave him total anonymity – although he was asked for his opinion on a spinal injury, a neck crick and a dislocated shoulder.

'Are you okay?' I asked him after we'd sat through three journeys around 'It's A Small World', a cheesy boat-ride through animated countries of the world that came with a musical accompaniment so grating that you'd happily take out the speakers by firing Huey, Dewey and Louie at them from a large cannon.

'Yeah, I'm great. You know, it's strange, all these years I've been here and I've never done any of the tourist stuff, but the boys just make it all great. And you. I'm so glad you came, Carly.'

I know. It was so nice of me to have arrived on his doorstep in a bedraggled state with two children in tow, cluttered up his house, forced him to call in favours from friends, almost got him arrested by two male LAPD officers who probably answered to the names Cilla and Whitney on their days off, and then subjected him to long queues, blistering heat, and conversations with large stuffed creatures called Mr Chip Monk.

And the strange thing was it all seemed so natural. I'm sure that if casual passers-by had paid us any attention they'd have thought that we looked like the nicest family from Milwaukee that they'd ever seen. Several times I had to remind myself that this wasn't real life. Me, Sam, the boys, all this fun. Real life was, in fact, being married to a workaholic and battering the door of a Wacky Warehouse at two minutes before opening time on a freezing Saturday morning, begging to be allowed in.

The boys were just in their element. Sure, there'd been a couple of minor spats fuelled by E-number overload and sleep deprivation, but in the main they were somewhere on the 'over the moon' side of the happiness scale, something they conveyed in no uncertain terms to their father on the two occasions each day that I dialled his number then gave them the phone. Petty, I know, but I had come to the decision that I wasn't going to speak to him until I was sure I could converse without swearing or making threats that could possibly land me an ASBO.

Other than chronic immaturity on my part, however, the weekend had been perfect. Bliss. I couldn't remember when the boys or I had last had such a great time, and since I grew up with my granny reminding me on a daily basis that 'You're not long on this earth, so you might as well enjoy it', it kind of reinforced the fact that I'd been in a rut for the last few years and it was time to take the bull by the horns and embrace life, excitement and a wee bit of thrilling danger again.

Talking of which . . .

Late Sunday night, Sam and I lay on sun-loungers out by his pool, joy in heart, stars in sky and beer in hand. We'd decided to pass on the karaoke as, much as we enjoyed their company, we did realise that the LAPD had other insignificant matters like gang warfare and serial looting to deal with.

The setting was perfect and we'd slumbered into the kind of comfortable silence that friends who've known each other forever find easy. I still had that bubbly, excited feeling in my stomach as I contemplated the fact that Ike Tusker could actually call me at some point during the next week with news that could potentially change our lives forever in a great way – if you didn't take into account divorce and the fact that our children would come from a broken home. Ah, I was being glib. Despite Mark being up there with serial killers and traffic wardens on my list of favourite people, I was still convinced that we'd get over this and that he'd come around to my way of thinking.

Mark and I were a team. No one had ever got in the middle of us and I was sure that we were solid. Unbreakable.

'Carly, have you ever wondered?'

'Wandered where?' I said, a bit flummoxed at being snapped from my contemplations.

'*Wondered.* Wondered about us. Wondered if we'd have made it if you hadn't left Hong Kong. Or if you'd come back sooner.'

I thought about it for a few moments. Shit, I hated these conversations. Nostalgia should be banned. There was nothing worse than probing the What Ifs of past romantic interactions to bring on a migraine and teenage urges to do irresponsible things involving tongues.

'Sure. Sometimes.'

'And?'

I laughed that nervous kind of giggle that I'm prone to do in moments of great sadness (example: funerals), stress (example: long queue in the supermarket) and when I'm trying to avert a potentially embarrassing/dangerous/foolish situation (example: amazing ex-boyfriend, feelings of wanton lust, starry night, husband being a prick, not had sex for a long time).

'And I think I would have driven you crazy. I was an erratic, hopeless case with the attention span of the average chicken and you were far more mature and

133

grounded. You knew what you were about. Me? I'm *still* making it up as I go along and cocking up on a regular basis. And anyway, if we'd worked out you'd still be living in Hong Kong earning a pittance, and you'd never have taken the journey that ended with you living here and having this really crap life of riches, opportunity and glory.'

I couldn't look at him. I couldn't. Where were Cilla and Whitney when I needed them?

Silence again. Only not so much comfortable as toe-curlingly excruciating this time. As usual, after a few minutes I caved.

'And what about you? Do you ever wonder?' I whispered. This was what I imagined it felt like to stand on a ledge half a mile up, waiting to do a bungee jump. I was on the edge of a precipice and had no faith whatsoever in how I would react if I was plunged into the unknown. Please say no. Please. Just say, 'Nope, lucky escape, I reckon. If things had worked out between us I'd never have got to shag 384 of the world's richest women and I wouldn't have missed that for the world.'

More silence. Stomach in knots. Body rigid. Staring at sky because I can't bear to look him in the tanned, long-eyelashed, sculptured-cheeked, bloody gorgeous face.

Aaaargh! Right, either that was a very large insect crawling up my arm or it was his fingertips. There was definitely contact, there was definitely something – very slowly, very gently and so very fucking erotically that my ovaries were singing the 'Hallelujah Chorus' – moving up my arm.

And I'd lost the ability to breathe. Animals with the smallest brains on the planet could breathe, and yet I'd momentarily completely forgotten the basics of air intake.

'Carly . . .'

I was turning pink through lack of oxygen and my skeletal system was turning to mush. I was blancmange. Mary, Mother of God, saint of the blessed virgins and all things non-tampered-with in a sexual manner, help me now.

'Carly . . .'

'Carly . . .'

I suddenly realised it was a woman's voice who was saying my name. LA – city of dreams, where nothing is impossible and Mary, Mother of God does house calls.

'Carly? Are you okay?' She was in front of me now, but instead of flowing robes and halos, it was Eliza and Motorola.

'Your mobile phone was ringing so I answered it. It's someone called Kate.'

'Thanks, Eliza,' I gasped, as I jumped up and took the phone. 'I'll, er, just go check on the boys while I'm talking to Kate,' I whispered to Sam, while backing off in the manner of an armed robber in front of a SWAT team.

I turned and walked briskly into the house.

'Kate, I love you. I *so* love you I can't even begin to tell you how much I love you,' I whispered into the phone.

She groaned. 'Eew, I think I preferred it when I

thought you'd dumped me for someone who earns ten mil a movie. Less than a week in LA and you're already all huggy-kissy, let's share our emotions and hug. If you've already joined the local Kabbalah centre I'm coming over there to get you.'

'Nope, worse than that. But I'll tell you when I see you – it's one for gin and accompanying hand actions. Anyway, how's you?'

'Everything's great, we miss you, but listen, I'm going to be quick because my brood will descend for breakfast any minute and it's costing me a limb a minute to call. I'm worried about Mark.'

'Can I just remind you that you're supposed to be *my* friend and that involves unswaying loyalty in times of marital strife?'

'Come on, Carly, he's miserable. I took him round some dinner last night . . .'

That's Kate. She thinks about everyone else, genuinely cares about people and would never turn her back on a friend in need. Which is absolutely no use at all when you want her to call your husband a tosser and assault him with a kitchen implement.

'. . . and he's really pissed off, Carly.'

'He *should* be pissed off. He's the one who is being completely non-supportive and downright bloody stubborn.'

'And are you being the pot or the kettle today?' she replied.

'Oh, come on, Kate, even you, paragon of stability and intelligent choices, thought I'd be crazy not to come here.'

'True,' she agreed. 'But, you know, I can see Mark's point as well. Carly, he's not trying to hold you back; he's just trying to hold things together. If he lost income or, God forbid, his job just because he went charging over to LA on a whim then that would have a huge impact on you as a family. In his roundabout way he's just trying to do the right thing for you and the boys.'

'How much did he pay you, Judas?'

'Can't say, but rumours that I left your house with three bottles of wine and a George Foreman Lean Machine may well be true. Look, make the peace with him. He's missing the boys, he's missing you and he's run out of Pot Noodles – the poor man's destitute.'

'He's also being a complete arse. And Kate, I understand what you're saying, but he's furious with me for coming here. As far as Mark's concerned we could quite happily spend the rest of our lives in that rut of an existence that we'd fallen into. I'm not ready to give up on dreams yet. Although granted the Liam Neeson one might be slightly out of reach now. Talking of which, he tried to cop a feel in a flash hotel the other day.'

'*You're kidding!!!*'

'Of course I am, but the difference is that here it could happen and that's what makes this trip so fantastic. Thanks for trying to help, Kate, but honestly, I'm not sure Mark and I are ever going to agree on how we should live our lives. But we'll work it out. Eventually. Hopefully when I'm a multi-millionaire movie screenwriter with more diamonds than Elizabeth Taylor's poodle.'

She sighed, obviously deciding to go away and

formulate another form of attack in her new capacity as my private marriage-guidance counsellor. She changed the subject.

'Talking of movie stars, how's my favourite actor then?'

'Tom Cruise is fine.'

She laughed. 'Yeew – that man would need an industrial whisk to get my hormones swirling. How's Sam?'

'Fine.'

'Fine?'

'Fine.'

'Oh no.'

'What?'

'Oh no. Carly, you haven't!'

I gave an indignant snort. 'Of course I haven't. He's an old comfy friend and I'm a responsible mother of two who would never dream of jeopardising her marriage or breaking her vows, and quite frankly I can't believe that you even considered that I might do something like that.'

Long pause.

'So you're thinking about it then?' she replied.

I groaned and caved simultaneously. 'All the time! Oh Kate, at this rate I'll be right behind Michael Douglas at Sex Addicts Anonymous. If you could parcel up some firm resolve and send it over I'd much appreciate it.'

'Carly, be careful,' she warned gently.

'I will. And don't worry, I won't do anything stupid.'

'Promise?'

'I promise.'

And as I hung up and wandered into the bedroom to check on the boys, I knew that I definitely meant it. Definitely. Without a doubt.

I crawled in between my sons and kissed both of them on the nose.

Yes, I definitely meant it, I thought as I snuggled down under the duvet. But probably best if I stayed away from temptation just in case.

I completely ignored Sam's searching look when I marched into the kitchen the next morning with Benny on my back and Mac on my front, both of them squealing with laughter.

'Uncle Sam, Uncle Sam, it's a mummy sandwich!' Mac shrieked, before Sam grabbed him, turned him upside-down and tickled him until there was a definite risk of flooding.

'Donut!' commanded Benny, pointing to the bagels that were heaped on the counter, already toasted.

'That's a bagel, honey,' I corrected him.

'Nope, donut,' argued Benny, before picking up one with banana slices on it and wolfing it down. I was astonished. Benny was the boy who refused point-blank to try anything new. Mark and I had tried every form of bribery, coercion and corruption only to be met with a defiant shake of the head and jaws that required a crowbar to open them.

'Actually, that's my fault,' Sam whispered. 'He didn't want to try one yesterday but after I assured him that it was just a kind of donut like the ones I'd seen him eat at your place he gave it a try.'

We both glanced over at Benny, face now smeared with banana.

'And I think he likes it,' Sam grinned.

As if it couldn't get any worse, the demigod now has a natural talent with children.

'Can we go and see Spiderman again today, Uncle Sam, can we, can we, can we?' Mac asked, his wee face a mask of optimism.

'*Spiderman, Spiderman . . .*' sang bagel boy.

Sam hesitated, his demeanour making it obvious that the answer was going to be no.

Mac sensed it and waded straight in with another request.

'Or Batman – Batman would be great,' he asked eagerly.

'*Da na na na, Da na na na . . .*' piped up Benny.

'Erm . . .' Sam started, trying to find the words to let them down gently.

'Superman! We love Superman! Can we go and see Superman, Uncle Sam, can we, can we, *please*?'

The desperation was creeping into Mac's voice now and Benny looked totally flummoxed. The superhero jukebox had just realised that it didn't contain the theme tune to Superman. His shoulders slumped and he was totally crestfallen for about three seconds, before childhood resilience kicked in and he just sang the first verse of 'Twinkle Twinkle Little Star' instead.

'Erm . . . sorry, guys, but I have to work today.'

I was glad that the door of the fridge was in between Sam and I so he couldn't see my face. Work? He hadn't mentioned anything about work.

I rearranged my expression into a sunny grin and popped it out from behind the door. 'Work? I thought you were a fully paid-up dosser these days,' I said in the manner of the glib and irreverent.

'I am, but the director of my next movie wants to meet up today to go over the schedule and brief me on the locations.'

Oh, that was okay then. I mean, if I had a fiver for every time I had a last-minute meeting with a director to discuss flying first class around the world then I'd be a rich woman.

'Great,' I gushed, not paying attention to the plastic maple syrup bottle that I was subconsciously squeezing in my hand.

'Mum, the syrup's dripping!' Mac shouted.

Sam tossed me a cloth. Great. And I was worried about the kids being messy. I ducked back into the fridge to sob in private.

'Don't worry about being bored, though ...' Sam continued. Somehow I thought boredom was the least of our worries. The house had a pool. Dinghies. Unconquered alligators. A tennis court. A five-a-side football pitch and a driveway so long we could spend the whole day just skateboarding up and down it. Boredom wouldn't be an issue. The fact that I feared we'd just chased a Hollywood A-lister out of his own home was slightly more of a problem.

I realised Sam was still speaking.

'. . . because you can either stay here or take the other car and go exploring. I could draw you up a list of places worth visiting.'

Mac burst into tears. 'But I want to go with you, Uncle Sam, can I, can I, can I?'

Me too, me too. Thankfully I'm pretty sure I didn't say that out loud.

Sam picked Mac up and gave him a hug. 'Tell you what, when I get back how about I teach you to dive in the swimming pool.'

Mac eyed him suspiciously. 'Without holding my nose?'

'Without holding your nose,' Sam promised.

'Okay, then,' Mac agreed, his protruding bottom lip gradually returning to a normal position. Meanwhile, over in the fridge, mine was still hitting the Spanish-marble floor tiles. I didn't want Sam to go out on his own today. We'd had such a great time since we arrived that I wanted our little escape from reality to continue a bit longer – although preferably without the bit where we got all deep and meaningful about our feelings.

I couldn't help wondering if this had indeed been planned or if he was so pissed off with me for ducking out on him last night that he'd just decided to avoid me. Or maybe he was embarrassed about dredging up the past. Maybe he'd only done it because he'd had a few beers and was getting melancholy and now he regretted it. Or maybe he was just getting totally pissed off having his house overtaken by an ex-girlfriend and two small creatures who created a disproportional amount of mess, noise and chaos. And we'd only been there for a weekend! Since Mark had spat his dummy and not come, I hadn't really considered looking for a hotel, but perhaps now I should. Despite break-ups, broken hearts and a very unusual career choice, Sam and I had managed to stay friends for almost fifteen years and I didn't want something trivial, like chronic irritation with family-style chaos, to spoil that now.

On the other hand, maybe I was being a paranoid, neurotic twat and he really did have a long-standing arrangement to meet his new director. Strange that he hadn't mentioned it before, though.

An hour later the boys were fed, washed and changed into their outdoor clothes. For the second time. When I got them ready the first time there was some kind of dispute over a glass of fresh orange juice that resulted in Benny wearing a guilty expression and Mac wearing the juice.

Sam took me out, past the Jaguar convertible that we'd been using since we got there, to the garage. He bleeped a button to make it open. The door slid up to reveal a shiny black Porsche and a colossal 4x4. Bloody hell, if I had that on the school run at home I'd scare the shit out of the twin-set and pearl brigade in their Land Rovers.

Sam reversed out the 4x4 (which he informed me was actually called an SUV), then gave me the keys. 'It's all yours,' he said with a grin. 'Unless, of course, you'd rather have the Porsche.'

'Of course I'd rather have the Porsche. And I'm sure the LAPD will turn a blind eye to the fact that I've strapped the kids onto the roof so they don't spill their Ribena on the calfskin seats.'

He laughed. And unlike the rest of the male population of Los Angeles, his eyes did crease up at the sides in a very cute fashion. He turned to walk back into the house.

'Sam,' I called after him, a little hesitantly. 'We're okay, aren't we?'

He stopped in his tracks, turned, came back over and kissed my head.

'Of course we're okay, you nut. We'll always be okay.'

He spun on his heel again and went back into the house, looking – as far as I could tell – like a man who was definitely not okay.

Mother's Beach, take two. I had a choice. I could take two children under six on a tour of the cultural high spots of Los Angeles with the view to educating them in the fine arts and widening their intellectual spectrum, or we could doss back down at the beach, eat pretzels and play Frisbee until our arms fell off. No contest. My children's inherent distaste for anything resembling learning, combined with the fact that driving on the wrong side of the road had already created near misses with four lampposts, three roller-bladers and a party of senior citizens made the beach a no-brainer. As we pulled back into the car park I marvelled at the number of people jogging past – hundreds of them. They were like locusts, although of course, this being LA, they were locusts in designer headbands and lip-gloss. Including the blokes. Joggers had always had a detrimental effect on my mental stability. At home there were a few who regularly trotted up and down our street and every time they passed I had an overwhelming urge to throw things in their general direction. However, there's one thing that's even worse than people who jog and that's *couples* who jog. Barbie and Ken lookalikes in matching Lycra, all healthy complexions and smug smiles. If I ever build a gun turret on my roof you'll know why.

Strangely, though, in LA it didn't bother me in the least. It's almost like it was part of the scenery, a national pastime as opposed to a hobby that was designed with the one and only intention of getting right on my hooters.

I might even take it up, I pondered as I laid out our towels. Nah, that would just be really naff and shallow. Just because I was in LA didn't mean I was going to start acting like a native, I decided, as I propped my mocha chocca skinny vanilla cappuccino with an espresso twist next to my cinnamon roll and my copy of *Us* magazine.

I reached into my bag for my mobile phone, clicked it on to vibrate and put it in the pocket of my shorts – the call from Ike Tusker could be orgasmic in more ways than one – then joined the boys on the play structure. It took me a few moments to realise that the demographic of the people around the beach on a weekday was completely different to our previous weekend visit. Gone were the picture-perfect families, and instead the beach looked like a crowd scene in the *L Word*: a sea of women. And they seemed to be split into three distinct camps. One camp was the kids, dozens of under-fives swarming all over the place in packs. Then over on one set of benches were what looked like nannies: about fifteen young women engrossed in manic chatter in what sounded like Spanish or Portuguese. And I'd like to claim some expertise in that area, having once spent a fortnight in Benidorm.

On the other benches were groups of what appeared to be mothers: some of them in sweat pants and yoga gear, with shiny faces and an aura of karmic serenity, others the frazzled-faced types who'd obviously reached boiling point before deciding that fresh air and the expulsion of small child's energy in an ergonomically designed play area was preferable to an illicit glass of wine and twenty fags out the back door.

The thought jolted my memory. I suddenly realised that only a week ago I'd been sitting on my back step having a cigarette, contemplating my general dissatis-faction with the lack of excitement in my life and strug-gling with a gnawing premonition that something out of the ordinary was about to happen. Well hello to the paranormal proclivities of Cosmic Cooper! In the space of a week I'd had the career break of a lifetime, taken one son out of preschool and the other out of nursery, said goodbye to my friends, travelled to LA, been reunited with an old flame, adopted a millionaire lifestyle, met a Hollywood high-flyer, had impure thoughts about said old flame, parted company with my husband on a yet-to-be-established basis and Liam Neeson had copped a feel (in my dreams).

I hadn't so much grabbed the bull by the horns as ridden him until he pegged out from exhaustion.

And it was far from over. Any minute now that phone call could come, the one call that would lead to a whole new life. I reached into my shorts and checked that my phone was still there. I resisted the urge to pull it out, look at the screen and bang it against my hand a few times to check that it was definitely working. It was like being fifteen again and waiting for the boy you'd snogged in the bus shelter the night before to call. Even then it was a certain Mark Barwick who was tugging on my heart strings. Nothing new there, then.

Watching Benny as he slid down the chute backwards on his belly, I could swear that there was a resemblance to his father that I'd never noticed before. Mark would love it here. The sun, the sea, his boys squealing with joy as they alternated between climbing over the play structure and trying to win the dollar I'd promised to whoever managed to dig up our lost camera.

It was his loss. I just hoped that he realised it and made an effort to put things right, before he lost a whole lot more.

'Mum, Mum, I found it, I found it!' Mac shrieked. He charged up to me clutching a sand-covered camera. *A* camera. Not *our* camera. This one was a swanky Pentax whereas ours was a swanky one by a Taiwanese company with a non-recognisable title. It seemed that burying cameras was a popular pastime around here. I gave him a kiss, told him his dollar was safe and sent him back to dig up more. At this rate we could get a profitable business going – Dodgy Cameras R Us.

A few hours, three cameras, two odd boots, four Tupperware dishes and a thong (swiftly returned to whence it was found) later, I took my phone out of my pocket, checked the screen, then banged it a few times on my palm. No calls. Not one. Where the hell was Ike Tusker? Probably off schmoozing Tom Cruise and telling Pamela bloody Anderson that she looked gorgeous.

I checked my watch. Four o'clock. If he was going to call he'd have done it before now. Damn! Yes, I did realise that it was only Monday and he'd said he wouldn't have any news until the middle of the week, but I have the same relationship with patience that I do with, say, Nepalese panpipes.

I called Kate and she answered on the third ring.

'Kate, it's me – can you call me back on my mobile straight away please?' I said, dispensing with little frivolities like 'Hello' and 'How are you?'

Two seconds later it rang. I pressed receive.

'Oh, fuck, it's working,' I swore into the phone.

'Am I even supposed to pretend that I know what you're on about?' she asked.

'Sorry, honey, I was hoping my phone wasn't working,' I replied.

There was a long pause, then, '*Er, right*. Makes perfect sense. I'm always hoping my laptop will crash and the pressure cooker will explode.' Her tone was somewhere between incredulous and calling Care in the Community for advice. 'Carly, I'm going to go now, because it's midnight and I've got this weird little habit called sleep. But, er, you might want to think about consulting an expert. I think you've been under a little too much strain lately.'

She hung up. Fab. Now my best pal thinks I'm certifiable – add her to the list. I rounded up the kids and took them home, not a little apprehensive about seeing Sam.

I needn't have worried. I pressed the bleeper to open the electronic gates (and incidentally, I think it would be highly immature to press the bleeper, drive in a few yards, reverse back out, let the gates close, press the bleeper, drive in a few yards, reverse back out, let the gates close, press the beeper . . . for at least half an hour just because it's you and your kids' idea of a jolly jape. I'd never do anything like that. Never. Honest officer – and if any lurking paps had photographic evidence of this I was prepared to buy the negatives), before noticing a couple of unfamiliar cars and one very swish sporty thingy. Jojo. The house was empty, so we went out to the swimming pool and *eugh*, I wished I hadn't bothered. There was Jojo, Patron Saint of Physical Bloody Perfection, and four of her pals who all had identically perfect bodies. If this lot were at the Last Supper it would consist of green salads all round, skip the wine, make the water Perrier and hold the bread because they're all on the South Beach Diet. Personally I prefer the Blackpool Beach diet: fish and chips with a buttered roll and don't spare the Vimto.

Sam introduced me to Deedee, CeeCee, Mimi and Bibi . . . or whatever they were called – I lost interest and the will to live after the first one said, 'Wow, flares – they are, like, soooo retro', when I was under the impression that they were distinctly trendy. In motherland, where I normally reside, anything less than two years old is distinctly trendy. She then proceeded to regale me with the story of how she found her 'best

149

skinny jeans ever' in a chichi boutique in Westwood, and they *only* cost three hundred dollars, before giving me a twirl to model said skinny jeans. I responded in the manner that such blatant superficiality, materialism and downright pain-in-the-arseness demanded – feigned interest and told her she simply must give me the name of the shop so that I could charge right down the next morning to snap up a pair for myself. I believe several residents of the Pacific Palisades suburb of Los Angeles reported random bolts of lightning around that very instant.

While I'd been gabbing to the entire cast of *America's Next Top Model*, the boys had jumped into the pool with Sam and Jojo. Traitors. They shouted at me to join them but there was about as much chance of me revealing my pallid, post-pregnancy body as there was of Deedee and CeeCee nipping out for a Big Mac and fries.

Instead, I hauled the boys inside, dried them off, and then sat them at the table in the kitchen while I made dinner. Sam popped in to refill his beer.

'Any word from Ike?' he asked. I shook my head, trying not to look like I was in mourning.

'Hey, don't worry, it's early days yet.'

'I know, I know, I'm fine about it. Really. I'm not anxious at all,' I said anxiously. God, now I knew why Julia Roberts got £20 million just for stepping outside her trailer – this acting lark wasn't as easy as it looked. And was it my imagination or did Sam seem to be acting a bit weird too? No wonder. Here was Mr Big Shot superstar, his house full of hot babes, and he was in the kitchen having to be polite to houseguests that were now approaching squatter status. He wandered back out to the pool and I plonked down a cordon bleu feast of cucumber, corn, tomatoes and potato waffles in front of the boys. After dinner they wanted to go back out to the pool, but I vetoed it. Schoolday warnings that if you went swimming within an hour of eating you would sink, drown or – worse – vomit in the pool in front of the fourth-year boys, had given me a phobia about after-dinner dips.

Instead we got out craft paper, crayons and tracing paper and proceeded to make a stunning collage of summer scenes. Oh, okay, I lie. We slumped down in front of back-to-back *Scooby-Doo* episodes, Mac on one side of me, Benny on the other. We remained in that prone position for at least an hour, before Jojo appeared.

'Hi guys,' she said with a sparkly, singy, Claudia Schiffery grin.

'Hi Jojo,' the boys responded in unison, both giving her big cheesy smiles. Ten minutes of water polo and they're anyone's.

'Sorry, we're not coming out to the pool, Jojo. I hope you don't think we're being rude, but it's just that the boys have a routine. Dinner, potentially terrifying cartoons featuring talking dogs who eat junk food, then bed.'

She laughed. 'Not at all. *Scooby-Doo*'s my favourite.' And with that, she settled down on the other side of Benny and watched the next two episodes.

Urgh, it was SO irritating. My former love for Jojo

had been dispelled the minute I'd walked in and seen her in a bikini, and now *this*. There was nothing worse than blatant bloody niceness to put a damper on rampant jealousy.

Sam found us all there a couple of hours later, both boys now sleeping, and Jojo and I engrossed in an old episode of *Miami Vice*. I asked him to give me a hand to lift the boys into bed. In the darkness of the bedroom, in a whisper, he said, 'Sorry about last night – too much beer, too much sun and a bit of homesickness and nostalgia thrown in. Hope I didn't embarrass you as much as I embarrassed myself.'

I snorted quietly – which, incidentally, isn't an easy thing to do. 'Don't be crazy,' I said with a flippant giggle. 'I didn't pay any attention anyway. You always did talk crap.'

So there it was. He was mortified. He'd suffered from an attack of Budweiser Gob and that's why he'd been dying to escape that morning.

'Thanks, Carly.'

'No problem. Listen, I'm just going to crash out with the boys just now – all that lying on my arse doing nothing at the beach has totally knackered me. Say goodnight to Jojo for me. And I'll see you in the morning.'

'Er, actually you won't. I'm sorry, hon, but I've got more meetings tomorrow. I'll be out all day.'

Okay, two options here once again. My sensible, pragmatic head, usually only relied upon in times of school parent nights and court appearances, was saying that these meetings had been planned for a long time, he'd genuinely forgotten to mention them before, they had no connection whatsoever to our arrival here and, more specifically, him feeling that he'd made a tit of himself with the whole arm-rubbing/Budweiser Gob incident. One that he really regretted. However, my paranoid, neurotic head, usually only relied upon on a daily basis during all waking hours, was screaming that he was still avoiding me, we were totally getting under his feet, on his nerves and generally just interfering with his life on all levels. And, let's face it, he'd been generous enough already.

As I snuggled down in between two small boys who were doing impressions of hyperactive squids and squashing me into a six-inch space in the middle, I decided that I'd sort it out the next day. There was no getting away from it – something had to change before our friendship was seriously dented. And hadn't I already filled my quota of 'pissing off members of the male species' this month? A stray foot whacked me on the face. The Gods of All with Dangly Bits were obviously getting their little people to do their dirty work for them.

Yep, something had to change.

CARLY CALLING . . .

Carly to Kate and Carol:

No word yet frm Hlwd big shot - u r
there4 stil my VBFs. Miss u. Cxxx

Kate:

Just as well - Nws Of Wrld says ur
not famous enuf 4 kiss & tell - but
say they'll giv me £20K for scud photos
with Kate Moss.

Carol:

Sorry, who r u? Ur name is not in my
contact list.

★ *Step Seven* ★

Nope, not one thing changed. Nothing. Nada. Zilch. I felt like I was stuck in Groundhog Day as the Tuesday, the Wednesday and the Thursday followed exactly the same pattern as the Monday. I'd get up, Sam would leave straight after breakfast (which usually involved my boys spilling at least one item of food/drink and a full discussion about their early-morning bowel movements), we'd head for the beach, hang out there all day, Ike Tusker wouldn't call, we'd get back to a house full of people then I'd take the kids to bed. On the Tuesday night there was a brief blip of abnormality as I wrote my weekly column for *Family Values* magazine and emailed it in using Sam's laptop – an act that did require a modicum of basic communication with my host. That aside, Sam and I had all the conversational interaction as those couples who have been married for twenty years and go to Harvester restaurants where they eat sausage and mash in total silence.

Things were no better on the husband front. I retained a dignified (petty), noble (immature) silence where my next of kin was concerned. Let him stew. Not once had he asked the boys to pass the phone to me, so I'd have to have electric probes on my nipples before I'd capitulate to him.

By Friday I was really beginning to panic. By lunchtime there had still been no phone call from Ike and only passing small talk with the other women at the beach was keeping me from going off my head with the stress of it. I even had a twenty-minute chat to a lovely, rotund, 50-something nanny called Consuela who spoke no English whatsoever. As far as I was concerned we were discussing the merits of baseball caps versus sunhats for the under fives, but as far as she was concerned we were probably discussing the aesthetic appeal of Elton John's hair transplant.

The other consolation was that the boys were having a great time. They'd made loads of pals and were, apparently, now official members of the management committee of the Marina del Rey Superhero Worship Society.

Two o'clock. By now, as far as I'd been led to believe, the whole of LA had bunked off early and headed for the golf course or the beach, so I figured that, for this week at least, my American dream was stuck in limbo.

And who knew if it would ever resurface?

I had to face facts: there was a distinct possibility that this whole debacle had been for nothing. Oh, I couldn't even contemplate the indignity of it. Imagine going home with my tail between my legs and admitting I'd been a fool. I'd have to change my name by deed poll to Mrs H. E. Optimist.

Hopeless Effing to my friends.

Mark would have a smug look on his face for at least the next ten years. That's if he was still around. Chances are he'd get so sick of all my new debt that he'd bugger off into the unknown. Or back into the loins of the chick from the typing pool.

Why hadn't he called? Why? Bollocks, bollocks, bollo— What the hell was that trembling in my nethers? Whey-hey!

My heart soared as I snatched the phone out of my shorts, flipped it open and ...

'Good afternoon, is that Carly Cooper?' an American voice drawled.

Squeak. In my head I said yes, but only a high-pitched exclamation made it as far as my vocal cords.

'This is Stefan from Ike Tusker's office.'

Squeak. Here it was. The big one. Mark Barwick, I bloody told you so! It was coming, any minute, the next few seconds were going to change my—

'I'd like to make an appointment for Mr Tusker to call you.'

What?

'An appointment? To call me? I'm sorry, I don't understand.'

I detected a very slight tremble of irritation on the other end of the line.

'Mr Tusker would like to speak with you and he'd like to set up a time that's mutually convenient.'

Er, right. So this was a phone call to plan a phone call. Not getting it, not liking it, but like those people who refused to convert to metric, I suspected that resistance was futile.

'Erm, any time. Now. Half an hour. Whenever. I'm free all day today, tomorrow, and the next few days. I have a lunch with Arnold Schwarzenegger a week next Tuesday, but apart from that I'm pretty flexible.'

We were in LA – how would he know that Schwarzenegger wasn't a close personal friend?

Pause.

'Okay, I've checked Mr Tusker's schedule and he has seven minutes this afternoon from 16.04 – would that be convenient?'

'That would definitely be convenient.'

Gleeeeeeeeee! Fantastic! Ike Tusker wanted to speak to me! Please God, I solemnly promise that for the rest of my life I will put money in those Salvation Army envelopes that come through the door if you please, *please* make this good news.

I rounded up the boys – time for a sharp exit. I didn't want to be engaged in a highbrow, movie-type conversation with one of the biggest players in Hollywood while having a small boy dangling from my back squealing, 'Ninja Turtles! Into the water, Master Shredder!'

I headed back to Sam's, hoping fervently that Eliza would be there and wouldn't mind keeping an eye on the boys for seven minutes from 16.04.

To my surprise, and I suspect his too, Sam was already there. Something that I wish I'd known before the boys and I strutted into the house singing a rousing version of 'Hi Ho Hi Ho, It's Off to Work We Go'. With actions. Even more surprisingly, he was alone. He must have given the supermodel apostles the day off. Not that I would have cared – I was far too excited to let pert bosoms spoil my day.

'Sam, Sam,' I screeched. 'Ike Tusker's office called and made an appointment for him to call me. Incidentally, what's that all about – appointments to call?'

He grinned. 'Yeah, they all do that here. So what happened?'

'Don't know – he's calling me back at 16.04. What do you think – good news or bad?'

'Good. Definitely good.'

Excellent. If there was anyone who knew this town and this business it was Sam. He had an acute mind and his experience with these people would only make his perceptions even more informed and razor-sharp.

'Why do you think it's good?' I wanted substantiated facts, real-life precedents and anecdotal evidence. He shrugged his shoulders.

'Dunno. Just got a feeling.'

Right then. Good enough for me.

I checked my watch – still a while to go. The boys had gone off in search of Eliza (after I'd checked the doors to the pool were locked – I'd been having recurring moments of panic about them going swimming with the alligators without adult supervision). Sam had pulled a carton of juice and various food-like ingredients out of the fridge and was busy concocting a sandwich that was the approximate height of Benny. I don't know how he did it. I thought bread was listed as a Class A drug in California. Shouldn't he be on the Atkins or in the Zone or . . . Oh, I don't know, but I was pretty sure he shouldn't be scoffing a whole loaf in one sitting; yet there he was, the man with the body of a finely tuned athlete, worshipping at the temple of Hovis. Those arms, perfectly formed with biceps like melons. That chest, pumped and defined. Those abs – oh God those abs – I could spend all day just counting every one of those perfectly toned little bumps. Thighs. Thighs. Thighs. Sorry, got stuck there for a moment.

'What are you thinking?'

Those thighs. Those thighs. Those . . .

'What're you thinking?'

Thighs.

'CARLY!'

'What? Where? What is it?'

Sam was staring at me quizzically.

'What are you thinking? You're in a world of your own there.'

'Oh, erm, sorry. Just . . . thinking. About Ike Tusker and what he'll say.'

'Oh. Erm, thought so,' Sam replied uncomfortably, before taking a huge bite out of his sandwich.

This was hopeless. What had happened to us? We'd always had such an easy relationship, had always been able to tell each other everything, and now there was a really strange atmosphere between us. I had absolutely no idea what he was thinking but I had a feeling that I wouldn't like it. Even during our darkest days as a couple we'd still talked, still cared, still understood each other. Now? Accidental strangers.

I momentarily considered going for a soak in the bath and using that tried and tested manner of relationship therapy: avoidance of major issues. Well, it seemed to be working well for my husband.

But Sam had been good to us. Besides, I had a niggling worry that the sandwich might be a sign of some kind of anxiety-related comfort eating, and if so I thought I'd better address the problem before the only role he was fit to play was Elvis in his later years.

'Sam, I was thinking. It's been so brilliant of you to let us stay here but I don't want to out-stay our welcome. We're disrupting your life and filling the house with mayhem. I really appreciate everything you've done, but we're in the way here – so maybe tomorrow, if it's okay with you, I'll ask Eliza to help me find a hotel.'

He looked stunned. Oh shit, I'd offended him. He thought he'd been hiding the fact that we were getting on his tits really well and now I'd made it obvious that I'd sensed it.

It was ages before he spoke, mainly due to the mouthful of sandwich. Finally, he swallowed, then spoke. 'Do you . . . *want* to move out?'

'No, it's not that I desperately want to move out – it's just that I love you, Sam . . .'

He choked. I ignored the bit of cucumber that shot across the room and pressed on.

'. . . You're one of my best friends. But, you know, that doesn't mean that we won't get on each other's nerves if we're together too much.'

I was trying to make this easy for him.

'I mean, Carol is one of my closest friends, we've known each other all our lives, we're even related now, but if we're together for any longer than eight hours at a time I get a nervous tic and an overwhelming urge to staple up her mouth.'

He laughed. At least I think it was a laugh. It might have been a minor choke. God, this was excruciating. Say something. Just say something.

Zzzzzzzzz. Phone! Phone! I panicked, snatched up the phone, dropped it, snatched it up again, pressed a button, held it to my ear, then turned it around so it was the right way up.

'Hello?'

'This is Stefan from Ike Tusker's office. I have Mr Tusker for you now.'

I'm not a religious woman but I suddenly knew how a lowly parish priest felt when he was granted an audience with the Pope.

'Carly!' Ike's voice boomed on to the line.

'Hi Ike, how are you?' Damn. Why was I wasting my time with pleasantries when I'd already been warned that I only had seven minutes in the presence of His Holiness? Give me the news; just give it to me straight. My nerves were jangling and my buttocks were clenched.

'Great, Carly, just great. Listen, I've had some feedback on the book.'

Come on, come on . . .

'A few of the studios have passed – just not the right thing for them just now.'

Come on . . .

'And two of the actors I sent it to have passed too. Still waiting to hear from a couple of them, though. Julia is on location in Morocco and the communications aren't great.'

Okay, stop now. Don't want to hear any more. Bubble had well and truly burst and I'd be picking gum out of my hair for the next ten years.

'But we've had interest from three parties: Global, GMG Studios and Dreamtime would all like to meet you.'

'Fantastic, Ike, I'm thrilled about that. Can you get your people to fax my people with the proposed schedule and I'll get back to you to confirm availability?'

A very efficient, appropriate reply, which, true to form, came out as, 'Eeeeeeeeeeeeeeeekkkkkk!!!!!!'

A few moments later, having regained the power of speech and discovered that two of the meetings would take place on the Thursday and the third one on the Friday of the following week, I pressed the end button on the phone.

'Well?' Sam was waiting with an expectant grin. I repeated the conversation, trying not to sound like a stunt double for Minnie Mouse, but unable to stop myself lunging into his arms at the end, spinning him round in circles and then jumping on the spot as I squeezed the life out of him. If he didn't have heartburn now it would be a miracle.

I was doing a jig, making the most of the feelings of sheer and utter bliss right up until . . . *stop!*

Suddenly I realised that I was standing with my arms around Sam Morton, my nipples were squashed against his torso, my head was somewhere between his pecs and he was breathing on my hair. What the hell was wrong with the air-conditioning? Had he forgotten to put money in the electricity meter?

'I'm so chuffed for you, babe,' he announced. 'You deserve it. And when they meet you they'll love you.'

'Mmchm.' That's all I could say as my face was still immersed somewhere in his chest cavity.

'And for the record, I LOVE having you all here, I DON'T want you to move out, and you can STAY for as long as you want.'

I retrieved my skull.

'Are you sure, Sam? Because, honestly, I won't be offended.'

'I'm sure. Actually, I've got an idea. Your first meeting isn't until next Thursday, right?'

'Right.'

'Soooo. How would you and the boys fancy taking a little trip? With me, that is.'

Let me think – another weekend on the admittedly sunny delights of Mother's Beach or a mystery adventure with one of my favourite people on earth? I resisted the urge to chew on one of his nipples while I contemplated the dilemma.

'Oh, I think a wee trip would be lovely,' I announced, just as Mac and Benny came thundering in.

'Hey guys, how would you like to go somewhere really, really cool?' Sam asked them.

'How cool?' Mac eyed him suspiciously.

'*Very* cool,' Sam answered.

It wasn't enough – Mac needed a bit more. 'Can we take the alligator?'

Sam thought about it for a moment, then nodded. 'We can take the alligator.'

'Yay!' they chorused, with much jumping up and

down and clapping of hands. A week here and I don't think they'd stopped grinning for more than a few seconds. They were having an absolute blast. And stressful career moves and confusing relationships with ex-boyfriends aside, so was I. And now it was only going to get even better because we were going on a jaunt. A trip. Which, unlike my temperature at that precise moment, was going to be very, very cool indeed.

Family Values *Magazine*

PUTTING THE YUMMY IN MUMMY
THIS WEEK . . .
CHILDREN'S SPECIAL TOYS

Children often form strong emotional attachments to special objects or toys. Don't worry if your favourite cashmere stole goes missing – chances are your little darling has commandeered it because it's soft, comforting and reassuring.

Boys, too, are prone to deep affections for their favourite teddy, train or blanket. This is all a perfectly natural stage in the development process, and don't fear, ladies, they do grow out of it! Your little angel will not be clutching on to Poopoo the stuffed Pomeranian when he takes his first steps through those vaulted doors at Eton or Harrow. Although he will always have a soft spot in his heart for his first Harrods teddy.

Indeed, far from being cause for concern, your child's attachment to that inanimate object conveys that they are loving, gentle and already developing the capacity to nurture. What's more, they often choose objects that comfort them because they remind them of their home or family. It might be the touch, the smell, or indeed, perhaps they even think their new favourite friend looks like Mummy or Daddy! Mothers of Barbie lovers, rejoice and congratulate yourself that the last little nip and tuck worked wonders.

Whatever the cause, indulge their little foible. Allow them to carry the object of their affection with them at all times. A gentle word with an understanding vicar and there will always be room at the end of the pew for a large purple dinosaur. Although, British Airways first-class cabin crew may not be quite so obliging.

Treat your little darling's toy like an item of value. Which indeed it is – it's adding to the richness and depth of your child's personality.

Now surely that's something worth treasuring?

★ *Step Eight* ★

I do realise that I'm often too quick to jump to conclusions and occasionally need to pay more attention to what people are saying, but in my defence I don't think that there are many people who wouldn't have misconstrued the finer details of our weekend destination. We were in California. The sun was shining. People wore flip-flops. There were half-naked bodies everywhere, usually with wheels attached to their feet. It was like one great big tampon advert. And yes, our trip was indeed destined to be very cool. As in polar bear's arse. Because we were going . . .

'Skiing,' Sam announced the following morning when I checked what to throw into my suitcase.

'*Skiing?*' I replied incredulously. It was official – he was on mind-altering drugs. I was under the impression that skiing required snow, and unless four foot of white stuff had poured down onto Pacific Palisades for the first time in living memory, then I was struggling with the practicalities of the trip.

I'd also, at this point, like to make a confession: I'd rather have had my teeth knocked out with a jousting pole than go skiing. What, exactly, was the point of going all the way up a bloody great hill just to come back down it again at speed? And don't even get me started on hill-walkers, but suffice to say that I'm convinced they need psychological help and I can quite understand why a disproportionate number of them are single.

Skiing is my idea of sheer bloody torture: cold, wet and energetic. Skiing wasn't a holiday, it was a sentence.

I was gutted. My idea of a fun trip is lying on a sun-lounger, eating chicken-in-a-basket, drinking cocktails with elaborate fruit garnishes and reading steamy bonk-busters penned by my biological mother.

Never, at any point, have I had the desire to dress in a duvet and strange hat and throw myself off a moun-tain.

However, I was aware that it would have been churlish, petty and ungrateful to object. But I did anyway.

'But Sam, I don't have any of the gear for skiing – no clothes, no hats, no co-ordination, no courage what-soever . . .'

'Don't worry, we'll get it all there. And we'll hire kit for the boys too.'

Oh God, the boys. Up a mountain. With sharp sticks. I could almost hear the police helicopters circling over-head.

A short while later I was on the Liam Gallagher side of chirpy when we all clambered into the car, but I slapped a smile on my face and resolved to make the most of it. At least it would be a great story to tell the grandchildren. If I survived the thousand-metre fall and ever came out of the coma.

We stopped at one of the outposts of Jojo's planetary home and stocked up on coffee, juice and muffins.

'Won't we get this at the airport?' I asked Sam, slightly puzzled.

'What airport?'

'Skiing. Snow. Airport. Big plane to take us there.'

He laughed. 'We're not flying, we're driving. We're going to Mammoth Mountain – it's a brilliant ski resort about five hours north of here.'

I had to admire him. Now I knew why Sam Morton had found fame and glory as a fearless action hero. He didn't flinch as he scaled mountains. He could take on ten karate-chopping baddies without batting an eyelid. He fought to the death to save small countries from tyrannical terrorists. And he voluntarily decided to spend five hours in a car with two small children.

Mammoth Mountain. It sounded amazing. I couldn't deny there was a little tremor of excitement running through me. We were going on a road trip! It was like *Thelma and Louise* – only it was Sam and me in the front, Mac and Benny behind us, and an inflatable alligator called Archie sticking out the back window.

And Sam seemed to be acting pretty normally again. The awkwardness of the last few days had evaporated and he was back to his lovely, funny self. I'm sure men have hormonal cycles every month as well.

He gave me a map to follow the route. We were to take the Interstate 5 North, to the State Route 14 North, to the US 395 North, to the State Route 203 North –

307 miles in total. Simple. If you were a satellite navigation system or a Sherpa.

Soon the densely populated Los Angeles was behind us, the spaces getting more open with every passing mile. We kept the kids as amused as possible. We sang every song in our not insignificant repertoire, we told jokes, we played I Spy, Animal Alphabets and Who Am I? (a frazzled mother with an aversion to extreme sports). We stopped 435 times for small boys to pee.

There was momentary excitement when we passed a huge field where the airlines send their decommissioned planes to die: row upon row upon row of aeroplanes of all shapes, sizes and nationalities. The boys were ecstatic. Cue toilet stop number 436. And then a few miles later ... nothing! Absolutely nothing for miles. We were smack in the middle of the Mojave Desert, on a narrow road and with not another car in sight. On we travelled on our epic journey, four fearless explorers and an alligator. But we had no idea just how exciting our expedition was about to become. We cleared the desert and drove on until it happened. It was the moment that I knew I'd made it. Never mind that I'd trotted off to LA in search of the American dream and planned to offer movie producers my kidneys if they would only turn one of my novels into a big-screen production. Forget the fact that I was now en route to a top ski resort where I'd no doubt spend a week looking like a Michelin Man on planks. This was the defining moment of my trip: the glamour, the glitz, the ultimate thrill. As we drove up the deserted highway, the sign appeared like an oasis in the desert in front of me. 'Welcome To Pearsonville, the Hub Cap Capital of the World.'

Yes, I know a top spot when I see it. I was giddy with excitement. Maybe hubcaps are like cats and always make their way back home. If so, I was potentially only minutes away from being reunited with the ones that were nicked off my Fiat 126 one miserable night in Peckham in 1988.

Despite my pleadings, movie-star-at-the-wheel refused to park up and we pressed on to Mammoth Mountain, with just one stop at a small town to buy winter clothes and change out of our LA togs. It was hard to believe that we'd had breakfast in the sun and now we were up to our knees in snow.

Two hundred shouts of 'Are we nearly there yet?' later (four from the kids in the back of the car, the rest from me), we finally reached ski utopia. 'Awesome,' gasped Mac in the back.

Great. A week in LA and already he had the vernacular of an *OC* extra.

But he did have a point – it was a magnificent sight. Huge expanses of perfect powdered snow, dozens of hi-tech ski lifts, and lots of rosy-cheeked people wandering around with skis thrown effortlessly across their shoulders. The reality of what I'd let myself in for immediately set in. It was an intimidating prospect for someone whose only experience of being on the piste was an adolescent school trip to Aviemore where I pleaded frostbite so that I could stay on the bus all day snogging my boyfriend. I believe he was called Mark Barwick. No idea where he is now.

I had a momentary pang of guilt – here we were blazing a trail to a new adventure and he was at home slogging his guts out at work.

Okay, guilt pang over. I did say it was only a short one. I dialled his mobile number, gave the phone to Mac and let him bring his dad up-to-date with the new developments. I'm not sure he understood quite why we were taking an alligator to a ski resort.

The manager was waiting for us when we checked into a hotel called The Village and he greeted Sam like a long-lost friend before informing him that his usual suite was ready. It was an impressive gesture of customer service that I was sure would be adopted by the staff at the Glasgow Travel Inn next time I went there.

I wondered if I would ever get used to the fact that the entire movie-going world fawned over Sam like he really had saved the planet from destruction by a deadly meteorite before going on to invent a nuclear heating system that prevented the coming of the second Ice Age. That's when he wasn't reforming the national justice system and getting the knickers off Nicole Kidman.

Taking all this into account, it was highly un-cool that I gasped out loud when we entered our room. Or should I say *rooms*. It was the most amazing suite – pardon me, *condominium* – I'd ever seen. There was a fabulous oak open-plan kitchen, a dining area that could seat the twelve supermodel apostles and a lounge area with a huge roaring fire – all decorated in rustic tones and luxurious fabrics. There were three bedrooms, two on one side of the lounge (one with twin beds, one with a double bed, both with en suites) and a huge master suite with a super-kingsize bed, dressing area and bathroom on the other side of the lounge.

'You take the master suite and I'll bunk in with the boys,' I offered, very conscious that this must be costing him an absolute fortune, and even if I emptied my overdraft I'd still struggle to pay for one night here.

'Don't be daft, you and the boys take the master – the bed's bigger. I'll sleep in the room at the end with the double bed.'

Why did it make me feel slightly better that he wasn't going to be sleeping directly on the other side of the wall?

Quick change and then we set off to explore the town. The boys were in their element – snowballs, snowmen, and little sleighs that were really cute until you tried to pull them with seven stone of little boys sitting on top.

We stopped for dinner in Lakanuki, a gorgeous, wintery, cosy – er, Hawaiian themed – restaurant. Hawaii. In the snow. Who said Americans had no sense of irony?

The boys crashed out within ten minutes of getting back to the condo. I was on page eight of their favourite book, called *I Don't Want to Grow Up* (don't listen to my husband – it's not my autobiography) when I realised they'd both slipped into slumbers. I kissed their noses and pulled the covers over them. Benny automatically turned on his side and threw an arm over Mac, cuddling in close to him. A huge wave of love and gratitude engulfed me. How had I got this lucky?

I wandered back through into the lounge and saw that Sam had poured me a glass of wine. From the noise coming from the bathroom, I guessed he was in the shower. I lifted the wine and noticed a door off the corner of the living room and immediately realised what that meant – toxins. Fab! I grappled in my handbag for my ciggies. Since smoking was punishable by death in most areas of LA, I was still on the same pack that I'd opened the day we'd arrived. My lungs were probably in shock.

I opened the door to the balcony and took a huge gasp of breath. The temperature had fallen to about minus ten degrees, there were little crystal droplets in the air, the sky was awash with stars and in front of me was the most beautiful sight I'd ever seen in my life. The Village Square was littered with young trees, each one about ten feet tall, and all of them were lit with hundreds of tiny white twinkling lights. It was breath-taking. If Santa were real, this would be his garden.

It must have been the wine, the altitude or possibly the beginnings of PMT, but suddenly I was aware that tears were tripping down my cheeks. I'd never forget this moment. Never. It was the kind of perfection that didn't happen often in a lifetime. Damn Mark. I wanted him here with me. I wanted him to see this, to have this slotted into our scrapbook of memories that we'd trot out in between bingo and basket-weaving in the nursing home. Damn him for not having the balls to take a chance on this. Damn him for not loving me enough to do this for me.

'Hey . . . you okay there?' came a soft, gentle voice.

Damn him for his complete lack of jealousy. Damn him for subjecting me to a weekend in five-star luxury in the most beautiful place on earth with my second favourite man on the planet.

'Mmmm,' I replied. 'It's just so . . . beautiful.'

'So are you.'

Oh, damn, damn, fucking damn.

He was just being friendly. He was just being Sam. He was just breathing on the back of my neck.

He stood behind me and put his arms around me; slightly unfortunate for his cashmere robe that he didn't notice I had a cigarette in one hand. It was only a small hole. I crossed my fingers that the robe wasn't super-flammable, in which case he might spontaneously combust and several major movie studios would have lawyers with my name at the top of their hit list.

His arms still wrapped around me, he kissed the top of my head. I said nothing, but held my breath, acutely aware that I had just inhaled a cloud of Silk Cut and exhalation would create a whole 'Puff the Magic Dragon' effect and ruin the moment.

Wait a minute, what moment?

He was just being friendly. Very, very friendly. About as friendly as you could get without the exchange of body fluids.

And, in that moment, every single pore of my body wanted to be very, very friendly right back. And I was prepared to negotiate on the body fluids thing.

There was a long silence. Actually, inside my head there was a raging barney going on as my conscience and my libido kicked the crap out of each other, but on the outside all was calm.

'I'm off to bed, hon, early start tomorrow,' he said softly, then unravelled his arms and went back inside. In the red corner, my conscience now had its hands on hips and a smug expression, while in the blue corner my libido was hyperventilating into a paper bag.

For a moment, I thought ... well, it doesn't really matter what I thought. The reality was that Sam really was just being friendly after all.

The next morning, I woke to find myself alone in the bed. I had a moment of panic, before I heard copious giggling in the lounge. I wandered through to see Sam and the boys looking like prototypes of Snowboarding Action Man.

'The hotel sent up the ski-suits I ordered – what do you think?' Sam gestured to Mac and Benny who immediately adopted ski-like poses and beaming grins.

'I think my plans for a day of eating chocolates and drinking wine in a picturesque ski lodge just bit the dust.'

How true. After a quick call to my lawyer to make sure my will was up-to-date, they forced me into my ski suit and before I knew it I was defying death on a gondola, headed to a height that shouldn't be attempted without the aid of a Cessna and a parachute. Sam had already booked the boys into junior ski school, so we took them there and waited until they got settled with their instructor: a springy, competent-looking young woman called Heidi.

When they went a whole ten minutes without even looking to see if we were still there, we about-turned and made for the slopes.

'Er, Sam, can you actually ski?'

'Yeah, I had to learn for *Ice Patrol*,' he answered, quoting his 100-million-dollar-grossing action flick from the year before.

'But I thought you were in a lab developing an electric sub-structure for the planet throughout that whole movie.'

'Carly, where was the lab?'

Aah, I remembered now. Halfway up a bloody great mountain in the Alps. The closing scene had been a re-creation of the famous James Bond ski scene but with Sam blasting all the baddies off the mountain with a Scud missile before making a spectacular three-hundred-yard jump and landing next to Renée Zellweger's Aston Martin. Bet Renée Zellweger never looked like a Teletubby in a sleeping bag, I pondered, as I waddled to the perilous terrain of the beginners' slopes.

Sam spent the first hour teaching me the basics. Skis on. Skis off. Crouch down. Stand up. Posture. Loose knees. Don't lean back. Snowplough. Snowplough. SNOWPLOUGH!!!! Crash. Cue three-course meal of snow and sincere apologies to injured passers-by.

But then something up there with curing leprosy and walking on water happened – I somehow managed to stay upright for a whole five minutes. It was all the incentive I needed. Soon my mammoth buttocks were whizzing down that mountain, striking the fear of God into anyone in my path. There were a few more apologies to hapless bystanders who inadvertently acted as my 'stop barrier' at the bottom, but two small incidents of minor concussion aside, the whole experience was exhilarating.

Another few glides down the mountain and I was convinced I could ski like a pro – although I have a sneaking suspicion that they don't close their eyes, launch themselves forward and then pray like their life depends on it while screaming 'shit, shit, shit' until coming to a crashing halt at the bottom.

As I lumbered over to collect Mac and Benny at the end of the day, there was a definite spring in my ski – yes, Big Mama Cooper was obviously a natural-born athlete. I might have had more falls than Niagara, but I'd made it through the whole day without a single visit to the nearest casualty department. I couldn't wait to pass on my newfound expertise to my offspring. Ah, they were going to be so grateful that their mother could guide them through the complexities of winter sports.

'Mum, look what I can do!' cried Mac the minute he spotted me. I donned my best indulgent expression, prepared to act delighted that he'd learned how to stand up on his skis.

He shot away from the top of the kids' slope, slalomed around three poles, did a jump and then executed a perfect stop at the bottom.

'Me too, Mummy, me too,' screeched Benny, who then proceeded to follow his brother down the hill without falling once. Fab. One day in ski school and they were the Swiss Alpine Synchronised Ski Team.

Suddenly my achievements didn't look quite so impressive. Perhaps in future I should just skip the skiing and book a long weekend in the Hub Cap Capital of the World.

Sam and I gave them a rousing ovation, copious hugs and then we all headed back to the hotel.

An hour later, I felt like I'd been wrestling with Archie the alligator. Every muscle in my body appeared to have been designed for someone at least six inches shorter than me and I was seizing up. I couldn't put my foot down flat because my Achilles heel was threatening to snap. I couldn't sit down for fear of my thighs breaking in two. And don't even get me started on my mammoths, which had clearly been put through the shrink cycle in a tumble-drier. I was in agony. Even a long soak in the Jacuzzi didn't return me to the less-than-two-high-strength-paracetamol side of sheer agony.

Luckily the boys were as exhausted as me, and after a few slices of called-in pizza we left Sam watching a sporty thingy and went off to bed.

I sent a quick text to Kate: 'Went skiing today – it was fantastic!'

A reply came straight back. 'Get off the drugs.'

I suddenly realised that I hadn't told her we were coming to Mammoth.

What a day. Carly Cooper, unapologetic sun-lounger potato and all-round holiday beached whale had learned to ski. Bite my sore buttocks, Snow Suit Action Barbie.

I fell asleep, aching, exhausted but strangely proud.

Unfortunately, next morning I woke up rigid. Completely rigid.

'Sam,' I called calmly, determined not to make a drama out of a definite crisis. He padded in with Mac and Benny in tow. 'I don't want to alarm you, but I think I'm paralysed.'

He laughed. If he's ever up for a part in *ER*, remind me to address his bedside manner.

'Carly, how long is it since you did any form of exercise?' he asked in a decidedly mocking tone.

'Do you want it in years or decades?' I replied with a groan.

'You're not paralysed, you're unfit.'

Well, no shit, Sherlock. Smug pals could be so irritating. However, even more upsetting was a smug pal who – deep breath, deep breath, I was having palpitations now – was only wearing jeans and had nothing on his perfectly sculpted torso. And he hadn't shaved yet, so his face was all gorgeously crinkly. Oh, the things I could do if I wasn't a married woman. Or paralysed from the neck down.

I couldn't help but wonder if this was yet another stroke of divine intervention from Mary, the Blessed Virgin. Although what she was doing in a ski resort with only those flowing robes between her and certain hypothermia, I'll never know.

Sam recruited the boys as his assistants and between the three of them they managed to haul me to an upright position.

'Send me back to the aeroplane graveyard and let me die in peace curled up to a Virgin Atlantic 747,' I begged, to much hilarity from the testosterone posse. Benny and Mac were collapsed in heaps of giggles now. That was it – no pocket money until their voices broke.

'Carly, there's only one thing that'll sort you out.'

'A general anaesthetic?'

He shook his head. 'Worse than that, I'm afraid. I've seen this condition here before and the cure is painful, traumatic and decidedly risky.'

'Sam, don't say I'm going back up that bloody mountain.'

'Okay, I won't say it. But if you could just get your kit together as quickly as possible because me and the boys are missing valuable snow time here and we're keen to get back up there,' he said with a chuckle.

The audacity! To presume that *he* could tell *me* what my children wanted. Those boys spent nine months in my womb and I knew them inside out. I knew their feelings, their wants and their desires. And their soft spots when it came to blatant blackmail.

'Guys, how about we spend the day on the sofas today and we'll watch *Scooby-Doo* all day?' I said in a tantalising tone. Take that, Sam Morton! Watch and weep.

The boys grinned.

That's it, boys, you know you want to.

Then they looked at each other.

Come on, boys, snuggle in beside me.

Then they looked back at me.

You don't have to thank me now. I'm your mother, I'm supposed to be this great.

182

And, in perfect synchronicity, said, 'Naaaaah! Skiing, skiing, skiing.'

Crap, they were chanting. Heidi wasn't a ski instructor, she was the black witch responsible for recruitment to a sinister cult that demanded twelve hours per day of snow worship.

I knew when I was outvoted. After some gentle rotations, stretching and manipulations, I vaguely regained the power of my legs and managed to break into a stagger. With help from the children of darkness, I climbed back into my suit and off we went again. I was sore, I was weak and my children had been possessed by a paranormal force. Mark didn't know what he was missing.

'You know what you need, don't you?' Sam asked me the following lunchtime. Yep, I was on my third day up that mountain. I still ached from head to toe. My skin was a subtle shade of beetroot except for two white circles around my eyes where my goggles sat. When I took my hat off my hair looked like straw hanging out of a skip. I had bruising in places that required three mirrors set at conflicting angles to see. And I know I'm supposed to say, 'Oh, but it was all so worth it because the exhilaration of roaring down that mountain had taken me to a higher spiritual plane and made me want to have a lesbian love-in with Mother Nature.' But the truth was that, much as I was beginning to accept that skiing could be a fun way to spend the day (as opposed to, say, working down a mine or being involved in a hostage situation), I had come to the conclusion that

I'd far rather spend my day lying in a prone position with a piña colada. Oh, hark. Less than a fortnight ago I was living a life of perpetual drudgery and now I was getting picky about what kind of rich and famous pastime I'd rather partake in.

I realised that Sam was still waiting for an answer.

'Oh, sorry – I thought that was a hypothetical question. Erm, what do I need . . . ?'

'A pamper,' he said with a grin.

You should never argue with a man who's holding a gun, a knife, or vouchers for spa treatments.

We checked on the boys, who were happy tucking into lunch with all their new pals at the ski school, then headed back down to the main lodge. Half an hour later I was naked, except for a towel covering my privates, and being gently massaged with oils and lotions.

'Better?' Sam murmured.

'Mmmmm,' I murmured.

Did I forget to mention that a naked Sam was lying next to me? Thankfully, three feet of space, two towels and two six-foot Swedish male masseurs were between us. The receptionist had obviously assumed we were partners and booked us into a double treatment room. Not that it mattered, I supposed. Sam had seen me naked hundreds of times. Although granted that was before I'd married someone else and expelled small children from my birthing canal. And while we were definitely in the scud, we couldn't actually see any of our dangling bits or areas with small curly hairs due to strategically placed textiles.

Still, I wondered if I'd just fallen flat on my face over some kind of invisible adultery trip wire. How would I feel if it were Mark lying here with another woman next to him? Homicidal, was the first word that came into my head.

I couldn't bear it. I'd hate it. I would be furious, hurt and devastated. Saint Carly of the Blessed Martyrdom would weep, wail and then do illegal things involving contact between hot wax and husband's pubes.

I'd be gutted. This was wrong, I realised. So, so wrong. What was I thinking? Or forgetting to think? Shouldn't I be keeping some kind of check on what was appropriate behaviour for a married woman? A married woman who loved her husband? I suddenly wanted to get up, get dressed, and go home.

I had a mental image of Mark standing in front of me, right there, right then. And his face was . . .

Totally impassive. He said hi to Sam, shook his hand and then had a twenty-minute chat with the masseurs about the transport links in Gothenburg.

My husband's lack of any kind of jealousy gene was reassuring, admirable and bore great testament to his grounded sense of self. It also drove me fucking crazy. I understood his logic, though, having had it explained to me on numerous occasions when questioned as to why I could threaten to give blow jobs to the entire Chelsea football squad and he wouldn't bat an eyelid.

'Carly, I trust you. Would you ever do anything that would hurt me?'

'No,' I would answer. Well, you do, don't you? Even Henry the Eighth wouldn't have piped up with, 'Er,

185

actually, I'll shag everything in sight then decapitate you, but don't worry, it'll be over in a flash and you won't feel a thing.'

Anyway, I meant it. I couldn't ever imagine wanting to do anything with another man that I couldn't do with my husband. I know, I just have to read back over the last hundred pages, but in my defence these discussions took place before the whole LA/desertion/half-naked-on-a-massage-table saga began.

Which brought me back to the present. Why was I feeling uncomfortable about this when I knew that Mark wouldn't mind?

Another factor of mitigation suddenly came to mind that removed my doubts. If this were Mark lying here with Kate or Carol, it wouldn't ruffle my feathers in the least. They were friends, we were friends, and it would all be perfectly harmless and innocent. Just like this was. Sam and I were friends. Lifelong friends. My husband knew him well and would realise that there was nothing suspicious in the least about this situation. It was utterly innocuous. I had nothing to worry about. Nothing. I wasn't pole-vaulting over any kind of marital boundary or jeopardising my husband's feelings in any way. It was fine that I was lying here next to Sam. It didn't matter that I could reach out and touch those arms. Or that my foot could easily wander across and rub up and down those perfect calves. Or that . . .

'Could you turn over now please,' said Sven of the gentle rub, raising the towel slightly from my body so that I could roll onto my back without losing my dignity.

I obliged. Although I think I blew the dignity bit when Sven let the towel float back down and it looked like Billy Smart had parked two of his circus tents side by side on my upper torso.

Now, *that* Mark might just object to.

'Mummy, I never, ever want to go home,' Mac declared sleepily in his bed later that night.

'Why not?' I asked.

'Because I love it here, Mum. I can ski and swim and I'm never leaving Archie,' he announced, pulling the covers up over Archie's two front legs, but leaving his snout poking out from between the sheets. If burglars broke in during the night they'd be traumatised for life.

'But what about all your friends at home? You'd really miss them.'

He eyed me like I was crazy. 'But Mum, I've got loads of new friends here.'

There goes my son – flighty, superficial and shallower than a puddle in the Gobi.

'They sleeping?' asked Sam when I returned to the lounge, walking for the first time in days without the general posture of a rodeo star with a groin strain.

I nodded.

'They're great kids,' he said as he handed me a glass of wine.

'Thanks. I know I'm biased, but I agree. And I'll still be proud of them when I'm smuggling in nail files concealed in sultana cakes in a bid to help them escape.'

Then, 'They like you,' I added with a grin. 'Mac said

something about "same mental age" or something like that.'

He raised one eyebrow. 'How dare you! Do you know who I am?'

'Jude Law?'

He ignored me. 'I'm a really important movie-star person who must be shamelessly pandered to for every moment of the day.'

'Yeah, well I'll pander you right after I've increased my chances of dying a premature death with a face that looks like it's made of cowhide. I'm nipping out for a quick ciggie.'

He frowned in mock disapproval. 'Those things will kill you.'

I spun round, sloshing a few drops of wine on the angora carpet. 'Can I just point out the irony of that statement coming from a man who's been dragging me up bloody mountains all week and forcing me to hurtle down them at break-neck speed? I think I'd rather take my chances with Mr Marlboro,' I said, laughing at his cheek.

I grabbed a rich red chenille throw from the sofa and headed out onto the balcony. I sat on one of the two chairs out there, careful to wrap the blanket around my posterior area, lest I spend the remainder of my trip of a lifetime with piles. I pulled my knees up to my chest and lit a cigarette, awestruck again by the sheer magnificence of the view. Straight ahead I spotted a couple climbing off the gondola, arms around each other, laughing at some shared joke. They looked like they were in love. Or was I just romanticising everything because this was undoubtedly the most romantic place on earth?

The most romantic place on earth.

The most physically gorgeous man on earth.

Who loves children, animals and alligators. And me.

Or at least he did once and still does when he's had too many Budweisers.

How did I ever find myself in this insane situation? The strangest thing about it was that it felt so . . . *normal*.

I was actually sad that we were leaving the next day. The only consolation was that it was another day closer to my meetings with the movie companies. A shiver of excitement made my stomach flip. Another day closer to potentially the most exciting career-break imaginable. 'Carly Cooper, who's she?' the crowds would ask. 'Oh, you know – Jackie Collins's daughter. That writing lark must be in the blood.'

I smiled as I stubbed the cigarette out in a metal ashtray on the floor. I'd lost the feeling in my feet and several fingers so it was probably time to go back inside. It struck me that this was the first night that Sam and I had actually spent alone together since we got there. My injuries and strains had caused me to crash out with the boys every night in a paracetamol-induced coma. I checked my watch. Eight o'clock. So what would we do for the next few hours? Music? Nope, too romantic. That would be like eating a starter and abstaining from main course and pudding. TV? Possibly, but surely we could think of something a little more intellectual than staring at a box all night. Games? We could have jolly japes and play games. Although I couldn't guarantee that I could stop my libido demanding sixteen rounds of strip poker.

Perhaps we should stick to the TV after all. Perhaps we could choose a DVD – anything with no sex, no romance and no scenes starring Sam Morton naked would do.

I opened the door to go back inside. Three things happened instantaneously:

1. I noticed that music was playing. Luther Vandross. Fuck. I'd forgotten how much Sam loved Luther. We used to play that all the time when we were together. Together as in a 'couple' way, not 'platonic friends with two children and an inflatable reptile'.
2. Sam was lying on the couch, with one leg slung over the back, reading what looked like a script. He was now wearing a white T-shirt and jeans, his hair almost gold in the light of the dozens of candles that were lit all around the roaring fire. Why do we say that fires roar? It was actually completely silent. The only thing that was roaring was . . .
3. My libido – and the yell went along the lines of 'Where are those playing cards? Strip poker NOW!'

Sam took his eyes off the script and transferred them to me, an act that was decidedly uncomfortable as I'd been struck by that intermittent paralysis thing again and I was rooted to the spot, incapable of doing anything except staring back.

He put the script down, still staring, his expression soft, almost tentative.

Thank Christ I was paralysed or it would have been like a magnetic beam drawing me towards the light. I really needed to stop watching *Star Wars* with the kids.

The kids! This was the point where, if this were a movie, one of the kids would wander in all sleepy-eyed and ask for a drink of water or announce that they'd just vomited over the duvet.

Nope. No kids. Even Mary the Blessed Virgin seemed to have deserted me. My motor functions had shut down and my heart sounded like the Paddington Express, yet there wasn't even the slightest sign of a divine intervention.

He got up from the sofa and walked towards me. In seconds I was eye-to-eye with his pecs. He raised my chin and leaned down and kissed me, so lightly I almost didn't feel our lips meeting for what must only have been a split second. Och, that was fine. I'd kissed him much harder than that every time he walked through the door on a visit to Mark and me. This wasn't wrong. It was just a wee peck. A friendly smacker. A . . . a full-blown case of denial.

Mark. Mark. Oh, God, what on earth was I doing? Mark. Sam. If I picked either of them out of a lucky bag at that exact moment I'd have been equally as happy. How wrong was that? When did I start to put Sam on the same footing as my husband?

'Carly, we need to . . . talk.'

I groaned, still rooted to the spot and looking at that beautiful face.

'I know.'

He put his hand up and ran a finger down my face,

then rested his hand on my neck. He was fighting dirty now. He knew that ever since I'd seen Richard Gere do that in *An Officer and a Gentleman* when I was fourteen it had become the single most sexy thing a man could do to me, guaranteed to make me melt, make my heart race and make my bra unhook itself and catapult a distance of up to ten feet.

Silence.

'I can't believe I'm stuck for words,' he eventually whispered. 'It's just that . . . Carly, you've no idea what I want to do to you right now.'

Oh, I think I could hazard a guess.

'Does it involve playing cards?'

'What?' he asked, his bewilderment obvious.

I giggled. I've no idea why, because there was absolutely nothing funny about this. It was the nervous giggle, the one that forced my Auntie Maud to ask me to leave Uncle Joseph's funeral on that black day in 1985.

I reached up and gently removed his hand from my neck. I couldn't concentrate when it was causing a small part of my brain to sing 'Love Lift Us Up Where We Belong' at a volume so high it could wake the kids.

'You're right, we need to talk,' I told him softly, 'but I can't do it when I'm so close I can see your heart beating.'

I took his hand and led him over to the dining table, motioning him to sit down. Stalling for time, I grabbed a mug and poured myself a coffee from the pot that was sitting on the machine, then I sat directly opposite him. Good point: There was now three feet of oak between us. Bad point: When had our fingers inter-locked?

He spoke first.

'I think I'm falling in love with you again.'

Great. I was glad he'd decided to gradually work up to the serious stuff.

'You are?'

He nodded. I groaned. And my head fell onto the table. Eventually, I lifted it again and almost gasped when I saw the raw emotion on his face. I'd seen Sam look at me that way before: when he asked me to marry him; when he begged me not to leave Hong Kong; and then years later when he wanted us to give our relationship another try.

'Sam, we can't do this.'

'Tell me you don't want to, and I promise I won't say anything else.'

Mouth open, nothing coming out. My voice had buggered off with my self-discipline, my morals and my senses.

'Carly?'

He squeezed my hand. My emergency voice mechanism eventually kicked in.

'Sam, I don't know. I just don't know. I was a mess when I came here. Mark and I are crap just now. Actually, we've been pretty crap for a while now. And life just didn't turn out the way I thought it would. Suburban mother, that's me. No decadence, no excitement, no drama, just the same stuff day in and day out. And then you pop up again and suddenly I'm here and Ike Tusker is my new best friend and I'm having breakfast in the Peninsula and living a life that's, well, the life that I always wanted to have. And I'm living it with you.' There was a pause while my brain caught up with what was coming out of my mouth. Then, 'And it's perfect,' I whispered, as a huge tear dropped down my cheek. Oh no. As previous incidents have shown, my crying isn't pretty, or poignant, or cute. I only cry with full-scale snot and racking sobs. I bit my tongue.

He leaned over and wiped away the tear, then took my hand again. 'And are you ... are you ... how do you feel about me now?'

I shrugged my shoulders. 'I don't know. I can't separate this life, this experience, the chronic state of my marriage, the excitement of the film stuff, the hope ... I don't know what's real and what isn't. And I don't trust myself to figure it out. I love you, Sam. But I can't tell if it's the same love I've always felt for you or if it's grown into something new. But I do know that ...'

I stopped. I couldn't say it. If Mary, Mother of God was whooping it up on that bloody ski slope outside instead of being in here where she was needed then I hoped an altercation with a crash barrier was looming.

'What?' he probed gently.

'I want to make love to you.'

I swear I heard a loud bang and a female's scream.

I'd said it. I wanted him. I wanted to do slow, frantic, beautiful, dirty, amazing things to him.

'I want to make love to you,' I repeated, just to make sure he'd heard me since he hadn't responded by leaping over the table, throwing me on the floor and ripping my kit off.

After about three and a half months, by which time my heart had stopped beating, I'd decomposed into a pile of bones and it had turned to spring outside, he finally spoke.

'I want to make love to you too.'

He reached over and did the Richard Gere face thing again.

'But we can't,' he whispered, looking sadder than I'd ever seen him.

'OH, FOR FUCK'S SAKE!' That wasn't me screaming, that was my clitoris, in total despair, disbelief and not just a little disappointment.

Fortunately, my mouth stayed silent. He was right. I knew he was. If I made love to him then things would be changed that could never be unchanged. Our beautiful, amazing friendship would either grow into something more or be destroyed. Sleeping with Sam would be a fatal blow to my marriage. Mark was the most stable, easy-going, non-jealous guy I'd ever met but I knew that would change if I ever broke his trust, and I was sure he'd take his stable, easy-going, non-jealous self as far away from me as possible. But most of all . . .

'I know we can't. My boys.' I didn't have to explain. Sam knew me. He knew how I felt about my family. And it all boiled down to this: if I was going to change my boys' futures by breaking up their family then I had to be sure, absolutely positive that it was absolutely right. It had to be the very best thing for them as well as me. More so.

And I couldn't risk making the wrong decision just

because a small part of my genital anatomy was now marching up and down the table in front of me wearing a sandwich board that said, 'Victim of Neglect – Demand Adoption to a New Home.'

'You've no idea how hard this is, Sam,' I told him, unable to keep the sadness from my voice.

He smiled ruefully. 'You think?'

'So what do we do next?'

He thought for a few moments. 'We just carry on. Don't worry, I'm not going to get all lovesick and pine at the window every time you leave the room.'

I made my best disappointed face. 'Well, that's shite – there was I hoping for rose petals, poetry and stalking to a level that's punishable by a custodial sentence.'

We both laughed, not so much breaking the ice as melting the top layer.

'I'm not going to give you ultimatums or deadlines or demands, Carly. You know how I feel. I couldn't go on any longer without telling you. And you have to know, I feel pretty crap about this too. I like Mark. And I don't want to cause anybody any hurt. But I had to tell you.'

'Is that what all those disappearing acts were about last week?'

He shrugged his shoulders in the manner of a fourteen-year-old who'd just been caught with the entire *Hustler* back-catalogue stashed under his bed.

'I just needed some time to think, so I dragged my meetings out a bit. But honestly, I've got a really heavy schedule for the next week or so, so don't get all paranoid if I'm not around.'

Huh. As if I'd ever get all paranoid and neurotic. At least not during sleeping hours.

'Listen, in case I forget to say it at any time, thank you.'

'What for?' he asked.

'For bringing us here, for loving my boys, for loving me – in a fully clothed way. For just being amazing. And for understanding why I'm not butt-naked and swinging from that light-shade right now. I do love you, Sam. Can I ask one last thing?'

'Anything.'

'Can you switch off Luther? I can resist you, but Luther? I have my doubts.'

We lay on the couch cuddled up for the rest of the night watching back-to-back episodes of *CSI Miami*. There was nothing like autopsies, body parts and random killings to quell the libido. Thank God.

Later that night, as I lay in bed with Mac's feet in my face and Benny snoring at a volume that could cause an avalanche, it occurred to me that the stakes of my life had just got higher. Everything hung on the meetings with the movie companies. If one of them went my way and we got a film deal, then that could mean moving to LA permanently. Would I be able to make Mark come over here? Without deploying tranquillising drugs, shackles and a large trunk? Or would it be the final death knell on our marriage? If he did come over here, would he hate it? Let's face it, Mark didn't do superficiality. He was more likely to stick needles in his eyes than pick up a celebrity magazine or take an interest in movie-star gossip.

And if he didn't come over, what then? A long-distance relationship? Yeah, right. I'd been here two weeks and I'd already had a near miss in the sexual department. If I was here on my own permanently there was no way that my restraint and discipline would stand up to the pressure.

So that left . . . What? Separation? Divorce? Sam? Sure, I could just move on in with Sam and play happy families. But how did I really feel about him? Did I love him enough to make a permanent relationship work? What if we tried and it didn't last – what kind of crap mother would that make me? I'd then have subjected the boys to TWO father figures only for neither of them to work out.

Oh, listen to me. One bit of lust and I already had Sam and me married, divorced and my kids in therapy.

I heard footsteps padding around in the condo. Sam must be up getting a drink.

For a split second I wondered if he'd come through but I knew he wouldn't. Sam would never pressure me. Whatever happened from here on in was going to be down to me. I had to make the decisions and the moves. Mac kicked me in the face, as if reminding me of his presence. Okay, I was just getting to you. Because whatever I decided had to be the best thing for the three of us. And right at that very moment, I had absolutely no idea what the best thing was.

CARLY CALLING . . .

Carly to Kate and Carol:

Survivd the skiing but storm brewng.
Wish u wer here - need moral compass,
pals and padlock 4 nethers. Help.

Kate:

Oh crap, knew this wd happn. DO NOT
do anythg stupid. Do Not! Think pure
thots & if that fails think thrush.
Legs crosd yet? Anywy, need 2 talk -
call me 18r. Kxxx

Carol:

Carol:

Carol:

No reply from Carol. Strange.

★ Step Nine ★

'*Mum, Benny's got his foot on my half of the seat!*'
'*Haven't.*'
'*Have.*'
'*Haven't.*'
'*Have.*'

'What's the penalty in LA for child abandonment?' I asked Sam. 'Because whatever it is, it's worth it.'

It had been the journey from hell. The kids were overexcited, exhausted and suffering from arguably the worst childhood affliction imaginable: dead batteries in the Game Boy.

If I could have managed it, I'd have chewed off my own ears. I now understood why taxi drivers have soundproof glass between the front and back sections of their cabs.

'*Mac!!*' Benny shouted in ear-splitting ire at something or another – perhaps a spare toe dangling into his personal space.

'MY NAME IS NOT MAC!' said Mac. Or at least a child who looked very like the one I'd given birth to and called by that name.

'So what's your name then?' I asked him.

'Doctor Octopus.'

'But Doctor Octopus is a baddie.'

'I know. I want to be a baddie now. Being a goodie is boring.'

Oh, sweet Jesus, he'd gone over to the dark side. I just hoped we could get him back or it would be Doctor Octopus today, tomorrow a drug-dealing service and a stable of women who charged by the hour.

'Think I should be concerned?' I asked Sam, who, after all, did have experience of the 'charging by the hour' bit.

'Nah. I play an intergalactic lawyer in my next movie – I'll make sure he only gets parole.'

'MUM, Doctor Octopus just hit me!'

I zoned out. I glanced at Sam to see if his knuckles were white and his jaw was clenched, but he looked remarkably calm. He'd make a great father one day. Oh, I wasn't even going to go down that train of thought again. I'd stored the whole Sam/Me/Naked/Relationship saga in the 'On Hold' file. I wasn't even going to give it another thought. That wasn't to say I wouldn't occasionally look at his body in a lustful manner – after all, I was married, not dead – but my priority had to be the studio meetings and I'd resolved to stop ruminating and fretting about everything else for the time being. There was nothing I could do about Sam being amazing. There was nothing I could do about my husband being a twat. And there was nothing I could do about the fact that Benny had Doctor Octopus in a headlock. Actually, there was, but on the bright side it was keeping them quiet.

Sam was fairly nonchalant too, but then, this had a precedent. Years before, when the whole 'I'm a male hooker' debacle came out and put the kibosh on us reigniting our relationship, we'd gone to Thailand for an extended holiday and had weeks of non-sexual bliss together. We were good at platonic. Hadn't we once spent weeks on a tropical island without so much as a tickly fumble? And Sam was the type of guy who, now that he'd shared his feelings and got everything out in the open, would let destiny take its course instead of trying to force it. I'd always thought he was a wise old head on young, perfectly formed, tanned shoulders.

Still, it was a relief when Sam's home appeared in front of us. Only one lone photographer at the entrance today – the others must have sussed that Sam was out of town and gone off to stalk Leonardo DiCaprio instead.

Thankfully, as we drove through the electronic gates, Sam put Benny's squeals of 'Go back, do again, do again,' down to fatigue and possible concussion resulting from Doctor Octopus scudding him with a ski boot. It was already almost seven o'clock – time for the boys to be in bed. As we headed up the driveway, I was mentally planning a quick but healthy dinner for the kids (chicken with vegetables that I would pretend not to see when they got sneaked into the bin) then a dip in the bath, then bed.

After which, I'd have a long soak myself, perhaps a light dinner with Sam out by the pool and then an early night so that I was fresh and alert for my big day. I was ready. So ready. Nothing but nothing was going to stand in my way, I resolved.

Then I noticed that something was standing in my way.

Eliza. She'd come out to greet us and help us in with our assorted baggage, child, arch evil nemesis and alligator.

I gave her a kiss on the cheek. 'Hi there,' I greeted her.

'Eliza!' screamed the boys as they rushed into her arms. They'd known her for a fortnight yet already she was Mary Poppins.

She grabbed Archie from the boot of the car.

'I have some news for you.'

Silence.

'Carly,' she added.

I jolted.

'Oh, sorry – I thought you were talking to Archie. Apologies. It's just that we've been doing it all weekend. He's become the pet we never had. Or wanted. Anyway, news? Me?'

'Ike Tusker's office called. He told me not to disturb you in Mammoth.'

My stomach started to turn. Ike Tusker! That must mean he had more meetings lined up for me.

'He said your meetings have been cancelled . . .'

The kick, when it came, almost doubled me in two. Oh no.

'. . . and rescheduled for next week, Monday and Tuesday.'

Knees like jelly, giddy relief. And actually, that probably wasn't a bad thing because it would give me even more time to prepare. I could spend the whole weekend relaxing and maybe even fit in a wee bit of pampering. I could bribe Jojo into giving me another overhaul with the promise of more *Miami Vice*. I could take up yoga. Get in touch with my higher self. Top up my karma so that the cosmos would deliver wondrous things – like a movie deal and a face free of wrinkles . . .

'Although he did say that the delay would mean that he couldn't accompany you as he'll be out of town, but he said that because they're just introductory meetings that wouldn't be a problem.'

Okay. Fine. I could do that. After all, how scary could major movie moguls be? I decided to overlook the fact that they were the kind of people who were responsible for things like *Alien*, Freddy Krueger and *Armageddon*.

'Thanks, Eliza.'

'And also . . .' she started, unable to disguise a definite grin. 'You have company.'

It took a second to sink in. Company. Whitney and Cilla from the LAPD back for an encore? No, their squad car would have been in the drive.

Company? I looked at Sam; there was a distinct tension in his eyes.

It seemed like everyone stopped for a second, no one sure how to react. Then reality caught up with me. Company. Company! That could only mean one thing – the one person I'd been hoping and praying would get their act together for long enough to do the decent thing and get over here. The person who'd been on my mind since the moment I got here (with the slight exception of a few minutes when my mind was being controlled by anatomy of the genital orientation).

Oh, I was so ready for company. I was so ready for . . .

'Hi honey,' came the voice. My eyes darted over to the doorway. 'Did ya miss me?'

There, in total, complete, resounding Technicolor splendour was . . . Carol!

I didn't know whether to laugh or cry. Carol! Oh. My. God. I ran over and threw my arms around her, swiftly followed by two boys screaming, 'Auntie Carol, Auntie Carol!'

My heart was still racing. I'd been so sure for a split second there that it was going to be my bloody knight in shining armour, sweeping in on a big dramatic entrance to save our marriage from the clutches of doom. Hah! If God loved an optimist then I just got a free ticket for the big white gates.

Meanwhile, I wondered if poor Eliza realised she'd just been trumped in the boys' shallow scale of affection. There was no contest. To them, their favourite aunt meant love, attention and, most importantly, new toys.

Carol laughed as she lifted them up and hugged them simultaneously. Not bad for a woman who makes Kate Moss look meaty.

'I've got toys for you inside, my darlings,' she said as they squealed with delight.

I joined in the group hug. 'I'm so glad to see you,' I murmured. Then, aware that Sam was far enough away that he couldn't hear, I continued, 'I've got so much to tell you. And I swear to God I want a medal for my powers of restrai—'

'Great,' she interrupted, shrieking so loudly that she startled the kids. Had she been mainlining caffeine again? She definitely had a manic look about her.

'Anyway, I have a present for you too,' she said in a distinctly odd voice.

'Carol, you shouldn't have,' I scolded her. After all, I'd only been away for two weeks.

'You know something, you could be right,' she said, her eyes darting from me to Sam then back to me again.

I laughed. 'Okay, if it's Gucci I'll accept it. Just to make you feel better, of course.'

'It's not Gucci, I'm afraid. It's . . .'

'It's me.'

It took me a few moments to register that her voice had dropped a few octaves. Or that it was now coming from the direction of the door. Or that, if I listened real close, I could hear a low, slow exhalation coming from Sam. Or that my children were now screaming like they were on a roller coaster at a totally vertical angle.

There was no drama and no sweeping. And the jury was definitely still out on whether he would save our marriage from the clutches of doom.

But Mark Barwick had come to the party.

'I know my powers of perception are not known for their reliability, but do you want to tell me what's going on with you and Sam?'

Busted.

But then I knew that already. Mark had barely got past the 'Hi honey, I've pined for you every moment of the day . . .' bit (okay, so I made that up, but he did say hello) when he held up 'exhibit for the prosecution number one' – *heat* magazine. And there, in full Technicolor, was a picture of me kissing Sam as I got out of his car at the Peninsula Hotel. And no, the mercenary gits hadn't got my good side. On pages three, four and five were step-by-step snaps of what happened next – the walk across the foyer, the stumble, the fall . . . all underneath the headline '*Drunken shame of Morton's new lady*'. With the subheading, '*Honey, hooker or hired help? Just who is Morton's new unstable gal-pal?*'

Fame at last – and it consisted of grainy photographs of an episode that left me with skinned knees. So that's what Kate wanted to talk to me about – 'Hi hon, don't know how to break it to you but your arse is all over *heat*.'

Of course, Mark wasn't bothered in the least about the mag. He was already on the way over when he picked it up from a newsagent's at Heathrow.

And anyway, he was smart enough to know it was all nonsense.

But Carol . . . well, as she always says, there's no smoke without matches.

She'd cornered me in the kitchen on the pretence that we were replenishing everyone's drinks. Eliza had gone home for the night, after rearranging the household sleeping arrangements. Mark had been moved into my room, the boys had been moved to a smaller room next door, and Carol was further along the corridor.

'So, Hawaii, wow!' I said breezily, remarking on her announcement that she'd just decided to come for a few days' stopover en route to Honolulu for a Pringle photo-shoot. Jumpers. On the beach.

'Don't avoid the question,' she hissed.

Woah. I peeked out of the window to check where everyone was. Mark and Sam were sitting by the pool having a beer. A sight that I'd have thought was perfectly normal a few weeks ago, but that now made me want to have a long lie down in a dark room with an oxygen tank. Mark and I hadn't had two minutes alone since the big reunion a couple of hours earlier. There had been one awkward hug/kiss thing, which would have been excruciating had the kids not glued over the fact that we had no idea how to react to each other. It was difficult to be passionate, even if we'd been so inclined, when there were small children hanging from limbs.

Now Benny and Doctor Octopus were playing in the pool, despite the fact that it was way past their bedtime and darkness had fallen. Thankfully, Sam had installed more floodlights than most Premiership football teams.

Okay, the coast was clear and my interrogator was waiting.

'Come on, what's going on with you two?' she probed again.

'Do you want the truth? Or shall I fob you off with something innocuous until I can get into a witness protection programme?'

'Truth.'

'I don't know. I honestly don't know. Okay, here's the short version – chapter and verse would take too long. Sam thinks he might be falling in love with me. I've no idea how I feel about him any more, apart from the definite, irrefutable fact that I could spend at least a fortnight doing filthy things to him. I don't know where things stand with Mark and me, but I'm skidding across that thin line between love and hate on an hourly basis. And everything could depend on what happens with the movie studios because they might want me to move out here and how would Mark feel about that? Let me tell you – colonic irrigation would have more appeal. And meanwhile, I love it here, Carol, I love it so much. It's an amazing life. I could live here forever. And so could the boys. Look at them! I haven't seen them this happy since they flooded the kitchen to make an indoor paddling pool. But anyway, nothing has happened between Sam and me that involved contact with internal organs. I promise. And I don't have my fingers crossed,' I finished, holding up my hands as evidence.

'That was the short version?' she asked archly.

I nodded. 'What do you think? Be objective, but bear in mind that I'm your sister-in-law and that means love, devotion and free babysitting.'

She leaned back against the worktop and gave the impression of serious thought. Although Carol is a model so she can conjure up any expression at will – what looked like 'deep, emotional, pensive contemplation' on the outside could quite easily be 'wonder how many calories are in that fajita' on the inside.

'I think you're stuck between a rock and a stone,' she

observed meaningfully. She continued, 'I know that Kate feels sorry for Mark, but I'm with you. I'd be gutted if Cal didn't support me in something that was really important to me. But Sam? Dangerous move, Carly. You should really think about it before you do anything crazy.' She glanced off in the direction of the window. Sam was now standing up on the diving board, every muscle gleaming in the moonlight. 'Aw, fuck it, go for crazy, he's bloody gorgeous.'

I laughed and gave her a hug. 'Crude, superficial and completely lacking in morals – I'm so glad you're here.'

Mark put the boys to bed, both of them having an internal tussle between exhaustion and excitement. One day they would have the emotional maturity to pick up on the tense vibes that were definitely present. Actually, cancel that – they're male, so perhaps not. I was just thankful that Carol was there to be outrageous, witty and keep the conversation flowing. Sam, to his credit, acted completely normally. But then, that calibre of acting skill was why he was in movies and not washing-powder commercials. Occasionally, our eyes would meet and I'd catch just a glance of a smile. Mark, on the other hand, found it difficult even to look at me. The mountain may have come to Mohammad but it was obviously still extremely pissed off.

Sam and Carol made their excuses and went off to bed around midnight.

Showdown time.

I half-expected to hear death knells sounding in the Hollywood Hills.

He was already in bed when I came out of the

bathroom. I stripped and climbed in beside him. He didn't move – just lay there, staring at the ceiling. Now, until a few weeks before that point in our lives, there were very few things that irritated me about my husband. However, as I may have mentioned before, his ability to ignore an argument drove me nuts. He would quite happily have laid there staring at the ceiling for twenty minutes until he nodded off to sleep, leaving words unspoken, insults unhurled and ornaments unbroken.

Unfortunately, I couldn't.

'How long are you here for?' I asked him.

'Two weeks. Took annual leave.'

Okay, so he hadn't chucked his job in blind faith that I was going to be Spielberg's right-hand woman, but that was fine. A fortnight was a start.

I decided to go for the white-flag approach.

'I'm glad you came.'

'You didn't leave me any choice. How could I stay away from my boys for a month?'

White flag shredded.

'Ah, so you didn't dash over here because you couldn't live without me a moment longer?' There was a definite edge to my voice.

'Look, Carly, we are never going to agree on this one. Did I miss you? Yes, I did. Was storming over here on a whim completely irresponsible? Sure it was. But that's you. Spontaneous, adventurous, irresponsible.'

How come when he said those things it didn't sound like a compliment?

'Mark, you can't stay pissed off with me forever. You're here now. Let's make the most of it. We could

211

even try acting like we're married and madly in love and see what happens.' I tried desperately to lighten the atmosphere. 'You might get to like it.'

He smiled and at last his voice softened into something approaching light-hearted. 'You're right. I might. Wouldn't bet on it, though.'

I reached under the duvet and squeezed his right nipple. Hard.

'Tell me you love me or the nipple's coming off.'

His knees reflexively came up as he tried to squirm out of my grip.

'I love you,' he screeched. Victory was mine. I let go, then reached out and ran my finger across his chest. I really was so glad he was here. At that moment I wanted more than anything to work things out.

He reached over and pushed my hair back from my face.

'I do love you,' he repeated, before leaning over to kiss me.

'I love you too,' I whispered. 'And I just want things to be the way they used to be. Between us, I mean.'

'Me too,' he replied. He put his arm around me and pulled me in tight, holding me for an age, as if he couldn't bear to let me go. Oh how amazing that felt – to be back in his arms, to feel his breath against my skin, to hear his . . . zzzzzzzzzzzzzzzzzzzz.

I opened one eye and squinted up. Yep, he was sleeping. Unconscious. Zonked.

I was wide awake, horny, deflated.

Yep, things were indeed *exactly* the way they used to be.

Family Values *Magazine*

PUTTING THE YUMMY IN MUMMY
THIS WEEK . . . FAMILY OUTINGS

As we all know, education doesn't stop when that school bell rings and your nanny whisks your child home. Or, in the case of boarders, when your offspring return for a short break at home.

Children learn from a multitude of experiences and one such occasion is the family excursion. Happy, family days are a bonding experience for your offspring, allowing them to experience the delights of their parents' company and instilling in them an appreciation of the rich experiences they will come to understand more fully as they move towards adulthood.

Plant a seed of love for the arts with a trip to a museum or gallery.

Encourage an interest in music with a jaunt to the opera or ballet.

Indulge in those joyful English traditions: afternoon tea at the Ritz, horse riding in Richmond Park, a day of history at Windsor Castle.

Or for the more fearless and adventurous among you, a camping expedition is a fine way to view the joys of nature first-hand. Pack up your Cath Kidston tent, your Barbour jacket and your mohair rug and head for the great outdoors (for safety reasons we would recommend that this is done in the grounds of your own home or that of a friend – if you do venture further afield, it is essential to avoid campsites that offer entertainment, licensed facilities and static homes, as these are often frequented by unsavoury characters).

However you choose to spend the day, do remember to pre-empt your trip with a visit to the Farmers' Market for supplies of freshly prepared organic treats, because as we all know, when it comes to children, a healthy body is a healthy mind.

Enjoy your day of family fun – and, at the end of it, congratulate yourself that you've added to the texture and depth of your child's education. And as we all know ladies, education is like fine wine, good company and household help - you can never have too much.'

★ *Step Ten* ★

'Mum, can I change my name again?' asked Mac hopefully.

'Of course you can – let me guess, you want to be Buzz Lightyear?'

'To infinity and beyond!' yelled Benny while swinging his Buzz pants and holding one fist in the air in a super-hero-like pose.

'Nope, Evil Emperor Zurg.'

Bugger. It didn't bode well for a day of good behaviour, brotherly relations and pristine manners. Helpful, though, if we decided to invade a neighbouring country.

It was the day after Mark and Carol had arrived and we'd succumbed to Carol's demands for an LA 'experience'. I was hoping for a wander along the Hollywood Walk of Fame. Or a jolly down to Venice beach to watch the body-builders in the outdoor gym get sand up their gluteus maximus.

'Shopping on Rodeo Drive, baby, then I've booked a table at the Ivy,' she announced.

Okay, mothers of the world, this one is for you. In this situation would you:

1. say, 'Fabulous!', shrug on a little D&G number and head for the shops; or
2. point out the pitfalls of a day of shopping and a posh lunch with two children under five in a clear and concise manner along the lines of 'I'd rather have my pubes plucked out with a Dyson'.

Buzz decked Zurg with a stiletto in Versace. Zurg retaliated by using a Louis Vuitton umbrella as a lightsaber and attempting to decapitate the saviour of the galaxy in full view of three shop assistants, a security guard and one of Rod Stewart's ex-wives. The tall blonde one.

Mark missed all of this as he was doing the standard bloke thing and standing outside the shop, checking his watch every five minutes while suffering from an acute case of terminal boredom. Unfortunately, this made him look like a bodyguard, and as a result Japanese tourists flocked into every shop we were in and then vented their general irritation that Carol and I weren't Diaz and Barrymore, Cruz and Hayek, or even former members of the Spice Girls. Although we did murder a chorus of '2 Become 1' in the middle of Prada in an attempt to pacify them.

And not one moment of that was more embarrassing than lunch at West Hollywood's favourite star-bedecked eatery.

Carol had secured the table on the very exclusive patio courtesy of an old modelling chum who was on first-name terms with the restaurant manager. So far, so name-droppingly, hobnobbingly glam. We were in celebrity-spotting heaven!

Carol had the shrimp salad along with a peek at Charlie Sheen, a possible Rob Lowe and a definite Heather Locklear. I had the pasta of the day, with a long stare at Lindsay Lohan, a grin at Christina Aguilera and a peruse of Pamela Anderson. Then we discovered that my Pam and Carol's Heather was the same person – well, we could only see her from the back (and incidentally, she needed her roots done).

The boys were impeccably behaved and had pizza and a five-dollar bribe each. And Mark had a great big bowl of boredom – celebrity-spotting had never been his thing.

It was all going along swimmingly until Carol gasped and leaned towards me. 'Babe, you are soooo going to love me,' she hissed.

'What? In a sisterly fashion or are we talking Rosie O'Donnell meets Ellen?'

And that's when my sister-in-law, the former Scottish supermodel, drew herself up to her full height, tossed back her auburn tendrils, swaggered over to a couple of blokes sitting three tables behind me, slapped on her very best grin and purred, 'Mr Neeson, my friend is a huge fan – would you mind autographing our menu?'

Oh. My. God. I held my breath. My stomach turned. My head spun. Right up until Gabriel Byrne asked her if she was from some shite MTV spoof show and stormed off in a huff.

I begged the kids to assault each other just to create a diversion, but no – for the first time in life they were verging on bloody sainthood. A fact that Mark offered in desperate mitigation when the manager asked us to leave. Apparently talking to the celebs is banned and mistaking them for someone else ranks just above treason on the Hollywood Talk of Shame.

As I said . . . bugger.

Next day we'd learned our lesson so we left our choice of destination up to the boys. An hour later we were on a repeat trip to Disneyland. It would have been churlish to object – after all, they'd experienced the thrills and excitement with their Uncle Sam so it was great that their father was getting to share it this time around.

Besides, I loved the rides, the atmosphere, and the unadulterated optimism of the theme parks. Although I was beginning to get homicidal tendencies towards all large creatures containing grown men.

As expected, since it was their life story, the Buzz Lightyear show was the highlight for the boys. We found it difficult to share their devotion. As the final song entered yet another chorus, Carol leaned in close and whispered, 'Is it just me who wants to kick the shit out of Buzz?'

I checked Mac was out of earshot. 'I presume you are talking about the one murdering that song on the stage?' I checked.

She nodded.

'Start punching and please never, ever stop,' I retorted hopefully.

I looked at Mark, sitting next to me with Benny on his shoulders and Mac on his knee. He was laughing at Benny, who was now copying the actions of the characters in the show. It was great to see him relaxing and enjoying himself. It struck me that this was the first time in years that we'd spent more than a few hours together without one of us being asleep. And it felt great. It did. Maybe this would be the jolt we needed to remind us that life was about love, about each other, and not just about shagging in forty-seven different positions on a daily basis or not.

Although, depending on location, work demands and general bendiness, that might be nice occasionally.

Groan, I was back to sex again.

I was becoming obsessed. I'd experienced this syndrome before. Whenever I went on a diet, I could quite happily commit armed robbery in a bakery for an iced fruit slice. Whenever I decided to have a month-long alcohol detox, I started hallucinating that vases were morphing into bottles of Asti Spumante. Now, since Mark had arrived, I'd been obsessed with sex.

Location? Idyllic. Work demands? Zero. General bendiness? Adequate. And had he put out? Not once. Not even a quickie.

And it didn't help when Sam was around, oozing wit, charm and pheromones that were sending psychic messages to my erogenous zones every time I ventured within a hundred yards of him. It was a blessing that he had pleaded prior social commitments and opted not to come with us on our theme-park expeditions, because there isn't an ovary in the land that wouldn't leap at the sight of him coming off the log flume with his T-shirt soaked and clinging to every inch of him.

Later that night, I cracked. As we climbed into bed after another convivial evening by the poolside with the boys, Carol, and Sam, I knew that I couldn't go another night without confronting the problem. But how to approach it? Should I just pounce on in there and initiate lustful groping? Or should I kiss him and refuse to stop until he took it a stage further? Or perhaps we should talk about it, like a sort of theory test before we tackled the practicalities.

I immediately ruled out pouncing. The last time I pounced it led to a sulk, a crushed ego and a repetitive strain injury. All mine.

Likewise, the seduction by suction probably wasn't wise either – too much of a risk that he'd fall asleep midway through.

'Mark, do you ever wonder what happened to our sex life?'

Yep, I even said it out loud.

There was a long pause. Then, just when I was about to weep because he'd fallen asleep on me again, he finally spoke.

'I guess it's not been that great lately.' Mark Barwick, Golden Globe Winner 2006 in the category of Best Understatement in a Dramatic Situation.

'Why is that?' I asked, in as non-accusatory a tone as I could manage when everything below the neck was screaming, 'Hurry up and get to the tickly bit!'

Another long silence. I had to bite my lip not to butt in and give him a twenty-five-point analysis of why we hadn't had great sex since the Eighties. Okay, maybe it just felt that long.

'I don't know,' he answered earnestly. 'Kids, work, exhaustion, time . . .' Then, in a lighter tone, '. . . a wife who's on the other side of the Atlantic.'

I laughed. 'Yeah, yeah, blame me. Well, listen, just so you know – I'm easy, okay? You don't even have to ask twice. Or once, for that matter. Just start the fondling stuff and I'll get the picture and join in.'

'Am I being reprimanded here?' he said as he playfully tugged my arm so that I fell over on top of him.

'You are. Is it working?'

'Consider me repentant,' he whispered as he flipped me over then climbed on top of me. He leaned down and kissed first my left ear, then my right. Then he moved on to my cheeks, my eyes, my neck, downwards to my . . .

Hallelujah, Hallelujah, Hallelujah, Hallelujah, Halle-ee-ee-ee-lujah!

I gasped with the sheer delight of it as he sucked on my nipples, slowly and gently at first, then more insistent, sucking harder and harder. By the time he got to Dyson level I was buckling with waves of sheer ecstasy and my lower body was limbo-dancing of its own accord. If I were a bloke, it would have been called premature ejaculation. But since I was lucky enough to have female chromosomes it was simply called 'fantastic – first of many'.

I put my fingers into his hair and pulled him upwards, before he had any notion of carrying on further south. I know cunnilingus gets great press but to be honest I think it's overrated. If I stare at the ceiling for too long I start getting thoughts of decorating and I've yet to come up with a spine-tingling fantasy involving B&Q.

When his face reached mine, I kissed him, then

pushed him over before climbing on top. I eased his hands up over his head, wrapping his fingers around the bars that were very conveniently located on the headboard. I wondered if Sam had chosen that bed for that reason. Sam. Oh God, Sam. I closed my eyes as I guided Sam's – I mean *Mark's* – cock inside me. He groaned as I sat back, one hand reaching behind me to grab his balls. I licked the fingers of my other hand then traced the outline of my nipples, all the time gyrating up and down, up and down.

'Oh, fuck, I missed you,' he groaned. Well, given the circumstances I should think so really.

I held a finger to his lips. 'Sssh.'

I didn't want him to speak. I wanted no conversation, no talking dirty, no sweet nothings, I wanted absolutely nothing to break the spell as Sam and I – aaargh – *Mark* and I rode towards a complete and utter simultaneous, thundering lip bite.

Yep, lip bite. It's a parent thing. The last thing you want during or immediately after sex is for a wee set of feet to pad into the room, attached to a child who's wailing because he 'heard a scary noise'.

So what, in the old days, was a simultaneous exclamation of orgasmic delight was now contained as much as possible by biting the bottom lip at the crucial moment. Thus sex is never a good idea if you're prone to cold sores or planning on eating something spicy the next day.

But right at that moment I couldn't have given a toss about the next day. As I felt Sam coming inside me, his hands now escaped from the headboard and clutching my hips, I felt a surrender that was pure joy. Oh, shit, I said Sam again, didn't I? Thankfully, not out loud.

Mark reached up and pulled me down on top of him, both hands clutching my face as he kissed me softly, tenderly on the lips.

'I love you, Carly,' he whispered gently, his voice raw with emotion.

'I love you too,' I replied

Mark, definitely Mark.

Wasn't it?

The following morning we woke to chills and torrential rain.

Kidding.

The sun, as per glorious usual, was high in the sky and it was a gorgeous eighty degrees.

We met around the breakfast table to plan our entertainment strategy for the day.

'Count me out, folks – much as I'd love to visit Disney yet again, I've got a game of football organised. I play for a British team against the Americans and it's competitive stuff – if I didn't show up they'd lynch me.'

'Where's the game?' Carol asked.

'Rod Stewart's.'

'Oh. I didn't know he had a stadium named after him,' Carol replied, perplexed.

'He doesn't – it's at his house. Sometimes we play at Robbie's, but today it's Rod's.'

'Sam, do you love me?' she asked in a seductive voice.

He grinned. 'Course I do, you know that.'

'Then let me be the team physio. I'm great with groin strains, I promise.'

'Babe, that's a great idea,' Sam replied, as Carol visibly glowed, 'but we've already got a physio.'

'Could I take her out without a weapon?'

'Doubt it. "She" is a "he" and he's built like a tank.'

He grabbed a bottle of water out of the fridge, kissed Carol and me on the cheek, kissed the boys on the top of the head and said goodbye to Mark. 'Good luck, mate – another day with these two,' he gestured to Carol and me.

'Yeah, well, my wife and a supermodel – it's a tough job.'

Oh, cute reply. I loved that man.

'Tell Robbie and Rod what they missed today!' Carol demanded.

'I will, I promise,' he assured her, before going off to socialise with the people I normally only encountered in celebrity magazines.

Oh, what a life. I loved that man as well.

My stomach gave a minor lurch. This dual-affection syndrome had to stop. I was married to Mark. He was sitting three feet away from me. If we were Vulcans he'd already have divorced me because he'd have picked up on my mental infidelity.

'Okay, I don't want to be bossy,' Carol piped up – a strange statement because she was always bossy. 'But I've got a plan. How about we spend the whole weekend at the beach and if the boys complain we'll just keep feeding them ice cream.'

'Yes, yes, yes,' screamed Mac and Benny, who had no

idea what they were excited about but figured that it involved a beach and ice cream so it couldn't be that bad.

I almost felt like an LA native as we drove along through Santa Monica into Venice and then on into Marina del Rey, passing the huge mansions in the Silver Strand area. Thankfully, Mark was at the wheel so we hadn't crashed once yet.

'On your left is Nicolas Cage's house, we might drop in for coffee and a chat later. On your right we have the mansion rumoured to belong to one of the cast of *Friends*. Next door to that is Robert Downey Jr's pad and after that we have Pamela Anderson's – if you look closely you'll see her bras on the washing line acting as windsocks for the nearby Los Angeles Airport.'

'Carly, are you making all of this up?' Carol asked.

'Absolutely all of it.'

'Well, carry on, you're doing a great job.'

By the time we reached Mother's Beach we'd passed the homes of Kevin Costner and Colin Farrell, seen Julia Robert weeding her garden, spied Catherine Zeta-Jones pulling her G-string out of her arse while gabbing to Arnold Schwarzenegger and spotted Marlon Brando out jogging – although Mark did point out that Mr Brando died in 2004.

However, while Mark might not have been impressed by my tour of LA, he loved the beach. It was the usual weekend assortment of picture-perfect Californian families, and packs of joggers swarming around the walkways like some kind of anti-fat militia squad. I wondered where all the nannies and soccer moms that were there during the week went at the weekends – hopefully they all got up to something deliciously scandalous that would give them another whole week's worth of gossip for their beach pals.

Mark immediately trotted off to play Frisbee with Benny and Darth Vader. Yes, he'd changed his name again and was now feeling the force. Or it might just have been the scrambled egg he'd had for breakfast.

As always, Carol turned every head on the beach. Her career might, as she often said, be in its dim-lit years, but she still had that whole shiny, stunning, late-Eighties supermodel thing going on and you could see people trying to work out who she used to be. Elle? Cindy? Miss America Porn Scandal?

She stripped down to a tiny swimsuit that showed every single inch of her perfectly toned body.

'Urgh. You know, I've never liked you,' I groaned. 'And I've absolutely no idea what my brother sees in you.'

'I'm great in bed,' she replied with a grin.

'Mmmm, me too.'

She stared at me quizzically for a second.

'Oh, I knew something was different. You've had sex! With another person present!' she exclaimed.

'Carol, could you shout that a little louder – I think the bloke in the leopard-skin Speedos might not have heard you. Holy shit, what's Peter Stringfellow doing in LA?'

She giggled as she dived down next to me. 'So?'

'Carol, I am not going to discuss my sex life with you – it might have escaped your notice but we're not eighteen any more.'

'That bad?'

'No, it was actually great. Apart from the bit where I fantasised about someone else.'

'Fuck, please don't mention Liam Neeson again,' she groaned. 'So who was it? Bruce Willis? George Clooney? Brad Pitt? . . . I always go for Brad. How Gwynie could go for that bloke in Coldplay after him, I'll never know.'

'Are you finished?'

'Yep, did I guess it right?'

'It was Sam. I fantasised about Sam the whole time. I even made Mark stop talking because it was distracting me from the things I was doing to a man who was lying a hundred yards away in a different part of the house. I'm sick, Carol. Sick, sick, sick.'

'Did you tell Mark?'

'Of course I did. Right after I ripped his heart out and jumped on it. Don't be so bloody stupid.'

There was a silence for a moment, then as always, I caved.

'What do think?' I asked her anxiously. I actually did value Carol's opinion. She always told it as she heard it and called a spade a hoe.

'Well, you know what they say, my love – two's company, three's a divorce. So what are you going to do?'

I shrugged my shoulders. 'Work it out. Hopefully this holiday will be what Mark and I need to get our relationship back together again. I really, really want it to work. And not just because of the boys, but also for the sake of how bloody brilliant we used to be. Honestly, Carol, if he were the person he was when things were great between us then we wouldn't even be having this conversation. But ever since the kids were born, he's been . . . *old*. It's like he's quite happy to settle for the life of an old married couple. And I'm not. I love him, but I'm bored with what our life has become – same stuff day in and day out, no conversation, no sex, no passion. And I know that makes me sound like a fickle cow, but it's the truth. I'm not ready to be old. Wrinkled, yes. But a life with no intimacy, no joy? This trip has proved that I'm not ready for that.'

'Maybe he isn't either – he just hasn't realised it yet.'

'I hope so, Carol. Anyway, we're going to have the next fortnight together so we'll have loads of time to work things out. And we will. I know we will.'

'And Sam?'

'Don't ask. I think he's keeping out of our way. He feels as bad about all this as I do, although obviously for different reasons. You know Sam; he's a decent guy. He hates the fact that he's getting in the middle of a relationship. I just wish he wouldn't show up when I was having sex with my husband.'

'What's that about your husband?' Mark asked.

We'd been too busy blethering to notice that Mark had come up behind us.

'I was just saying that he's an absolutely gorgeous guy, wickedly intelligent and amazing in bed . . .'

'Did you mention my Trivial Pursuit skills? I'm great at Trivial Pursuit.'

'Who is fan-fucking-tastic at Trivial Pursuit.'

He bowed slightly, accepting the adulation.

I was shocked and stunned. If I wasn't mistaken,

we'd just witnessed the rebirth of Mark Barwick's sense of humour. His sense of humour! The thing that had made me fall madly in love with him aged twelve. The thing that had first got my knickers off aged . . . actually, I'm saying nothing in case my children read this one day. And the sense of humour that stopped him from divorcing me in times of PMT or shopping.

A little surge of joy manifested itself in a huge grin. We would work it out. All we needed was a little time together and we'd be fine.

'What are you laughing at?' he asked.

I couldn't tell him – this wasn't the time to be making him self-conscious about his behaviour by commenting on it.

'Nothing,' I replied.

'Tell me . . .'

Oh, the pressure. I racked my brain for a suitable answer. Something that would make me grin, that was frivolous, hilarious, ridiculous . . .

'I think that's Peter Stringfellow over there in those leopard-skin Speedos.'

CARLY CALLING . . .

Kate to Carly:

So ws Mrk arrvng good surprise? All ok?

Carly:

Had sex. Earth movd. San Andreas fault now unstable.

Kate:

Lip bite?

Carly:

Requiring stiches & poss plastic surgry.

Kate:

Congrats. If u cm home lookn like Joan Rivers wl kno ur a nympho. Gd lck 2day, fngrs crssd 4 u. Just b urself.

Carly:

Hopeless, disorganisd, talk pish?

Kate:

Good point ... be som1 else. Luv ya, Kxxx

★ Step Eleven ★

'How do I look?' I asked the assorted menfolk when I appeared for breakfast on Monday morning. Or perhaps it should be lunch, because Jojo had been there since 6 a.m., feeding me mocha chocca vanilla skinny twisty thingys while transforming me into a recognisable human being.

'Jojo, move in with me. Please. I never want you to leave my side ever again.'

'I think your husband might object,' she said with a laugh.

'Oh, I doubt it somehow.' When Jojo had come into our bedroom and shaken me awake that morning, Mark had stirred, opened one eye, spotted this goddess and I'm sure I heard him say something about Christmas and giving thanks to the Lord. All those years we'd been together and I'd never realised he was religious.

I still had trouble believing that I had someone to come 'fix' me for meetings, but Sam and Jojo insisted that it was the way things were done here. It was going to have to stop, though, before I came to depend on

Jojo so much that she had to drag me around, clutching on to her ankle and refusing to let go.

Mark scanned me top to bottom when I did a twirl at the breakfast table.

'You look good,' he declared.

'Good?'

'Good. Why do you look disappointed?'

I wondered if it was the perfectly made-up, super-glossy, artfully coloured glum expression that was giving me away.

'Because I was going for "fabulous" or "fantastic"', I replied. I know, childish and petulant.

'Mummy, you are fab-lee-ous!' said Benny proudly. Oh, how I loved my boy. Right up until he hugged me and got jam-covered fingers stuck in my hair.

I'd miss them. Mark had already decided he was going to take them down to Mother's Beach for the next two days to let me go and play at dressed-up, grown-up, potential movie screenwriter.

'Sam, can you give me a taxi number please – I should get going.'

I checked my watch. I was two hours early for my first meeting with Dave Marino, Head of Development at Global Studios. I'd been hoping that Sam would be able to go with me to the studios but when we'd dropped Carol at the airport the night before he announced that he'd be flying to Vegas this morning to do some promotional events for the movie that he had coming out the following month.

Mmmmm, I was cynical. Paranoid head took over. I dreaded the thought that we were forcing the man out of his own home. I swapped over to intelligent, practical head. Sam was a movie star. He would be staying in the finest suite in the finest hotel in the city and having every need pandered to. He would eat fine food, drink fine wine and watch damn fine lap dancers. Somehow, I didn't think it would be a cross too heavy to bear.

'Don't take a taxi, take the Porsche,' he replied.

'The Porsche? Sam, I'm not to be trusted with the washing machine and you want me to drive a hundred-thousand-dollar car? That's the equivalent of a house where I grew up. And besides, not only am I likely to wrap it around a lamppost, but it'll be a lamppost in the wrong area of town because I'm bound to get lost. When I'm supposed to be drinking coffee with Dave Marino I'll probably end up looting shops with gang members in South Central.'

'Okay, tell you what,' Sam acquiesced. 'I'll drop you off at Global on the way to the airport and you can get a cab back. There's a *Thomas Guide* in my office – that's a street map of the city. Take that and after your meeting, spend the afternoon driving the Porsche around getting used to it – that way, you'll be okay to use it tomorrow. Sorted.' A Porsche. That took 'sorted' to a whole new level.

I kissed the guys goodbye and set off with Sam. We weren't even at the end of the driveway when I blurted, 'I'm sorry.'

'For what?'

'For this. All of it. Arriving here, disrupting your life, causing chaos, Mark arriving, us. Everything. And now we're chasing you out of your own home.'

'You are not.'

'Okay, so if Mark wasn't here would you be going to Vegas?' I asked, totally confident of the answer.

'Yes.'

Oh.

'But I'd be taking you and the boys with me.'

Oh.

'Look, Carly, I just want to give you two some space to sort things out. It's awkward. For the first time in years I'm jealous – jealous when Mark touches you, when he speaks to you, when you go off to bed. I hate it. I'm sorry, but I hate it. All those years it didn't bother me in the least, but now . . . something's changed. And if I could un-change it I would because I know how messy this is. So I think it's better if I just stay out of the way for a while. You and Mark – if you can sort things out then you should.'

'And if we can't?'

'You've got my cell number.' He grinned.

I reached out and stroked his face.

'You are such a good man, Sam Morton.'

'Nah, I'm not really. If I was then I wouldn't have put us in this position in the first place.'

'If it's any consolation, I think I was shamelessly lusting after your body first.'

'Really?' he said, with accompanying movie-star grin.

'Yeah, but don't get too flattered, I also fancy Jack Nicholson and he's got a bus pass.'

'You wouldn't!' he asked with a scrunched-up, horri-fied face.

'All night long at many bendy angles,' I replied.

There was an easy, comfortable silence for a few moments while Sam attempted to rid himself of that mental picture before I decided to get to the really important stuff.

'So, tell me then – is it true that the casting couch is still the main method of recruitment in this town? Only I haven't been shopping for new undies yet and I don't want to scare anyone.'

'Hi, I'm here to collect Cameron's new script,' said a shiny male-model type wearing a delivery jacket. How come the delivery blokes back where I live didn't look like that? And who was Cameron? Diaz? Probably. Although in saying that it could have been Cameron Buttersworth the photocopier lady and I'd still have experienced a wee thrill.

Dave Marino's gorgeous receptionist handed over a large envelope.

'It's ready – here you go. You take care now,' she chirped in a singsong voice.

God, everybody was just so *nice*. I wondered if they went home at night, wrecked their houses and kicked holes in the walls while repeatedly screaming 'Fuck, fuck, fuck!' as some kind of antidote to all this niceness.

I'd been waiting for half an hour for Mr Marino, but I didn't mind in the least.

I know it's a cliché, but I wanted to pinch myself. This was it. Since I was a kid I'd dreamed of a life of glitz, glamour and fortune and I was moments away from meeting the man who could make it happen. If my biological mother could see me now, she'd know for sure that I was a chip off the old diamond-clad, big-hair-wearing block.

Even coming through security had been a thrill. Sam had dropped me at the studio gates, and I'd gone into a glass booth beside them. 'Carly Cooper,' I'd announced to the guard with the big gun behind the desk.

'Photo ID please!'

I'd showed him the very attractive photograph on my passport that made me look like an extra on *Prisoner: Cell Block H.*

He'd consulted his computer, and then hit a button. Beside him, a printer spat out my ID card.

'Yes, Miss Cooper, Mr Marino is expecting you.'

Me. Carly Cooper. Was expected. I felt giddy. I wondered if the guard with the big gun was trained in first aid and would know what to do when I fainted. And I sensed that asking if I could sit down and put my head between my knees might just get me ejected at speed.

He'd given me a map of the lot (oh, I'm there with the lingo!) and marked Marino's office. I'd set off, still waiting for a big hand to fall on my shoulder and someone to announce that I was trespassing and shouldn't be there.

I'd had to cut through several movie sets to get to the offices. It was incredibly bizarre turning a corner into New York's Times Square at Christmas, then turning another corner to discover that you're in Oklahoma. In 1746.

When I'd got to the building that housed Dave's office (we were already on first-name terms), I was, to be honest, a little disappointed. From the outside it looked like a warehouse. It was only a few licks of paint up from those Portakabins the police set up at murder sites. It was hard to tell if I was going to meet a Hollywood player or the cast of *The Bill*.

Inside, however, the transformation was astounding. I'd felt like I'd stumbled into a plantation house in Georgia – oak panels lined every wall, a huge chandelier hung from the middle of the reception and the exquisite oak furniture had definitely never seen the inside of IKEA.

The receptionist had instructed me to take a seat on a rich red velour chaise longue, and there I sat quite happily, while straining to overhear every word the receptionist muttered. I'd died and gone to superficial, movie-lover heaven.

I texted Kate. 'In office of Hollywood movie mogul!'

She replied, 'If you don't leave fingerprints or DNA then they'll never catch you.'

'Carly Cooper!' came a loud, contralto voice from a door on my right. I swung around to see a tall, dark-haired bloke in his late thirties, dressed in what looked like designer jeans and an open-necked pale blue silk shirt.

He was holding his arms out like I was a long-lost relative (a theory I ruled out as I was positive Jackie didn't have a son). My senses were reeling. How was I supposed to react? Was this Dave Marino? In which case, falling to the floor and offering to suck his toes might be a good place to start. Or perhaps it was his secretary or PA? Should I rush into those outstretched arms? Would a simple handshake seem rude?

I tried frantically to remember the briefing that Sam had given me on the people I would be meeting.

Meanwhile, friendly silk shirt was advancing.

'I feel like I want to hug you,' he announced with an accompanying thousand-kilowatt grin.

And he did.

I caught a whiff of Bvlgari aftershave –it was the one that Sam wore. Sam. Where was he when I needed him to educate me on the finer points of Hollywood etiquette?

'I loved the book. Loved it. Mercedes, did I tell you I loved that book?'

'You loved it,' replied shiny reception person.

At which point my shoes became hovercrafts and I started floating on air.

This was Dave. Head of Development at Global Studios. And he loved my book.

We sailed on through to his office, another feast of décor so extravagant and sumptuous that it was the kind of place I imagined that Elton John would come to die.

We sat down at a massive, ornate table that spanned almost an entire stretch of wall. On the other side of the office was a magnificent antique desk and two stunning overstuffed antique sofas, furniture that looked slightly out of place in a room that was decked in more movie posters than our local Odeon. Focus, Carly, focus, I chided myself. And do not make an inappropriate comment about that life-size cardboard cut-out of Uma Thurman.

He offered me a drink but I declined – I didn't trust myself not to spill it, leave ring marks on the table or do that very inelegant thing where you take a large gulp then choke and spray the entire room.

'So . . . loved the book. Loved it. Funny. Quick. Sharp, sharp, sharp,' he announced with accompanying finger clicks.

Great, great, great, thought I.

'So, tell me all about you.'

My astonishment just gained another layer. I was expecting a guy who looked like a stockbroker and a serious, intellectual, intimidating discussion, and instead I was having a girly chat with one of the blokes from *Queer Eye*.

'What do you want to know?' I asked.

'Everything – start with growing up and we'll take it from there – I just want to get inside the head of Carly Cooper.'

A head that was, at that moment, ready to explode with excitement. Surely that must mean he was interested in making me an offer? These guys had so many people banging on their doors that they surely wouldn't waste time with meetings that weren't going to lead somewhere?

Although why details of how I grew up had any relevance to the numbers of zeros on the cheque, I had no idea.

Nevertheless, I regaled him with tales of a Glasgow childhood, moving through my teenage years and into early adulthood. I was just approaching the point where the story of *Nipple Alert* started when he interrupted me.

'Do you smoke?' he asked.

Oh, crap – a test. In California the mere mention of the word Marlboro can result in forty environmentalists (with the emphasis on 'mentalist') descending and beating you to death with fag packets. Perhaps the studio had a policy of working only with non-smokers. My first instinct was, of course, to lie. But then I wondered if he somehow knew I smoked and wanted to test my honesty and integrity.

Doh! Now I knew how Mac and Benny felt when being interrogated about something they knew they'd done wrong but planned to lie their way out of.

'Erm, yes. Sometimes. Not many. But occasionally. Socially . . .'

Mouth open, ramblings coming out.

I waited for klaxons to sound, lights to flash and storm-troopers to burst in and hose me down with anti-nicotine spray.

But instead, 'Fantastic!' he whispered in a conspiratorial tone. 'Let's have a cigarette right now.'

'But I thought there was no smoking on the lot,' I replied, perplexed. I don't know what had given me that idea – perhaps the four-foot-high signs on every single wall promising ejection and death to all smokers.

He motioned me over to a window that had a packet of cigs on the ledge, offered me one and took one for himself. Just when I thought this meeting couldn't get any more bizarre, I was now hanging out of a window and giggling with the Head of Development of one of the most prestigious studios on the planet.

I was so on to a good thing here. I was so . . .

'Okay, so here's the thing, Carly.' *Finally*, he was going to contribute more to this meeting than prompts for the gory, salacious details of my life and black lungs.

'This is what we're going to do.'

'Write a huge big cheque and transform your life,' was the line I was waiting for.

'We're going to pass on *Nipple Alert.*'

Did he say *pass*? Was that movie-world lingo for 'snap up right now for an obscene amount of money'?

'We love it. Love it. But we've already got six rom coms in development and I think we're maxed out in that genre.'

You could have knocked me down with a Marlboro Light.

'But we love your writing. We love what you do and we love you.'

Fuck, this bloke just loved everything. Except cheques with his signature on them.

'The reason I wanted to meet you today is because I think we could work together on future projects. How would you feel about doing a dialogue polish on comedy projects?'

I pondered this for a moment, giving the grey matter time to regroup. He didn't want to buy my book, so goodbye fame and fortune. He did, however, want me to do some work for him on script polishing. Consulting my vast knowledge of the world of movie production, garnered from Jackie Collins's books and occasional chats with Sam, I knew that polishing was when a script was just about finished and they brought in someone to make the dialogue better.

Or something like that.

It definitely didn't involve Pledge and a duster, so it could only be good. Great, actually.

I started to get excited again. It might not be the jackpot but it was the equivalent of five numbers and the bonus ball. He was offering me a job with Global. Should I jump up and smother him with kisses now or wait until later?

'When would I start?' I asked in a voice that was on the helium side of normal.

He looked confused for a second. 'Actually, I don't have a specific project in mind at the moment. But with six scripts in development, we're definitely going to need you at some stage on a freelance basis. No guarantees, of course.'

So much for stardom being handed to me on a plate by Dave Marino. Instead I got deflation, dejection, and another step closer to lung cancer.

'Ah, he's a shrewd guy,' said Ike Tusker later when I called him on his cell phone to give him the lowdown on the meeting, while waiting at the studio entrance for a cab. 'He's spotted that you're good and he wants to keep you onside. No one in this town wants to be known as the person who rejected the next big movie, the next big actor or the next hot writer.'

'So do you think it'll lead to anything?'

'Possibly,' he replied.

My spirits soared.

'But possibly not.'

Spirits clutched their chest and keeled over.

'It's a crapshoot, honey, but at least Dave Marino knows who Carly Cooper is, and we might be able to use it as leverage later down the line. Now you go home, rest and call me tomorrow after your other meetings.'

I flopped back against the security booth as I disconnected the call. I felt like I'd just run a marathon – I was exhausted, disorientated and I had sweat marks in very unattractive places.

I allowed myself a moment of disappointment for the Hollywood break that hadn't quite transpired, then returned to giggly, thrilled mode when a huge limo drew up at the gates and stopped to be checked by security.

I tried my hardest to see who was inside while trying my hardest to act like I didn't care. Nothing. I couldn't see a thing through the smoked glass of the windows.

The security guard had a chat to the driver then the car started to move into the studio lot. As the back seat passed the booth the window rolled down.

'Morning, William,' shouted a female voice.

The security guard tipped his hat. 'Morning, Ms Winslet.'

I turned my head away so quickly I was left with whiplash. The last thing I needed was for her to think that her deranged park stalker had followed her overseas.

Thankfully, I don't think she saw me. And on my way back to Pacific Palisades, I pondered that brief episode.

Kate Winslet: limo-driven by chauffeur. Carly Cooper: taxi-driven erratically by a rally-driving maniac who spoke only in the national tongue of Kurdistan.

Sometimes the Gods just liked to rub it in.

Family Values *Magazine*

PUTTING THE YUMMY IN MUMMY
THIS WEEK . . .
A LITTLE HELP FROM OUR FRIENDS

It's happened to all of us – the car has broken down, the nanny has called in sick, and the heel on your Manolo Blahnik has broken on the way to that benefit you've been planning for months. Quelle horreur! *Girls, there's only one emergency service you can call when such disasters strike – your friends!*

It's often easy to take your chums for granted. Remember, they're there for the good times as well as the bad. So if it's been a while since you slipped into your favourite little Chloe number and headed out for fun with the femmes, then get on that BlackBerry right now and set up a date.

Actually, why not go one step further? Next time husband is away on business, call the agency, recruit some extra help, leave the housekeeper in charge and book a revitalising spa weekend with the girls. Go on, you deserve it. What could be better than a couple of days spent nourishing the important things in life: your soul, your skin and your sense of humour? Close your eyes and imagine it now: the sheer bliss of catching up with the gossip, sharing your worries and giggling until your face pack prevents it. Remember, ladies, husbands are fighting bigger fires and don't want to worry about our minor annoyances. Offload all those little irritations and let the fulfilment of female companionship remind you that we're the suffragettes of the new millennium: we're fearless, fabulous and always ready to support our sisterhood in their struggles.

(On that note, can I just thank everyone who joined my petition against the delay of the new Mulberry bag – the company has assured me it is looking into ways to increase production.)

And the best part of a break with the girls? When husband returns he'll find you refreshed in both body and mind. Isn't he lucky!

★ Step Twelve ★

'Wow, you're Carly Cooper, aren't you? I love the car! You know, you are such an inspiration. I think you're a great example of a woman in her thirties who decided to risk it all and go for the dream, and now look at you: Porsche, house in Pacific Palisades, and married to Liam Neeson. I wish I could be just like you.'

At which point, a middle-aged man in a Corvette drew up beside me and looked at me like my normal mode of dress should be white and have the words 'strait' and 'jacket' in the title. Aw, come on – didn't everyone talk to themselves in their rear-view mirror sometimes?

And anyway, like he could talk – he was a middle-aged bloke in a bomber jacket and a sports car, two facts that automatically barred him from making lifestyle judgements about anyone else.

The lights turned to red and I moved forward. Then stopped. Then moved forward. Then stopped. Shit, I'd never get used to these automatic left-hand-drive controls. I had all the co-ordination of a line dancer on Buckfast.

But hell, I was driving through LA in a Porsche, so how bad could it be?

After seventeen stops for consultations with my *Thomas Guide*, I finally saw the offices of Dreamtime looming in front of me. Ike Tusker's secretary, the jolly Stefan, had emailed me my schedule and he'd noted that there was underground parking at these offices, so I screeched around the side of the building and down into the car park – a manoeuvre that was executed in a state of mortal fear that driving on the opposite side of the road from normal would cause me to misjudge the barriers and leave a wing of Sam's car as a souvenir of my visit.

I stopped at the checkpoint and introduced myself, then frantically groped for the brake as the Porsche jumped forward. Then stopped again. Then jumped forward. Where the fuck was the handbrake?

The very nice security man ignored my ineptitude. He checked a list, found my name and directed me to park over at the faraway wall of the garage, in between a Ferrari and a Bentley. I bit my bottom lip and mentally did a calculation: if I wrecked both of them, I figured I could have the debt cleared by the time I was 126.

'Would you like me to park it for you, ma'am?' asked very nice security man.

I beamed. 'Am I allowed to kiss you?'

'That won't be necessary, ma'am,' he replied with just a faint hint of terror on his face.

I entered a very dramatic pink lift – if it were a shade on a colour chart it would be 'vulva' – and made my way up to the eleventh floor.

'Juliet Brookstein, please, I have an appointment.'

'And your name?'

'Carly Cooper.'

Operation Hollywood Break, take two.

I glanced around the reception area, trying my very best not to be awestruck by the huge water wall in front of me. A water wall. In the middle of a high-rise block. The whole space looked like it had been decorated by Ivana Trump on LSD.

My favourite thing, though, was yet another wall of movie posters, these ones featuring every film that Dreamtime had made, almost every one of which had been a success of blockbuster proportions. I pondered again how far I'd come – all the way from watching their movies with a rubber hot dog in a cardboard roll at the Chiswick multiplex, next to a group of fourteen teenagers with mobile phones that kept ringing, to looking at posters of the same movies in Dreamtime's offices. Glee and giddy excitement once again.

My stomach was doing flips and my heart was throbbing. I suddenly realised that I wanted to phone Sam. Or Kate. Or even Carol. Or anyone else who would take some joy from sharing the absurdity and sheer bloody optimism of this whole adventure.

Anyone except my husband.

I was sure he was trying. No, cancel that, he was definitely trying – trying to get right on my hooters. When I'd returned home the day before, bursting with the news of my first, admittedly anticlimactic meeting, he had still been at the beach with Mac and Benny.

I'd busied myself writing and filing my column while I waited for him to return.

And waited. And waited. My mind had gone into overdrive – after all, Mark didn't know LA, it was his first time out on his own and there were loads of crazy drivers out there.

Yep: pot, kettle.

Just when I had been considering calling my friends at the LAPD to file a 'missing persons and inflatable reptile' report, I'd heard the car crunch up the driveway.

'Mum!' screeched the boys as they piled out of the car, all shiny faces, spiky hair and filthy clothes. I'd wrapped them up in a huge hug then sent them on inside to find Eliza.

'Hey you, I was getting worried,' I'd said.

Now, here's where it gets a bit fuzzy. That statement could be construed in several ways, depending on the tone of voice used, the mood of the moment and the time of the month.

True, I had been worried sick, so I was possibly a little on the tetchy side. But on the other hand I was genuinely pleased to see him and looking forward to a long cosy night discussing our escapades of the day. So my story, and I'm sticking to it, is that it was said in a jovial, concerned and loving way.

Unfortunately, his brain had heard accusatory, narky and pissed off. The truth is probably somewhere in the middle. And of course, Mark being Mark had reacted by, well, *being Mark*. 'Look, Carly, it's been a long day, the boys have been a nightmare and I'm tired. I don't need the moaning, okay?'

'I wasn't moaning!' I'd moaned.

He'd shrugged his shoulders and turned on his heel, heading into the house. 'I'm going to check my emails,' he'd said, in a tone that definitely couldn't have been called jovial, concerned or loving.

Damn! How had that happened? We'd gone from hello to pissed off in seconds. This was the kind of stuff that happened to couples who didn't like each other any more, not Mark and I. We'd never been hostile. We'd never been disdainful. Even through those dark, dark days of new-babydom when we were dropping with exhaustion and our nerves were shredded we'd always managed to laugh and stay on the same side. Now it seemed like the distance between us was wider than Kate Winslet's limo.

An hour later, after sixteen attempts to peel the boys off the ceiling and settle them down for the night, I'd gone into Sam's office, where Mark was hunched over the computer.

'What did the boys have to eat today?'

This time I had been going for 'casual enquiry', but I'm prepared to admit that it may have come out as 'Jesus Christ, what have you been feeding them because they're completely hyperactive, I know that E-numbers are involved and I can't believe you'd be so bloody irresponsible and such a crap parent.'

There were heated words, stamping of feet and a slamming of door.

It had taken me a while to calm down, but eventually my fists unclenched. On my way to bed, only an hour after Mac and Benny had finally admitted defeat and fallen asleep, I'd popped my head in again, a white flag clenched between my teeth. Perhaps I was being a bit harsh. After all, Mark hadn't spent ten unaccompanied hours with the kids since, well, *ever*. Small Child Mania must have been a bit of a shock to the system for someone who usually spent his day having cappuccinos served to him by a secretary and holding civilised, orderly conversations with real grown-up adults. Time to cut him some slack. Anyway, it was only for one more day, then normal service would be resumed and we could have a semblance of a happy family holiday. We could explore, we could relax, we could shag like porn stars if it took our fancy. We could rediscover why we loved each other and spend all day celebrating the important things in life: marriage, children and Ben & Jerry's. I couldn't wait. But first . . .

'So do you want to hear about my meeting today?' I'd asked him in what I'd hoped was a manner that could not be construed as anything other than conciliatory.

He had taken his hands off the keyboard and turned around to face me.

'Sure.' It was fairly deadpan.

I'd jumped onto Sam's big red chenille office sofa. 'Well,' I started, 'when I got there, I gave my name to the security guard and he looked it up on the computer . . .'

Big mistake. I'd got him confused with my female pals, who would want every minute detail of such an extraordinary jaunt, right down to Dave Marino's inside-leg measurement and the colour of the studio toilet rolls.

Within moments Mark had had the glazed-over look that he usually adopts in times of shopping trips and discussions about anything to do with the female reproductive system.

'You're not interested in the least, are you?' I declared.

'Carly, I'm interested,' he argued, with a despairing, depressed sigh. 'What happened when you finally got to speak to him, did he make you an offer?'

'Yes.'

'Really?' For the first time there had been a little hint of perky. 'He wants to buy the movie rights for your book?'

'Er . . . not exactly.'

I'd filled him in on Marino's offer, aware with every passing sentence that it didn't seem quite so exciting any more.

When I'd finished, Mark looked confused.

'So let me check I understand this. He doesn't want your book, but he said that he might, possibly, maybe, use you to tweak someone else's work on a freelance basis in the future, but there are no guarantees and Ike thinks he might just be humouring you.'

'Not "humouring" exactly,' I'd replied indignantly.

'Sorry, "keeping you onside",' he'd countered.

'Erm . . . yes.'

'Oh. Bummer.'

Wait a minute – how had it gone from being great, exciting, super, smashing, and guess what, I met my best friend Kate Winslet, to *bummer*? Two words: Mark bloody Barwick. Okay, I know that was three, but swear words don't bloody count. Why did he always have to be so bloody sensible? As bloody usual. And I couldn't bloody stop saying bloody.

Just to check that I wasn't being unreasonably judgemental, I'd sneaked off and called Kate. She was surprisingly receptive considering my call came around the same time as the morning milk. I'd relayed the whole story to her from start to finish. At the end of every line, her gasps and 'and then what happened's got more enthusiastic, so that by the time her namesake's limo passed me at the security gate she was borderline orgasmic.

'Carly, that's fantastic! Oh God, I wish I'd been there. Tell me, were the loos flash? Did you see anyone else famous? When do you think he'll get in touch? And what did Mark say about it all?' she'd gushed, when I'd finally finished. As far as I can recall (from the very dim and distant past, because I am, after all, married to Mark Barwick) that is called '*being interested*'.

'"Bummer."'

'What?'

'"Bummer." Mark said "bummer".'

Kate had laughed.

'Nope,' I'd interjected, 'laughter definitely wasn't my reaction.'

'Oh, come on, Carly, he's just being Mark. Sensible. Stable. Not getting too excited until something is signed and sealed. He just doesn't want you to get too carried away in case nothing comes of it. He's trying to inject a bit of temperance because he's worried you'll be devastated later if it fizzles out.'

'That's one way of looking at it,' I'd replied huffily. Why did she always stick up for him in what should be times of female solidarity and mutual man-hating?

'And another way of looking at it is . . . ?' she'd prompted.

'He's a great big boring twat,' I'd replied.

'Succinct. Mature. Have you been spending a lot of time with the kids lately?'

'It drives me crazy, Kate. Why can't he throw caution to the wind and live on the wild side a little?'

'Because if he were exactly like you then you'd both be bankrupt, destitute and divorced.'

I really hated that she was always right.

'Look, just give him a break. He did come all the way over there for you, didn't he?'

I grunted.

'Then give him a chance, okay? Go jump his bones right now and have crazy make-up sex.'

Actually, that wasn't such a bad idea, I'd conceded. Right, time we got back on the same wavelength, if only on a physical level. I'd opened the bedroom door, determined to fish out my one set of matching bra and pants and go wow him with daring, lust and co-ordinating lingerie. Note to self: *still* haven't gone on a spree for the new knick-knacks.

He'd beaten me to it. The bedroom, that is, not the co-ordinating lingerie. He had already been there, under the covers . . . and was bordered on each side by a small boy.

Maybe that shopping trip would be a wasted journey.

*　　*　　*

'Carly?' came the voice, snapping my mind away from chronic self-pity and borderline martyrdom. 'Hi, I'm Juliet. It's great to meet you.'

I jumped up. 'And you, Juliet. Thanks for inviting me here.'

Okay, so it wasn't quite on the same scale of gushiness as Dave Marino's hugs, but it was nevertheless pleasant.

Juliet Brookstein, Vice President of Development for Dreamtime was, I guessed, in her early forties. Tall and slim, with a shoulder-length blonde bob and – gasp – no make-up, she had the kind of flawless features and easy poise that suggested she was utterly comfortable in her own skin. Even her clothes said comfort and class: black hipster jeans, black cowboy boots and a black cashmere polo-neck. She was calm, she was serene, but she had a steely edge that hinted of formidable strength. I suspected if she ever got into a fistfight with Dave Marino, the only stars he'd see would be of the concussion variety.

Her office was neat and surprisingly basic, with the exception of a huge pile of scripts that was languishing on the floor in one corner of the room. Each wall was lined with shelves that stretched from carpet to ceiling and groaned under the weight of thousands of books. Normally I'd be impressed, but Sam had already told me that many of his movie-industry pals installed libraries in their houses and then simply got interior designers to fill the bookshelves, while they themselves never read anything more in-depth than the *National Enquirer*. That said, Juliet didn't look like the type of woman who'd believe that aliens had abducted several members of European royalty and Courtney Love. Actually, maybe the last one wasn't such a stretch.

We sat down on two overstuffed chairs that were positioned on either side of a low coffee table. Right on cue, a stunning Asian girl in a black trouser suit appeared with a tray of coffee, water and fruit. LA – the land that time, coloured clothing and HobNobs forgot.

We made some casual chitchat, then just when I was settling back and getting ready for the 'so tell me all about yourself' bit, Juliet reached for a large bound book and pen. She leafed through the pages until she found what she was looking for.

'Okay, I have some questions that I'd like to go through with you . . .'

Oh, good grief, this was like a job interview. And I was rubbish at those. I just hoped she didn't ask me what my three major strengths were because 'shopping', 'making jelly', and 'spotting if a bloke is well-hung at a hundred yards' probably wouldn't impress.

Thankfully, the questions centred entirely around *Nipple Alert*. We talked over the characters, the plots and the dialogue. We discussed the settings: how would I feel if the main location was changed from London to New York – absolutely fine, as long as I was put up in the Waldorf-Astoria for the entire duration of the shoot. I might not have said that last bit out loud, but I definitely thought it.

She shared the difficulties that she envisaged – the fact that the manhunt takes place over several countries (very expensive to re-create and shoot) and the heroine ages fifteen years (many hours in make-up, unless of course you are Joan Collins, in which case you simply remove the bulldog clip from back of head. Once again, I didn't say that bit out loud).

We then chatted over the background of the story and she asked me the question that every journalist and my God-fearing granny had demanded to know when the book was first released – how much of it was auto-biographical. I stuck to the practised line that every-thing except the sex was real. I didn't want the press and Juliet to look at me in a new light and I didn't want my granny to have a stroke.

After an hour I was starting to feel quite heartened. She didn't have the manic gushiness of Marino (she hadn't told me she loved the book even once – sob) but at the same time she'd obviously done extensive research and work on it and seemed to have a genuine interest.

Was this it? Was Juliet going to be the one who gave me my first steps along the Hollywood Walk of Fame?

That oh-too-familiar bubble of excitement started to fizz again the longer the meeting lasted.

'Carly, let me tell you where I want to go with this from here,' she announced.

Fingers crossed. Please say you'll buy it. Please. Please. I've got houses in the sun to buy. A Porsche that'll need repairs by the end of the day. The under-sixes Alpine Synchronised Skiing Team to fund.

'I'm going to recommend this one to our board. I love it, I think it has originality, I think it has great humour, I love the characters and I think that with the right cast it would have mass appeal.'

Right then. Great. I think. So what did that mean exactly?

'Juliet, that's fantastic. So what will the process and timelines be from here on in and what do you need from me to make this work?'

Oh, would you listen to me with the lingo? Proof, if I ever needed it, that all those nights watching *Boston Legal* were not wasted. And I even managed to say all that while surreptitiously covering the stains from where I'd dribbled my coffee down my white blouse.

I called Ike from the underground car park to give him the update.

'So what did she say then?' he asked.

'Nothing. She said there was nothing she needed me to do – just to leave it all to her.'

'Hey, you did great, honey,' he bellowed. 'Okay, so I'll call a couple of my contacts on the board and just leverage a little extra pressure. Not that you need it, babe, cos you are smoking!'

I was, actually. I was puffing furiously on a Marlboro Light and Mr Nice Security Man was now giving me evil looks and reaching for his mace spray.

Okay, so it wasn't a deal, but it was going in the right direction.

I was bursting to tell someone else. Mark? Nope. If he called this one a 'bummer' I wouldn't be responsible for my actions. Sam. I dialled his number and he answered on the second ring.

'Sam, I've got news,' I screeched.

'Do I have to call my insurance company?' he said with a laugh. A gorgeous laugh. I missed him. I actually missed him.

'You do. The Porsche is currently scuba diving in the Pacific.'

He laughed again. That gorgeous . . . Just fill in the blanks.

I recounted the details of my meeting with Juliet, right up till the point where she said that she'd distribute details to the board and they'd meet to discuss it in around two weeks, but that she was optimistic her recommendation to buy would be accepted.

Eeeeeeeek!

'Babe, that's amazing. Congratulations! Juliet Brookstein is a smart lady with a great reputation, so if she's on your side then I think the odds are pretty good. I'm SO proud of you. I knew they'd love you.'

My eyes filled up. If I deleted the bit where it was Sam saying all this and replaced it with 'Mark', then life would be perfect. This was wrong, wrong, wrong.

'So how're you getting on in Vegas?' I asked.

'Missing you,' he answered, his voice raw and breaking up with emotion. Or that might just have been because I was still in the underground car park and the signal was dodgy.

'I miss you too,' I replied honestly. I did. Since Sam left I hadn't had one great big belly laugh, one moment of butterflies in my stomach.

'I'm going to go now,' I said. 'I have to get across town for my next meeting.'

'Is this the one at GMG?'

'Yep.'

'Okay, well, listen – Lee Stavorski is a real character so be prepared for the unexpected.'

'What do you mean, "character"?'

Silence.

'Sam? SAM?'

He was gone. Either he'd gone into a bad area or the anti-fag fascists – alerted by Mr Nice Security Man with the Mace Spray – were surrounding this area and hindering the signal at my end.

As I pulled out of the car park, right into the path of oncoming traffic, I cursed, panicked, then – when the honking of horns had stopped and I finally shook off the pissed-off lady in the station wagon who'd decided to chase me – pondered what Sam had meant.

He hadn't said it with too much foreboding so surely it wouldn't be too painful. After all, I'd had two meetings with movie bigwigs already and survived. I could cope with anything that Mr Stavorski threw at me. Anything at all.

CARLY CALLING . . .

Carly to Kate and Carol:

Gr8 mtg - fab lady, says she wl rec.
board 2 buy my script. Get the frocks
ready 4 the premiere!

Kate:

Bummer.

Carly to Kate:

Ur not funny.

Carol:

Well done, babe! V. proud of u. Hav 2
go - Hawaii shoot soooo hot, keep havin
2 drink cocktails 2 cool off. Barman
looks like Ben Affleck. Life tough.

Carly to Carol:

Bummer.

★ *Step Thirteen* ★

'Okay, you've got five minutes. Pitch it to me.'

I could cope with anything Lee Stavorski threw at me except this. What did he mean 'pitch it to him'? I'd discussed the preparation required for these meetings with Ike and he'd assured me that because he'd submitted my book to his 'close friends in the industry' and they'd read it before asking to see me, I wouldn't be required to do the standard new-movie-concept sales pitch.

Thanks to my annual subscription to *Variety* magazine I'd read many stories about these pitches over the years. There was an urban myth, which might well be founded on truth, that the shortest movie concept ever pitched was three words: Schwarzenegger. DeVito. Twins.

Now Lee Stavorski, a man whose physicality suggested he may well be a close relative of the afore-mentioned Mr DeVito, was sitting in his big flash leather chair, in his super-swanky minimalist office on the GMG Studios lot, asking me to pitch it to him. And if I wasn't mistaken, he had a slightly sadistic edge to the beaming smile that exposed ... drum roll, drum roll ... the only yellow, squinty teeth west of the Rocky Mountains.

I took a sip of water, playing for time.

I could pitch. I could. Come on, it was *my* book, I knew it inside-out. And hadn't I done a thousand sales pitches before? In my former life I'd been the best toilet-roll salesperson in the country. Oh yes, I was top of the pile when it came to bog rolls. I'd given endless presentations. I'd trained hundreds of reps to give endless presentations. And when it came right down to it, the techniques for pitching any kind of product are pretty much generic. Features, benefits, unique selling points, match all of above to customer needs and bingo – another order for two hundred pallets of extra-soft two-ply in magnolia goes trundling off to the customer's warehouse.

When it came to sales presentations, there was no real difference between something that led to hygienic bottoms and a multi-million-dollar movie production.

Think. Think. Oh hell, I was floundering. Features and benefits of the story I could pretty much manage – translated into movie speak that was a sharp, snappy synopsis. But after that I was lost. What bits should I highlight that would really spark his interest and take him from 'five minutes to impress me' to 'dollface, let's go have lunch at Trader Vic's. Oh, and by the way, would you like your limo to be black or pink?'

I gave a sparkly, confident grin as I took another sip of water and pretended to flick through the notepad I'd brought along. It was empty. I'd only shoved it in my bag to give me a slight air of efficiency.

'I'd be delighted to, Mr Stavorski. However, I know you're a busy man and I don't want to repeat anything you already know, so can I just ask how much of the original book you've actually read.'

'None of it,' he drawled. 'Honey, this is a chick flick. Do I look like the kind of guy who reads chick stuff? But do you know why I'm successful?'

Because of your stunning good looks, compassionate ways and dental plan?

He didn't even wait for an audible answer.

'Because I know how to tap into what makes people tick. I gave your book to my daughter . . .'

Good grief, he had spawned.

'. . . and she loved it. Said it was the rudest damn thing she'd read in years and damned funny too. So now I want you to tell me what I need to know.'

I considered, *Mr Stavorski, what you really need to know is that you require a dentist and a work-out regime. And that if you buy my book I will have your babies. As long as I can keep my eyes closed during the conception part.*

I could definitely feel my body temperature rising and I was sure my sweat glands had started to leak.

Right there, right then, I felt like a duck out of water. What the hell was I doing there on my own? How crazy had I been to think that I could just waltz in here, have a chat, then waltz back out with a contract in my pocket? There were people who had dedicated their whole lives to cracking Hollywood, and here was I, fresh from a hectic schedule of mothering, housework and prowling up the frozen-food aisle in Asda, thinking that I had a chance of pulling this off.

Nuts.

Stavorski was still staring at me with anticipation.

More nuts.

I needed a sensible, intelligent, educated resolution to this crisis. I decided to fake a burst appendix. If I keeled over right now he'd have to call the paramedics and they'd have me out of there in no time – then I could come back when I was more prepared. Hang on, I was a terrible actress – I would double over, scream with pain, contort my face and give my very best impression of an appendix-like problem (was the appendix on the right or the left?) and it would probably come across as something completely different, like chronic constipation.

I'd go down in Hollywood folklore as the woman whose bowels seized in front of Lee Stavorski.

He was *still* looking at me with an expectant expression. Although I could now see a slight hint of wariness. Oh, this was all going to end so badly. The mortification of it. I'd have to leave here right now and go directly to LAX, fly home and never darken Tinseltown's gilded door again.

Then I had a revelation. It was like a blinding beam of light leading me to the promised land of articulate speech and superior presentation skills. Juliet Brookstein. Juliet Brookstein had pulled out several aspects of the book for further discussion – so surely they must be the pertinent areas. Surely, if I gave a synopsis of the book then summarised and recapped the points that Juliet had raised for discussion, then I had a good chance of, if not hitting the bulls-eye, then at least getting on the Hollywood dartboard.

My arse left my chair like it was on fire. I could do this. Of course I could. I gave Mr Stavorski my very best grin then launched into a spiel. Those heady days of corporate presentations on the absorption levels of quilted three-ply came flooding right back. I gave an overview of my novel, then further comments on all the subjects that Juliet had raised: the characters, the plot, the settings, the market, what set this apart from every other rom com out there . . .

And Stavorski was warming. I could see it in his eyes and in the hint of a smile that was playing around his lips. Maybe I wouldn't have to offer up my womb after all.

I finished with a smiley flourish and asked if he had any questions.

He was quiet for a few moments, his gaze never leaving mine. I started to feel distinctly uncomfortable. Had I made a complete pork mammal's ear of it? Had my professionalism not reached his exacting standards (I quickly discounted this one – after all, he was the man who couldn't even be bothered reading the book in the first place)?

'I like you.'

What? It took me by surprise. Did he mean 'like' in a 'You are the most talented woman to ever stand in front of me, I'm buying this book, making a movie and I'm calling Meryl Streep this minute?' Or in a 'Good move wearing the matching undies because I want you to get your kit off and spread-eagle yourself across my desk in a lustful manner this very minute.'

'And I like the sound of what you've got there.'

Phew, he was still on the book. Thank God – the desk was glass and I wasn't sure it could take my weight.

'Here's what I want you to do: back here two weeks from now with a treatment and a script. Doesn't need to be a whole one – first fifty pages will do. I just want to get a real good feel for the characters and the dialogue. Whaddya think?'

What did I think? I thought, 'You have got to be joking! What's a treatment? How do I write a fifty-page script?' The only script I'd ever written was for Mac's nativity play, Big Puddles Nursery, Christmas 2004.

Of course, I said none of this out loud.

It was crunch time. I could say no, leave and abandon this mad, crazy mission. Or I could give it a go – an option that was a logistical nightmare, a stress-induced heart attack in the making and sheer bloody madness.

So of course, the latter made perfect sense.

I held out my hand. 'Deal,' I said with what I hoped was a confident grin.

He took my paw and shook it.

'Deal,' he replied.

This was it. This really was, *finally*, my first step on the Hollywood Walk of Fame. Okay, so it was a baby step, but it felt good. It felt great! One day I would hopefully look back on this as being my big break. My first rung on the ladder.

As I wandered back towards the car park to collect the Porsche, another thought struck me. When I told

Mark that I'd have to spend the next fortnight working, it might just be the first step on the road towards divorce.

I was right. I could have closed my eyes really tight and worn a balaclava backwards and *still* seen it coming.

I'd given him a rundown on the day's activities and until I dropped the bombshell it had gone pretty well – he'd even managed to listen for almost an hour without glazing over. He'd asked informed, perceptive questions. And he'd thrown in an enthusiastic (if a little clichéd) 'Way to go – that's my girl' when I told him about the raging success of my spontaneous presentation.

He seemed keen, interested, and like he was making an effort. Right up until the shock almost induced a stroke.

'You're what? What are you talking about?'

I wondered whether repeating it all at the speed of a horse-racing commentator might soften the blow since he was bound to miss out on some pertinent words: like work, two, weeks, you, look, after, kids.

God, I hated doing this to him. I felt like he'd made a genuine concession coming over here, demonstrating that he was willing to go against his better judgement for the sake of our marriage, and now I'd just dumped a ton of manure on him from a very great height.

But I really had no choice.

After I'd left Stavorski's office, I'd immediately called Sam again. Actually, that's not strictly true. I'd waited until the panic attack had subsided, then I called him.

I told him what I'd agreed to and there was a sharp intake of breath – the one that furniture removal men do when they've got a piano at the bottom of a flight of stairs and reckon there's no chance of budging it.

'I warned you he was a bit of a character,' Sam had said, utterly unhelpfully.

'Sam, I thought you meant *"he's a bit of a character – wears odd socks and can't pronounce his r's"*. Or even, *"he's a bit of a character – might try to grope your arse every time you walk past him"*. I didn't realise you meant he was a character in the same sense as those slave-drivers who used to send children down mines.

'Sam, I'm panicking, help me.'

'Okay, let me think, let me think. I've got a mate who's a screenplay writer – I'll get him to come over to the house . . .'

'No! I don't want anyone else to help.'

'But why? Are you mad? Carly, you'll never write a treatment and fifty pages in a fortnight – not when you've never done it before. You'll *need* someone to help you.'

'Sam, I'm not letting anyone else do this. Number one: if someone else is involved then I'll feel like a fraud. Number two: I'm a fast worker. If I really pushed myself I could write the first draft of a novel in just a few weeks, and that's far more labour-intensive. For Christ's sake, Barbara Cartland used to churn out a Mills and Boon every fortnight and she had the chronic disadvantages of being 165 and having her eyelids weighed down with all that blue eyeshadow.

'If I'm going to do this, then I'm doing it myself.'

I had heard him groan. 'I'd forgotten how bloody-minded you were.'

'Sam, I promise that I'm not being stubborn. It's just that *Nipple Alert* is my book, it's the story of my life, and nobody knows it better than me. If anyone else became involved then I'd have to explain it all to them and go through it with them and that would take days, and if it wasn't exactly perfect I'd hate it.

'Just tell me, strictly speaking, is it possible to do this in the time-frame he's given me?'

'Strictly speaking, forgoing basic bodily functions like eating and sleeping, and with the aid of perform-ance-enhancing drugs?'

'Yes,' I'd replied with my fingers crossed and my brow furrowed. If I'd had Botox it would have surren-dered under the pressure by now.

'Yes.'

'It's possible?' I'd checked.

'Yes. But you'll need a miracle, Carly.'

'Oh, miracles are a doddle, I do them at least twice a day. Once when I fit into my jeans and then again when I somehow get Mac and Benny through a whole day without a visit to Casualty.'

'How're they doing?' he had said, his voice softening.

'Great. Mark's had them down at Mother's Beach for the last two days. They love it there – they've got a whole group of pals already. Mac says he's never going home.'

Long, long pause . . . and then a slightly strained, 'And what does Mark say to that?'

'Oh, he just ignores it – Mac's got a history of rash

and unreasonable demands. So far this week he's wanted to fly a helicopter, go deep-sea diving and adopt a Teenage Mutant Ninja Turtle. And he's still not reverted to "Mac" yet. He informed us this morning that he's now called Lex Luthor.'

He'd laughed, then said, 'I miss them.'

'They miss you too.'

Silence. I hadn't said a word, I promise. I swear on my wedding ring – the one that had been burning a hole in my finger – that I'd made no inappropriate comments. At least not out loud.

'And how are you and Mark doing?'

For the last few years, every time Sam and I had spoken on the phone, he'd always say, 'How are things with you and Mark?' An innocent question, born out of genuine interest and friendship.

This time it hadn't seemed quite so innocent.

'I'm not sure. Some good, some not so good. And I think it's about to go rapidly downhill when I tell him about my new workload. Talking of which . . .' I'd said, happy to steer the conversation back into safer terri-tory, 'where do I actually start with this treatment and script, Sam? Just give me a wee clue and I'll take it from there.'

He'd thought for a moment.

'Okay, here's what to do. Go into my office and in the filing cabinet next to the bookshelf you'll find a file marked "Treatments". Read that – it's movie treatments I've been sent over the years. Some of them have got notes in the margins that might help too.'

Great. Halfway there already, I'd thought.

'But that's only ten per cent of it, Carly . . .'

I had always been crap at maths.

'The script is going to be the hard bit. Go onto my PC and open up a programme file called "Final Draft". That's script-writing software – it automatically formats everything for you. There's also a whole shelf of scripts in there, so read through them to get a feel for it. Then go into the top drawer on the right-hand side of my desk and there's a DVD called *Syd Field's Screenwriting Workshop*. Watch that. It tells you everything you'll need to know to get started. You already have the raw material, so you're a few steps ahead of the game . . .'

'Positive words at last,' I'd interjected joyously.

'But you're still fucking mental.'

I had still been giggling when I'd hung up. I could do this. I could.

Couldn't I?

'Carly, there is no way on earth you're going to be able to do this. It's madness!' Mark yelped. 'People study for years to become screenwriters – you will not be able to do it in a fortnight, Carly, it's impossible.'

'Mark, I can, I promise. I can learn the script format and I already have the material – the action and dialogue is all in my book, all I have to do is adapt just under half of it into about fifty pages of script. Which is about fifty minutes of screen time. See, I already have some experience with this.'

I didn't tell him that I had absolutely no idea what any of my last statement meant – my 'experience' consisted of watching the Syd Field DVD once while waiting for my next of kin to return from the beach, and it hadn't all quite sunk in yet.

'Will it be easy? No. But I can do it, Mark. If you'll help me,' I pleaded.

He started pacing up and down the kitchen going from the fridge to the cooker, back to the fridge, to the cooker, swearing repetitively ... It was like watching Gordon Ramsay on fast-forward.

'Help you how?' He was raising his voice now. I waited for the building to start shaking and the San Andreas Fault to crack all the way to Mexico. Mark Barwick NEVER raised his voice – that was my job in our relationship. Mark didn't do shouting. And now there was definite amplification. Dear God, what had I done to him?

'By taking care of the boys for me. All day. Every day. Until you leave.'

He went grey. I wondered if the marble floor tiles would crack under the pressure of twelve stone of hunk hitting it at speed. I decided to put a positive spin on it.

'Actually, you'll probably enjoy it because they're great company these days.'

Cue bad sitcom moment.

'Waaaaaaaaahhhhhhhhhh.'

Benny came flying through the door, wailing like a soap star. I scooped him up as Mark's eyes widened.

'Is he okay?'

I nodded. This was a 'I'm a victim of injustice and I'm not getting my own way' cry, as opposed to 'I've fallen off my bike and I have several broken bones'.

At what point do mothers attain the ability to identify and analyse their children's crying? I reckon it must get slipped in somewhere between the epidural and the post-birth tea and toast.

'Mac hit me with the ball!' he screamed.

'Aw, honey, it's only a ball. I'm sure it isn't that sore,' I said soothingly while administering medicinal kisses.

'IS sore,' he protested. 'Hard ball!'

I looked at Mark quizzically. Hard ball? Was this something he'd bought them at the beach? The only hard ball I could think of was a cricket ball and I didn't think there'd be too much of a market for them in downtown LA.

'What hard ball, sweetheart?' I prompted.

'Shiny ball,' he wailed.

Shiny ball? Now I was completely confused. Hard, shiny ball?

Oh. No.

When the penny dropped it was joined by my stomach. There was only one hard, shiny ball in this house.

'Mark, go get Lex – I mean, *Mac* – right now. Now!'

'Why? What is it?' he asked anxiously.

'He's playing touch football with Sam's Golden Globe.'

He turned and raced off in the direction of the loud crashing noises. And as he went, I heard a distinct, disdainful echo of, 'Yep, they're *great company* these days.'

Family Values *Magazine*

PUTTING THE YUMMY IN MUMMY
THIS WEEK . . . MAINTAINING A
WORK/FAMILY BALANCE

We're all juggling far too many things these days, and for those of us who choose to work and bring up our family at the same time it can be especially fretful. Sometimes there just aren't enough hours in the day, and of course there is the guilt – we all know what it's like to miss little Cosmo's poetry recital because we've got a crucial board meeting in Zurich on the same day. But ladies, banish those negative feelings by reminding yourself that by working you are giving your child a dynamic, successful role model to aspire to. There are positives and negatives of both full-time motherhood and combining motherhood with a busy career, and I'd say that both options can work wonderfully if the most important factor is present: BALANCE.

For a working mother it's crucial to get the balance right, and to do this takes planning and preparation and delegation, delegation, delegation. Housework? Engage more cleaning staff. Cooking? Employ a house-

keeper. Or for those with a little extra in their budget, a chef is a wonderful investment. Childcare? A nanny is, of course, indispensable, and a tutor can be invaluable for those older children who are laden down with the grindstone of homework.

Try when possible to leave for work after the children have gone to school, and to return home no later than 6 p.m., thus allowing you time to share in the stories of their day. And ladies, no matter how important the task, never, ever work in the evening. That's YOU time and it's FAMILY time.

And you'll need to recharge those batteries for another tough, demanding but ultimately rewarding day of work and family life.

★ Step Fourteen ★

'Ding dong!'

It was 7 a.m. on Sunday, day five of my frantic work-induced isolation from the world. I was frazzled, confused, disheartened, and I now understood why Batman installed a Batphone in the Batcave. This was about the seventy-eighth time I'd called Sam to ask him a question about some technicality or other of the script-writing process and my button-pressing finger was red raw. If this was going to continue then we definitely needed a direct line.

He answered on the second ring, but before he could even speak I heard that very familiar, distinct *ding dong* in the background, followed by an announcement that I couldn't quite make out.

'Are you in an airport, Sam?'

'I am.'

Great – he must be coming back.

After day one of studying the technicalities of script writing, all my stoic resolve about not letting anyone help me had crumpled into a pile of desperation. At this rate I'd soon be dragging the postman in to explain the concept of 'plot points'. Actually, that wasn't so far-fetched. The postman was probably only delivering the mail until his first blockbuster got snapped up, since everyone but *everyone* in this town was just an Oscar winner waiting to happen. You'll notice I said Oscar and not Golden Globe. We were still trying to find somewhere that did invisible mending for Sam's pride and joy.

I was desperate to ask Sam to call his script-writing mate and appoint him as cavalry, but I was too embarrassed and – okay, I admit it – too stubborn and proud to confess defeat. But now, no need – my script expert in shining armour was on his way home.

'So when will you be back?' I asked with just a slightly overenthusiastic gush.

'Carly, I'm not coming home, I'm going to Italy. George has been bugging me for ages to visit, so I thought this was probably a good opportunity.'

I was speechless. I read *Hello!* I read *OK!* George. Italy. It had to be Clooney. Sun. Gorgeous. In swimming trunks. Drool at mouth.

I think Sam interpreted my silence as disappointment – which it was, of course. But I'm not sure it was solely for the reasons he suspected.

'I'm sorry, Carly. I just think it's better that I stay out of the way right now. And to be honest, I could do with the break.'

I didn't argue. Actually, if I deployed my sensible head for a few moments, I had to agree that it was probably the best thing. Tensions in the house were already on the vicelike-grip side of tight, so the last thing we needed were any confusing emotional under-tones. Or should I say, any *more* confusing emotional undertones. So I put on my best breezy voice and asked him for clarification on a couple of screenplay-type things and then hung up. And I decided to completely ignore the dull ache that I felt in my stomach for a few seconds when I said goodbye.

Must have been that bagel I had for breakfast.

Later that day, he called me back. 'How are you getting on?' he asked. 'You sounded really pissed off earlier – I was worried about you.' Oh, he was a complete bastard, that Sam Morton. There was nothing worse than a gorgeous, caring, lovely (I was going to throw in 'hung like a donkey' but I thought it might spoil the moment) movie star having the absolute audacity to phone up and be all sensitive, loving and absolutely bloody perfect.

There was another bong noise. 'Carly, listen to this.'

'Ladies and gentlemen, this is your captain speaking. Just giving you an update on our progress across the Atlantic . . .'

'Sam! SAM! Stop rubbing it in, you evil git!' I wailed down the phone.

'How many seats does the plane have?' I asked when he put the phone back to his ear.

'Six big leather ones. And a sofa. And a bed in the other room.'

'Do you have a telly?'

'Four. Plasma screens.'

'What's the food like?'

'Perfection. The chef has three Michelin stars.'

I groaned. 'Sam, I think I've got a hard-on.'

The sound of his laughter made me smile. A feeling of dread started creeping up from my toes. I was going to have to address what was bubbling between us – the ostrich impersonation couldn't go on forever. As soon as the script was finished. One thing at a time.

'Anyway, tell me where you're up to with Operation Big Cheque.'

That was the name we'd given to this whole fiasco the day before in a bid to motivate and inspire me. I still wasn't sure if it was working.

'Okay, I've finished the treatment.'

'Wow, that was fast!'

'I cheated,' I confessed. 'To be honest, once I discovered that a "treatment" was basically a description of what happens in the story, I realised that it wasn't too different from the synopsis I wrote for the original book, so I called Kate and asked her to pop into my house and email all my *Nipple Alert* stuff over to me. Then I stayed up most of last night tweaking it and I think we're good to go on that now.'

Sam's voice dropped a few octaves. 'You do know I love it when you do that American-lingo thing, don't you?' he said. I detected disparagement.

'Piss off and stop mocking the afflicted. If it's good enough for Oprah . . .

'Anyway, I'm starting the script now. I've studied the theory on the DVDs and books, I've read loads of the scripts in your office, I've asked you 676 questions and I'm in a mild state of confusion and panic - so I figure it's a good time to start.'

'Carly, most of the scriptwriters I know are in a permanent state of confusion and panic,' he said encouragingly.

'Then I was born to do this!' I declared positively. 'And I will. Just as soon as my telephone stalker goes back to luxuriating in his flash private jet and stops harassing poor plebs like me. Now go away before I'm overtaken with jealousy and turn a mild shade of Shrek.'

I put the phone down and stared at the computer. And stared. And stared. Then I got up, wandered around in circles, then sat back down again. And stared at the computer. A few minutes later I got up again and this time went to the loo, where I sat, contemplating, for at least half an hour. I checked my reflection in the mirror.

Carly Cooper, Miss Glasgow Bag Lady 2007. My eyes were puffy through lack of sleep. My hair had forgotten what a hairdryer looked like and I'd been wearing the same clothes for two days. Don't judge me harshly, please – clothes selection takes valuable minutes from each day and it was time I didn't have. Thank God for Eliza bringing in food every few hours or the skeletal model apostles would have a new recruit.

I went back into Sam's office and poured a coffee from the pot that was on the hotplate. I sat back down and stared at the computer. A coffee machine in his office – how flash was that? Then I decided that the desk was dusty, so I took everything except the PC off it, then used the sleeve of my jumper to polish it until it gleamed. I put everything back on the desk. Then I ran my fingers over my eyebrows. Yep, they definitely needed plucking. Now where were my tweezers? I had to pluck them that very moment. It couldn't wait for another minute. I was slipping, I chided myself. I'd let my new eyebrow regime go to hell.

Writer's block.

Argh! It had been so long since I'd written my last book that I'd forgotten the agony that is writer's block. It must be like childbirth – once you get to the end of labour you forget the pain.

When I had written *Nipple Alert*, I'd had the cleanest house in London. I'd sit down to write and four hours later I'd have done two loads of washing, disinfected every inch of the bathroom, tidied all my cupboards and cut the grass.

It's a rare idiosyncrasy of the writing profession. I mean, I've never heard of astronaut block. Or dinner-lady block. And the only blockage that plumbers encounter involves a dodgy beef vindaloo, a U-bend, and a bill for fifty quid an hour.

Come on, Carly, get it together. You can do this. You *have* to do this.

I put the coffee cup down and shook my shoulders like an athlete limbering up. Come on, girl, time to get serious. I placed my hands above the keyboard, took a deep breath, made contact, and then . . . Whoosh. My fingers were like speeding bullets as they came to life in a flurry of determination and productivity.

A few seconds later, I sat back to contemplate the fruits of my labours. There it was, in full glorious, fabulous brilliance . . .

www.eBay.com

And I was already on the 'handbags – closing in one

hour with no offers' page. Oooooh, my attention was taken by a natty wee red leather number that . . .

What was I thinking? I was in the middle of the most pressurised situation in my career, and I was about to buy a bag that would make me look like one of Santa's little helpers for no other reason than it would take my mind off the fact that I had writer's block.

I pressed the square on the top right corner of the screen and closed it down. I opened up my novel and read right to the end of the first chapter. I'd already worked out that the best idea was to pretty much stick to the original framework of *Nipple Alert*, so as not to lose the plot completely. In every sense.

Time to work. No more procrastination. I conjured up the one thing that would motivate me to such an extent that I wouldn't be tempted even for one second to go back onto eBay every ten minutes to check the offer price on that handbag – my family.

My boys, first and foremost. But also Mark. I was doing this for Mark. More accurately, I was doing this for that glorious moment when I'd be able to tell him that it had all paid off and the fruits of my labours were going to bring us everything we'd ever dreamed of: financial stability, freedom from the rat race, time to spend together as a family, a ten-foot paddling pool . . . actually, that last one was only on the boys' wish list.

And I'd give the whole speech with a big smug grin and then add 'na na na na boo boo, ya big unsupportive twat' to the end.

Bitter. Immature. Unnecessary.

But it was enough to get the fingers flying and the brain in gear. A couple of hours later I sat back, grinned and pressed 'save'. I'd done it. I'd had more false starts than a nervous swimmer, and I hadn't quite mastered every function of the software so all the characters currently had the same name, but those technical hitches aside, I'd completed the very first page of my very first ever script on the way to my very own star on the Hollywood Walk of Fame.

And it felt great.

I checked my watch – 5.45 p.m. Great timing, the boys would be back any minute.

I couldn't resist a wee surge of excitement. I might look like I'd been dragged through a Hollywood hedge backwards, but I had page one of my script, my husband, my boys, and, now that I'd finally got started, a definite feeling of optimism about getting the screenplay finished. It might be the biggest load of tosh Lee Stavorski had ever had the misfortune to read and he might use it for nothing more than lighting the end of his big phallic cigar, but at least I'd be able to say that I'd done it.

And that would make all this worth it. God, I was missing spending time with the boys.

Since I'd started working, we'd fallen into a routine. I'd get up in the morning and work for an hour or so, then when the boys finally roused I'd feed them and get them dressed. Mark would appear after his shower, and then he'd pack the boys and assorted accoutrements into the car, pausing, as demanded by Mac, to mourn the departure of Archie, who'd been sent to the great

286

alligator park in the sky by a stiletto in the beach car park. It was Lex Luthor's first experience of losing a family member and he wasn't taking it well.

The man-van would then ride off into the sunrise, not to be seen again until 6 p.m. when it would come trundling back up the drive full of exhausted, happy people. And Mark.

Eliza normally finished around five, so I'd slave over a hot telephone, calling in whatever feast the kids would like for tea. Oh, I know it was sheer indulgence, but cooking time detracted from the valuable two hours that I got to spend with the kids before they got packed off to bed. And anyway, this was exceptional circumstances – although I was going to have to put them in some kind of 'gastronomic decompression chamber' before we went home and returned to a stable, healthy diet with a takeaway treat once a week.

In my defence, though, it's not as if the takeaway food I was ordering was junk.

Oh, I know – I'm attempting a feeble justification to stop Jamie Oliver adding me to his hit list.

I could call up the local veggie shop and they'd send up four delicious mouth-watering salads all prepared and ready to eat.

I could. I didn't, but I definitely could.

Instead I usually plumped – with plump being the operative word – for a great little Italian on Sunset who did gorgeous chicken, pasta and pizza with freshly baked focaccia breads and a salad on the side. And it would all arrive, ready garnished and plated, just waiting to be put in front of Mac and Benny (who would be slipping into a fatigue-induced fog by that time) and their non-communicative parents.

It's not that Mark and I weren't talking. It's just that it was hard to have an in-depth conversation when you were in separate rooms. While I ate with the kids, he'd normally disappear with his dinner into Sam's office to take advantage of the only two hours in the day that the computer was free. Same old Mark – he never could quite cut the umbilical cord that connected him to his work. We'd once been on holiday in Egypt and he'd nipped out of Tutankhamen's tomb to take a call from a screeching female in Essex who was apoplectic because her former business partner had buggered off with the company Bentley. She got it back eventually but Mark never did get to see how Tut departed the earth.

I didn't dare disturb him while he was in there working, so I just ate with the kids, sometimes played with them in the pool, trounced them at Connect Four, watched a bit of TV, then read them stories until it was time to kiss them goodnight.

Cue change of rooms. By the time I'd come out of the boys' bedroom, Mark had cleared out of the office to let me start working again. Sometimes he'd go and crash out in Sam's home cinema to watch a DVD. Or have a float in the hot tub under the stars. Or chill in the electronic massage chair. Yes, I could see why he thought LA life sucked.

Or sometimes he'd just go and sit out by the pool with a beer and a book. On the first night I'd gone out to see him. 'Thanks for today,' I'd said, because I did truly appreciate the fact that he was going along with this and taking the kids out of my hair so that I could get on with the work. Although, here's the thing – permission to have minor rant about the inequality in parental relationships. When I had the boys all day on a Saturday because he had to work extra hours, did he ever come home, snog my face off and thank me? Nope. He came home and asked what was for tea. So how come I felt I should show gratitude for something that, if the roles were reversed, would be taken for granted? However, I did, for once, have the sense to keep such mildly irritating issues to myself, being cognisant of the fact that our relationship did, at present, have all the stability of a vibrator on a skateboard.

Anyway, back to that first night. He'd put the book down (a good start), smiled and shrugged his shoulders. 'S'okay.' Articulate.

'I really appreciate this, you know,' said I, not so much lying as exaggerating ever so slightly in the name of ceasefire maintenance.

He'd looked at me for a moment, then opened his mouth to speak. Nothing came out.

I'd sat on his knee and kissed him. 'I love you,' I'd whispered. Don't say I don't try.

'How's it going?' he'd asked.

'Slowly. Haven't got a clue what I'm doing, to be honest.'

Silence.

'Well, you'd better get back to it because the sooner you get finished the sooner we can have some time together.'

It hadn't been said in an angry or nasty tone, it was

just pragmatic. Pragmatically irritating the life out of me.

'You're right,' I'd said through gritted teeth, as I jumped off his knee and about-turned.

'And I love you too,' he'd said when I was about ten feet away.

I turned and grinned at him. 'Thanks. I needed that.'

'Any time,' he'd replied.

And so, as dawn fell that evening, not a single cheap shot had been fired. That was Wednesday; it was now Sunday and the truce had held up. On the few occasions when our ships did pass in the night there would be a quick kiss, a smile, and maybe even, God forbid, the occasional locking of lips. Apart from that one time when he grabbed me, threw me down on the sunlounger and shagged me in twenty-six different positions. But he'd been asleep when I had that little fantasy, late one night while waiting for a new pot of coffee to brew, so that didn't count.

Suddenly I heard a commotion outside – lots of thundering wee feet and shouts of 'Muuuuuuuuum! Where are you?'

I wandered out into the hall and followed the noise. 'Muuuuuuuuuuuuuuuum!!!!!!' came more shrieks from the other side of the house.

I didn't panic – the mother sensor had kicked in again and I realised that they were happy squeals, not 'Come quick, I've just decapitated my brother.'

I found them already out at the pool, Mac and Benny in the shallow end endeavouring to mount an inflatable reptile of indeterminate origins, while Mark held the tail, his own head thrown back as he roared with laughter.

A week at the beach had darkened his skin, lightened his hair, and he had a couple of days' growth on his chin. Mark had always been handsome, but . . . hello! Ovaries in spin cycle.

'Look, Mum, look, Mum, it's Rex!' screeched Mac.

'And Rex is . . . ?' I asked vaguely, frantically racking my brain for a Blue Peter reference that would help to identify the creature in front of me.

'A dinosaur! Mandy at the barbecue said it's a Tyrannosaurus Rex and *everybody* knows that!'

Except me, apparently. And don't let my ignorance of planetary evolution distract you from the most crucial two words in that sentence.

Mandy? Barbecue?

Dame Judi Dench couldn't have put on a better act than the one I had going at that very minute. I kept a huge smile on my face the whole time as I walked around the pool to the shallow end, sat down on the edge and dangled my feet in.

'That's great, guys!'

'Do you like Rex, Mum, do you do you do you?' Mac gasped.

'I do, Mac – he's gorgeous.'

Mac's eyes widened in fury.

'Green Goblin,' Mark whispered out of the corner of his mouth.

'I mean, Mr Goblin,' I back-pedalled furiously.

'I've got a new name too, Mummy,' declared Benny coyly. Well, this was new. Inevitable, but new. I dreaded to think. Since his favourite characters in the whole world were Scooby-Doo and Sponge Bob Square Pants, I had an impending feeling of doom.

'And what's that, honey?' I crossed my fingers behind my back.

'Mac. I'm called Mac now.'

So Mac was the Green Goblin and Benny was Mac. I was beginning to think my family had issues that could see a psychologist's children through college.

'Well, Mac and Green – can I call you Green?' He nodded. 'Okay, Mac and Green, Mum needs millions and millions of hugs and kisses or it's broccoli for tea.' You can't beat blatant threats when it comes to effective child-rearing.

They crossed the pool like tornadoes and smothered me in hugs, kisses and chlorinated water.

When they splashed off with Rex in tow, Mark waded over towards me. I expected him to quickly tap me in the manner of two wrestlers in a tag-team bout, then head inside to lose himself in the fascinating world of his email inbox, but instead he stopped at the edge, pulled himself up and sat next to me.

My brain immediately switched to the really important stuff – like . . . like . . . how incredibly fit he looked in those blue swim shorts.

'Good day?' I asked him, going for innocuous and cheery but probably hitting somewhere on the line between slightly deranged and bunny-boiler.

'Yeah, we had a great time – the boys just love Mother's Beach. Every time I suggest we go elsewhere they overrule me.'

Three things struck me about that sentence. Number one: Mark was being light-hearted. Number two: It was possibly the longest sentence he'd uttered to me all week. Make that 'month'. Number three: Years working in nightclubs in my wild youth had resulted in very minor damage to my hearing, but even with my reduced audio capacity I was pretty fucking sure he hadn't mentioned the words 'Mandy' or 'barbecue'.

A pause stretched out as I tried to work out the best way to formulate my next question. Unlike Mark, I have been known to occasionally tango with the big green monster. Not to an obsessive, private-detective-on-the-payroll level – I was more at the 'occasionally just happens to scroll through the messages on his mobile but of course I trust him' stage.

And it goes without saying that I checked his pockets before I took his suits to the dry-cleaners, but that's not suspicion, it's just loss prevention.

'So . . . Mandy?' Short, simple, and if you listened really clearly you could hear the slightest hint of aggressive undertones.

'Oh, one of the mothers who goes to the beach during the week. She decided to have a barbecue there today and we were invited.'

My danger radar was flashing like a strobe light. I could be wrong, but as far as I had ascertained, there was one crowd of women who went there during the week – all nannies, mums and grans – and a very different crowd who went at weekends. Today was Sunday, so why would one of the weekday mums make the effort to go on an extra day? Unless . . . Oh, I was writing too much – my imagination was on overdrive. I surreptitiously took a deep breath and shook off my cloak of doom. It was bound to be completely innocent. I'm sure there was a very simple explanation. And maybe Mandy was the one in her late fifties who was no stranger to KFC. I wouldn't even dignify this train of thought with any further discussion. None. It ended right there. Definitely.

'So is she the older lady who goes most days?' I asked casually.

'Erm, no. She's probably about late thirties.'

'Black hair?'

'No, blonde.'

'Married?'

'Single.'

'Little girl?'

'No, boy.' The feeling of fear was rising in my stomach and threatening to choke me. Dear God, if I never, ever ask you for anything again, please make his name be anything but Zac.

'Oh, the little boy called Joshua?' I asked.

'No, Zac.'

Zac. An obnoxious little brat who had scudded Benny with a fishing pole on our first day there. The one whose mother made armed robbers seem fairly inoffensive. And Charlize Theron look plain.

Sob. And now she was contriving to have romantic little tête-à-têtes with my husband.

'And the reason for her barbecue was . . . ?'

'Oh, it wasn't *her* barbecue,' he corrected me. 'Most of the women who go during the week were there too. Apparently they do this every now and then just for the social aspects. And because I'd been telling them you were working so hard they invited us too. It was great. The boys just love all their little pals down there now – they're going to be so upset when we leave.'

With that, he climbed up and wrapped a towel around himself. 'Anyway, better go and check my mail before you need to go back into the office. The kids won't need dinner – they ate late at the barbecue. And they each had two pieces of Mandy's banana bread.'

Off he went in the direction of the house, leaving my emotions on spin cycle, setting: high.

Emotion one: The jealousy that had subsided with the explanation that it was a barbecue en masse had peaked again with the news that the cow baked bread. I mean, please!

Emotion two: Gratitude – I still appreciated how Mark was helping me out.

Emotion three: Admiration. He seemed to have really got to grips with having the kids all day and was suddenly acting more chilled-out than I'd seen him in years. He was even integrating with strangers. And cows.

Emotion four: Surprise. We'd actually just had something approaching a fairly normal conversation between a married couple.

Emotion five: Dread. Complete and utter dread. He'd said those three little words.

When. We. Leave.

I knew I was going to have to confront that particular

little demon at some point, but I'd been fairly success-fully managing to avoid it so far.

Sure, I knew none of this life was real. This wasn't our home, or our cars, or our neighbourhood. Mac wasn't at preschool and Benny wasn't at nursery so we were living in a little blur of holiday fever. Mark wasn't trudging off to work every day so he was starting to emerge from his normal zombie-like state. Eliza wasn't mine. Although she would be when I drugged her, kidnapped her, then brainwashed her into thinking she must never again leave my side.

And I was Carly Cooper, skint, average author and naff columnist; not Carly Cooper, Hollywood screen-writer and woman of means.

Every single aspect of our current lives was an illu-sion, and definitely temporary. Mark was due to leave on Wednesday. That was only three days from now. Eliza had offered to look after the boys from then until I got the screenplay finished and delivered to Lee Stavorski six days later, but I couldn't possibly take advantage of all her time like that. I'd thought perhaps if she could watch them in the mornings then I could take over in the afternoons and then work again when they were in bed at night. It wouldn't be easy, but it was manageable as long as I got the majority of the work done while Mark was still here. Three more days. Three more days with my husband here. Which meant three more days until Sam came home. Nine days until I met Lee Stavorski again. And nine days until I learned my fate. In less than ten days' time my whole life could change beyond recognition. I could get a deal and thus a new life would be handed to me on a plate. I could get no deal – cue sound of plate smashing. I could go home. I could stay here. That might possibly lead to divorce, or it might not. I could possibly work out how I felt about Sam. I could decide to forget him and open my life up to completely new experiences. I could have a go at persuading Jojo to have a lipstick-lesbian affair with me. If I could find my make-up bag.

Or I could just admit defeat and slide back into my old life of suburban mediocrity. Good points: For one, I'd be back in the Wonderbra-adorned bosoms of my friends and would no longer be missing them desperately. Bad points: Too many to mention.

I shuddered – bugger it, my pals would visit. I'd rather chew my own nipples than go back. I'd had a taste of something so much more amazing and I wanted it so badly. Pandora's box hadn't just been opened, it had been cracked in half and then fed through a chipper.

A gush of water landed on me as the boys ventured over to my side of the pool again. I knew it was impossible, but they looked like they'd grown dramatically in the month that they'd been here. And despite being dipped in a vat of factor 50 ten times every day, they had a slight tint to their skin that made them look even more adorable. I didn't want to take them away from all this. LA wasn't the Promised Land – it had as many downsides as anywhere else – but this little nook of perfection that we lived in was such a great environment for them.

And if nothing else, the last month had convinced me, without one iota of a doubt, that I wanted to live somewhere sunny. So if it wasn't going to be LA then I'd have to find somewhere else that offered an outdoor life for them.

Of course, this was all just a pipe dream because without some kind of financial miracle we were back to domestic drudgery.

Actually, there was another way . . . Sam.

'Mum, what does extinct mean?' shouted the Green Goblin as he and Benny/Mac/Confused waded towards me.

'Why? Where did you hear that?' I replied, grateful to be called back to the real world.

They were almost at my feet by now. 'Mandy told us. When she gave me Rex she said that dinosaurs were extinct.'

My blood began to simmer – Gas Mark 5, leave for twenty minutes until uncontrollable jealousy boils over.

'Extinct means that there aren't any around any more – they're all dead.'

'How did they all die?' B/M/C asked, his eyes like saucers.

I motioned to them to come closer. They crept in, their intrigue almost tangible.

'If I tell you, do you promise to tell Mandy?' I stage-whispered.

They both nodded.

'You promise?' I repeated. 'You'll tell her the minute you get to the beach tomorrow?'

More nods.

'Okay, this is what happened. Once upon a time, there were only three dinosaurs left in the whole wide world. A mummy dinosaur, a daddy dinosaur and another lady dinosaur.'

Their mouths were wide open in anticipation.

'And then the very naughty lady dinosaur stole the daddy dinosaur, so the mummy dinosaur thumped her. Then the lady dinosaur ran away and the mummy dinosaur and the daddy dinosaur didn't make any more babies so no more dinosaurs were born.'

'Wow,' gasped Green.

'Did you get all that?' I checked.

They nodded furiously. 'The lady dinosaur stole the daddy dinosaur so the mummy dinosaur thumped her,' repeated Mac. I mean Green.

Christian names aside, how well did I know my son – he only ever remembered the beginning of any story.

'I bet Mandy would love to hear that story,' I reminded him.

'I'll tell her, Mum, I promise.'

CARLY CALLING . . .

Carol to Carly:

Cal misd me so he's flown ovr here –
we're goin 2 hav 2nd honeymoon. Ur
brothr is amazing!

Carly:

bog off, u smug boot.

Carol:

So glad that u r sharing in my happiness ...

Carly:

Hope u get cystitis.

Carol:

Aw, knife thro heart. But I kno ur havin hard time so I wont rub it in. Did I tell you he brought me diamond eternity ring and swore undying love?

Carly:

I've nevr likd u. Pls don't contact me again til ur life is in toilet and I can gloat. Thank u.

★ Step Fifteen ★

'Mandy sent this banana bread home for you. She baked it herself,' Mark said when they returned from the beach on Tuesday night. He handed it over to me and I plonked it down on the kitchen worktop.

'Oh, how sweet of her,' I enthused. 'I love banana bread. The people here are just *so* friendly.'

'You know, I've found the very same thing,' he agreed.

'Oh, I bet you have, honey,' I said, reaching up to give him a peck on the cheek. I suddenly caught myself. Jesus, when had we started pecking? Pecking was what your granny did to you at Christmas, leaving a trail of Avon scarlet lipstick that didn't come off until Boxing Day. Or was that just mine?

'I'm just going into the office – won't be long,' he announced.

Mac and Benny had climbed up at the breakfast bar, which had probably required the entire annual marble output of a small Italian quarry to produce.

'Boys, did you tell Mandy the dinosaur story?' I whispered.

302

They nodded.

'Yesterday, like you told us,' Mac confirmed.

Ah, explained a lot. As soon as their backs were turned I slipped the banana bread into the waste disposal. I was willing to bet my one pair of designer jeans that she'd spat in that while she was making it. Oh, she was playing dirty, I just knew it.

'Guys, listen, tonight is Dad's last night, so what do you say we treat him to our very, very favourite thing.'

'Pizza!' they shouted in unison, with beaming grins that made them look like the precocious kids on the adverts for diarrhoea medication that seemed to run on American television on a perpetual basis.

I raided one of the drawers for the pizza menu and called in an order. Mark appeared at my back as I hung up the phone.

'So what's for tea tonight then?' he asked.

'Well,' I replied huskily as I wrapped my arms around his neck. It was his last night – I was going for ten out of ten for effort. 'I thought that since it was your last night, me and the boys would treat you to some pizza.'

I reached up to kiss him – and we're talking a full-scale, sink-plunging snog – when he whipped his head around to face the boys, and instead of lip-locking passion I got ear-wax inhalation.

'My last night?' he asked the boys, his eyebrows raised. Oh, this wasn't good. We all knew that my eyebrows were the main disciplinary force in this family – for Mark to put his into action meant a serious misdemeanour had been committed.

Both the boys had their heads bowed and were

slinking down off their seats, imitating the general demeanour of a serial killer who had been caught with suspicious-looking chops in the fridge.

'What's going on?' I asked, baffled.

'Run for it,' Mac shouted to Benny before they took off like said serial killer was behind them.

The minute they disappeared out of sight, Mark burst into fits of giggles. *Giggles*. And outside there was a blue moon, it was raining frogs and Elvis was cleaning the pool.

'What?' I spluttered. The giggles were infectious and I was having one of those bizarre moments where you're in fits of laughter but you've absolutely no idea what the joke is.

'This isn't my last night.'

'It isn't?' The shock killed the laughter. So what did that mean? He'd decided to stay? He'd decided that we were all going to stay here and take our chances in the Tinseltown crapshoot?

'I've postponed my flight . . .'

Okay, so it wasn't cancelled. But postponed was good. Postponed was *great*. Another month or so here should give me time to make some kind of progress on the career front.

'. . . until Sunday . . .'

Sunday? He'd postponed the flight for a *whole* four days.

'. . . and I'd already told the boys so they knew fine well that tonight wasn't my last night – they just lied for the pizza, little buggers.'

Why was he still laughing? Could he not see that the

four presidents carved into the rock at Mount Rushmore had more expression on their faces than I did at that very moment?

My face was a frozen, immobile mask. I was Melanie bloody Griffith after a Botox top-up.

'So why postpone the flight? Why Sunday?' I interrupted his little bout of isolated hilarity-for-one.

'Because I thought you could do with another couple of days to focus on your script. But work-wise I could only swing the rest of the week. The partners are already grumbling that I've been away for so long.' He reached into the fridge and took out a beer. 'Honestly, Carly, there's shitloads of stuff piling up – I'm going to be working round the clock for the next month. Still, at least we'll be back to some semblance of normality by then.'

'What do you mean?'

This was bizarre. Mark was chatting like this was a casual, everyday conversation, whereas I had all the levity of lead. He was being so completely matter-of-fact.

'Because if you're coming home next Wednesday . . .'

What? At what point had I said that I was coming home next Wednesday?

'. . . then we'll be back into our old routine within a few weeks. I tell you something, though, I'm definitely going to make some changes.'

Okay, I'm listening. Did they involve radical lifestyle alterations and long-distance haulage?

'I'm definitely, definitely not working on Saturdays any more. At least, unless it's absolutely necessary –

which it will be until I clear my backlog. But after that weekends are going to be strictly family time.'

I momentarily wondered if there was a way that I could get Mandy's skanky banana bread out of the waste disposal and ram it down his throat.

'Mark, stop! Just stop!'

He spun around, taken aback by the vehemence in my tone.

'Mark, what makes you think I'm coming home next Wednesday?'

He looked stunned. 'Because . . . because that's when your return ticket is booked for! And because you'll have had your meeting by then and you'll know the result of that.'

'Mark, tickets can be changed. I booked the return date before I even got here, but things are different now. I've made progress! What if they offer to buy my book? And my script? You expect me to just get on a plane and come straight home?'

The temperature in the room had just plummeted by about twenty degrees. Freak LA weather conditions.

'Carly, you may not have noticed, but this is the technological age. You could write the rest of the script at home. If you were commissioned to do more work, you could do that at home too. That's why email was invented.' His voice was absolutely calm, absolutely cool.

I, on the other hand, felt like I was in a sauna in the Arctic – a chilly atmosphere, but I was sweating like a stuck pig and just as happy.

'Mark, I don't want to go home next Wednesday. If you ever bloody spoke to me you'd know that I don't

306

want to go home. At all. I want to stay. I want this – this life! Or at least to give it a damn good go. I don't want to come back next week, next month or maybe even next bloody year!'

He looked like I'd slapped him. Then, after an interminable silence, during which I had to grind my teeth together not to barrage him with all the reasons that he was being a total twat, he spoke.

'Carly, you are living in a dream world.'

'I know! And I bloody like it here.'

'Carly, how can we live in LA? Huh? Come on then, Miss I Want to Live in Hollywood – give me your grand master-plan!'

There was a slight problem with that request – i.e. distinct lack of plan, grand master or otherwise.

'I haven't fully worked it out yet,' I declared defiantly.

'Well, there's a surprise. Carly, there is no plan! If you stay here you have no guaranteed income. None. And I can't come and work here because, although it might have escaped your notice, I'm a lawyer. I practise British law. British law that's been totally and completely bloody irrelevant in America since the fourth of July 1776.' I hated that he did that. I hated that he could summon up historical facts and throw them into arguments whenever it suited him. Only the other day he had the language skills of Benny, and now he was suddenly Mr Eloquent 2007. And he was still speaking . . .

'Thus I couldn't get a job, we couldn't support our family, and last time I checked they did not allow you to live here for free. And don't even get me started on immigration requirements, but I will point out that your tourist visa only lasts for three months.'

'But if I worked for a studio they could help me get one for longer. That's what happened to Sam.'

'Carly, Sam didn't have two kids and a partner with a job that wasn't transferable. I cannot come and live here. Ever. Unless we were completely financially independent and had a million quid tucked away in the bank. And let me tell you, we're pretty far away from that at the moment – about a million quid away, to be exact.' So much for the ceasefire.

'And I hate to point out another small flaw in your plan, but you don't work for a studio.'

'But I might.'

He was getting really frustrated now. There was a vein in the side of his neck that was bulging like a beach ball.

'And Mac needs to get back – what about school?'

'They have schools here.'

'Carly, I'm not even going to discuss this any more,' he announced angrily. Then, in a gentler tone, 'I'm not denying this is a great life, Carly. But it's not our life.'

He spun on his heel and marched off.

I slumped against the worktop. He was right. This wasn't our life. But I wanted it to be. And it wasn't even for the money or the flash houses. To be honest, I wouldn't have cared if we lived in a one-bedroom shack on the beach. Not that there *were* any of those – this was LA, not Bora Bora – but you get my meaning. I just loved the excitement of all this. The sheer bloody madness of it. And when I was 102 and lying on my deathbed in the nursing home next to Mark, I knew that if I hadn't at least tried my damnedest to go for the life I'd always dreamed of then my dying words to him would involve profanity and castigation.

The buzzer for the security system kicked into life. I checked the screen to see a teenager in a baseball cap and a Dominos uniform clutching a pizza.

I pressed the button.

'Pizza delivery,' he announced. 'I've got a sixteen-inch Celebration with extra everything.'

I bet he wowed the ladies down the disco on a Saturday night with that chat-up line.

I buzzed him in. I just hoped the boys were hungry, because I'd suddenly lost my appetite.

We have much to be grateful for in this world. Technological advances. The wonder of modern medicine. And the complete and utter lifesaver that is *Scooby-Doo*. We all crashed out in the den, pizza on the coffee table, and *Scooby-Doo* valiantly masked the fact that Mark and I couldn't even look at each other.

It was a relief when the pesky kids triumphed and I packed my two off to bed. Mark had already left the room by the time I returned. Sod him. I didn't even want to talk to him. I headed straight for the office and sat down to work, an act that was hindered slightly by the fact that I was in the middle of writing a comedy scene, and right at that moment I felt about as funny as botulism.

I slogged on until the early hours, then capitulated

to the need for contact with a human being who actually liked me. I texted Sam, who was still languishing in the sheer bloody deprivation of a palatial villa on the banks of Lake Como.

'Mark now leaving Sunday. Sorry.'

Concise. Apologetic.

Half an hour later the reply came back. Strange. Sam always answered almost instantaneously. He was the only person I have ever seen texting with his index finger – and a super-fast one at that. It was a talent he'd acquired in his last job by . . . nope, didn't even want to go there.

'No problem. U ok?'

'No.'

I definitely wasn't okay.

'U want me 2 come home?'

Did I? I thought about it for a moment. I did. I wanted some fun. I wanted some laughs. I wanted to chat to someone who was interested. I wanted someone to help me get from page ten of my script to page thirty and check that it wouldn't get me laughed out of town.

But I had to be realistic – if Sam came home just now the atmosphere in the house would be unbearable. And it was already unbearable enough.

My phone beeped again. Since I hadn't replied, Sam must have thought there was a problem with the message and re-sent it.

'U want me 2 come home?'

'No,' I replied. Then I suddenly had the thought that since this was actually *his* five-million-dollar palatial pad we were dossing in, that answer probably wasn't

the best one. It was like we were holding his house in a siege situation.

'*I mean, YES. It's ur house. Sorry. Brain addled, not thinking str8.*'

A message came right back. '*Think I'll stay here another few days. Will come back Monday.*'

Monday. Five more days. One day before I met with Lee Stavorski again. That meant one hour for Sam to read my script, two minutes to break it gently to me that it was crap, forty-five minutes for me to have a complete meltdown, and twenty-two hours and thirteen minutes for me to frantically rewrite it. Doddle.

I poured another of my endless cups of coffee, flicked the computer off standby and started typing again. Sitting worrying about this wasn't going to get it done.

I just had to focus, forget about all the turmoil, mainline some more high-grade caffeine and keep typing.

And phone my pals for moral support. Kate answered on the third ring.

'Kate, it's me. I'm going to tell you what's happened and you have to swear that you'll take my side, defend my motivations, and say "Mark – what a prick he is!" every time I stop for breath.'

'I'm good on the second one, but a bit shaky on numbers one and three – do you want to hang up and go phone one of your other best pals?' I got the distinct impression she wasn't taking this seriously.

Miraculously, for the woman who usually defends my husband at all costs, I got all the way to the end of the story without her telling me that I was being unreasonable, harsh and bloody-minded.

'So there you go – what do you think?' I asked her after an outpouring that would have put a daytime talk show to shame.

'I think you're being unreasonable, harsh and bloody-minded.'

'Why?' I replied petulantly. Okay, really I knew why – I was stubborn, not thick – but I figured hearing it from someone else might help with absorption and acceptance.

'Carly, he came all the way over there. He's watched the boys for a whole week on his own. My Bruce struggles to get my three dressed in the morning. Now he's delayed his flight back to help you even more. He's absolutely right about moving over there or anywhere else that he can't work. You'd end up spending your life on the corner of a junction holding up a sign saying "WILL WRITE FOR FOOD".'

'I have got money.'

'Where?'

'On my credit cards. I've one with a ten-grand limit that I haven't even used yet. And there's a grand of credit left on my secret one too.'

'Carly, credit cards do *not* count, on the grounds that Visa, MasterCard and American Express are not in the habit of donating money. And I understand that this is your dream, honey, but maybe it's just not your time yet.'

'It'll never be my time if I don't take a chance on this, Kate.'

312

'It will. You're getting there. Look how far you've come already – a month in Hollywood and they're already letting you past security. They obviously don't know about your criminal record.'

'I was seven, it was pickled onion crisps and they let me off with a caution. After I'd cried a lot.'

'Yeah, you were lucky. Anyway, don't be too harsh on Mark – this is all hard for him too. He just wants his wife back.'

'She's gone. I stabbed her to death with a kebab skewer after too much time waiting in the pissing rain for buses to come sent me into a psychotic frenzy.'

'Ah the road to crime. One day shoplifting, the next day murder with a kebab skewer. Happens all the time. Anyway, I have to run – some of us do actually have to work for a living. Go be nice to your husband. And tell him he owes me another large kitchen tool for acting as his official PR manager once again.'

'Okay, the yoghurt-maker is yours. His mother gave me it for Christmas last year. I never liked her.'

There was laughter, then silence. I missed Kate. I missed Carol. I missed my brother Cal. And Michael. I even missed my mother.

But much as I missed them all, I wasn't ready to go home. No matter what Mark said.

I looked down at my computer screen. Page thirty. Twenty more to go. Twenty pages of script that I was sure an experienced screenwriter could rattle off on his lunch break.

'Experienced' being the key word there – I was

getting a migraine just thinking about it. Although that could have just been a reaction to too much coffee.

Migraine or no migraine, I had to keep going. Because if there was one thing, *one thing*, that was going to save me in all of this, it was the success of this script. I just had to keep my head down and my spirits up – the latter of which would probably be aided by avoiding my husband as much as possible. I knew Mark was right. I knew he was sensible. I knew he was being a responsible adult.

But I was going to be a screenwriter.

And the last time I checked, that was a lot more fun than being a grown-up.

'Mum, I never want to be a grown-up.'

'Why not, honey?'

'Because you have to do really yucky things.'

'Like what?'

'Like clean up when Benny pees the bed. And eat baspargarus . . .'

'Asparagus.'

'That's what I said. Baspargarus.'

'Okay. And what else?'

'And kiss girls. Yuk! I hate girls.'

'I'll remind you that you said that when you're eighteen.'

'Why?'

'Don't ask. I'm your mother, by that time embarrassing you will be my full-time job.'

'Daddy kisses Mandy.'

Ziiiiiiiiiiiiiiiip! Rewind. *Daddy kissed . . . ?*

'What was that, honey?'

'Daddy kissed Mandy.'

'Where?'

'On the b—'

Fuck me dead, I was about to have a heart attack.

'Beach.'

Oh, thank God. Bottom or boob would have put me in casualty.

'No, I mean, *where* did he kiss her. On the lips?'

'What name shall I have today, Mummy? Have I been Doctor Octopus before?'

Curse small children with the attention span of something that lives in a bowl.

'Yes, you have. So where did he kiss her?'

'Doctor Octopus doesn't kiss girls,' he said in a 'duh, I can't believe you didn't know that' voice.

I counted to ten. I did it in time with my heartbeat so it was over in about 2.3 seconds.

'Where. Did. Daddy. Kiss. Mandy?'

There. Even Mac couldn't misinterpret that one. I squeezed my eyes shut tight, fearful of the answer. How had I managed to go from eating baspargarus to a potentially life-changing moment in less time than it took to make a cup of tea? I could hear Oprah's voice in the background. 'So, Carly, how did you first find out that your husband had been unfaithful?'

'There.'

I opened my eyes, but Mac's hands were already back down on the worktop. Shit, I'd missed it. Where? Where did he point to?

'Do that again, Mac.'

'Nope.'

'No telly for a week,' I warned.

'Oh, okay. It was there.' He pointed to his cheek. Relief. Sweet, giddy, sodding relief. I felt faint.

'What was there?' came a voice from the doorway. I turned around just as Mark came in with a holdall over his shoulder.

'Oh, nothing. Mac was just telling me a story about Doctor Octopus.'

'Mum's telling lies!' said Mac with an astonished gasp.

I threw him the glare of death. He clammed up immediately and automatically searched for the nearest exit.

I turned to face Mark. 'So . . . you're ready?'

'Yep, taxi will be here any minute.'

Silence.

'Thanks. For coming here, I mean. And for staying longer.'

I tried my hardest to make it sound like I meant it, and deep down I did. Really, really deep down. On a surface level, where I much preferred to exist, I was still annoyed with him for going home at all. I was sure he could have swung another week, another fortnight even, but when I'd put this to him the night before, in the only proper conversation we'd had since the blow-out on Tuesday, he'd been really dismissive.

'And then what, Carly? Another three weeks? Another four? It'll never be enough. You want to live here and it's not possible. And if I stay here any longer then the work piles up even more at home and so do the debts.

My company appreciates me, but I think paying me while I'm swanning it up thousands of miles away might stretch their appreciation just a little too far.'

The buzzer went on the security system.

'Good luck with the meeting on Tuesday. Let me know how it goes.'

'I will.'

I could feel the tears welling up. Don't cry. Don't cry. Don't ... go. Please don't go. He wouldn't leave us. I just knew he wouldn't. He was bluffing. Wasn't he?

'Better go.'

Wrong again.

He scooped up Mac while I shouted to Benny, who tore himself away from a *Scooby-Doo* omnibus and wandered through. When he saw that Mark was leaving he burst into tears.

'Don't go, Daddy, me miss you.' He threw his arms around Mark's leg. Ever the drama queen, Mac decided that since there was an inkling of the theatrical, he was going to join in too. The two of them were clutching on to Mark, sobbing their hearts out and refusing to let go.

Where the hell had this come from? When we left the UK they'd been positively nonchalant about leaving their daddy for a few weeks, and now they were clinging on to him like he was their life source.

But I was still holding it together. Just. I was taking my mind off the emotion of the situation by wondering if Sam had a crowbar in the garage that would prise small children from a departing parent, when I suddenly caught Mark's face. Or, rather, the huge big tear that was running down it.

I had never, *never* in my life seen Mark Barwick cry. Never. Not even when John Potts battered him with an ice-hockey stick back in 1982. Or when he'd crashed his Ford Cortina into next-door's lamppost the week after he passed his driving test in 1985.

Everything stopped. Everything came to a crashing halt, as my husband bowed his head and used his shoulder to wipe away the moisture from his cheek.

I just wanted to reach out and pull him towards me, to tell him that everything was going to be okay and that I loved him. I wanted to, I really did.

Right up until the moment that he sniffed really loudly and said, 'Come on, guys, don't be sad. Daddy has to go back and go to work, but don't worry, I'll see you when you get home.'

He raised his head and stared straight at me.

'When you get home on Wednesday.'

'Wednesday?' said Mac, not comprehending the implications. 'How many sleeps?'

'Three sleeps,' said Mark.

'Three sleeps!' Mac repeated, then burst into tears again. 'I. Don't. Want. To. Go. Home.'

That's my boy. I knew exactly how he felt. And, of course, Benny, whose sole purpose in life was to copy everything his big brother said and did, immediately launched into a chorus of 'I don't want to go home' too.

I lifted Benny up and put him on one hip, then scooped Mac off Mark and on to the other hip. Mark was still staring at me, as if trying to read my thoughts.

It was easy, but I decided to help him out anyway.

Mac didn't want to go home. Benny didn't want to go home.

'I don't want to go home either,' I whispered. There. I'd said it. I'd finally said it.

Mark's eyes fell to his shoes and stayed there for a few excruciatingly long seconds. Eventually, he lifted his head.

'You know what you're saying? What this will do to us?'

I bit my lip so hard I tasted blood. And not in a good way.

Then . . . then I nodded.

Without another word, he turned and left. Just like that. Gone.

But even as huge big fat tears ran down my face, I knew I'd done the right thing. Even if the cost of staying might be a high price to pay.

Family Values *Magazine*

PUTTING THE YUMMY IN MUMMY
THIS WEEK ...
THE SEXUAL SOUL WITHIN

We've got so much to thank those Sex and the City *girls for! The fashion, the lifestyle trends, and most of all – the sex talk! Oh yes, ladies, say it loud and say it proud (checking first to make sure the housekeeper is not within earshot) – 'I have a clitoris and I know how to find it.'*

Sadly, however, many men still need a flashlight and a diagram – so, girls, the time has come to take control. No more unsatisfactory fumbles with the lights out. No more lying back and thinking of Harvey Nicks. Leave the missionary position to those who choose a career in religious service.

Take control of cunnilingus, organise your orgasms and titillate your tickly bits – and if you don't have the equipment necessary for that last suggestion then it can be purchased very discreetly from several high-profile internet sites.

Yes, the days when the only rabbit in the house was soft, furry and wore a Dior collar are long gone. Let's throw off those inhibitions and revel in the physical delights of a great sex life. Gone are the days when we waited for our partners to initiate intercourse. When husband comes home tonight, surprise him by answering the door wearing nothing but Chanel No. 5. Seduce him in the shower, join him in the Jacuzzi, attack him on the Aga – and as for the window-seat? I'll leave that one to your naughty imaginations!

Oh, the advantages are endless – the radiant glow, the satisfied partner, the inner contentment. But the best part? You guessed it, girls – sex burns off 550 calories an hour. Now there's a fitness regime with additional perks!

★ Step Sixteen ★

I always wondered what the Earth would be like after Armageddon and now I knew. As I stumbled out into the new world, I squinted against the sun, my eyes unused to the light after all that time spent locked in isolated semi-darkness. I stumbled on, up through the dense foliage, until I encountered another life form, one that bore a terrifying resemblance to a creature from another long-ago time.

Okay, so his name was Rex, he was plastic, and the foliage was nothing more threatening than the land-scaped gardens around Sam's pool, but the fact remains that I'd finally, finally, after what seemed like centuries, been released from Sam's office. I'd finished the script. Finished it. Drum-roll and trumpets please.

'Hi, Carly, how's it going?' Eliza, chief cook, babysitter and Nobel Peace Prize nominee shouted over to me. That woman was a genius. She'd managed to keep the boys occupied and on the non-violent side of brother-ly interaction for over 24 hours.

'I finished, Eliza, I finished!' was my joyous reply, before giving her a huge hug.

'Oh, that's great, Carly. Sam will be so pleased too. He just called to say he'd be here in five minutes.'

I blew kisses to the boys in the pool and told them that they had five more minutes to play before it would be time to change for tea, then made my way out to the front door.

When Sam came into sight, the huge involuntary grin on my face was matched only by the huge grin on his. The break had obviously suited him. He was tanned, bright-eyed and his hair was even blonder. He was physical perfection in the shape of six foot and two inches of hunka hunka burnin' love.

I was standing at the door as he got out of the car and I had a momentary glimmer of discomfort. What was the etiquette in situations like this? Should I run over, hug him and generally treat him in the manner of someone returning from a tour of duty?

Should I casually say hi and give him a quick peck on the cheek? I was, after all, very practised in the pecking department.

Or should I take off all my clothes, lie down in the hallway and make his entrance particularly spectacular? I would like to point out that that particular suggestion was brought to the party by the organs in my reproductive area.

I went for big hug, small kiss on lips and a continuation of the huge grin.

'Where are the boys?' he asked.

'Pool with Eliza.'

'Mark gone?'

'Yes.' Our gaze held for a few moments. Nope, I wasn't

ready for this. I'd only just broken out of incarceration and discovered a brave new world; I was still far too traumatised to deal with emotional entanglements. I swiftly changed the subject. 'So, how was the trip? What was the house like? Describe the toilets and who else was there?'

That's what I loved about Sam – he described things, places and events like a girl. If it had been Mark, the answer would have been 'fine', 'great', 'functional' and 'never noticed'. Sam, however, went into full chapter and glorious verse on every detail. I listened with utter fascination, devouring every word, until he mentioned that Cameron King had joined them.

'Cameron King, as in Jojo's boyfriend?' I asked him.

'Yep. Think things are a bit rocky there, though – he's decided to direct my next movie and she's not too chuffed about it.'

Now I was totally confused.

'But I thought you told me that Bob Slazer was directing your next movie?'

'He was. Past tense. Creative differences with the studio so he's opted out. That's the way it is in this town – everyone is dispensable and every project is liable to go tits-up at any moment. That's why people here are, in the majority, barking. Anyway, Cameron's signed up now, but Jojo's not pleased, even though he's got her contracted to run make-up.'

'But why? All those months away in a glamorous location . . . sounds fabulous to me.'

Honestly, some people just didn't know when they had it good.

'They've moved shooting to Serbia.'

Oh. Well, thermals could be fashionable.

We wandered outside to see the boys. I shoved my hands deep in my pockets in a bid to fight off an overwhelming urge to hold his hand.

The boys' feelings, however, were a little more straightforward.

'UNCLE SAM!!!!' they screamed. Glazing companies suddenly got a huge rush of business as windows shattered all over Pacific Palisades.

They clamoured out of the pool, rushed over and gave him the full 'jumping up and down until bladder control was threatened' welcome. And they couldn't wait to show off Rex.

'Wow, guys, he's great! Did Mum get him for you?'

'Nope, Mandy. And Daddy kissed Mandy.'

Sam looked at me quizzically.

'Don't ask,' I told him dismissively.

'Right, boys, who wants fajitas for dinner?' Eliza asked.

'Yeeeeeaaaah,' they chorused.

'Pardon?' I prompted sternly.

'Yeeeeeaaaah pleeease!' they replied.

If they were going to speak like they were Californian surf dudes, then they could at least do it politely.

Sam and I dried off the boys, helped them get changed, and then we all had dinner together. Or at least, they all ate. I couldn't. Nerves had kicked in. Terror had settled. If I decided to start a new life in the brave new world, was I going to be able to earn a living there?

*   *   *

'Ladies and gentlemen of the jury, in the case of Hollywood versus Carly Cooper, for the crime of "Writing a script that's fit for the shredder" – do you find Ms Cooper guilty or not guilty?'

Silence. Fifty pages of script. Two weeks' worth of work. Several new stress-induced wrinkles. And now it was crunch time. The verdict.

I stared at Sam – not exactly a hardship, but at that moment it was the scariest sight in the world. He was bowing over the script and hadn't moved for the last ten minutes. I wondered if he'd fallen asleep. After all, I did have a previous history of men nodding off at vital moments.

Finally, after another few minutes that lasted at least a week and a half, he raised his head and smiled. 'It's good.'

'Good?' Was that like 'nice'? Or 'lovely'? Because if so I'd be really disappointed because I was definitely going for fan-fucking-tastic.

'Fantastic, in fact,' Sam said with a grin.

And the verdict was in! Not guilty! It was good. Fantastic. Yee-hah, as they say in some American counties where first cousins are allowed to marry.

'Really?' I replied.

'Really. But it still needs a few minor tweaks. Nothing we won't be able to sort out before you meet Stavorski, though.'

Tweaks were good. Tweaks I could do. I was overcome with a huge burst of adrenalin and happiness. I'd done it. I'd actually written a script. Okay, half of one. Two weeks of blood, sweat and buckets of tears and it was done.

I suddenly realised that my body position had changed. From sitting upright on a big overstuffed chair in Sam's office, I'd been catapulted across the room and was now practically sitting on top of him on the sofa, hugging him like my life depended on it.

'Thank you, thank you, thank you! I love you!' I squealed with sheer bloody happiness. Then my brain caught up with what my bionic gob was saying and pressed the intruder alarms, causing all power to the gums and lips to shut down. I stared at him, my mouth stuck open, nothing coming out.

'Do you?' he asked gently.

Was this it? Was this the moment where my ostrich head had to come out of that sand and face the realities of our changing relationship?

Nope.

The emergency generator kicked in and I regained my speech motor functions.

'Sam, don't. Not now. It's all too . . . complicated.'

'You're right, I'm sorry. I don't know why I said that. I'd made my mind up that I wasn't going to say a single word about us unless you raised it first. I still feel crap about this situation, Carly. I feel crap about Mark, I feel crap about you being all churned up. I'm sorry.'

'Muuuuuuuum. Darth Vader kicked me,' came an indignant shriek from the telly room.

'Darth Vader?' Sam asked me.

'Yep, he went over to the dark side. I actually miss the whole Superhero thing – Benny has not sung once since Mac changed sides because none of the villains have their own theme tunes. It's tragic and blatantly

327

unfair. I think it calls for union involvement – get the bad guys a tune and some better PR.'

The phone rang and Sam answered it while I went off to check on whether or not Benny still had all of his limbs. The guys were sitting at either side of the sofa, enjoying their post-dinner TV hour. I plonked down in the middle of them and they both automatically switched the way that they were leaning so that they snuggled into me. I'd never stop feeling lucky. All those years of fertility treatment and despair, and now I had not one but two gorgeous little boys. And I would never, never take them for granted.

I kissed the tops of their heads. They didn't even raise their eyes from the screen – good to see that their male genes were functioning normally.

There had been a definite difference in their demeanour today. Apart from their spectacular welcoming committee for their favourite uncle, they seemed a bit lethargic, a bit less sparkly than normal. I put it down to the fact that they'd been by Sam's pool all day with Eliza instead of racing around with all their pals down at Mother's Beach. They were having withdrawal symptoms. That was it, withdrawal symptoms.

'I miss Daddy, Mummy,' murmured Mac.

'I know, Darthie, I miss him too.' I did. When I wasn't busy with the whole uncontrollable sulks and petulance thing.

Sam wandered in, phone in hand. 'It's Ike – he wants to speak to you too.'

I took the phone. 'Hi Ike,' I said warmly. I liked Ike. True, I'd only actually met him once, but his occasional phone calls of one hundred per cent pure optimism and encouragement had gone a long way to sustain me over the last fortnight.

'So I hear the script's done and it's brilliant. Genius!'

I laughed. 'So Mr Morton tells me. He may just be trying to save my feelings, though – there's nothing worse than a disappointed woman.'

'Honey, I wouldn't know,' he replied, sending me into peals of laughter. You couldn't beat confidence.

'Okay, babe, so I'm getting back into town tomorrow afternoon, so as soon as you're finished with Stavorski, call me.'

'I will,' I promised.

'And good luck. Not that you need it – you'll blow him away.'

And I thought that kind of stuff didn't go on any more. Still, if that's what it took . . .

'Ready?' Sam asked.

I nodded, smiled and shouted, 'Yep, let's do it!'

In my mind.

In reality I shook my head, grimaced and said, 'Put your foot down and keep going, I've changed my mind.'

He laughed and turned off the ignition. 'Go on, it'll be great. *You'll* be great. You'll have Stavorski eating out of your hand.'

Ooh, mental image, foul taste in mouth.

We were sitting outside the security gates at GMG Studios and my heart was beating so loudly I sounded like the drum section on a parade. This was it. I was about to face a life-defining moment. The next hour could change the whole course of my entire life. And I was so glad that Sam was there with me offering support and gentle encouragement.

'Carly, if you don't get out the car, I'm going to have to drag you. Now go. Go, you mad woman.'

Gentle.

I took a deep breath. 'Okay, wish me luck,' I said.

He leaned over and kissed my cheek in a purely platonic way. After his little outburst the day before, he'd been a paragon of model behaviour right up until we fell into bed (separately) at 2 a.m. after a few hours of tweaking. Platonic tweaking. Sam's suggestions had been perceptive and the script was all the better for it. In fact as far as I could tell, it might even be, as Sam said, quite good. This morning he'd been supportive and sweet. He'd even told me I was gorgeous despite the fact that I hadn't recruited the services of the lovely Jojo. I felt she'd helped me enough and I didn't want to take advantage of her generosity. Unfortunately, the result was I looked like Mac had given me a quick blow-dry and Benny had applied my make-up.

'Good luck,' he said. 'I'm not going to be far away – just meeting Jojo for a coffee down on Wilshire Boulevard, so buzz me as soon as you come out and I'll come back for you.'

I nodded, then climbed out. I pulled out Sam's very poshest briefcase from the back of the car. He'd insisted I take it as a good-luck charm.

I waved him goodbye and blew him a kiss, then straightened up. Okay. This was it. I was a cosmopolitan woman of the world and I was about to crack Hollywood. With my thighs, if necessary.

Head up, shoulders back, hips a-swayin' and strut, strut, strut over to the security booth.

'Good morning again,' I said to the same security guard who'd been on shift when I last visited. He obviously had absolutely no recollection of ever meeting me. Well, I was Carly Cooper, not Sharon Stone.

That thought suddenly gave me another idea for persuasive negotiating tactics, but damn! I was wearing trousers.

'Just one moment please,' said security man, then he tapped, tapped, tapped on his computer. A thrill was gurgling away in my stomach. I was nearly there. My moment of truth . . .

'Er, sorry, Ms Cooper, but could you have a seat for a moment over there please?'

He directed me to two little seats on the opposite wall of the booth. This hadn't happened last time. Oh well, probably just a computer malfunction.

Security man picked up the phone and dialled a number. I was out of earshot so I couldn't quite make out what he was saying. A minute later, he replaced the handset and came over to me.

'Ma'am, you're definitely waiting to see Mr Stavorski?'

I nodded.

'I'm afraid Mr Stavorski isn't available today.' Oh, bollocks. All that build-up, all that work, all that unnecessary neurotic worry and now the bloody twat was off sick.

'Oh, that's okay,' I replied with a smile – after all, it wasn't the security guard's fault that my life ambition had just been trampled on by Danny DeVito's wee brother.

'I'll call his secretary later to reschedule,' I told him.

'Ma'am, I don't think that will be possible. You see, Mr Stavorski doesn't work here any more.'

For the second time in a month, in front of an innocent, unsuspecting security guard, I had a desperate urge to put my head between my knees.

'Honey, I don't fucking believe it! He was fired. Studio thought he'd lost his edge. Only just got back into the office and found out myself.'

'So what does that mean, Ike? We need to wait for his replacement to take a look at my script?'

There was an ominous silence.

I was Carly Cooper, twenty storeys up on the metaphorical Hollywood high-rise, hanging on for dear life and desperate not to fall and land with a resounding thump on my arse. My ten fingers were clinging on by a thread.

'Actually, it doesn't work that way, honey.'

Nine fingers.

'But why? Do you mean it'll go on hold?'

'Erm, no. That's not how it works either.'

Eight fingers.

'Carly, as far as GMG are concerned you were Lee Stavorski's project. Now he's on the highway, and that means you are too. No one else in that studio will touch you now.'

Seven fingers.

Think. Think. This could *not* be the end of my American dream. No! It just bloody couldn't. Hang on, hang on . . .

'Ike, we've still got Juliet Brookstein. She said she'd come back to us with an answer this week.'

See! There was still hope.

Silence. Oh crap, six fingers.

'Honey, there was a message from Juliet waiting for me when I got back today.'

Flat tone, no cheer whatsoever.

Five fingers.

'She says she loves it. Loves it. But her board has decided to pass on this one.'

Four fingers.

'But, but, they make loads of rom coms, so perhaps I could show them my other book. Maybe they'd buy that one, Ike, it's great!'

Desperation had taken over completely and I was now panicking big-time.

Three fingers.

'Sorry, Carly, they think rom coms are over. They've decided to diversify into reality TV.'

Two fingers.

'Any other ideas, Ike? Anything?'

One finger.

'Honey, I think we've just got to put this one down to experience. We've made progress. People know who you are now. And I think it's time to put this one aside and come back from a different angle. Maybe write another book, or finish that script and I'll pass that around. But this deal, honey? I think this one is dead for now.'

Splat.

'But hey, don't be disheartened, babe, there's always next time.'

I snapped my phone shut. Goodbye, Cliché Man.

My whole body felt numb. Apart from my stomach, which was going like a hamster on a spinning wheel and a diet of E-numbers.

That was it. It was over. I'd finally woken up from the Hollywood dream.

I wanted to cry. I really, really wanted to cry. Then I noticed I already was. And I was also starting to attract strange looks from passers-by.

I opened my phone again and pressed a speed-dial key. Sam answered straight away.

'Sam, please come and get me. No. I'll tell you later. Just come for me, please. I want to go home. Home to your house.'

CARLY CALLING . . .

Fastphone to Ms. C. Cooper:

Sorry to inform you that you have exceeded your call and message limit for this month. Please call Fastphone customer services to increase your account limit. Further usage will not be allowed until this issue has been rectified.

Thank you, Fastphone Customer Services.

★ Step Seventeen ★

'You sure you don't want me to come?' Sam asked. 'I'm happy to cancel my meetings this morning.'

I shook my head. 'Thanks, Sam, but to be honest I'd quite like to spend some time with the boys on my own. I've missed them the last couple of weeks.'

It was the morning after the day before. Twenty-four hours ago I'd been beside myself with excitement at what the day could bring. Now all my day held in store was contemplation, a repetitive strain injury on my Frisbee arm and sand in places that it shouldn't be.

I'd been so incredibly stupid. Why had I even thought for a minute that I could just arrive here and the movie world would treat me like a long-lost relative and welcome me with open arms and a monthly trust fund? I'd been so pathetically unrealistic. Or optimistic. I still wasn't sure which. And the craziest thing about the whole situation, the one factor that had left me wondering if there was some kind of genetic affliction that had taken control of my brain, was that I had a horrible feeling that if I could rewind the last few weeks I'd probably do exactly the same things all over again.

I loaded the boys into the car and set off for the beach. For the first time since I'd arrived in LA I didn't sing that really annoying Sheryl Crow song when I rode down Santa Monica Boulevard. I didn't sing the fantastic one by the Lighthouse Family when we passed Ocean Drive. I was too busy veering between 'What Becomes of the Broken Hearted' and 'I Will Survive'. If there had been a song called 'Little Old Self Pity Me' I'd have been whistling that too.

Bollocks. Bloody, bloody, bloody bollocks.

I still hadn't told Mark. My stomach flipped at the very thought of it. He'd called me the night before but I'd just bluffed him and told him that the meeting had been postponed for a couple of days. Big bolt of lightning. Bluff? Who am I kidding? That wasn't a bluff – a bluff is what you did at poker when you were trying to hold on to your last tenner. What I'd done to Mark was tell him a great big whopping lie. The kind of lie that, had it come out of Mac or Benny's mouth, would have resulted in them being grounded for a month and all their toys dispatched to the nearest Oxfam shop.

'So you're not coming home tomorrow then?' he had asked.

'No, Mark, I'm not coming home tomorrow. I've changed the tickets and left them open. I have to wait to find out what's happening and then I'll let you know.'

'Fine. Can I talk to the boys?'

Fine. That was it. 'Fine', in a distinctly fractious tone.

But then, I hardly had the moral high-ground, did I? The moral high-ground had turned into an avalanche the minute I'd started telling great big whoppers.

This couldn't go on forever. I was going to have to make my mind up about what I was going to do and then face the consequences. It was decision time – head had been surgically extricated from sand.

I still didn't want to go home. The thought of going back to the monotony and drudgery of normal life did absolutely nothing for me. How would I feel about giving up on my dreams when I was back in the UK? How would Mark and I ever get our relationship back on track? And how would I cope with knowing that the only chance of me coming face-to-face with Jackie Collins was if she took up selling Avon and wandered down our street?

Point one: Answer – devastated.

Point three: Answer – devastated.

Point two: Answer – I had absolutely no idea. Had Mark and I given up? We'd somehow become one of those couples who'd just completely grown apart and woken up one morning realising they had nothing left in common any more.

And then there was Sam. Gorgeous, adorable Sam.

Finally, *finally* I had to do a bit of soul-searching and ask myself the tough questions that I'd been putting off since the moment I'd realised that there could be more to us than just friends. Could we be happy together?

There, I'd said it.

Could Sam Morton and I be happy together?

And the truth was . . . we probably could. We'd be happy. We'd have a great life. We'd have absolutely amazing, bend-me-backwards sex and I'd permanently walk like a cowboy.

I was pretty sure that there should be a huge BUT after the analysis of the Sam situation – however, right at that very moment I couldn't think what it was.

'Mum, are we ever going to get out?' Mac demanded.

I suddenly realised that I was sitting stationary in the beach car park. It was lucky Mac had jolted me or I could have sat there in a pensive trance for the rest of the day.

'Sorry, guys,' I told them, turning round to make my apologies face-to-face.

That's when I realised that Benny was wearing a scuba mask. Fabulous. I needed a Samaritans counsellor and instead I got a Navy Seal. I unloaded everything from the car and we – Mum, Mac and Scuba Boy – traipsed down to the sand. 'Hi Mac, hi Benny!' came a rousing chorus of calls from assorted small children. My boys raised their hands in greeting, before hi-fiving those within arm's reach. Lord. They'd gone from the Alpine Synchronised Ski Team to the Mother's Beach Volleyball Team overnight.

It took me a few seconds to realise that something was strange. At first I couldn't put my finger on it. It was, it was . . . why was everyone staring at me? About thirty assorted humans of the female variety had their eyes trained on my moving form and not in a friendly way. It was at that moment in every B-movie Western where the hero cowboy looks up to see 4,000 Apaches advancing swiftly in his direction.

And something else was strange. They looked different somehow.

'Hi there! Great to see you again.'

'Muuuuum, Zac just hit me!' Benny shouted.

Ah, little Zac. So that meant there was a greater than evens chance that the singsong voice behind me was emanating from the extra-wide gob of . . .

'Hi Mandy. How are you? Thank you so much for the banana bread, it was delicious. You're too, too sweet,' I wittered.

But then marzipan was too, too sweet and it made me want to vomit. As if life hadn't pissed on me enough in the last twenty-four hours, now I was making small talk with Mandy.

'Oh, it was my pleasure. Come sit down here, it'll be nice to have a chat,' she whined.

I considered my options. I could risk scaring every child in the immediate vicinity by choking myself to death on Benny's scuba pipe, or I could sit with Mandy.

It was a tough choice. If only those kids weren't there . . .

'So . . .' she began, in the same voice my mother uses when she's pretending that she *doesn't* really want to know something that she desperately *does* want to know about.

'. . . How's Mark?'

Ah. Paws off, banana tart.

'He's fine, thank you.'

'And . . . did he go back to the UK then?' she asked, still in that sickly tone. I wondered, if I applied pressure to her windpipe, would her tone of voice change? I doubted it, but I was willing to give it a try.

'Yes, he did. He left on Sunday.'

Her face fell. I let that hang in the air for a few

moments. You know, right up close she wasn't that gorgeous. Okay, she was, but her pores could do with work.

'Something wrong, Mandy?' I asked sweetly. Cruel, I know, but this woman had kissed my husband and tried to bribe my children with inflatable reptiles – I had cause for cruelty.

'No, it's just . . . Carly, can I be totally frank with you?'

She looked so earnest, so serious.

If her next words were, 'I shagged your husband on a daily basis and now I'm up the duff with twins,' I had the feeling that this wouldn't be such a fun game any more.

I nodded, slightly fearfully.

'It's just that . . .' she began, then paused, struggling for words. Bad feeling. Real bad feeling about this. 'It's just that . . . we'd all kind of got to like him around here. He brightened things up a bit. Every day, same crowd of girls, then suddenly along comes Mark with his cute accent and funny ways and it just kinda brightened the place up a bit. D'ya mind if I tell the others?'

I shook my head in a kind of shock-induced zombie trance. Funny ways? Mark Barwick?

'Mark did leave on Sunday, girls,' she shouted over to the rest of the crowd. There was a general groan. This was surreal. Bizarre.

Then I realised what was different about most of the women. Full make-up. Hair groomed to perfection. Comfy trackies out, rock-chick jeans in. Either some reality makeover show had descended on Mother's

Beach or . . . or . . . nope, I couldn't even contemplate it. But . . . bloody hell, even *Consuela* was wearing lip-gloss.

'He made us laugh. And he was so great with the kids.' Then she giggled. 'At least, he was after the first day when the two of them got a little . . . *carried away.*'

Carried away? My boys didn't do 'carried away'. They went straight from angelic to demonic, and didn't even stop to pick up a 'get-out-of-borstal-free card'.

I summoned up the memory of that first day he'd gone solo with them. When he came home he was in a foul mood and I'd just dismissed it. Now I understood – a whole day with the boys when they were seriously playing up could have made Mother Teresa crack and head for the gin bottle.

'Anyway, tell him we were all asking after him. To be perfectly frank, and *please* don't take offence, but I think some of the girls were rather *taken* with him. Well, he's not exactly hard on the eyes.'

Incredible. Absolutely incredible. Mark Barwick had left Sam's house every morning and somewhere in between Pacific Palisades and Mother's Beach he'd been transformed into the Diet Coke guy.

Good grief, was Mandy ever going to stop talking?

'Oh, and tell him that I did get engaged to Bob at the weekend – Mark was such a good listener when I was deliberating last week and it was great to talk it through with someone who was completely impartial.'

That's when I knew this had to be a set-up. There were cameras in the sand bunkers and Ashton Kutcher was about to jump out and tell me I'd been junked. Or punked. Or whatever it was he did when he wasn't interfering with Demi Moore.

The person she was describing wasn't Mark. Well, it was ... it was ... *Mark*. The old Mark. The Mark I married. The fun, interested, sexy, lovely, decent man that I'd married and somehow turned into a walking zombie.

And at that moment I realised something else.

Benny was thumping Mac with a tennis racket. I just ignored them. That was nothing to do with the big realisation.

What had suddenly come to me was ... Sam. We could have a great life. We could be happy together. We could ... well, you know the other bits. But he would never be Mark. And the absolute truth was that the only man I had ever wanted to live the rest of my life with was the old Mark.

'Mandy, can I ask you a very personal question?'

She looked slightly taken aback. 'Sure,' she conceded cagily.

'Mandy ... can I kiss you?'

Family Values *Magazine*

PUTTING THE YUMMY IN MUMMY THIS WEEK . . . ME, MYSELF, MOI

Ladies, ponder this question – 'Who are you?' Are you someone's wife? Someone's mother? Someone's daughter? Just a name on a listing in Debrett's*? Or are you just 'you' – in all your individual, beautifully groomed glory?*

It's so easy these days to forget that the most important person in your life is you (although Anastasia, that genius of the perfectly plucked eyebrow, does come a close second). You are more than just someone's appendage – you are a vibrant, sexy, gorgeous woman who should take as good a care of herself as she does of others. Be your own best friend and celebrate yourself in all your unique wonder.

Just because you are a wife doesn't mean that you should deny your beauty in the presence of other men. Rejoice in it! Flaunt that sexuality! Remember what our mothers taught us on that first pre-pubescent trip to Chanel? That's right, girlies – sometimes it's wonderful to look, even if you can't touch!

And similarly, don't deny your dreams and aspirations just because you have a family to take care of.

Always remember that the concept of staff was invented for a very good reason.

So if you have often dreamed of climbing Kilimanjaro? Then whiz down to the local rock-climbing club and sign up for lessons.

Do you think wistfully of a career in couture? Then research your subject by hitting the shows in Milan, Paris, New York and London.

Do you feel unfulfilled in your marriage and find yourself wondering if your Mr Right has become Mr Wrong? Then put yourself first! Do what's right for you! Remember, life is short and only you can control your destiny.

Who am I? I am me, myself, moi – my very own best friend.

★ Step Eighteen ★

'Ding dong.'

I smiled at Sam. 'Time to go through. Come on, boys, let's go get that aeroplane.'

Benny jumped up and grabbed his Spiderman backpack. Mac just ignored me.

'Mac, come on, honey, we have to go.'

He'd been like this for two days now, since I announced to him on the way back from the beach that we were going home.

Going home.

Strange thing number 232 that had happened to me in the last couple of days: the phrase 'going home' didn't fill me with dread any more. In fact, while it didn't exactly make me want to throw a party, drink rum and limbo dance under the living-room coffee table, in a small, strange way (number 233) I was actually kind of looking forward to it. Or rather, kind of looking forward to seeing Mark.

The old Mark. And if he was still buried deep beneath the constraints of work, stress and monotony, then I was just going to have to apply gentle force with a jackhammer and break him out. He was still in there somewhere; I was sure of it. I'd just spent the last couple of years forgetting to look.

I'd never thought I was completely blameless, but I'd realised over the last couple of days that I had more to answer for than I'd first realised when it came to the erosion of our marriage. I'd bemoaned Mark's neglect in showing any interest or support towards my career.

Pot. Kettle.

When I'd last asked Mark about his work, I think that we were wearing shoulder pads, leg-warmers and George Michael was still straight.

And okay, I'd made half-hearted efforts to reignite our sex life, but that was only after about two years of chronic neglect, and then only when it suited me. Small, helpful details like making sure we were both awake at the time had been casually overlooked.

So when I'd called him on Wednesday afternoon and told him I was coming home, it felt right. Actually, I didn't tell him, I told the answering machine, because he wasn't in, but it still felt right.

Because I knew that the truth was that somewhere amid my work, house, kids and the general necessities of life, I'd stopped making an effort. And so had he. But I honestly, truly didn't think that it was over. It couldn't be. Because I loved him.

And more importantly than that, he was my boys' dad. We were a family. And that alone warranted another try – even if one of the smaller members of that very family was currently trying to chain himself to the airport restaurant table with plastic handcuffs.

He'd get over it eventually. Although I might have to talk to him in an American accent and feed him nothing but pizza and Hershey bars for a few weeks to help with the transition.

It wasn't as if we wouldn't be back. I was sure we would, eventually. Maybe I'd finally finish that script. Maybe I'd write another book and come over to try to pitch it. Maybe I'd find out where Lee Stavorski was working as a Danny DeVito impersonator and come back over to punch him for losing me what could have been two glorious weeks of my life.

Actually, in a way I was grateful for the lesson. Hollywood had chewed me up and spat me out, but at least I now understood the game rules a bit more.

Rule number one: Don't get your hopes up until the cheque is cashed.

I wondered if I'd feel differently now if I'd been offered a fantastic deal to stay. Maybe. Possibly. But I'd never know, because this was fate giving me a push in the direction that was right for me.

The hardest thing about our departure was telling Sam. But he knew. Deep down, he'd probably known all along.

I'd waited until the boys were in bed on the Wednesday night then taken a beer out to him. He was lying on a lounger by the pool, reading a script by floodlight.

I lay on the lounger next to him, desperately trying to think of the right way to phrase everything that I was feeling.

'You're going home, aren't you?'

Gorgeous, smart, sexy *and* psychic.

'How did you know?'

'Mac told me.'

Scratch that last bit.

'I have to. I still love him, Sam.'

'I know that.'

'I'm so, so sorry.'

'So is this the end of us?' I asked. 'Friendship over?'

There was a protracted silence. Doom. I knew this would happen – play with fire and you'll spoil the broth, as Carol was fond of saying.

'No. Carly, we've been either friends or lovers for the best part of twenty years. Last time you left me you broke my heart by marrying Mark, but we got over it. This time you're going back to Mark, and we'll get over that too. We have to – I've got godfather duties to perform. Who else will buy Benny his first hooker?'

I spluttered my wine all down the front of my T-shirt – which kind of spoiled the poignancy of the moment.

'And I know it would never have worked,' he added.

He did? Why wouldn't it have worked? I mean, it was perfectly okay for *me* to be sure that it wouldn't work out, but he was supposed to be lying here trying to convince me that we were soul mates separated at birth.

'Because Mark's the love of your life.'

True.

'And you'd never have brought your boys to the other end of the world and deprived them of their father on a permanent basis.'

Also true.

'And everything that makes you unhappy in your life is fixable without me. You don't *need* me to live, Carly. You can live without me.'

True. Sadly.

'And because . . .'

In the name of the unstoppable gob! How many reasons did he have? I'd have been cool with him quitting after number one.

'And because . . . I did a lot of thinking when I was in Italy, and I realised that I'd done exactly the same as you. I'd let my life slide into a rut – too much work, no fun, no love . . . and then you appeared and suddenly I was laughing again, and it felt so great, and I wanted to do filthy things to you . . .'

Past tense! Oh, cruel, cruel blow.

'. . . and I think that for a minute there we got our love for each other confused with a different kind of love. But I think we've worked that out. We should never be more than friends, Carly. That's what we're meant to be.'

I didn't feel it necessary to inform him that my clitoris had, at that point, just tracked down a big gun and shot itself.

He held out his hand. 'But I will always love you, Carly.'

'And I'll always love you too.'

As friends, I thought to myself. Definitely as friends. There could never, ever be anything more.

Could there?

*   *   *

'Ding Dong. This is the last call for all remaining passengers travelling to London . . .'

'Hurry, Sam, hurry.'

Fuck. If there were any paparazzi lurking they were going to be able to retire on this one. Sam Morton, A-list movie star, lying on the floor trying to saw through a pair of plastic handcuffs with a knife.

Finally, he broke through and released one crying little boy from the clutches of the furniture demon.

'I'm sorry, Mummy,' Mac wailed.

'That's okay, honey. It's okay,' I consoled him. Okay, so I should have grounded him for a fortnight for being so bloody silly but the wee soul had given himself a genuine fright when he thought he'd be forever stuck in the salubrious surroundings of LAX.

'Thanks, Sam,' I said when he clambered back to his feet.

'No problem. I freed an entire race from religious oppression when I played Moses, so a wee boy in handcuffs was a walk in the park.'

I laughed.

'Thanks anyway. For everything, Sam. Everything.'

I reached up and touched his face.

'Mum, why are you crying?' Benny asked.

I sniffed loudly. 'I'm not.'

'Are.'

Sam and I smiled at each other.

'So . . . Nothing I can do to change your mind then?' he asked.

'Not unless you can magic-up a hot-shot producer with a six-figure sum for my debut script.'

'Nope, all out of them, I'm afraid.'

I leaned over and kissed him. Then . . .

Why did my bloody phone always ring at the worst possible moments? If this was Kate I was having my yoghurt-maker back.

'Carly Cooper,' I said in a terse voice.

'Carly, this is Dave Marino at Global. Listen, I've got a script here that's just come across my desk and it's crying out for you. I love it. I just love it. But I'll love it even more once you've polished it up for me. It's a big one, hon, over a hundred-mil budget so we've got a bit of room on the fee. Only thing is they're already on location. We'd need you on a plane en route to Hawaii tonight, and we're talking snappy, snappy, snappy. Whaddya think, hon, will it fly? Tell me you're in, Carly Cooper. Tell me you're in.'

★ Step Nineteen ★

My stomach churned as I stepped off the plane.

I'd done it. I'd actually done it.

Right up until the last moment I wasn't sure that it was the right thing to do.

After all, how often does that kind of crossroads come along in your life?

Someone smart once said that life was what happened when you were busy making other plans. That was exactly what had happened to me. I planned to stay with Mark forever. I planned to crack Hollywood. I planned to do lots of things and somehow life just always got in the way.

But then, that's when you rely on destiny to throw you a curveball that, after the concussion wears off, will show you which way you're supposed to be travelling.

And in my case it did.

Dave Marino's offer had come out of the blue. It was sensational. The stuff that dreams are made of. Especially mine. It was the screenplay for *Husbands and Lovers*. Yep, the bonkbuster written by Jackie Collins, my spiritual mother, was being made into a movie. And they wanted me – *me!* – to work on the script.

In Jackie's holiday home in Hawaii.

So I made the decision. There and then, in that crowded restaurant in LAX, I made the biggest decision of my life. Sure, it would involve sacrifices. There would probably be times when I regretted it. And it was never going to be an easy decision to live with.

But who the fuck liked easy?

The most important thing was that I had a gut instinct it would be worth it. And when I saw Mac and Benny charging up the arrivals corridor and knocking their father clean on his arse, I knew it definitely was.

He hugged me for a long, long time. And so tightly I gave serious consideration as to whether he was trying to suffocate me in plain view of a thousand people so that he could later plead that it was an accident at the tribunal.

He leaned down and squeezed the boys.

'I'm so glad you came back,' he said eventually, with a definite catch in his voice.

'Don't be crazy,' I gasped, 'there was never any doubt that we'd come back.'

That banging noise is the gates of heaven slamming shut. Look, it was only a white lie – I was a reformed character, but that didn't make me perfect.

'Come on, let's go home,' I told him. 'Let's just go home.'

He took my hand and we walked off, towards the airport doors, walking back towards our old life.

Or at least, that's what would have happened if he hadn't said, 'Erm, Carly, there's something I have to tell you about that.'

'What?'

No! Don't tell me our house had buggering flooded again. Those freaking pipes were a nightmare. Or burnt down. How the hell had he managed to burn the house down when his idea of cooking was boiling a kettle for a Pot Noodle? Shit, an electrical fault within the kettle. That's it, I was suing Kenwood. They might be a multi-million-pound corporation, but . . .

'There are boxes, lots of them, all over the house. I really didn't think that you'd come home so I've already started packing up.'

I tried to breathe but someone had seemingly removed my windpipe. Packing up? Was he leaving me? I'd just knocked back Jackie bloody Collins for him and now he was *leaving*?

One word sprang immediately to mind. 'Divorce.'

Actually, there were a few more, but if I repeated them Mark would have grounds for an injunction.

'Wh— Wh— Wh—'

I was actually just gasping for air, but he interpreted that as a 'Why?'

'Carly, you were right. I realised it when I got back from LA. You know, I saw my boys more in those two and a half weeks than I've done in the last three years. My own children are growing up and I didn't even know them. What is that all about?'

I had absolutely no idea. I was both mute and vacant.

'And what had happened to us? We were a divorce

355

court waiting to happen. And I'm a lawyer, for Christ's sake, so I know how much that costs.'

Still speechless. Nodding now.

'Actually, strictly speaking, I *was* a lawyer. I quit my job.'

'You what?' I meant it to be a quiet gasp, but it came out as a roar so loud that several dozen people stopped to stare.

'I quit my job. Or at least took a sabbatical for a year. I can decide then whether I want to go back. There are a few things to tie up so I finish at the end of the month. Michael is going to rent our house – Cal and Carol have finally evicted him. So I'm boxing up everything that's personal, breakable or pawnable.'

He reached over and stroked my pink face.

'I just want to be with you and the boys, Carly. Those days down at Mother's Beach were so fantastic. Except for the first one, but that's another story.'

I finally found my voice. 'I heard. Mandy and the girls asked me to tell you that they missed talking to you.'

'They do? I kind of miss talking to them. In a very macho way, of course,' he said with a grin.

'Of course.'

'It just all reminded me of what real life was like. Or, at least, should be like.'

It was incredible. Somewhere between London, LA and back to London again, Mark Barwick, high-flying workaholic lawyer had morphed into Cool Dude Ken, the one that came complete with surfboard, scuba set and three-quarter-length flowery shorts.

Talking of which, Benny was going to have to take

that scuba mask off sooner or later otherwise his gradu-
ation photos were going to be highly unusual. I glanced
down at my sons, who were patiently sitting on our
suitcase waiting for their parents to stop gabbing. Which
we would. Just as soon as I got my head around the
logistics of their father's mid-life crisis.

'Honey, I have never loved you more than I do at
this very minute. Or at least, as much as I will after I've
had you drug-tested and confirmed that you're clean.
But your sabbatical plus my overloaded credit cards
equals poverty. Where are we supposed to live?'

'Beverly Hills.'

'What?' I gasped.

He reached into his inside pocket and pulled out
tickets – four of them.

'Flights back to LA, a month from now, for all of us.
I intended to rent an apartment, but I spoke to Sam
this morning and he said that a director pal of his was
going on location . . .'

'Cameron King,' I interjected.

'. . . and was looking for someone to house-sit for a
few months. That girl Jojo called back a wee while later
to say that she'd love you to do it, if you didn't mind.'

Mind? The world was going mad. Completely mad.
Maybe it was me who'd inhaled some mind-altering
substance and we were actually already halfway home
at this very minute, stopping to pick up essentials like
milk, bread, and another fix from the local dealer.

'Oh, and she said to tell you that Sam was having
dinner with one of the apostles tonight. Does that make
any sense?'

'Perfect sense.' Go, Sam.

'Okay. So the house is sorted. But we'll still need money . . .'

Sold the car . . .

'Visas?'

'Our tourist visas will last for three months. We can possibly extend them to six. By that time, you'll be working for a studio. Or if not, then we'll go somewhere else. It'll be an adventure, Carly. One great big sodding adventure!'

Tears started to flow down my face. Huge great rivers of them. Guilt had kicked in. I couldn't carry on with this. I couldn't let him do this after everything that had happened. I checked to see that the boys weren't listening then whispered . . .

'Mark, I need to tell you something. While we were in LA, I had impure thoughts about Sam. I'm so, so sorry.'

Mark's gorgeous brow furrowed. Ecstasy had turned to torment in a split second. For the first time in all these years together it was *me* who had burst *his* bubble.

'Did you do anything about it?' he replied, deathly quiet.

'No. I thought about it, but I didn't. I promise. Oh, Mark, I'm sorry.'

Eventually, after an eternity, he spoke. But it was so quiet that I couldn't hear him.

'What?' I asked him. This was it. This was where he told me that I was a manky tart and I should never darken his door again. Presuming he ever got another door, that is, since our present one seemed to be in the hands of an estate agency.

'I had impure thoughts about Mandy.'

The bastard! But hey: goose, gander.

'Did you do anything about it?'

'No. A decision I was glad of when I discovered her boyfriend . . .'

'Fiancé,' I corrected him.

He grinned. 'She said yes? Great. Well, her *fiancé* plays American football for the LA Raiders – he'd have killed me.

'Carly, we wouldn't have been human if we'd never thought about anyone else – our marriage was dying. But now it's okay. Isn't it?'

I nodded. The sobs were starting to subside now, good news on the snot front for Mark, because at that moment I leaned over and kissed him. Kissed him like I hadn't done in years. And he kissed me back.

Hallelujah! Hallelujah! Hallelujah!

It was coming from the general direction of my ovaries. How predictable was I?

I suddenly had an overwhelming urge to be horizontal in a dark room.

'Let's go home. Now. Quickly. Can you carry my bag?'

'Sure,' he said, picking it up and grabbing Benny's free hand with his.

I took Benny's other hand, then reached for Mac. 'Come on, Mac, time to go.'

'I'm not Mac.'

Here we go.

'Fine! But even Darth Vader has to take his mother's hand in a busy airport.'

'Not Darth any more.'

'Who are you?'

'Batman!'

My life was now complete. I had my husband back, Benny was happy and my oldest son had returned to the right side of the law.

'Da na na na Da na na na Da na na na Da na na na BATMAN!' screeched Benny.

Bliss. Sheer bloody bliss.

It was so blissful in fact, that as we strolled off towards the exit I didn't even hear my phone ringing.

Mark grabbed it out of my bag and answered it. He held it out to me. 'It's Kate.'

I took the phone. She must have known all about this and she hadn't said a word. But I knew how happy she'd be for me.

'Kate! Can't talk, babe, but let me tell you, ORGASMIC! Slap my thigh, colour me happy and sheer bloody orgasmic. I'll be home in an hour or so and I'll pop right in!'

'I'm sorry?' she said in what sounded like a very confused voice.

Perhaps Mark hadn't told her after all. She was talking again – I strained to hear her over the noise of the terminal.

'I think you might have me mixed up with someone else. This is Kate. Kate Winslet. We met a few months ago in Richmond Park and you gave me a copy of your book. I'm so sorry it's taken me so long to contact you but I've just had a chance to read it and . . .'

Read on for an exclusive extract from Shari Low's new novel, coming in 2008 . . .

Prologue

The Daily Globe. 22nd June 2006

Deputy Prime Minister John Prescott today announced that, in line with European legislation, the government has decided to ease restrictions currently placed on the operation of brothels within the UK.

In this controversial move, it is proposed that from July 1st this year, local authorities will have the power to license and oversee premises engaged in the business of providing sex for cash (or other means of payment).

Announcing the new regulations, Mr Prescott made this statement.

"It has been clear for some time that current legislation pertaining to the adult entertainment industry is neither realistic nor effective. In recent years we have seen dramatic increases both in the number of arrests for prostitution and the influx of sex trade workers from other EU countries. This government has concluded that the only progressive, sensible way forward is to legitimise this industry, therefore allowing it to be controlled and regulated.

I'd like to give my firm commitment that I will personally monitor the success of the new guidelines and intend to be fully involved in the forthcoming months in the evolution of policies to further develop this sector."

Chancellor Gordon Brown has issued no comment on the matter but it is thought that he is in favour of the move and has instructed the Department of Revenue & Customs to initiate the administrative procedures to ensure full financial transparency and accountability within the industry.

Prime Minister Tony Blair's views are not yet known. Mr Blair is now on day 57 of his stay at The Priory for an unknown condition. However his wife Cherie, currently on a very lucrative two-month speaking tour of the US, claims that he is making progress and hopes to resume his role as Prime Minister in the near future.

Chapter 1 – Tom, Harry, Forget about Dick

"So you mean, like, a penis embargo?"

"Correct," replied Roxy. "I'm going to be an official willy-free zone. I'm on a twelve-step male-genital detox programme – step number one, boyfriend is history. Step number two, I quit my job. Step number three, I recruit my best friend to help me get a new job. Er, Ginny, honey, that's you."

There was a pause so pregnant it could have applied to social services for free milk vouchers and child benefit.

Roxy waited for a reaction. None. *Nada*. Ok, so this wasn't going to plan. Normally she could rely on Ginny to react in exactly the way she'd been reacting to everything Roxy said since they were sitting side by side in the playpen.

Act one: Rolling of eyes.

Act two: Loud tutting noise.

Act three: Adopts the approximate expression of someone who has just discovered that she is chewing a wasp.

Act four: Capitulates, offers sympathy, then digs friend out of big hole.

But no. Ginny was staring mournfully into space, as if she'd slipped into one of those cosmic, out of body trances that pass the time while you're waiting in the bank queue or having a smear test.

"Ginny?" she probed, attempting to snap her friend's focus back to the most important thing in life – her.

"What?"

"Didn't you hear me? I need help. Ginny, I'm single, I'm unemployed, I'm devastated . . . I'm desperate!"

From her cramp-inducing position on a tatty beanbag (circa 1990), Ginny looked over at her clapped-out single bed and the female reclining on it – probably the least desperate-looking woman she had ever set eyes on. Roxy's jet-black hair hung in sleek, shiny slates from the middle parting to her shoulder bones. Her perfect, size 12, über-toned frame was adorned in her standard uniform of black Prada bootcut trousers, a black Nicole Farhi, cashmere roll neck and lethal, 4-inch, stiletto, Gina boots. Skin: flawless. Nails: perfectly plastic. Make up: subtle. Breasts: pert. And Ginny just knew without looking that there were no hairs on her legs, no hard skin on her feet and her nethers had applied for residence in Brazil.

There was no doubt about it: Roxy Galloway was channelling Angelina Jolie.

Ginny Wallis, meanwhile, was channelling the bag lady who sat outside Superdrug on an inner tube flogging jewellery she'd made out of string and discarded scratchcards.

She sighed wearily, so immune to Roxy's perpetual

melodramas that she'd slipped into a moment of reflection instead of participating in the panic. The contrast of her glam, glitzy, cutting-edge friend with the greyness of Ginny's life somehow highlighted the fact that Ginny was twenty-seven and still living at home in a bedroom that hadn't changed since the nineties. The duvet was a tribute to the golden days when boy bands ruled the world. If the carpet ever revisited its former life it would have been baby pink and orange – now, ten years of spills and wear later, it was a delicate shade of road kill. Even woodworm would shun the furniture. And the curtains were obviously designed by someone on LSD, bought by someone on crack and then hung by someone on two bottles of cider and a Lambert & Butler that Roxy had stolen from her mother's handbag.

And they paid for that wild, drunken, teenage night of fabric-hanging by being grounded for a month and having their Christmas Top Shop vouchers confiscated.

Urgh, it was depressing. She pulled a bit of fluff off her hoodie.

"Roxy, when did I become so old that I thought jogging bottoms and sweatshirts were acceptable as everyday outerwear?"

"Honey, until four o'clock this afternoon when I resigned from my erstwhile employment, I worked with people who thought PVC nurses' uniforms, nipple rings and five-inch Perspex platforms were acceptable everyday outerwear."

Roxy's bottom lip trembled. "Oh, I miss them," she

wailed. "Have I made a mistake?" I mean, it was a prestigious career in the hospitality industry . . ."

"Roxy, you worked in a whore house," Ginny interjected, with a tut and a roll of the eyes. Phew. Normal service was almost resumed. All they needed was the wasp-chewing face and they were back on track to Moral Support Central.

"An international, classy, extremely exclusive entertainment club, if you don't mind."

Actually Ginny did mind. It wasn't that she was a prude, it's just that, well, she'd never understood Roxy's career choice. Receptionist at the Seismic Lounge – *guaranteed to make the earth move.* Yep, whatever marketing genius had thought up that slogan was probably now enjoying a fulfilling career flipping burgers. Or making scratchcard jewellery next to the bag lady outside Superdrug.

Roxy had been ecstatic when she got the job. The club opened the day after the government legalised brothels – definitely some insider information at work there – and it was on one of the most prestigious streets in Mayfair. Four hours of copulation cost the same as a second-hand Corsa, the girls all spoke with accents that could crack windows and the sex toys came gold-plated. It oozed class and made no apologies for targeting only the extremely wealthy. It even employed chauffeurs to collect the clients in blacked-out Range Rovers and bring them in through a private underground car park so that the paparazzi never got a recognisable shot. Actually, that wasn't true – Stephen Knight, notorious B-list movie star, usually arrived in his open-top Aston Martin DB7 and parked it right outside the door. He was obviously channelling Charlie Sheen.

To Roxy, it was all so decadently glamorous. Short of becoming a fake-tan consultant or adopting a serial football-player-shagging habit, it seemed like the easiest way to hob-nob with the rich and/or famous on a daily basis. And the bonus was that as receptionist, she only had to meet, greet and keep the customer record cards up to date. The money was great, the tips were outstanding and unlike the rest of the girls, cystitis didn't play havoc with her pay packet.

She loved it – at least to start with. But over the last couple of months it had all seemed a little too repetitive. The same faces week after week, the endless stream of girls (who invariably quit once they'd earned enough to buy a flat, finished university or received an irresistible offer of marriage from a blue-blooded, upper-class, Eton-educated arms dealer) and the rising scepticism after yet another client did an "at home with the happy family" spread in *Hello!*. Roxy had to admit it – the job was wearing down her trust in men and turning the loving act of sex into a business transaction. Did you enjoy your ejaculation, sir? Oh, lovely – now would that be Visa, MasterCard or American Express?

She just wanted to be like normal people (porn stars and penile implant specialists aside) and experience a daily life that wasn't controlled or influenced by actions of the male reproductive organ.

She could probably have struggled on for another couple of months, but the latest devastation in her love life had tipped her over the edge. She winced. She still couldn't believe that after two years of devotion, Felix was history. Gone. Past tense.

But after spending three days submerged in hysterical mourning she decided that no man was worth a 45% increase in wrinkles caused by perpetual sobbing.

She would never, ever mention his name again.

Ever.

Except in a blatant ploy to get help and sympathy from a bored, indifferent best friend . . .

"God, Ginny, you're *so* self-absorbed. I'm experiencing such emotional devastation that I've put off having my roots done, I can't face going out and I'm so bitter that my karma has gone all to fuck. I mean, how would you feel if you were not only unemployed, but you'd caught the love of your life shagging the local florist?" she wailed. "And he didn't even have the decency to send me a bunch of bloody flowers."

Ginny nodded in what she hoped vaguely resembled a sympathetic expression. It lasted about three seconds before the truth tunnelled to freedom.

"He was a twat anyway."

"He was not!" Roxy protested.

"Was."

"Was not."

Ginny sighed. "You do realise that we're twenty-seven? Apparently we should have given up on childish, petty, pantomime dialogue somewhere around puberty. Remind me again why we're friends."

She had a point. More than twenty years of friendship,

based on having absolutely nothing in common other than the fact that they were born on the same day and their mothers were distantly related.

"Helloooooooooooo, girlies." The sing-song shriek came from downstairs and was accompanied by a slamming door and the smell of chow mein.

Said girlies groaned. "How can you be related to someone who sounds like that? You know, you really have to move out of your mother's house, Gin – it's obscene that you still live here at your age."

"And is *my* favourite girlie still up there too?" screeched another voice, which to the untrained ear sounded very like the first one.

Roxy sighed. "And how can I be related to someone who sounds like that?"

Then louder, "Yes, Mum, I'll be down in a minute."

"I've got your favourite here, sweetie – prawn crackers and crispy chicken. We thought we'd all have dinner together."

"Gin, do you think our mothers are having a lesbian affair? I haven't seen them apart since about 1974. Urgh, mental image, my mother muff-diving . . . don't think I can face those prawn crackers now. And I'm not buying that my mother moved in here just for the companionship."

Gin giggled. "You have a sex-obsessed, twisted mind. They're not lovers, they're cousins."

"About third cousins, four times removed. I've met people in public toilets who are closer relations than that. But think about it. Since my dad popped his clogs and your dad popped Mrs Fleming from the fish shop, they've been joined at the hip. Urgh, another mental thought that I could live without."

"They're *cousins*!" shrieked Ginny, smacking Roxy with a threadbare, heart-shaped pink pillow, and *still* her perfect hair didn't move an inch out of place.

"Come on then, let's go join them. But when we're finished you have to help me update my CV and find a new job, Gin – you know I'm hopeless at that kind of stuff."

"And what am I, a careers officer?" Ginny replied indignantly.

"You work in a library! There're loads of job information advice thingies in there. Right in between dog-eared editions of the Kama Sutra and books on dealing with the menopause. I need you to help me decide what I'm going to do. Maybe I should take a year out and travel a bit. Or go back to university. I only had one year left to do before . . . well . . . before . . ."

"Before you got caught giving the philosophy professor a blow job. Under a podium. During a lecture."

"Thanks for the recap," Roxy retorted dryly.

"Girlies!!!" came another shriek from downstairs.

Ginny groaned. "You know, Rox, you're right – I have to move out of here. I need to stop wearing clothes with 'sweat' in the title, and I need to shred the apron strings."

Suddenly, a rousing chorus of "You Can Leave Your Hat On," filled the room.

"Rox, either your arse is singing or that's the naffest ringtone I've ever heard."

Roxy ignored her and checked the screen.

"Shit. Shit. Bloody shit. It's Sam at the Seismic."

"What did he say when you resigned?"

"Actually I just left a note. Couldn't face them."

To Ginny, this didn't exactly come as a newsflash. It was vintage Roxy. Roxy, who couldn't face up to life's unpleasantries if her Fendi Baguette depended on it. It had been the same their whole lives. Roxy couldn't tell a boy she didn't like him any more so she sent Ginny. Roxy never did her homework, she just copied Ginny's. Roxy didn't want to tell her mother she was leaving home, so she did a midnight flit. Ginny carried the bags. Crazy, impetuous, dramatic, spontaneous, endlessly fucking irritating, Roxy.

Still, at least Roxy would never be boring, Ginny thought dolefully. Would anyone ever call *her* spontaneous? Her life CV could fill one paragraph: Same job since she left school ten years ago, same boyfriend for twelve years, still lived in the same village she'd lived in all her life, with her mother, in a bedroom that she hadn't decorated since before the millennium. She was so ponderous that she took two weeks to decide to order something out of a catalogue and that was with the safety net of a money-back guarantee.

Boring? Check. Restrained? Check. Dead? It was pretty close . . .

Roxy was blustering into the phone. "But I don't know anyone who can cover it! Ok. Ok. I understand. Ok. I'll get back to you. Sorry, Sam."

She snapped the phone shut.

"Fuck."

"Problem?"

"He says I can't just walk out – something about a one-month notice period, blah, blah, blah. He sounds really pissed off. Apparently Sascha has gone off with herpes and Tilly has been barricaded in a hotel by the *News of the World* because she's doing a kiss and tell on some MP this week, so they've got no one to cover for me. He says I'll lose my holiday pay and my salary and, oh I don't know, a bloody kidney if I'm not at the desk tomorrow. So much for turning over a new leaf."

She looked at her watch. "The new, penis-avoiding me lasted for a whole eight hours . . ."

"I'll do it."

"And now Felix will know where to find me and he'll come begging me to take him back."

"I'll do it."

"And I tell you, if he pitches up with a bunch of petunias I'll shove them up his . . . what?"

"I'll do it."

"Do what?"

"Cover your shift at the Seismic. Sam's the guy I met at your birthday party, right? The one who helped me fill the vol-au-vents?"

Roxy groaned. "Still can't believe you brought vol-au-vents to my party. Thank God Gordon Ramsay didn't make it or you'd have had his stroke on your conscience. Anyway, Sam, party, so?"

"Well, he was nice. Said if I ever decided to move into the city I should check in with him to see if there were any vacancies. Of course, I was wearing your clothes, your jewellery and your shoes at the time, so he probably thought I was Miss Cosmopolitan Girl About Town. Anyway, if it's only for a month, surely he wouldn't mind?"

"But even if it was ok with Sam, what about your job? Where will you live? You can't commute, the hours are too irregular."

"I'll move into your place."

"And I would live . . .?"

"Here."

"You're kidding me."

Ginny's inspiration was gathering speed. Suddenly this seemed like the best idea she'd ever had. *Spontaneous?* She could be spontaneous. Her enthusiasm bubbled. Spontaneous was her middle name. Actually it was Violet, after her mother, but that wasn't the point.

"I'm not. Come on, Roxy – it totally works! That gives you a month to sort out what you're going to do with your life and heal that devastated soul. You can live here and you can take my place in the library. You said it yourself, it's the best place to research your future options."

"But they'd never let me."

"Course they would. Hold on, I'll ask the manager." Ginny opened her bedroom door.

"Muuuuum, is it ok if Roxy takes my place at the library for a few days?"

"Course it is, dear. Now, hurry up, or I'll have to microwave your hoi sin sauce."

"That's settled then. Come on, you know what to do there, you covered my holidays."

"That was in about 1998!"

"Trust me, nothing's changed. What shift are you supposed to be on tomorrow?"

"Er, noon till eight," replied Roxy, tentatively. She had a horrible feeling that for the first time in her life she was being out-manoeuvred. The library. One month. God, she could smell the boredom.

But then, she couldn't face London again. She needed a break. She needed to be away from the Seismic, away from memories of Felix, away from the constant pressure to be nice to grown men who paid for women half their age to attach probes to their testicles.

"Ok, I'll do it. On one condition . . ."

"Name it," said Ginny.

"I'm changing that duvet. If I'm going to sleep with Westlife, then I want them to have working parts."

<u>Win a two-night mid-week Spa Break for 2 people at</u>

CHAMPNEYS

HEALTH RESORTS

Champneys. The place to *be* . . .

Champneys Health Resorts, in conjunction with AVON, are offering you and a friend the chance to win a luxury two-night break at either the glamorous Forest Mere in Hampshire, the modern Springs in Leicestershire or the cozy Henlow in Bedfordshire, all set in sweeping countryside.

They offer elegant and luxurious accommodation, healthy cuisine, the latest fitness regimes, as well as the most indulgent and pampering beauty treatments around. Your stay includes two nights' luxury accommodation, an indulgent body massage and a relaxing facial each, unlimited use of all facilities, plus all meals.

We are also offering all readers a 15% discount at Champneys. Book online at www.champneys.com and enter promotional code 'rav07' in the online reservations section.

To enter this free prize draw, simply answer the question below and then visit <u>www.avon-books.co.uk/spabreak</u> or send your postal entry to AVON Champneys Promotion, c/o WDMP, 116 Putney Bridge Road, Putney, London, SW15 2NQ.

In *The Motherhood Walk of Fame*, which US city does Carly Cooper fly to in search of fame and fortune ?

A) New York
B) Los Angeles
C) Miami

Terms and Conditions

061279573